A STRANGE FATE AWAITED IN THE GUISE OF PASSION IMMORTAL...

He almost pulled me into the drawing room, firmly closing the doors behind us. Then he turned and placed both hands on my shoulders. He said, "I have waited for you for a very long time...."

"We have known each other only a few weeks."

"Much longer than that. Much, much longer. In some previous existence, I am certain, for the moment I first saw you I knew we were predestined for each other...."

His arms slipped from my shoulders to my back, drawing me close, pressing my body against his. He whispered excitedly, "I know you feel as I do ... the heat, the longing ... that is desire, my darling; a physical need, an ache, a yearning that can be satisfied in only one way, with one person."

We kissed.

THE EAGLE AT THE GATE

RONA RANDALL

AVON
PUBLISHERS OF BARD, CAMELOT AND DISCUS BOOKS

First American Edition 1978

AVON BOOKS
A division of
The Hearst Corporation
959 Eighth Avenue
New York, New York 10019
Copyright © 1978 by Rona Randall
Published by arrangement with Coward, McCann & Geoghegan
Library of Congress Catalog Card Number: 77-10062
ISBN: 0-380-42846-6

All rights reserved, which includes the right
to reproduce this book or portions thereof in
any form whatsoever. For information address
Coward, McCann and Geoghegan, Inc., 200 Madison Avenue,
New York, New York 10016

First Avon Printing, February, 1979

AVON TRADEMARK REG. PAT. OFF. AND IN
OTHER COUNTRIES, MARCA REGISTRADA, HECHO EN
U.S.A.

Printed in the U.S.A.

To my much loved family—
  Freddie,
  Paul,
  Celia,
  Rebecca,
  and
  Patrick

ONE

ONE

My passionate desire to live at Abbotswood began imperceptibly, but grew as relentlessly as a fever in the blood. Neither my father's anxiety nor Red Deakon's mockery could have halted my obsession once I set eyes upon the place; but at that time the red-haired ruler of Deakon's Forge had not come into my life, so I was free of his disturbing personality, and my father's opposition could be dismissed because, not being born into such a world, he could not comprehend the fascination it held for me.

But I had not been born into it either, so my immediate desire to belong there seemed illogical even to me. Nevertheless, I felt an instinctive need to identify myself with the place. Perhaps it was the security of it, or the pattern of life it represented, that sparked such ambition in me; the basic need to belong, to put down roots, which the footloose theatrical world I came from had always denied me.

The odd thing was that until I saw Abbotswood I had never been consciously aware of any such need. I had thought myself content with our roving life until I met David Hillyard and, through him, came to Abbotswood. Not even my father's reluctance to go near the place and, when there, his anxiety to get away could touch me then. Insidiously the house and the people in it reached out and took hold of me.

Naturally I hid my reaction from my father because I knew he would be disappointed, even hurt, although there was no reason why he should be. It was unlikely that I would ever set eyes on the place again once that memorable visit was over. Perhaps it was merely the excitement of glimpsing a world so remote from our own which captured my imagination, or so I told myself.

Whatever the reason, I succumbed—enchanted, I believed, but no more than that. This was a diversion in our lives, a glimpse of a more elegant and exciting world, the sort of world into which Gaiety girls and other professional beauties sometimes married, but never the daughters of touring Shakespearean actors because not only did the young bloods rarely bother to see us perform, but we had no permanent theatre in London where high society could even notice us. In this year of 1902 we were the troubadours of the road and, therefore, like wandering Gypsies.

But one type of audience we could always count on—a largely feminine one which came to see and to sigh over Charles Coleman's renowned profile and to swoon at the sound of his voice, and well could I understand this because although my father was known as a matinee idol, I considered him something greater than that. When he stood by the footlights and the flickering gas jets at his feet threw revealing shadows onto his handsome face and he smiled that dazzling smile way up to the back of the gods ("Always play to the gallery, my dear—if you don't, you're finished!"), I would stand in the wings, my heart bursting with pride, and when the tabs swished together, he would turn and hold out his hand to me.

"Quickly, my dear! *Quickly!*"

I would run onstage then and seize his proffered hand, and all the time he would be gesticulating with the other toward the prompt corner and urging, *"Take 'em up again, Barney, take 'em up!"* And Barney, the stage manager, would obey at once. (Curtain calls could be doubled that way.) Then would come the familiar sound, the *swoosh*, the rush of air, and together we would step down to the footlights and bow, and smile, and bow, and smile again, and I knew that my father's heart was in it, despite the histrionic touch and for all that he made a joke of it, and if the company resented this refocusing of the limelight, they just had to put up with it. My father was actor-manager of the Thespian Players and could therefore do as he pleased, so when he bypassed the second lead, or even the leading lady, in my favour, they dared not protest even though I ranked as a lesser member of the company. This final appearance at the footlights, holding his daughter by the hand, his face alight with pride and affection, was the climax of my father's performance and never failed to bring down the house.

And when the tabs swished together again finally, he would hug me and declare, "They love us, Aphra. They love us!"

"They love *you*, Papa."

That always pleased him because more than anything in life my father wanted to be loved. My mother had loved him unstintingly, and when she died from pneumonia following a prolonged stay in damp theatrical digs in Dublin, it was inevitable that I should continue where she left off. I know full well that he turned to other women for physical solace—I had been born on the road and knew the facts of life from an early age—but for the family affection he so badly needed he turned to me more and more.

He never married again. Everyone was surprised about that, but not I. No woman could really take my mother's place, and he didn't pretend that any woman could, no matter how frequently he dallied with one or how close an association he formed. There had been only one Petronella in the world for him. "With a name like that," he had once said to me, half in jest, half in earnest, "how could I ever settle down with an Ethel or a Mabel or an Alice? I would be forever comparing even their names!"

My mother, who in her turn had a very romantic one who christened her daughter Petronella after the heroine of one of her favourite romantic novels, was equally insistent that I should have an unusual name in an age which produced nothing more imaginative than Daisy or Violet or Rose. And of all things, she found it on a memorial brass set into the stone floor of a small country church in Kent.

My parents had been playing Canterbury at the time and had hired a trap one afternoon when there was no matinee, and gone bowling out into the countryside, and found this tiny church beside a river, and wandered in. And when my mother saw the memorial brass and read the inscription, she declared, "If our child is a girl, I am sure she will be just like that saintly creature!"

Years later, when my father and I were also playing Canterbury, he took me to the church, and I read the

inscription for myself, puzzling a little over the mediaeval
Vs for Us.

> HERE LYETH BVRYED YE BODY OF APHRA NEVTON
> WIFE OF MEDRITH NEVTON GENT. & DAUGHTER
> OF HENRY CREWYS ESQ. WHO SCARCELY HAVING
> ARRIVED TO 21 YEARES OF AGE YET FVLLY
> ATTAYNED PERFECTION IN MANY VERTVES.
> DEPARTED THIS FRAYLE LIFE YE IX OF JANV. 1611.

The armorial bearings above were broken and worn away, but poor little Aphra's image was well preserved. There she lay, hands together in prayer and wistful face gazing heavenward, wearing very early-seventeenth-century dress and a starched ruff; sad but tremendously appealing.

The name seemed to suit her, but did it suit me? And how optimistic my dear mamma had been to imagine that I might grow up in Aphra's saintly image! So virtuous a name seemed out of place in the theatre. Besides, I did not much care for the sound of it, perhaps because it reminded me of its sad association.

But I felt better when my father said, "Dear Petronella —I could hardly spoil her pleasure by telling her that the name also belonged to one of the most notorious women of the seventeenth century—Aphra Behn, a scandalous creature who defied her generation by writing shocking Restoration plays and salacious novels. She also led a dubious life, during which she enchanted Charles the First, became a spy, and was even clapped into the debtors' prison, but finished up in Westminster Abbey for all that."

Somehow that made me feel better. It would be easy to live a more virtuous life than the scandalous Aphra Behn because I could never write a salacious novel if I tried and would certainly have no opportunity to become a spy. But my poor little namesake, lying beneath the stones of that ancient church, somehow lingered with me forever after. Had she secretly yearned for a life in which the achievement of "many virtues" was *not* the ultimate aim? A life like mine, with irresponsible actors and a precarious future, unconventional and thoroughly disapproved of by respectable members of society?

But I did not even suspect, on that memorable day,

that Kent was to play an even greater part in my fate. As we left the country church and drove quietly back to Canterbury, my father was unusually silent, and when I glanced at his face, some instinct warned me to be silent, too. His eyes had that faraway look which frequently came into them after my mother's death, and I knew that this reminder of her had gone deep, despite his inconsequential remarks about the less virtuous of the two Aphras. I now suspected that he had thrown in those remarks to lighten what would otherwise have been a poignant moment or perhaps to avoid displaying emotion. But driving back to the theatre, he was unable to hide it. He had stepped back into the past that afternoon, and consequently the present was less easy to bear.

So I was glad when Barney came hurrying to meet us with that beaming smile on his face which always heralded good news. His excitement was plain.

"Mr. Coleman, sir, I've been trying to find you all afternoon! Went round to your lodgings, I did, but your landlady didn't even know where you'd gone, more's the pity. A gentleman's been to see you, sir, with a rare proposition. He wants you to take the company to perform at some swanky place for some celebration or other, the owner's birthday or something. Now where *did* I put that piece of paper wot I writ it all down on?"

My father smiled and shook his head indulgently. We were well acquainted with Barney's forgetfulness, but also with his enthusiasm, which lit his wizened face at this moment.

"Can you remember the name of the place, Barney? If so, that might recall other details."

"Something to do with an abbot or a monk, if I remember rightly—I've got it! Abbotswood! Abbotswood, beyond Hythe, he said. And here's me bit of paper, Mr. Coleman, sir, with the gent's name all writ down."

But my father scarcely glanced at it. It seemed to me that his face had become even more still and withdrawn than during our drive home. I wished he could shed this melancholy detachment and take a delight in this unusual booking, as I did. To act before an invited audience in what sounded like a beautiful and possibly aristocratic setting was something to get excited about, especially at the end of a tour with no further engagements ahead of us. But Barney had to speak three times before my father jerked to attention, and I stood there, wondering what caused this deep abstraction in his mind. Silence on the way home because thoughts of my mother had taken hold of him was one thing, but this complete withdrawal was another.

"I said the gent'll be coming back, Mr. Coleman, sir. He said he'll call at the stage door after this evening's performance."

"Then he will be wasting his time." My father tore up the piece of paper and tossed the scraps aside; then without another word he walked on to his dressing room.

I ran after him.

"Papa! Please! It sounds interesting and unusual, and the company could do with an extra date. You're not turning your back on it, surely?"

Of course, he wasn't. No actor-manager rejected a firm booking.

He answered peremptorily, "There's no money in one-night stands. Transporting scenery and costumes and props, not to mention the cast, swallows any meagre profit."

"This wouldn't be meagre, sir." Barney was hurrying along beside us. "Wait until you hear the booking fee—three times wot we've ever been offered just for one single performance! And we wouldn't have to pay for transport—all that would be taken care of, the gentleman said, and carriages sent to convey the company to Abbotswood, *and* the cast would be guests in the house itself. It's a great house, sir, a noble house—"

"And how do you know that, Barney?"

My father had reached his cramped dressing room, where flickering gas jets surrounded a fly-marked mirror. His make-up box lay open before it, and wig stands and costumes stood in orderly array along one wall. Clancy, his dresser, was already laying out Prospero's costume.

Barney continued eagerly, "I checked, sir. Thought you'd want to have all perticklers as soon as you got here. 'Twere easy enough. One of the resident stagehands is a Kentish man, and he was mightily impressed. One of the great houses of Kent, he called it, though mebbee that was just his local pride, but it's certainly an ancient house. The late master was Sir William Bentine, but he died years ago, and his daughter-in-law lives there now; her brother, too—this gent wot called."

"Spare me the family history, Barney."

It was unlike my father to be so curt, especially with Barney, who was his mainstay. He rarely lost his temper even at rehearsals, which earned the loyalty of actors and actresses alike, so they forgave his whims and his foibles. So naturally I stared in astonishment when he snapped at Barney.

"Well, *I* am interested, Barney, dear," I declared, and was satisfied because my father noticed the reproach in my voice and knew it was directed at him.

He said contritely, "Sorry, Barney, I have a headache," but I didn't believe him. I knew the familiar signs of my father's headaches—the crease between the brows, the frown of pain. There were no such signs now, only that air of abstraction which seemed to have nothing to do with his memories of my mother, though why I should think that I had no idea.

Barney said at once that he would have some tea brought along, which meant he would fetch it himself. Barney was general runabout to the company and had been with it ever since its formation, starting as callboy and assistant to props, then becoming ASM and finally full SM, but actually doing a great deal more than that. He had the sharp intelligence of the true Cockney and used it, so that gradually he undertook a lot of responsibility one way and another, even acting as road manager as well as stage manager when touring. But no task was ever too menial for him, even fetching tea.

My father was adamant. "When this man returns—what was his name, Barney? Bentine, did you say?"

"No, Mr. Coleman, sir. Bentine was the name of the gent wot used to own Abbotswood, the one whose daughter-in-law succeeded him. This one, her brother, is called Hillyard."

"Well, when this Mr. Hillyard returns, tell him I thank him for the invitation, but regret we cannot accept."

Barney gasped, and so did I.

"But—but what reason shall I give, sir? He knows it's the end of the tour—"

My father said sharply, "And how does he know that?"

Barney shrugged. "Couldn't say, sir, but know he does.

'Since the company will be free,' he said. 'I have no doubt this date will be very convenient.' ...."

"The devil he did!"

"And he was right, sir, wasn't he? It *is* the end of the run, and until you book up another, we'll have to be glad of even one-night stands. And we'll be lucky if we get offers as generous as this. Everyone agrees, and everyone's that excited—"

My father interrupted, "Everyone? The rest of the cast, you mean? And how did they come to hear about it?"

Barney looked reproachful. "If you think I talked out of turn, Mr. Coleman, sir, you oughta know me better'n that, just as you oughta know that before a closing performance the cast is in the theatre nearly all day, packing their skips and so forth, because the place has to be vacated by midnight, so there's no time for all that after the curtain comes down at eleven. So there the lot of us were, knocking off for a cuppa onstage, and in this gent walks, straight through the stage door and into the wings. The stage doorkeeper was off duty, so there weren't nothing to stop him, and *were* we all glad about that! It isn't every day an offer like this comes breezing right in! And he made a real impression, I can tell you, for all he was so quiet and unassuminglike. Didn't set himself out to be persuasive, didn't paint a wonderful picture of the place he was inviting us to, just said 'Abbotswood' as if everyone should know of it. Miss Lorrimer was overjoyed, and Mr. Mayfield, too. But so was everyone. When the gent had gone, they all went wild, and who can blame them? It'll be a good finish-up to the tour, Mr. Coleman, sir, and every one of us could do with the money."

"What you are saying is that I owe it to the company to accept."

"Well, sir, it isn't for me to tell you that, is it?"

My father made no reply, and Barney went away to fetch the tea.

"He is right, Papa. You do owe it to the company. Why do you hesitate?"

"I am merely considering it," my father hedged, which failed to convince me, but when he added that he would give his decision after tonight's performance, I had to be content. In the eighteen years of my life I had learned when and when not to pester him.

The Eagle at the Gate

He was forced to reach a decision before the final curtain. Somehow the news of his refusal spread through the theatre, and during the last interval a delegation presented itself at his dressing-room door, headed by Elizabeth Lorrimer, his leading lady, and George Mayfield, the second lead, and supported by the rest of the company en masse. I wanted to stand aside from all this, feeling it disloyal to support either one side or the other, but inwardly as surprised and confused as the rest of the cast.

Only Elizabeth and George and Barney were able to get inside my father's restricted dressing room, lead accommodation as it was. This theatre in Canterbury was old and inadequate, particularly backstage, so the rest of us had to be content with straining our ears in the passage outside, but some of the cast allowed me to push my way through to the foreground, hoping I would add my persuasion through the open door.

Elizabeth Lorrimer was at her most elegant and haughty as she demanded, "Charles, is it actually *true* that you refuse to let us perform at one of the most prominent stately homes of England?"

"It isn't one of the most prominent, and it isn't a stately home. It is merely a large country house—"

"And how do you know that, pray?"

"I recall sepia pictures of the place in the *Spectator* and the *Tatler* from time to time."

George Mayfield put in, "Then you know it isn't merely a country house, but a mansion. But the important thing is that you owe it to the company to accept a good and generous booking which we are lucky to get right at the end of a tour. Every London theatre has a full bill, so there is no hope of getting into a new show, or even of getting a fill-in, while the Thespians are idle. And what chance of other engagements is there for Shakespearean actors like us? The immortal Bard is not so popular as melodrama and music hall these days."

I squeezed through the dressing-room door and interrupted. "Even one night's booking would help everyone, Papa, including us. Can you really afford to say no?"

I looked at him in pleading, and he looked back at me, and I knew that all the persuasion we were putting forward was really unnecessary because he was aware of these facts already. But still he was reluctant.

"Why?" I demanded.

I saw his mouth open and close on an answer and then finally open again.

"Very well," he said abruptly. "I will accept, provided you perform in my place, George. An understudy can take your part. For myself, I prefer to go home. This tour has fatigued me."

George Mayfield's face lit up, then dropped visibly when Barney put in, "Won't do, sir. The gent said the offer depended on your appearing. Seems the lady of the house is an admirer of yours."

My father displayed none of the normal actor's gratification at that. He fell silent again, his face unreadable. I pushed past Elizabeth and George and placed my hand on his shoulder, shaking it slightly.

"Please, Papa, *please!*"

He looked up at me, patted my hand, and said abruptly, "Very well. I leave it to you, Barney, to handle all arrangements, and you, Aphra, to give my decision to Mr. Hillyard. Tell him we will repeat *The Tempest* since costumes and scenery for the rest of our repertoire are packed and ready for loading."

"You mean you are not going to meet him personally?" George Mayfield demanded in shocked tones. "That's very discourteous, Charles."

"So long as Hillyard gets the acceptance which he appears to be taking for granted, I don't imagine he will consider it so."

"In that case, I, as second lead, should receive him."

"Certainly not!" Elizabeth was indignant. "Let me remind you, George, that *I* am leading lady of this company and therefore take precedence over any supporting lead."

My father said quietly, "Aphra is my daughter, and I appoint her to represent me. Take it or leave it. I can retract my decision before the man arrives, if need be."

He picked up a stick of No. 9 and began to retouch his makeup before the flyblown mirror, his back toward us. There was an implacability about it which said all too plainly that he would fulfil his threat if pushed, so nobody pushed. Elizabeth Lorrimer shrugged again and murmured something inaudible, but she was at least pacified because the booking would go through, and George Mayfield, so long as acceptance was assured, was willing to put up no further opposition. Everyone departed quietly, satisfied because his moment of panic, the panic which every actor feels when a good booking seems to be slipping from his grasp, had passed.

I was left alone with my father.

"Thank you, Papa. You've made the right decision, and everyone is grateful, I'm sure."

"You, too, Aphra? But I don't want gratitude from you. All I want is for you to be happy, and if performing at this country mansion pleases you, well then, it pleases me."

"But don't you think you should give Mr. Hillyard your acceptance personally? Surely, you want to meet him?"

"I shall meet him at Abbotswood. That will be time enough."

My father used to say there were more dramas in life than could ever be performed upon a stage and that by the time a man died the curtain rose and fell many times. I should have remembered those words as I went to meet David Hillyard, but unlike the theatre, life gives us no warning when a curtain is about to rise, so how could I even suspect that I was about to enter the most important, the most far-reaching, and ultimately the most terrifying phase of my life?

The callboy had summoned me to the Green Room, where Mr. Hillyard waited, and on the way there I met Barney, so we went along together. Later I wished I had been able to make my entry alone; it would have been good to enjoy that meeting without Barney's alert eyes taking in every detail. Even though he did it in the most kindly fashion, I knew he observed the way in which Mr. Hillyard raised my hand to his lips, kissing it lightly but meaningfully as he glanced at me. There was admiration there, but not flattery; appreciation, but not invitation. Because I was familiar with the advances of men who considered touring actresses conveniently passing game, the respect behind Mr. Hillyard's courtesy was pleasing.

Here was no Stage Door Johnny with a bouquet, a flattering gift, and an invitation to dine in a private room (complete with chaise longue and a maid to unlace me) at the best local hotel. Here was a man who, I knew instinctively, made no practice of pursuing actresses. The Green Room was unfamiliar ground to him. He did not fit into the background in the way accustomed mashers did, and his gallantry bore no exaggerated overtures. He kissed my hand because it was the correct way for a gentleman to greet a lady, holding the fingers without any suggestive pressure, lifting them with respect instead of illicit anticipation. But the admiration was there, nonetheless, and I liked it.

"Miss Coleman, may I congratulate you on your performance? You are the most delightful Ariel I have ever seen."

"How many times have you seen *The Tempest* then?"

"No less than four—twice in London, once in Paris, and again in Vienna, where I was educated. And I even saw a lesser production of it in Corfu—that is reputed to be the island Shakespeare used for *The Tempest*, as I am sure you know, so it was included in a Festival programme last year when King Edward came to the throne. The Greeks cannot do justice to our dramatists—they should stick to their own great classics—but it was a courteous gesture on their part, an acknowledgement of the British influence on the island."

Barney stood boggling, greatly impressed by this sophisticated flow of words which revealed how travelled and cultured the speaker was. I too was impressed, although I endeavoured to display only a polite interest. I would have hated this man of the world to suspect that I had never travelled farther than a day trip to Ostend.

But worldly as he apparently was, he did not look it. There was no blasé air about him, no foppishness, no Burlington Bertie touch. He was good-looking in a quiet fashion, with pale blond hair which seemed to emphasize his pale well-bred features. His figure was slim and of medium height, which made him slightly taller than I. My head, I noticed, reached just below his shoulder, and that shoulder was elegantly clad in suiting which bespoke of Savile Row. There was no air of the country squire about him or, in contrast, of the Piccadilly Dandy, and he had the most charming smile I had ever met in a man.

I don't suppose I fell in love with him at that moment,

The Eagle at the Gate

but I took a big step toward it. His quiet manner and lack of affectation were in such contrast with the acting fraternity into which I had been born that he charmed me at once. I was accustomed to the lavish endearments bandied about amongst theatricals, all so superficial that they were meaningless other than as an expression of light-hearted affection; this man, I knew, would be incapable of artificiality or flippancy. A woman would know just where she stood with him, and the feeling would be good.

"My father begs you to excuse him, Mr. Hillyard. He is somewhat fatigued. But he asks me to tell you that he is very happy to accept your invitation to perform at Abbotswood."

The lie was essential for courtesy's sake, and I relegated my father's reluctance to the back of my mind.

David Hillyard nodded without surprise, and I was reminded of my father's remark that acceptance had been taken for granted. But Mr. Hillyard, I thought, was not a man to display his feeling too obviously, and when his eyes smiled into mine, I knew he was as pleased as I.

"Good," he said. "My sister will be glad. It is her invitation really, since she is mistress of Abbotswood. I merely conveyed it on her behalf."

"My father suggests that we repeat *The Tempest* and hopes this idea will be acceptable."

"*The Tempest* will be admirable, and now that May is on us it can be performed in the grounds. We have a natural open-air theatre on the south side, consisting of a wide area of lawn with a background of oaks."

"That sounds delightful."

"The audience will consist of family friends, county dignitaries and local society, plus visitors from the metropolis, all invited to celeberate my sister's fortieth birthday. I am delighted that she fell in with my suggestion. She should have come out of her shell long ago."

I was tempted to ask what had forced her into it, but refrained. There was so much I wanted to know. Was his sister married and, what was suddenly more important, was he?

"Are you a large family?" I ventured.

He shook his head. "Just the three of us—myself, my sister Claudia, and my cousin Harriet. Claudia is Mrs.

Bentine, daughter-in-law of the late owner, Sir William. It was a conferred title and, therefore, not hereditary. Not that my sister is concerned about that; she is content as mistress of Abbotswood, which is her greatest pride."

"And—her husband?"

"She is a widow."

Barney's discreet cough reminded us that we were not alone and that there were practicalities to discuss. I also knew it was a hint to me that the theatre had to be vacated within the hour. I could hear heavy sounds of scenery being dismantled and stage props being hauled about, work which should be done under the diligent eye of the stage manager, so no wonder Barney wanted to get down to business and to tie up this singular booking as quickly as possible. While he discussed essentials, I poured wine into glasses which stood on a wide table, the usual accompaniment to meetings in the Green Room, but suddenly I was conscious of its inferior quality and that David Hillyard must be accustomed to much better vintages, as my father was. Sometimes I wondered where my father had acquired his knowledge of wines. He always insisted that the company's finances could not run to the best just for Green Room consumption, but only the best was good enough for himself.

Barney's voice interrupted my thought.

"And carriages for the actors, sir. You mentioned something about supplying these."

"Indeed, yes. Tell me how many are in the cast, and transport will be provided accordingly."

"In *The Tempest*, sir, eleven main characters, but then there are two lords, three chief spirits, nymphs and reapers and mariners, a boatswain and ship's master, and other spirits attending on Prospero. Quite a company altogether, sir, plus dressers and stage crew and a wardrobe mistress. The lesser players act as understudies and, of course, double up for small parts, so we don't carry any dead wood, as it were, but all in all we number well over thirty."

David Hillyard was not the least perturbed. "I estimated so. All will be conveyed, but owing to the number of house-guests I am afraid that only the acting members of the company can be accommodated in Abbotswood itself; the rest will be put up over the mews and in cottages on the estate—quite comfortably furnished, I assure you—and your stage crew will be lodged in the village. I have made all necessary arrangements, which I trust will be satisfactory."

Barney murmured something about being sure they would. I could see a light of satisfaction in his eyes as he downed his wine at a gulp, and as I sipped mine, I reflected that David Hillyard had indeed been confident of that acceptance.

"My sister has put the east wing at the disposal of the acting members," he continued. "I propose to convey you all to Abbotswood tomorrow, Sunday, and the performance will take place on Monday, starting late in the afternoon to make the most of the evening light. That will leave the whole of the morning for any rehearsal Mr. Coleman may desire, and for that the company may use the big hall. I shall allow no one to intrude during that time."

I said I was sure my father would appreciate that and added that it was good of him to accommodate us all so well.

"Both my sister and I are anxious that you should be comfortable. Creature comforts must be important to people of a creative and artistic nature."

How little he knew about third-rate theatrical lodgings, I thought wryly. The east wing of a country mansion would be luxury indeed to travelling players.

He finished his wine, bowed slightly, and made his farewell, but before leaving, he said to me, "I myself will convey you and your father to Abbotswood. I already have the address of your lodgings and will call for you there. The rest of the conveyances will be sent direct to the theatre, so will the company please assemble outside the main doors at ten o'clock tomorrow morning?"

"My!" Barney exclaimed after the man's well-tailored figure had departed. "Hasn't forgotten a thing, has he, Miss Aphra? Planned it all down to the last detail. Just like a campaign. . . . "

TWO

The cavalcade which set off from Canterbury the next day must have impressed the inhabitants and caused a stir in every village through which it passed. There were landaus, victorias, wagonettes, buggies, traps and flies, as well as sturdy wagons equipped with wooden seats for the stage crew and luggage. The whole procession had an air of a large-scale picnic, for in addition to transport, the Hillyards had provided refreshment for the travellers. There were hampers containing wine and delicacies, although the journey was little over twenty miles, but the horses were slow, and on such a day as this no one was in the mood for haste. A stop was made halfway along the old Roman road, and rugs were spread beside a stream. We passed the party, David Hillyard and I, as we drove by in one of Abbotswood's best carriages.

That we should be travelling alone instead of with my father was an unexpected development, but no more unexpected than his announcement, at breakfast that morning, that he would not be accompanying us but would arrive at Abbotswood in time for the performance on Monday, having business to attend to in Folkestone that day. "There is a possibility that the manager of the Hippodrome there will book us for the autumn. It would be a good opening date for a new tour, and while we are in the vicinity, it seems wise to take advantage of a personal call. Folkestone is only about four miles from Hythe."

There was nothing I could say to that, although I was again left to make my father's excuses to Mr. Hillyard, but I certainly expressed my opinion about the next surprise he sprang.

He had decided to let George Mayfield play Prospero, he himself switching to the role of Caliban. "George has wanted to play Prospero for a long time and deserves a chance. I imagine he will be delighted."

George, who was lodging in the same house as ourselves, certainly was. He promised to rehearse the part as soon as the company arrived at Abbotswood and set off jauntily for the theatre to join the travelling party. Only then did I round on my father.

"*You* . . . play Caliban! You know perfectly well that Prospero is one of your most successful roles!"

"There is no reason why I shouldn't be equally successful as the unfortunate slave."

"There is every reason! The audience will expect to see you as you are, handsome and elegant and dignified, not as a hairy monster!"

My father laughed, kissed me lightly, and told me not to fret. "I am growing older, my dear—fifty next birthday. It is time I stopped being the matinee idol and concentrated on character parts. Besides, I have wanted to play Caliban for a long time."

"You have never said so."

"I am saying so now. As much as George deserves a chance to play Prospero, *I* deserve a chance to experiment. Do you doubt my ability?" he finished on a teasing note.

Of course, I didn't. My father knew every major Shakespearean rôle by heart; he had stood in for other actors at rehearsals and never even needed the prompt copy. But I was illogically disappointed. Without realising it, I had been looking forward to seeing him play Prospero against the setting of a beautiful country mansion. The background would be admirable, and the audience promised to be very different from our usual provincial one. Perhaps I had also anticipated the final moment when he would draw his daughter onstage from the wings and present her with pride to this distinguished gathering, and I would look up at his handsome profile and think how wonderful he was. . . .

I would still think him wonderful, of course, but would we make such an appealing picture with his handsome looks disguised beyond all recognition?

However, my protests met only with amusement and so availed me nothing. A cab conveyed my father to the station long before David Hillyard was due to collect us, but before leaving, he suggested that Elizabeth Lorrimer should take his place on the drive to Abbotswood because he felt it desirable that I should be chaperoned, at which I laughed and declared that it would more likely be a case of *my* chaperoning *her*.

"Apart from the fact that she cannot resist flirting with any man, Papa, you must surely know that she has been having an affair with Miles Tregunter throughout this tour! They are not merely Ferdinand and Miranda onstage, you know, and you cannot fail to have noticed that whatever travel arrangements you make for the company, those two invariably finish up in the same railway compartment—hers. They will surely wish to travel together today."

"That would be most inappropriate. He ranks lower in the company than the leading lady."

I was well aware of that. Strict observance of theatrical precedence was an unwritten law. But I also knew that Elizabeth would no more welcome me as a travelling companion than I would welcome her. In David Hillyard's company she would consider me in the way, and I would undoubtedly feel it. No, I decided, I would leave the fair Elizabeth to her current favourite, and I skilfully led my father away from the subject, or so I thought, but when finally departing, he said, "What is this man Hillyard like? I don't care for the idea of your travelling alone with a stranger. You know I am always urging you to watch your step through life and never to take people at their face value. There can be menace behind a mask, remember."

It was a habit of my father's to deliver such gems of wisdom, a favourite one being that there were always predators lurking like eagles at the gate, but at least he spared me that one now, merely repeating his wish that I should not travel alone with a man I knew nothing about and adding that two women together were always safer.

"Oh, come, Papa! There will be a whole stream of carriages driving in the same direction! Indeed, I wonder that Abbotswood can command so many. They must be a very rich family indeed. As to what Mr. Hillyard is like, to tell the truth he made little impression except that he was gentlemanly and quite old."

It was a lie, except for the gentlemanly part, but necessary if I were to allay my father's anxiety and get my own way.

"Old, my dear?"

"In his thirties, at least."

My father laughed and said, "What it must be like to be young! But I still insist that you be accompanied, and I am sure Elizabeth would like to travel with our host. She might even consider it her due. So don't forget."

I didn't forget, but I did nothing about it. Not for the world would I have missed the opportunity to drive alone with such a man. There was a streak of stubbornness in me which was not above scheming to get what I wanted, so when Mr. Hillyard drove up to that very ordinary terraced house in that very ordinary street (theatrical digs were never in the best areas), I was ready and waiting, watching from behind heavy Victorian lace curtains and taking care that they should not move and betray me.

What I saw was precisely what I expected, but even so it impressed me. A handsome maroon landau, drawn by a pair of greys which even I, ignorant as I was about horseflesh, recognised as thoroughbreds, drew into the pavement dead on time. That did not surprise me, either, for already I had plenty of evidence that this man was a man of his word and completely thorough. What he planned would always be carried out; what he promised would be fulfilled. It was only unreliable theatrical folk like my father who were unpredictable, and I was now faced with the task of explaining away this very characteristic yet again.

David Hillyard was understanding. "A new tour must obviously take priority over a casual booking, but I could have arranged for him to be driven over to Folkestone tomorrow morning. It is only a short journey from Abbotswood, and the theatre—it will be the Hippodrome, the only one there—won't be open on Sunday. At which hotel will your father be spending the night? I can send a carriage over for him."

I had to confess I had no idea.

"Never mind. I will drive to the theatre tomorrow morning and hope to contact him there and bring him to Abbotswood myself. I greatly look forward to meeting him. I have seen him act so many times. He is a man of outstanding ability and memorable looks."

This pleased me so much that I did not even think of asking where and when he had seen my father perform, and only later did it occur to me that it must have been farther afield than Canterbury, since this was a number two stand and my father usually played only number ones.

To close a tour with a number two was one thing, but to include it as a regular date was quite another. For me, this visit had been the first, but it was certainly one I was not likely to forget.

Was there ever such a day in my life? Had the sun ever shone more brightly, and had I ever been so aware of my own femininity and my companion's masculinity? Sitting beside him in my best gown of pink and white striped muslin, with a white straw boater trimmed with floating pink ribbons and a parasol of pale pink silk adorned with white lace ruffles, I was aware of nothing but happiness coupled with expectancy. That this day marked the opening of a new and wonderful chapter in my life I had not the slightest doubt. The mere fact that I was sitting in this splendid carriage with a man who epitomised everything that was lacking in my life—stability, wealth, position, and, more than all, conventionality—was enough to carry me up to the clouds. At that stage of my life conventionality was a most desirable thing. It held the attraction of the unknown for me. It was unassociated with theatrical lodgings, with anxiety over bookings, with secondhand clothes bought from theatrical "wardrobes," with periods of "resting" between tours and doing the rounds of the agents in the hope of obtaining a fill-in, with my father totting up accounts and his almost regular announcement that we would have to live more economically.

A theatrical life might appear to be glamorous, but the truth was quite the reverse. To me, a conventional life was the more desirable because I firmly believed that it lacked even a nodding acquaintance with such anxieties as ours, and I believed this because I glimpsed it every Sunday as we shunted toward our next date, our next lodging house. Through grimy train windows I saw the secure, comfortable homes of conventional people and envied them. I envied their neat gardens, their dog kennels, their vegetable plots, their cosily curtained windows, their front porches, their closed doors. Actually, to own a house, no matter how small, would be to own one's world.

So, to me, conventionality had a lot to be said for it. To step out of a world in which one never dared to contemplate the future into a world where one was not afraid to seemed a most desirable fate—and never more so than now.

"Tell me about yourself, Miss Coleman. Tell me about your life. It must be very interesting, even exciting. I hope you won't find Abbotswood tame by comparison."

David Hillyard was smiling at me. He had removed his grey bowler and placed it on the seat between us. The crown had a well-brushed nap, and the brim looked as if it had been carefully steamed and curled by an efficient valet. His gloves were of dove grey and immaculate; the hands inside them held the reins with confidence and ease. Confidence and ease were in every line of this man. Particularly his face. He had never known uncertainty in his life.

"There is nothing really exciting about it, Mr. Hillyard. It has stimulating moments, of course, such as when a performance is well received—"

"Or when your father brings you down to the footlights to present you to the audience. He always looks so proud when he does that."

"Always? You have seen him perform frequently then? It couldn't have been in Canterbury because he rarely accepts a booking there."

"I wonder why."

"Because it is a number two date. That means it isn't normally included in a number one tour."

"Then what brought him to Canterbury this time?"

I answered frankly, "Necessity. For the final week it was the best we could obtain."

"Which was fortunate for Abbotswood. And for me."

His eyes, frank and full of liking, ran over me, and I didn't mind at all.

"You look like sugar candy, Miss Coleman, all pink and white. Very delectable," he finished with a smile. I was so pleased that I felt my colour rise and hoped he would mistake it for a reflection of my pink parasol.

"Tell me more about theatrical tours—this placing of towns in categories, for instance. Why is it that Canterbury, a famous cathedral city, ranks only as a number two, when a lesser seaside resort like Folkestone apparently ranks as a number one?"

Why, indeed? The question should have occurred to me. Only my father's sudden departure had suggested that Folkestone was a desirable date; he had not actually stated that it was a number one, only that it would be a good place in which to start a tour. Sometimes we opened in second-ranking theatres as a tryout, but I had never known my father to go hurrying off to clinch anything less than a first. Not knowing the answer, I shrugged it off and was glad when David Hillyard didn't press the point, but I resolved to question my father about it as soon as I saw him again, for it now seemed a double discourtesy to our host to behave as he had done, avoiding a meeting for the second time.

The thought startled me. Was my father really trying to avoid a meeting with this man? Ridiculous. There was absolutely no reason why he should and absolutely none to make me wonder.

It was then that we overtook the rest of the party, or rather the last carriage in the procession. In a meadow beyond, the other members of the company were spreading rugs beside the stream, but the last carriage was travelling very leisurely, its occupants absorbed in each other. I recognised Elizabeth's back, sitting very proudly in her corner. She too carried a parasol to shield her complexion from the sun, but it was a finer parasol than mine—champagne silk adorned with massed flowers. It looked like a miniature garden, and so did her magnificent hat. Automatically my mind registered: *The Second Mrs. Tanqueray*, Birmingham, spring tour of last year... So Helen Rossiter, who played the lead, had been forced to sell her gowns from that show. Poor Helen, she couldn't be doing so well ... and they would cost her a lot to replace should she get another part requiring such clothes. The advantage of doing Shakespeare was that, being in costume, the actors did not have to supply their own.

As we overtook the carriage, I saw the rest of Elizabeth's outfit—a tightly fitting gown of heavy champagne moiré, lavishly trimmed with matching lace. Tiers of it cascaded from wrists and throat. Such a heavy costume must be extremely uncomfortable in this heat, I thought, especially since it demanded the tightest lacing, plus pads on the hips and beneath the armpits to make the waist look even smaller. No wonder she was sitting so erect. Her companion would find her whale-boned figure rigidly unbending on this particular journey; there could be no loosening of her stays, as on the Sunday trains.

But she certainly looked splendid, riding in an elegant victoria as if it were the state coach itself, with the enslaved Miles Tregunter as her prince consort. The fifteen-odd years between them only bore testimony to her eternal youth.

As we passed, she sat even more bolt upright, and I saw her surprised and speculative glance settle on my companion. She had not expected me to be travelling alone with this wealthy stranger who had walked onto the stage yesterday afternoon when all were gathered there for tea. I smiled and waved to her, but she had no time to acknowledge me, for Mr. Hillyard had bowed to her, and she was too busy bowing and smiling in return to bother with anyone else. Miles Tregunter frowned. He was a handsome, spoilt, and sulky youth who resented being eclipsed even for a passing greeting.

Before we finally passed, Elizabeth's eyes turned to me. There was fury there, and a question. *Where is your father?* they demanded. *And why wasn't I invited to travel in his place? I shall have a word or two to say to him on that score, make no mistake!*

Well, Aphra Coleman, I admonished secretly, you have only yourself to blame if he is angry. You shouldn't have been so selfish and scheming. But there was time enough to repent about that, and for the present I could continue to enjoy David Hillyard's exclusive company. It was unlikely to come my way again, so I resolved to make the most of it.

I lifted my hand to Elizabeth again, this time waving good-bye.

"Do you wish to stop and join the party, Miss Coleman?"

"No, indeed," I answered a shade too quickly. "That is —I am not in the least thirsty, and to tell the truth, it is a rare treat for me to take a country drive in such a vehicle as this." I glanced at the waiting carriages gathered on the verge, their horses cropping the grass and the drivers looking somewhat enviously at the picnickers. "Abbotswood's coach house must be very well stocked, Mr. Hillyard. And with such a variety of vehicles, too!"

"My dear Miss Coleman, we do not own them! Or only a few, that is. This landau, a brougham, the victoria Miss Lorrimer is traveling in, a couple of traps, and some wagonettes used by the staff. The rest I hired from surrounding villages."

"And they were all ready to be at your service, just like that?" I snapped my fingers lightly, as if giving an order.

"Indeed, no. I reserved the lot of them a fortnight ago"

"A fortnight! That was before the company even arrived in Canterbury. You must have been very sure that my father would accept your invitation."

"Not sure, but hopeful. There seemed to be no reason why he should refuse since your tour was in its last week and the company would therefore be free."

"But how did you know? I mean, how did you know it was the end of the tour?"

"How could I fail to? The theatre billing announced it. *'Final week of the Thespian Players' current Shakespearean tour! Don't miss this opportunity to see Charles Coleman as Prospero! Such a chance may never come your way again!'* I didn't believe that, of course. *The Tempest* is one of his most successful productions and Prospero one of his most successful parts, so I would consider it very surprising if he failed to appear in it again somewhere, sometime."

He looked at me with a teasing smile which, at the same time, was gentle and understanding. I think it was then that I first noticed the quality of that smile, the tenderness and sweetness of it, but it was by no means the last time it was to touch my heart.

Not surprisingly, we arrived at Abbotswood in advance of the rest of the company. Although we did not linger on the way, we did not hurry either, and this leisurely approach served as a kind of apéritif for what was to come. I relished every moment and found myself comparing this unusual Sunday with the normal Sundays in my life. From babyhood I had endured the slow train journeys which were the lot of touring actors, and I suppose it was from those days that I acquired the habit of window gazing into the world of other people and secretly envying them.

I would make up stories about them—the occupants of a wayside cottage could be anything from smallholders to farm labourers, with a warm hearth to toast their feet by on a cold Sunday afternoon while the troubadours of the road shivered in draughty railway carriages, or the owners of a fine house on a distant hill might have a brood of happy children to ride the ponies which must surely fill those stables I could glimpse at the side. The stories and the characters were endless because the houses I caught sight of during those journeys were endless, too.

No one knew of the dreams I wove. Even as a child I kept them to myself, perhaps because I did not want to distress my parents by seeming to be discontented with my lot—the lot which they had ordained for me. But the weaving of dreams persisted, and always I was in the centre of them—the young wife in a neat little suburban house; the young mother bringing up children in the country; the elegant mistress of a fine house in a fashionable district, playing hostess to her successful husband's business friends. These dreams provided security of a sort, wrapping me in a flimsy shawl of pretence but making me feel that there could be permanency in life.

Now, in 1902, nearly three hundred touring companies shunted their way north, south, east, and west of the British Isles every Sunday, whilst the rest of the inhabitants sat over their roast beef, devoured the scandals in the Sunday press, and took afternoon naps, and sometimes I wondered whether any other young actress passed her dreary Sabbaths in the same way as I or whether there was something odd about me, something unnatural which made me yearn for what I would certainly never have.

Theatrical people were a race apart; everyone knew that. Once the smell of greasepaint was in their nostrils and the call of the road echoed in their ears, none wanted any other way of life—or so they said. But sometimes, when we were shunted into a siding to wait for a passing train heading for our ultimate destination (depleted Sunday services never included direct trains to anywhere), my mother would get out her portable spirit stove to make tea, and I would wonder if she also might be playing a secret game, imagining herself in a nice bright kitchen in her own nice bright home, boiling water on a proper stove.

I never knew. All I did know was that wherever my father went, she was content to go, too, and when at last an obliging train came along and obligingly halted, and we were shunted out of the siding and hitched onto the end of it, she would calmly gather up the teacups and the brown earthenware teapot which always travelled with us, tip the tea leaves through the window onto the rail track, give us both a warm smile, and say, "There now, wasn't that good? I couldn't have made a better pot of tea in the kitchens of Buckingham Palace!"

"Miss Coleman, is anything wrong? You look sad. I trust you are not fatigued? This is my sister's favourite carriage. She insisted that I should use no other to bring you to Abbotswood. I should be distressed to think you were uncomfortable...."

I jerked back to the moment, shocked to find that my lashes were wet.

"No, no! I was just thinking, that was all. Dreaming. I have a deplorable habit of dreaming, Mr. Hillyard."

Again the gentle, understanding smile.

"Someday, Miss Coleman, I will discover what you dream about."

But none of my dreams had prepared me for Abbotswood. Only in pictures had I seen anything like it, for the trains of Edwardian England never travelled close to such properties or even skirted their boundaries. Only rarely did the turrets and towers of places like Arundel or Bodiam rise splendidly on the horizon, but castles like those seemed to have nothing to do with reality. One could not identify with them or imagine ordinary human beings—the nice, cosy, conventional kind—living there. Were there kitchens in such places, comfy bedrooms, family living rooms? Could a man put his feet up on the fender and puff smoke from behind his Sunday newspaper? I doubted it. Some ducal presence would preside there, complete with peer's robes of crimson velvet and ermine, and his duchess would never be without her coronet or at the very least a tiara, and they would dine in state at a vast table in a vast hall with fleets of flunkeys to wait on them—blissfully unaware of us antlike creatures shunting along in boxes on wheels in the valleys below.

That was what I imagined as a child. Such pictures awed me, but did not enchant. They conjured up no dreams of the kind of security I secretly yearned for, the security of a warm and happy home in which I would feel not only safe, but at ease. Never for a moment did I picture myself at ease amongst grandeur.

Abbotswood, of course, was not on a par with Arundel, home of the premier duke of England, nor had it been built as a fortress castle like Bodiam, but even so no railway tracks would have had the impertinence to run close enough for passengers to catch a glimpse of it, and even if they had, the surrounding acres, with their centuries-old trees, would have screened it from view. Mansions like Abbotswood had been built for privacy, and their situation ensured it.

The casual way in which David Hillyard drove through the gates suggested that he was approaching nothing spectacular, nothing grand. The action had an air of familiarity which reduced it to the level of the ordinary for him. But not for me.

The entrance was impressive, flanked by stone pillars linked by an arch, so that a solid frame was formed for the heavy iron gates which were opened by a lodgekeeper, who touched his forelock respectfully. His appearance immediately distracted my attention; otherwise, I might have noticed a detail which escaped me until later. As it was, my glance went to his small lodge, stone-built and with latticed panes to the windows. I thought it a most enviable property but naturally did not betray this. Not for nothing had I been trained as an actress from childhood. When the man inclined his head to me respectfully, I inclined mine graciously in return, with the right amount of hauteur and courtesy.

"Leave the gates open, Walker. There are other carriages following."

The order was given automatically, with the ease of someone accustomed to issuing commands. With an instinctive ability to note mannerisms and customs, I observed the way in which it was done. All knowledge was useful, and observation was never wasted. This was essential training for an actress and never failed to come in useful.

The landau moved on. We passed through the gates, and as we did so, I glanced up and saw the detail I had overlooked.

Carved in the centre of the stone arch was an eagle's head, so skilfully done that it looked predatory, menacing, too realistic for comfort. I jerked my glance away and saw the bird of prey again, reproduced in iron in the centre of each gate, but less sharply contoured so that it seemed less threatening than the jutting stone beak and outthrust claws overhead.

The next moment we were bowling through acres of parkland, then over a bridge leading to formal grounds beyond, then along a curving drive between massed rhododendrons already ablaze with colour. Giant oaks, sycamores, and horse chestnut trees gave an added background and effectively screened what was to come. Every curve promised a rising of the curtain until I was on tenterhooks to see what lay beyond. I did not merely feel that I was driving into another world. I knew it, and I was right, for as we rounded the last curve, the curtain rose so dramatically that my breath caught. Here was a house beautiful beyond my imagining. It had the air of a place which had been carefully planned, skilfully designed, and diligently preserved. To the right and left of the porticoed front entrance two long wings spread in creeper-covered charm, and shining sash windows rose four storeys high, diminishing in carefully balanced size, but those on the ground floor were in Queen Anne style, elegantly bowed, and so were those on the first floor, opening onto wrought-iron balconies. This was a house of dignity and elegance, and I loved it on sight. That predatory eagle's head above the gates had no association with it. I forgot it at once.

"Welcome to Abbotswood," David Hillyard said quietly. "You have no idea how long I have waited to bring you here."

THREE

I looked at him, startled, and he smiled. "I am not being presumptuous, Miss Coleman. Merely truthful."

His frankness encouraged me to the same.

"How long?" I asked breathlessly.

"For as long as I have been following the Thespian Players from town to town, city to city. You are not angry, I hope?"

"Should I be?"

"You might condemn me for practicing a certain subterfuge."

"You mean your story about the mistress of Abbotswood being an admirer of my father was untrue?"

"Is that what your stage manager said?"

"It was an impression he received from you."

"Then I am indeed to be condemned!" His smile was impenitent. "Alas, Miss Coleman, my sister, Claudia, has not been inside a theatre since the death of her husband, and that was very many years ago. The only entertainments she has watched since then have been those put on in the grounds of Abbotswood, amateur productions in aid of charity. Still, I haven't the slightest doubt she will enjoy meeting your father and seeing him act. But it was I who put the idea to her, and a good idea it was, for Abbotswood really is the ideal place in which to stage *The Tempest*. If your father had not suggested that particular production, I would have done so, for our outdoor theatre is the perfect setting. Lawrence, my late brother-in-law, used to stage many amateur productions. I believe there may still be faded pictures of them in existence; I don't know where. So at least my story had a basis of truth, and you must surely understand that a certain touch of guile was necessary. How could I approach your father with the request that he should bring his daughter to Abbotswood because I wanted to meet her ever since I first saw her at the Theatre Royal, Bristol? He would have doubted my motives, and understandably, but I trust you will not, Miss Coleman. They are ancient and honourable, believe me."

I did believe him, and suddenly I was happy in a way I had never experienced before.

The sound of wheels and hooves brought a couple of stableboys running from beyond the house. As their master reined the horses, they caught hold of bridles and bits and brought them to a halt. Then David jumped down and held out both hands to me. It was suddenly natural to think of him by his Christian name. Within a space of minutes formality seemed to have no place in our lives, though I knew we would continue to observe it.

The main double doors of the house opened as if by magic, and down the steps came a manservant, who collected my valise and stood dutifully aside as we mounted the steps ahead of him. At the entrance a white-haired butler inclined a dignified head and announced that Mrs. Bentine awaited us on the terrace and that luncheon would be served there just as soon as we were ready.

"A buffet has been set out in the dining hall for the company, but Mrs. Bentine thought you would wish to share something more intimate with your personal friends, sir." The man peered with shortsighted eyes at the empty carriage behind us and added delicately, "I take it the number will be for three instead of four, sir?"

"Quite so, Truman. Miss Coleman's father will be arriving later. And now I think she would like to freshen herself after the journey. Be good enough to summon Mrs. Stevens."

But Mrs. Stevens had already appeared. I saw the black-clad figure of a buxom housekeeper standing near the stairs and knew her rank at once, for the traditional costume of her station appeared regularly in Edwardian society drama.

She was a plump woman, whose bright eyes were too bright with curiosity to put me at ease. Given the opportunity, she would gossip, so I discouraged any such idea with a polite but remote smile and, gathering up my skirts, followed her upstairs. The treads were of stone, but the balusters were of wrought iron, picked out here and there in gold leaf. My admiring glance did not escape the housekeeper, who promptly said, "Made by Deakon's, of course, miss, and a very long time ago at that, but Master Red's workmanship is as fine today as in his forefathers'."

"Master Red?"

"Deakon, Miss. Of Deakon's Forge. The family has been in these parts even longer than the Bentines, who are newcomers, as you might say, having come here only three generations ago."

I discouraged any further confidences about her employers by making no reply, but those shrewd eyes missed nothing. The involuntary start I gave on being confronted with two immense stone eagles, standing like sentinels at the head of the great staircase, immediately brought further comment.

"The Bentine eagles, miss. They're a kind of symbol, here at Abbotswood. The late Sir William's father used to breed them in captivity. It weren't cruel, he said, and I understand he was a good, fair-minded man. They were confined to the woods, netted in, but with enough space for their needs, he always said, but I fancy Mr. Hillyard would disagree. Anyway, they all died off. Perhaps it weren't natural to shut them in, even in woods as big as these, or so my mother used to say. She was in service here, like her mother afore her, and I'm proud to carry on the tradition. My mother also used to tell me that the old gentleman considered eagles to be the proudest and most aristocratic creatures ever created, but somehow I don't fancy they'd be to everyone's liking, and as it turned out—" She broke off, changing the subject hastily. "Now we're in the east wing, miss, and I'm sure you'll all be comfortable here."

She opened a door.

"I trust you'll find this room to your liking. Your father's is next door." She hesitated. "Has he not come with you then?"

"He will arrive in time for the performance tomorrow."

She beamed. "Such excitement there is! Miss Harriet was telling me that Mr. Hillyard once took her to a matinee at Bristol, to see his Richard the Second. Very keen on acting is Miss Harriet. A little too much, I sometimes think, the way she goes on—"

She checked herself. Curious as I was, I did not question her, and when she asked if I thought I would be able to find my way downstairs or if I would like her to send a maid to conduct me, I said, with a confidence I did not wholly feel, that I was sure I would find my way, at which she nodded and said, "All you do is turn right out of this corridor, and then right again and then left, and you will come to the main stairs down to the hall. The terrace, where madam awaits you, runs across the back of the house, so once downstairs you just turn left again and go through the drawing room."

I thanked her and she closed the door behind her a little unwillingly. I guessed that she had wanted to linger for a chat and that she imagined I would be fair game because I was "in the profession." The thought annoyed me, but it also put me on my mettle. This might be the first time I had ever crossed the threshold of such a home as this, but no member of the household staff was going to suspect it.

Alone, I glanced around. I had never seen such a room, never had so spacious a bed all to myself, never slept beneath a canopy like that or between such sheets. I fingered them reverently, so soft and fine they were; then I replaced the bedcover and smoothed it in case any trace of my action should remain. Whatever I did, I must not betray myself. I must carry off every situation with ease and apparent confidence.

I moved from the bed to the dressing table and ran my hand over the smooth patina of the wood. How old was it? I wished my father were here to tell me. He was knowledgeable about furniture, knew exactly which period was associated with which style. On the rare occasions that we did not perform Shakespeare he varied the programme with Sheridan or other dramatists and knew precisely the correct furnishings each period required. The right pictures, too, and which artists had been painting at that particular time, which portrait painters. "A walking encyclopaedia, your Pa is," Barney sometimes said.

I crossed to the window, where a velvet-upholstered seat curved within the bay and matching curtains hung from ceiling to floor. I could not resist touching everything, relishing the loveliness of it all, and as I stood there, reverently stroking a curtain fold, something drew my glance outside, and I halted with my hand poised. Then I dropped it, for a man stood watching me from below, an amused smile on his face. He had flaming red hair, and I disliked him at once. More than disliked. I resented him because, infuriatingly, he had caught me out.

Abruptly I withdrew.

When I went downstairs, David was waiting in the hall. He put his hand beneath my elbow quite naturally, and quite naturally I allowed him to. I was glad of his nearness, glad of his moral support, for that distant encounter had unnerved me. Would Claudia Bentine see through me with the same uncanny perception? And how many other people in this household would guess that I was unaccustomed to such standards as these? In a brief moment of panic I experienced a longing for the free and easy atmosphere of the theatre and wished the rest of the company had arrived, so that I could hide amongst them. If Elizabeth Lorrimer wished to take the stage this weekend, I was more than willing to let her. She would carry it off with greater poise than I, and if she were awed by unaccustomed luxury, she would make sure that no mocking eyes observed it.

I wanted to ask who the disconcerting stranger was, but refrained.

"You look very lovely, Miss Coleman. Aphra. I always think of you as Aphra. My sister will be enchanted by you, as I am."

"I hardly expect a woman to react like a man—" I clipped the words off, slightly embarrassed and confused, and he laughed.

"She will be enchanted in a different way, of course." His clear, calm eyes looked down at me, and he continued. "I can't believe that I have actually succeeded in getting you here. While I admit that I had little anxiety about your father's acceptance, for it is logical that theatrical managements welcome bookings, I had a great deal when it came to wondering whether you, personally, would like me. I hope you do. I feel you do. And I hope you will continue to because I have no intention of allowing you to go out of my life. This meeting has taken too much planning and scheming."

I was lost for words. I felt the colour ebb and flow in

my cheeks. I felt a great deal more than that, and the feeling was as exciting as it was unfamiliar. Never before had the pressure of a man's hand beneath my elbow made me feel so self-conscious or my blood run so hotly, and when I felt composed enough to glance up at him, I saw that his face was very still and his eyes were intent.

So this is how it feels, I marvelled. This is how a man and a woman are drawn to each other. *This* is desire . . . the quickening . . . the longing. . . .

"Aphra," he said again. "Sweet Aphra. That is how I have thought of you ever since I first saw you walk upon a stage. That was as Ariel, too—the loveliest sprite I ever saw, and the most real. All other Ariels I have seen have been neither boy nor girl—quite sexless, as I suppose Ariel was meant to be—but you could never be that, never anything but completely feminine."

"In that case I have given a bad performance! An actress should never project her own personality. She should get into the skin of the part."

"I prefer that you remain in your own. It is a very beautiful skin."

I had no answer. The conversation seemed to be getting beyond me and to have advanced at an unpredictable pace, with sensuous undercurrents to which I responded but felt I should avoid. Nor had I expected this from a man who seemed so conventional and correct.

We had reached the terrace. I was both glad and sorry. Then the deep awareness which united us was broken as a tall, good-looking woman came toward us. Beyond her I was aware of others. Another woman—and the man who had regarded me with such mocking amusement as I stood at my window. I wanted to turn and run away, but David Hillyard's grasp of my elbow was firm.

"You have no need to fear Claudia," he said quietly. "She is the sweetest woman in the world."

And so she was. She had the same calm grey eyes as her brother, the same tranquillity, the same capacity to make one feel at ease.

The hand she held out to me was long and tapering. From the way she held it, palm downward and the fingers slightly drooping, I expected her handshake to be limp, but it was not, for as I accepted it, the palm turned and the fingers curved about my own with surprising strength.

"Welcome to Abbotswood, Miss Coleman."

Her voice was exactly as I should have expected from someone so poised and full of grace. Light, confident, and cultured. And apart from the eyes there was also another resemblance between herself and her brother—they were both fair-skinned and fair-haired, with symmetrical features which bore a strong family resemblance. It was surprising how features so very much alike could be decidedly feminine in one and decidedly masculine in the other.

And then the same features were approaching, but diminished into plainness, similar, yet somehow dissimilar, like a distorted reflection in a mirror, and I realised that the woman in the background had come forward and was waiting to be introduced. Her appearance was startling, like a grotesque caricature of Claudia Bentine. She was approximately the same height and slimness, but slightly younger, and it seemed to me that she had made some pathetic attempt to model herself on the elegant mistress of the house, at the same time striving to outdo her by wearing the maximum of adornment instead of pursuing simple good taste. Even her hair was exaggeratedly frizzed, seeming to crown her trailing gown of patterned voile like a bird's nest perched on a flowering bush. The final result of all this was bizarre and unbecoming.

Claudia Bentine said, "Harriet, dear, come and be introduced—" and took the oddly pathetic woman by the hand and drew her forward.

This time the handshake was indeed limp. Inert fingers lay within my own so that my grasp of them seemed almost too strong. I said, "You must be the cousin Mr. Hillyard told me about."

"What did he tell you about me?" she demanded quickly, then just as quickly her glance darted to the table in the background. "I see you are all lunching together, but I am being left out. I suppose that is because I am only a Hillyard and not a Bentine."

"I am a Hillyard, too," David reminded her.

"And the reason the table is set for four," Claudia said equably, "is that Miss Coleman and her father are joining me, and David also because he brought them."

So her brother had not yet mentioned my father's delayed arrival. I explained immediately, but as soon as I had spoken, I could have bitten back the words, because although not a flicker of expression touched Claudia Bentine's face, I knew she would have preferred this strange cousin not to know that there was to be a vacant place at table.

She turned quickly to the man, who throughout this meeting had not moved from his position at the far corner of the terrace. He was leaning negligently against the stone balustrade, watching us all.

"Then you, Red—will you take Mr. Coleman's place?"

Of course, I thought, he *would* be called Red. No name could have suited him better.

He left the balustrade and strolled toward us.

"My dear Claudia, I would be delighted were I only free, but alas!" He spread his hands, indicating how much he regretted having to leave her, but how unavoidable it was, at which she smiled and remarked that he need say no more. The implication of an amorous assignation was obvious and seemed entirely credible. If anyone had told me that the man was a womaniser, I would not have been surprised.

Then he was standing before me, looking down from a height which I found surprising. The foreshortened angle from my bedroom window had given no such impression.

Harriet Hillyard promptly clapped her hands and spun round, watching her floating voile skirts swirl about her feet, delighted as a child.

"Now you will *have* to include me, won't you, Claudia, because Miss Coleman will think you very rude if you do not, and you hate to be thought rude. Oh, I know there is a buffet for everyone else—I have been watching preparations all morning—but don't imagine I would enjoy it more, or tell me what a chance it would be for me to meet the rest of the Thespian Players, because it is Miss Coleman and her father that I want to meet, even though David has warned me that I must not bother them. He says they will be very busy, though why *they* should be and not the rest of the company, I don't understand."

"All the principal actors will be very much occupied," David told her.

I could tell from his voice that he had had much experience in dealing with his eccentric cousin.

His sister said, "My dear Harriet, of course you may lunch with us." Like David's, her voice was patient. Then she turned to me and said how disappointed she was to hear that my father had been delayed but that she looked forward to meeting him even more now that she had met his daughter.

"Do you resemble him, I wonder?"

"I am always told that I take after my mother."

David moved to a table bearing decanters and glasses and began pouring wine for us all, and then the man called Red was at my side, saying quietly, "Claudia forgot to introduce us. You must excuse her—she is a woman with much on her mind. My name is Deakon. It isn't my place to welcome you to Abbotswood since I don't live here, but I am confident that Hillyard has already done so. He is meticulous about everything."

"He is extremely kind, if that is what you mean."

The man smiled, and his eyes, which were the colour of dark amber, looked down at me with the same discernment that I had felt even from a distance. I wished he would go away. He made me feel uncomfortable.

I was glad when David came back. He held out a glass to me, and as he smiled, I realised that it was the shape of his mouth which lent gentleness to his face, for it was almost delicately formed, with the lips curving upward at the corners. For me, it held a potent appeal, and I found myself imagining what it would feel like against my own.

I forced my glance away and saw that Red Deakon was no longer at my side. He was bowing over Claudia's hand, and she was saying something about being grateful for his visit.

"It is good of you to give up so much of your time to what must seem to be no more than a whim on my part, but I have wanted to see those balconies, with those hideous eagles' heads, replaced for a very long time. How soon can you produce new designs?"

"Within a few weeks. I shall do them myself."

"How kind you are! I would scarcely have expected a firm like Deakon's to bother with so small an order."

"Replacing wrought-iron balconies is not exactly a small

order, but whatever the size, we value all work. From friends, particularly."

"Good-bye, then, for the present."

So he was leaving. I was glad of that, for it meant he was not a houseguest. I hoped I would have no further meeting with him, for although he had given not the slightest indication, I knew he had been watching me as I accepted the wine from David, and somehow I also knew that he had read my thoughts and interpreted them correctly, just as he had observed and correctly interpreted my stroking of the velvet curtains.

Refusing to be disconcerted by him anymore, I studied him with matching frankness as he came over and said good-bye. In the sunlight I saw that his eyes were not really the colour of amber, but that unusual shade of brown which sometimes accompanies red hair. There was nothing really exceptional about them or indeed about his features, which were not conventionally handsome. His hands lacked the grace of David's, nor were they so white and well cared for; they looked strong enough to grapple with the toughest manual work. His nose was high-bridged, and his forehead strong. I grudgingly admitted that it was also intelligent. The cheekbones were high, and the chin balanced them well. It also looked as strong as his hands, and the cleft in it somehow added to this impression. The mouth, well, as for that, the most that could be said for it was that it was resolute, with a touch which might be described as humorous but which, as far as I was concerned, I felt to be mocking. No, I did not like him.

"I am sorry our meeting has been so brief, Miss Coleman, but I shall be here for the performance tomorrow and hope for better fortune then."

He was gone before I could think of a suitable answer or excuse. But a man like that would dismiss any answer or excuse if he so wished.

"You don't look at all like an actress."

Harriet sounded disappointed.

"And what do you imagine an actress looks like?"

"Very painted and all dressed up."

I laughed.

"Wait until you see our leading lady. She will please you more than I. Not because she is 'very painted and all dressed up,' Miss Lorrimer knows just the right amount of makeup to use off stage, but because she is really quite lovely. Far lovelier than I."

"That is what I mean."

"Harriet, dear!" Claudia Bentine protested mildly.

"If Miss Lorrimer uses makeup, she cannot be a lady," Harriet continued relentlessly, "but it is well known that actresses are not ladies anyway."

Claudia turned to me with an apologetic smile. "You mustn't mind Harriet. She doesn't mean all she says."

"Oh, but I do! Miss Coleman *doesn't* look actressy, does she, David?"

"I think she looks just like herself, which is charming."

His glance to me endorsed his sister's warning not to heed Harriet's chatter.

Lunch was nearly over. Somehow I felt that my hostess was glad, and I understood why. Her voluble cousin could be exhausting. But I recalled my father once saying that it was from babbling mouths that one learned the truth and that people who guarded their tongues revealed nothing. On the other hand, empty vessels made the most sound, I reflected, and found myself trying to turn a deaf ear. It was the only way to withstand Harriet Hillyard's verbal onslaught, which continued in full spate.

"Lots of amateur theatricals are held at Abbotswood. I played Ophelia once and everyone said I was wonderful, though I would have preferred to play Juliet, although that is a sad part, too. I think it a pity that Shakespeare made them *both* die, but at least Juliet's death was the nicer because she did have a lover and Ophelia had none. Hamlet just told her to hie into a nunnery, so she went mad and drowned herself. Have you seen that beautiful picture of her floating in a stream, all covered in water lilies and reeds? *Such* a pity I could not appear like that, but no stream at Abbotswood runs anywhere near the dell where the outdoor theatre is. Have you ever played Ophelia, Miss Coleman? If not, I will coach you, if you like."

I thanked her, but said that I had played Ophelia many

times, *Hamlet* being one of the Thespian Players' regular productions.

"I can't imagine you in the part, with all that dark hair. Ophelia needs to be pale and golden, like me." I glanced at the woman's once-blond hair, made dull through too much frizzing with curling irons, then quickly away again. She was quite oblivious of my glance and ran on without interruption, "I have a photograph of myself as Ophelia—Hobson, the saddler in the village, is a very good amateur photographer and came to Abbotswood to take pictures of us all, didn't he, David? Oh, I forgot— you weren't there." She turned back to me. "David isn't interested in the theatre at all."

(*"I have been following the Thespian Players from town to town, city to city."* Not interested in the theatre?)

"You are wrong, Harriet. It interests me very much, but only the professional theatre, not the amateur."

"That is because you are no good at it. You lack my talent. Claudia's husband was very good, too, though I never saw him, of course. I wasn't living at Abbotswood then. I was away at school."

That startled me, and I found myself doing a swift calculation. Claudia Bentine was about to celebrate her fortieth birthday, and her cousin seemed only a few years younger. At what age had Claudia been married, if Harriet had still been a schoolgirl? And although in a certain stratum of society daughters had been sent away to finishing schools for twelve months or so before being presented at court, Harriet had no such air about her. What sort of school would turn out anyone so gauche?

I switched my attention back. She was saying something about Lawrence getting all the local people to take part, and David was saying no, that wasn't Lawrence, that was Jasper, his younger brother.

"It was not! How can you possibly know? You were away in Vienna. Only Claudia knows, because Lawrence was her husband. What marvellous times they must have had! Did you take part, too, Claudia? No—I suppose you didn't get much opportunity. You were hardly married long enough." The frizzed head turned back to me, and the voice continued artlessly. "Can you imagine anything more dramatic than being widowed after only nine months of marriage?"

I was so startled I could think of no answer. Nor did she give me time to make one. Her high-pitched, excitable voice ran straight on. "Even more dramatic was *how* she became a widow!"

David said sharply, "That will be enough, Harriet. You will upset Claudia."

"Indeed she will not," his sister said serenely. "Her chatter never upsets me. Nor does she mean it to, do you, Harriet?"

"Upset you? Why should you be upset? I should think a woman would scarcely remember a dead husband after more than twenty years. And you were only nineteen at the time. It must seem like another world, another life to you now."

Claudia Bentine merely smiled and made no answer. To me, she said that if I had no particular plans for the afternoon, she hoped I would feel free to enjoy Abbotswood at will. "The grounds have many pleasant walks, which I am sure my brother will be happy to show you."

Harriet immediately leaped out of her chair, catching one trailing sleeve, at which she tugged impatiently.

"No, no! *I* will show Miss Coleman everywhere. I have a lovely idea! I will take her down to the dell where we perform, and I will do my Ophelia for her."

I was thankful when David said firmly, "Some other time. Sunday is the only day Miss Coleman has a break from acting, and I intend to see that she enjoys it."

I didn't glance at Harriet Hillyard to see how she accepted that piece of news.

Going up to my room to change into walking slippers, I saw my father's carpetbag being carried into the room adjoining my own. It had been sent with the rest of the company's luggage, so I guessed that everyone had now arrived.

The manservant who had brought up my valise on arrival bobbed his head and departed. I went into the room, opened the carpetbag, which suddenly seemed even more ancient and more shabby in contrast with its present surroundings, and began to unpack my father's clothes. I was interrupted by a discreet cough from the doorway and looked up to see the white-haired butler standing there. He advanced with dignity, saying, "Your pardon, miss, but I serve as valet-butler here at Abbotswood, and Mr. Hillyard had asked me to unpack for Mr. Coleman."

I dropped my father's shirts as if caught in the act of stealing.

Glancing over my shoulder as I walked toward my room, I saw the man peering at the carpetbag with the careful scrutiny of the shortsighted, but I knew that even lack of sight did not conceal its shabbiness from him. He was fingering it with a curiosity which I resented, but there was nothing I could do but stroll nonchalantly away. As keenly as I was aware of the man's scrutiny of the carpetbag, I was aware that he was unpacking the rest of the clothes as if he were accustomed to handling garments far superior and certainly more plentiful. Like myself, my father had brought little for so short a visit, but I was disconcerted to notice that he had not troubled to include evening wear. In the eyes of the elderly retainer this omission was probably further betrayal, but to me it revealed that my father had no intention of accepting any but the most essential hospitality and certainly no intention of mixing socially after the performance, as might be expected.

I went into my own room thoughtfully, puzzled by this attitude and not a little displeased by it. Both David Hillyard and his sister were being very gracious, and it embarrassed me to think that it could go unappreciated. When my father arrived, he would surely realise what a mistake he was making in regarding this appearance at Abbotswood merely as a one-night stand. No ordinary professional booking ever included such hospitality as this, nor such accommodation.

I saw that my valise had been unpacked and my one evening gown—a simple Grecian affair which I had made over from a past production of *Antony and Cleopatra*—had been taken away for pressing. My toilet articles had been set out on the dressing table—the silver-backed brush and comb which had been my mother's, and the silver-topped perfume bottle which had been a wedding anniversary present to her from my father, and the miniature of her which went with me everywhere. They looked well on the rosewood table, modest as they were —but oh, Papa, I thought despairingly, as I unlaced my white high-heeled boots and slipped my feet into white kid pumps, did you *have* to behave so casually toward our hostess?

Without ceremony, my door clicked open.

"I thought this would be your room," said Elizabeth without any preamble. " 'They will have given *her* the best one,' I said to myself, 'considering she was conveyed here personally by Mr. Hillyard.' I suppose your father saw to that." She closed the door with a sharp little slam and stood facing me—not arms akimbo, for she would never adopt so ungraceful a pose, but truculently for all that.

"And may I ask, dear Aphra, precisely what your father is up to? You cannot deny he is up to *some*thing, and if anyone knows what it is, it must be you. And what in the name of heaven is he thinking of, allowing George Mayfield to play Prospero and he Caliban? I would dearly like to know."

So would I, I thought.

"George has been giving himself airs all day. Anyone would think *he* owned the Thespians now! And I hear *you* have been lunching privately with the family!"

"And how do you know that?"

"Simply enough, my dear. I enquired of that lofty butler, who graciously informed me that you were lunching on the terrace with Madam and her brother. I take that as a personal slight on the leading lady of the company."

"I am sure no slight was intended, and that I was only invited because my father is actor-manager."

That partially pacified her, but I was still out of favour. She sauntered about the room, examining it in detail and, I knew, mentally comparing it with the one allotted to herself.

I continued in conciliatory tones. "If you imagine my father arranged for me to be Mr. Hillyard's only passenger, you are wrong, Elizabeth. I was responsible for that."

She stared at me with raised eyebrows, and I rushed on. "Papa insisted that I should take you along as a chaperone, but I didn't want one. Nor did I think that you would want to act as one."

"I certainly would not. I am not *that* old! But how artful of you, my dear. You are turning out to be as dark a horse as your father."

"He serves as valet-butler and was quite annoyed when I started to unpack your bag—and I don't think he was very impressed by such a shabby thing. I saw him inspecting it, as if nothing so inferior had been brought to Abbotswood by any guest before."

"Servants are notoriously inquisitive, or so I have heard." My father was busy with the liner again. "Forgive me if I let you down, my dear, but I have a great affection for that bag. I have owned it all my life."

"You could have never let me down, Papa!" I hung my arms round his neck, regardless of his makeup, and he gave me a bearlike hug in return.

"I do wish you were not playing Caliban. I am always so proud of you onstage, you look so handsome."

"Only *on*stage?" he teased.

"Onstage *and* off, and well you know it! When we take that curtain call together—well, you don't know what it means to me. Tonight I will be cheated of that. I won't be able to look up and see your handsome profile and think how proud I am, with the audience clapping their hands off and admiring you, too. All I shall see, and all *they* will see, will be that hideous face disguising your own."

"Be proud of my acting instead, my dear. My Caliban may surprise you. I am more than a matinee idol, and it is time people realised it, including you," he teased.

There was a tap on the door.

"That will be George. I told Clancy to send him along. I hear he has been diligently rehearsing."

"Very diligently. He will make a good Prospero, but not so good as you."

My father smiled and called to him to enter.

It was not George Mayfield, but David Hillyard, looking as blond and serene as ever.

"Your dresser told me you had arrived, Mr. Coleman. Welcome to Abbotswood. I am sorry I missed you on the road."

My father's hand paused halfway to his face, a dark liner between the fingers. I wished he were looking his debonair self, instead of half disguised as Prospero's half-human slave. Then he dropped the liner into his makeup box and took David's proffered hand.

"On the road?" he echoed.

"My father—a dark horse!" I asked her, indignantly, what she meant.

"I expect you will find out someday, or as much as he will allow you to. The only woman who ever knew the secrets of his heart was Petronella." She strolled back to the door and then, with her hand on the knob, said casually, "And if you are thinking of going for a walk—I see you have donned walking pumps—I am afraid you will have to hurry. In his newfound grandeur George commanded Barney to put out a rehearsal call for four o'clock, and it is now nearly three. The man really *is* above himself," she finished with a yawn, and departed.

Abbotswood was a revelation to me. The graciousness, the dignity, the comfort and luxury, the smoothly run household in which everything seemed to be done with unobtrusive efficiency—all this impressed me and sparked a desire to live in such a way. Impossible, of course. This was no more than an interlude in my life and had to be accepted as such, but I would remember it forever and never again be content to weave dreams about cosy conventional houses in cosy conventional streets.

I think my first real envy of those who lived in homes such as Abbotswood stirred during that walk with David through spreading grounds and into the woods beyond —the woods in which eagles had once tried to spread their wings and failed. I could understand why. The trees grew thickly, encircling the entire estate, a prison for wild creatures whose instinct was to soar freely into the skies, looking for prey on which to swoop and kill. Abbotswood was not set in rugged Highland country where peaks and crags abounded, so no wonder such captivity put an end to the Bentine eagles. How had the man who considered them the proudest and most aristocratic creatures ever created failed to realise that they were predatory, too? I wondered as I walked through those woods with their crowding trees and their network of branches shutting out the sky. I could imagine the savage creatures destroying all other wildlife in their desperate quest for survival. The thought made me shiver slightly, so that David asked if I were cold.

"No, not cold, but these woods are so dark. Let us go back to the sun!"

The Eagle at the Gate 47

We turned in our tracks, and soon the gardens opened out ahead of us, with the dell where *The Tempest* was to be performed situated in a hollow to the left. Sweeping lawns rose from it, on which seats for the audience were being erected. It was a beautiful setting, and my father would appreciate it. To the right, more lawns spread as far as a high wall concealing a kitchen garden. There was an arch in the middle, containing a wrought-iron gate. And crowning everything stood the house, with its graceful wings spreading east and west, a picture of architectural beauty.

I stood still, my breath catching, wanting passionately to belong there—not to be an outsider or a mere visitor, but actually to *live* there. It did not seem an unnatural wish.

"You must be very proud of such a home," I said.

"It isn't mine to be proud of, nor is it ever likely to be. My sister is a Bentine, not I. She married into the family, and when her husband died, the name died, too. I manage affairs for her. There is a lot of work attached to a place like this, even though it isn't the size of many country estates. Abbotswood owns only one farm of a little under eight hundred acres, but of course, there are vast orchards as well in this fruit-growing country. The farm is mainly agricultural, with a certain amount of livestock as a sideline."

I could not imagine this man, with his immaculate hands, engaged in farming.

"It is run by a resident factor, of course, who is also responsible for the orchards. I hope you will be here at blossom time to see their beauty."

"We shall be on a spring tour, I have no doubt."

"You sound regretful."

I was, and knew that he was, too.

He slipped a hand beneath my elbow to help me across an ornamental stream, and as we continued toward the house, he kept hold of it, and although he went on talking about Abbotswood and the administrative work he handled, we were once again keenly aware of each other. But every step brought me nearer to the end of these magic moments and to the rehearsal, which must have already begun. Glancing at the fob watch on my bodice, I saw that it was already a quarter past four, but if George or Elizabeth or even dear Barney was vexed by my tardiness, I did not care. I was living only in this hour, wanting to capture it and treasure it for all time.

Idly my companion plucked a sprig of syringa and gave it to me, and as I lifted it to my nostrils to relish the perfume, something fluttered from between the petals. David caught it swiftly.

"A royal admiral! A perfect specimen, too. Look at the marks on its wings, the colour!"

Admiration lent excitement to his voice and apparently made him oblivious of the tremulous beating of the butterfly's wings against his hand, but I cried, "The poor thing is frightened! Let it go!"

"Not yet. Let us enjoy it a little longer."

"But it is terrified!"

"So it is—" His white hand threw the butterfly into the air, but regretfully, I thought. He watched its flight, a dancing pattern of brilliance in the sun, and when it settled once more, he captured it again. Now the beating of the wings was frantic, and he kept it a long time within a closely cupped palm, sniffing gently before releasing it again.

"For a moment," I said, "I thought you were not going to let it go at all."

"My dear Miss Coleman, do I look the kind of man who would trap a helpless creature—and keep it trapped?"

As I expected, the rehearsal had started, and true to his promise, David had ensured that no one should intrude, but as I slipped into the hall set aside for our use, I detected a figure seated in the shadows. I recognised that untidy mop of hair immediately and went over to join her. Somehow Harriet Hillyard must be persuaded to leave, for I could anticipate her interrupting should the impulse seize her.

"You will enjoy tomorrow's performance more if you don't watch the run-through," I whispered. "This is for Mr. Mayfield's benefit, to make sure he is word perfect. There is no glamour about this kind of rehearsal."

"Oh, I don't agree! When I played Ophelia, everyone said how glamorous I was, even at rehearsal. But I wish the company were presenting *Julius Caesar*. I do so enjoy that scene where the assassins fall on him. But I suppose Claudia forbade it."

"I don't understand."

"Well, naturally she wouldn't want it. She has never allowed it to be performed here again. We have a festival every year, in aid of church funds, and she lets people put on all sorts of things—dancing, pageants, concerts, and even musical comedies. The local operatic society did *Floradora* last year. It was lovely, but unfortunately there was no part for me." She preened slightly. "As you know, I am a serious actress. I could have been a great one had I been allowed to enter the profession, but that is what my dear mamma had against it—that it is called 'the profession,' which could be wrongly interpreted and often deserves to be, she said. Why are you theatrical people so immoral?"

"There are immoral people in every walk of life, but those in the limelight attract more attention. And now, Miss Hillyard, if you would be so kind—I see Miss Lorrimer frowning in our direction. Even whispers can disturb, and she likes complete silence when acting."

"Naturally. I do myself. But since it is only a run-through for Mr. Mayfield's benefit, why should *she* object? As I was saying, dear Claudia doesn't mind the local amateurs doing all those other things, and of course, she was terribly proud of my Ophelia, but *Julius Caesar* she will never permit."

I found it hard to follow the woman's vacillating mind and therefore made no reply. Silence, I vainly hoped, would discourage her, but it didn't. She leaned toward me confidentially and whispered, "O course, *The Tempest* is safer. No one is likely to get murdered this time."

I was too bewildered to answer, and she leant even closer and whispered even more dramatically, "Would you like to come down to the dell and see where it actually happened?"

"Where what happened?" I found myself whispering back.

"The stage murder, of course. The spot where Caesar was finally stabbed by Brutus. Or, I should say, Lawrence by his brother, Jasper."

FOUR

Before dinner that night, champagne was served in the long hall, to welcome the company. Extra staff had been brought up from the village.

"They always help during the annual fête—I am sure Harriet has told you all about that," Claudia said to me. "It is the highlight of the year for most of the villagers, and Abbotswood plays its part. But this weekend is even more special. It is the first time a professional company of actors has performed here and the first time the mistress of the house has reached her fortieth birthday," she finished with a laugh.

She looked about her, pleased to see that the cast were obviously enjoying themselves. I knew why they were. Such a booking as this was never likely to come our way again, so they were making the most of it.

"Such a pity your father could not be with us," she continued, "but at least that is a pleasure to which I can look forward." Drawing me slightly to one side, she added, "I wanted to snatch a moment or two alone with you, to warn you not to heed dear Harriet's chatter. She has a vivid imagination and pours out the most unlikely stories to people, all of which she believes at the time and promptly forgets—except the one about playing Ophelia, which she never did, of course. It is a conviction in her mind, and so we humour it. She does know certain passages; alas, not accurately. Her memory is very unreliable, poor soul. I hear she trespassed on the rehearsal this afternoon. David will take good care that she keeps well out of the way tomorrow. I hope she didn't tire you with her chatter or burden you with nonsensical stories?"

"None whatever," I lied. How could I announce that she had told me some fantastic tale about the murder of this woman's husband by his brother? And how could I possibly believe it?

"I am thankful for that. You see"—Claudia Bentine hesitated, then went on more confidentially—"I am sure it will not surprise you to learn that the poor dear soul is somewhat—well, retarded. You must have observed her feckless behaviour at luncheon. I lack the heart to be too severe with her; besides, we have been warned of the danger of it. Oh, yes, she has had treatment. Ever since girlhood, in fact, but nothing has done much good. She was born retarded, and she will remain so, but quite harmless, of course. Naturally I feel it my duty to take care of her. When she was left alone on her mother's death, everyone urged me to make other arrangements, but I could not bring myself to. Asylums are for the insane, and poor Harriet is not insane. There is room for her here at Abbotswood, and as far as I am concerned, she can stay here for the rest of her life."

"That is good of you."

"Good?" She looked surprised. "Not 'good,' my dear. Merely natural. Relations should always look after each other, and being childless, I like having someone to look after. And now *I* am monopolising you, and David is aware of it. . . ."

She smiled and moved on, and then her brother was beside me, his eyes eloquent. How different they were from the eyes of Red Deakon, I thought. Not penetrating and critical, but calm and thoughtful.

I found myself asking if Mr. Deakon were here, but only to make conversation in an attempt to cover my confusion. I had been conscious of inner delight ever since David Hillyard had admitted that his determination to bring the Thespian Players to Abbotswood had been merely a cover for his determination to bring me.

"Red Deakon? No, he is absent, but he will be here for the performance tomorrow, work permitting. He lives for that business, which was founded a couple of centuries ago by another Red Deakon, a blacksmith by trade who did very well out of the iron boom which flourished in East Sussex and West Kent. The Deakons came from Lamberhurst, where they manufactured the iron railings for St. Paul's Cathedral, and after that the business never looked back. They also produced all the wrought-iron balconies for Abbotswood, which were added to the original building by the first Bentine. But even ironwork can suffer the rav-

The Eagle at the Gate

ages of time, especially so close to the sea. That was why Red came over today. Corrosion has weakened them. Replacement will be a costly business, but being a personal friend, Red Deakon will do it for us at a very fair price—particularly for my sister, whom he greatly admires."

I could scarcely believe that money was a problem to owners of such property as this. I also seemed to recall that Claudia Bentine had referred to the replacement of the balconies as being no more than a whim on her part, owing to her dislike of "those hideous eagles' heads"—or was she averse to admitting to any financial pressure?

David Hillyard continued frankly, "You see, my sister has a problem—she never actually inherited Abbotswood, so she never inherited its income either. Lawrence Bentine was the elder son. The shock of his death caused his father to have a stroke. He was incapable of making a new will, in which he would undoubtedly have provided generously for Claudia. In fact, it is generally believed, and not without cause, that he would have cut his younger son out altogether, in which case Claudia would have become the legal mistress of Abbotswood. Jasper had never pleased his father in any way. But as it happened, Sir William failed to recover from the stroke. So his will was never revised."

"And the younger brother inherited?"

"Yes."

"And allowed your sister to remain—"

"Not exactly. She remained because it had become her rightful home, as Lawrence's wife, and her father-in-law would have wished her to stay. He was very fond of her and frequently said that Abbotswood could not have a better mistress. Nor would Jasper have opposed the idea. You see, he loved her, too."

Two brothers in love with the same young woman, the one marrying her and inheriting everything, and the other . . .

Would a man kill his brother for such a reason?

"But we talk of gloomy things, and this is not a night for gloom. Some more champagne, Miss Coleman?"

I thanked him but declined. He looked at me intently and said, "You seem preoccupied. What is on your mind?"

"Something your cousin told me today about Lawrence Bentine's death."

"So you know."

"Is it true?"

"Yes."

I had a vivid picture of Brutus killing Caesar in an English garden, of horror amidst loveliness, and an old man struck down by shock.

"Surely it was accidental?"

"That was the verdict. You are probably familiar with stage daggers—"

"The blade slides back into the hilt, thus appearing to go into the body."

"But on that occasion, it didn't. It penetrated the heart."

I shuddered. How many times did my father have the props checked and rechecked to avoid possible accidents, making sure, when genuine weapons were used, that blades were blunted and firearms rendered harmless? Perhaps amateurs were less thorough.

"What happened to Jasper Bentine?"

"He left Abbotswood shortly after the inquest and has never been traced. He has been 'missing, presumed dead' for a long time now, but there is always the possibility that he may be alive somewhere overseas. He has never dared draw on the income from Abbotswood's estates because that way he could have been traced, but neither has he dared to come back, so obviously he was guilty, despite the verdict. Had he remained and lived the thing down, the accident might really have been accepted as such, despite the scepticism of many, but in fleeing from the place, he condemned himself. But perhaps, in the long run, Claudia fared far worse. She has been condemned to the struggle of maintaining Abbotswood on the income left to her by her husband, whereas Jasper Bentine escaped not only punishment but his responsibilities, too. Fortunately the executors of Sir William's estate have allowed Claudia to draw on a fund set aside for essential repairs, but the value of such a fund decreases as time goes on, so that it cannot keep pace with demand. It is inadequate now."

I slept late, wakening next morning to the sound of wheels on gravel, far too many to herald the arrival of only one carriage, so I knew it was not my father driving up to the main entrance. In any case, he was not due until the afternoon, after keeping his appointment with the manager of the Hippodrome and then journeying to Hythe and from thence to Abbotswood.

The flurry of sounds, of voices, of commands, of laughter, of echoing hooves on the cobblestoned courtyard, of the snorting of horses and the jingle of martingale and harness, brought me barefoot to the window and held me transfixed. I watched fascinated, aware that I was seeing something of which, hitherto, I had only heard. Everyone knew about the country house parties which had become even more ostentatious since King Teddy had come to the throne. They typified the opulence and glitter of England's new society, but this procession outdid anything I could have imagined.

Into the courtyard streamed a procession of carriages, followed by wagonettes carrying servants and baggage. The carriages stopped at the main entrance, and the servants and luggage disappeared into an inner courtyard. Every man appeared to have brought his valet, and every woman her personal maid, not to mention mountains of luggage. I wondered how many times a day they intended to change their clothes.

That first procession consisted of about a dozen guests, each with his individual entourage, but throughout the morning others continued to arrive. Long before the last carriage bowled into the courtyard, David had departed to Folkestone to seek out my father, and after an early luncheon with the rest of the cast I set out to explore Abbotswood even further, starting with the orangery and from there to a sunken rose garden with an arbour in one corner. The sides and roof were of ornamental wrought iron, but the seat which ran round the interior was of stone.

I sat down, and as I spread my skirts, my fingers touched a rough patch, a pair of carved initials entwined with a heart. J and C. There was also a date—June 16, 1880. So lovers had once plighted their troth here.

I suppose it was inevitable that two names should spring to my mind—Jasper and Claudia. "Jasper loved her, too," David had said, but there had been no suggestion that she had loved him in return, and since she had forbidden any performance of Shakespeare's tragedy ever to be performed again because she could not bear the reminder of her husband's death, I could dismiss that idea as fanciful. And surely no married woman would be so indiscreet as to allow her initials to be carved, so close to home, with that of a lover? No, I decided, J and C must have belonged to others.

I left the arbour and strolled on, admiring the clipped yew hedges surrounding the sunken garden and the fine examples of topiary which lined the brick steps leading up from it at each end—chessmen, birds, pelicans and swans, all fashioned expertly from yew trees which had been carefully planted at regular intervals. All was in keeping with the pride of Abbotswood, and I could well understand Claudia Bentine's dedication to the place. Actually to belong here, I thought, would be the most marvellous thing in the world.

When I reached the house again, I met David returning from Folkestone, and it was then that I received my first surprise of the day. He was alone.

The second surprise was the news that the Hippodrome was closed and appeared to have been for some time. Boards announcing that the lease was for sale were prominently displayed.

"I fear your father was misled if he imagined that any booking was likely. No doubt he proceeded to Abbotswood as soon as he arrived at the theatre this morning and found it shut up. I must have missed him on the way."

I had no reply to that because I recalled that David had seen my father perform many times and would therefore have recognised him had they passed on the road, but I managed to say, "Poor Papa, what a wasted journey for him! But having no carriage, he must have decided to come by rail."

"I thought of that. At Folkestone Station I learned there was a train to Hythe within the hour, so I waited, hoping he would arrive to catch it, but the only passengers to board it were an elderly couple, and when I questioned the station staff, I gathered that no one resembling your father had caught an earlier one."

I was surprised because he had gone to such lengths to check on my father's movements, although such thoroughness seemed well in keeping with such a man. All I could do was thank him and say, with a confidence I no longer felt, that I was sure my father would arrive on time because he had never yet been late for a performance, but as

The Eagle at the Gate 57

I went upstairs to my room, I had to suppress a feeling of uneasiness.

One reason the Thespians had been accommodated in the east wing was that it was convenient for that part of the grounds which housed the open-air theatre, and since no dressing rooms were available, the cast could change and make up in their own rooms, using a side stair for access.

It was now only two hours to curtain-up. The performance was to start at five, to catch the full benefit of late summer-time, and after it was over, a party was to be held for houseguests and members of the company. My concern over my father's nonarrival deepened. What if he actually did not appear? An understudy could perform instead, but it would not be the same thing, and the damage to Charles Coleman's reputation would be undesirable. I now remembered, with deepening uneasiness, his reluctance to accept this booking and the feeling I had had that he was deliberately avoiding David Hillyard, although I could see no possible reason for either. But this news about the closure of the Folkestone theatre was the most puzzling thing of all. I could not believe that my father had not known of it, because *The Era*, the theatrical newspaper which no member of the profession ever missed, announced such things regularly. The journal featured all theatrical news, from the opening and closing of shows to the booking dates of tours, new productions, available dates at theatres, auditions and casting—in fact, anything and everything pertaining to the London and provincial theatre, so the sale of a theatrical lease was not likely to be overlooked.

I was very preoccupied as I changed and made up for Ariel. Elizabeth Lorrimer had declared that my father was up to something, and now it seemed that she was right. I was aware of alarm beneath my concern and tried to overcome it by memorising my lines.

I had scarcely reached:

> Not a soul
> but felt a fever of the mad and play'd
> Some tricks of desperation. . . .

when a sound next door caught my attention. It was a cough, and a familiar one. That was my third surprise of the day.

I flung open the communicating door and stared in astonishment at my father. There he was, sitting before the mirror, well embarked on the lengthy business of making up as Caliban.

"*Papa!* When did you arrive? No one told me—"

"Because no one saw me. I hired a carriage to bring me here. I felt the actor-manager of the Thespians should arrive in style but unfortunately it passed unnoticed."

He gave me that wry, conspiratorial smile which he used when enticing me to share final curtain calls with him, and all my anxiety fled at the sight of it. I might have known I could rely on him. Never in my life had he let me down.

"The main courtyard was blocked with carriages," he continued, "so I came in by the entrance to the east wing. I remembered you saying that we were to be accommodated there, and it was easy to find. All I had to do was consult the weather vane standing above the coach house. I was glad to avoid people. I was tired."

I saw then that beneath his partial makeup he looked more than tired. There were signs of strain which filled me with concern. I promptly crossed to a bell rope beside the fireplace.

"Food is what you need, Papa. I'll hazard a guess that you haven't bothered with refreshment, except the liquid kind, all day."

"You are wrong, my dear. Clancy brought me a tray—and a very good Châteauneuf-du-Pape. Abbotswood apparently keeps a good cellar. So you need not ring the bell."

"How did you find your room?"

"That was easy. It was logical that the principal room in the wing would be given to the principal of the company, and that was simple to find. Then Clancy came along with my costume, so I got him to bring me some food. He had already unpacked for me and was worried about my late arrival."

"It was Truman who unpacked for you."

My father was wielding a liner from nose to mouth. It paused momentarily as he repeated, "Truman?"

"Somewhere between Folkestone and Hythe, I imagine. At Sandgate there are two turnings leading to Abbotswood; we probably chose opposite ones. I am Hillyard. I expect your daughter has mentioned me to you."

"Indeed, yes, but what is this about missing me on the road?"

"Mr. Hillyard went to meet you, Papa. He went all the way to the theatre to collect you late this morning."

My father made no reply, and David said, "It must have been frustrating for you, calling there on the off chance and finding the theatre closed down. Those 'For Sale' boards appear to have been up for some time. And to think that you were forced to seek overnight accommodation, all for nothing! Had I known of your plans I could have prevented that, at least. You could have travelled here yesterday as arranged and driven into Folkestone this morning. That way you would have wasted only an hour or two of your time."

"I appreciate your thought, but as it happens, I wasted no time at all and was forced to seek no accommodation. Nor did I call at the theatre on any off chance. In fact, I had no need to go there, for the new lessee accommodated me, and we were able to attend to business on the spot. He is an hotelier—the Metropole on the Leas—making his first venture into the theatre. Contracts for the lease have been exchanged and completion date is not so far off, so he is wasting no time in negotiating bookings. Those 'For Sale' boards will be down soon, I have no doubt." My father turned to me. "He plans to turn the theatre into a number one booking, and we open our winter tour there late October. I thought *Cymbeline* would be a good choice and give you your first change to play Imogen."

"Splendid!" cried David. "That means you will come to this part of the world again." The words were directed at my father, but his glance at me, and somehow I knew my father did not miss it, even though he had turned back to his makeup.

"I came not only to welcome you, sir, but to see if you would like refreshment. But now I see you have had something. I hope it was sufficient and that the Châteauneuf was to your liking."

"Very much so."

"Then I shall have more sent up to you. Anything you

The Eagle at the Gate

need or want, you have only to ring for. Now I will disturb you no longer. I imagine that makeup requires a deal of concentration. By the way, my sister is looking forward to meeting you after the performance, and so are a great many of the guests."

To that my father made no reply, and David departed. In the mirror my father surveyed me shrewdly.

"You have taken a liking to that man, Aphra. Why?"

"Why not?" I hedged. "He is charming and very kind. You don't know how welcome he and his sister have made me, though I see no reason why they should."

"And I see no reason why they should not." The liner lay idle in my father's fingers. He watched me broodingly for a moment, then roused and demanded to know how I had been occupying myself, so I told him about yesterday's rehearsal.

"And what else besides? You have not been rehearsing all the time, surely?"

"Indeed, no. I have explored Abbotswood, and oh, Papa, you don't know how beautiful it is! Did you ever see such a place? Did you ever see such a room as this? And wait until you see mine!"

It was hard to tell, beneath the thick eyebrows and jutting brow which he was building up layer by layer, whether he really did frown, but somehow I felt that he did.

"Don't place too much store upon it, child, too much value. It isn't our world."

I said musingly, "But perhaps we will be invited again when we play Folkestone next October."

"We shall see," said my father in a tone which told me full well that he would see we were not.

Suddenly I flared. "Why are you behaving like this, Papa? Why didn't you want to come here? Why were you trying to avoid Mr. Hillyard? You seemed determined not to come to Abbotswood, but I cannot imagine why. I have never visited any place so wonderful or stayed in such a house—or ever had such a longing to remain anywhere."

He stared.

"If I thought you meant that, I would take you away at once."

"Papa!"

"I mean it, child. I have never wanted you to grow up

with a wrong sense of values, but if your first glimpse of luxury threatens to overwhelm you, I will do everything I can to bring you to your senses." His voice rose angrily. "We will leave this house at the first possible opportunity. If it could be tonight, nothing would please me more."

"You are being horrid, Papa. *And* ungrateful. And I think you have been most discourteous to Mr. Hillyard and his sister."

"I didn't come here to be sociable. I came to perform and perform I will—but no more than that. And the same applies to you. When we leave this place, I want you to forget you ever came near it."

"How can I? It is a beautiful, *beautiful* place! A glimpse of another world for me—"

"And that is how I wish it to remain. We will leave early in the morning. There is a train from Hythe to Folkestone, with a connection to London, at eight o'clock. I have already checked on it."

I was too aghast to answer. My hands trembled so much that I could scarcely control them. My father reached out and took hold of them firmly.

"Remember what I said, Aphra. Places like this, houses like this, people like this are not for you."

"Then what *is* for me?" I cried. "A life spent in third-rate lodging houses, pinching and scraping and dreaming of better things?"

"Is that what you do—dream of better things?" he asked gently. "I never thought, never suspected. . . ."

"I'm sorry, Papa, but how can I help it? Seeing all *this*, the way people can live, the way they *do* live. . . . But it hasn't started with this visit, believe me. Always I have had a hankering for something better, a life different from our own." I sobbed and tried to steady myself, and his kindly arms went round me.

"My dear child—my dear, dear child—" There was a helplessness in his voice and a kind of despair.

I clung to him. "Try to understand," I begged. "I never dreamt of a home like this, and now that I have seen it, I can imagine none more desirable. Imagine how it must feel to *belong* here!"

He put me aside—perhaps because there was another knock on the door.

Again, it was not George Mayfield. This time it was the white-haired butler, bearing a tray.

"I was asked to bring you this, sir. The cork has already been drawn. Do you desire a glass now?"

It was another bottle of the Châteauneuf, and I thought how typical it was of David Hillyard to be so thoughtful and felt even more indignant about my father's avoidance of him. When I came to think of it, he had been no more than conventionally polite when they finally did meet, and that made things worse because David had been friendliness itself. Now, when my father scarcely glanced at the servant, merely shaking his head as he concentrated once more on his makeup, my indignation became anger. It was unlike my father to be discourteous to anyone, and in such circumstances as these I was not ready to forgive him.

The old man put down the tray and departed. I crossed to my own door, saying coldly that it was time I got ready. I did not trust myself to say more; but as I reached my door, I heard the rattle of glass against glass, and when I turned, I was surprised to see how violently my father's hand shook. He drank deeply of the wine, as if needing its strength.

"Papa! You are unwell!"

"Tired, my dear. Just tired. The tour has been a long and strenuous one. A few days' rest at home and I shall be all right. And the sooner we get there, the better for both of us."

So he was still out of sympathy with my enchantment, still failed to understand it, still wanted to leave Abbotswood as soon as possible.

I went into my room, and closed the door.

FIVE

True to his resolve, we did leave early, and true to his resolve, he did not mix socially that night. Although the rest of the cast attended the party following the performance, my father, still wearing his Caliban makeup, merely put in a courtesy appearance, then disappeared, not even staying for the birthday toast to our hostess. In the crush of people I did not even see them meet.

Everyone praised his performance, but I and the rest of the cast knew it had been tragically below standard. To my chagrin, it was George Mayfield who stole the honours, which I might have expected since my father had virtually abdicated in his favour, but even so none of us had expected anything less than Charles Coleman at his best.

The uncertainty, the fluffing of his lines, the seeming inability to concentrate began toward the end of the second act, but even during the first one he had been slow and a little too laboured even for Caliban. Waiting in the wings between entrances, I had heard Barney mutter, "Your Pa seems a bit off tonight, Miss Aphra. Not himself at all. . . ."

I could do nothing but pray that only the cast realised what a bad performance he was giving.

It was during the first interval that he began to complain of thirst, which he appeased with some of the wine which Clancy brought from his room, but he continued to falter, to hesitate, to speak his lines indistinctly at times. The other actors quickly realised that he would have to be helped through the performance, and with the loyalty and generosity of theatrical folk they banded together to do so. Lapses of memory were covered for him, fluffed lines quickly drowned, wrong moves skilfully disguised, so that any clumsiness appeared to be merely part of the character of the subnormal slave. For the first time I was glad that George was playing Prospero. I could not have borne to watch my father offer anything less than his best in that part.

Despite my anxiety, I was keenly aware of the setting in which we performed and the glittering audience—the men in white ties and tails and the women bedecked in satins and jewels, with ospreyed headbands and ostrich feather fans, their backs naked to the waist in décolleté gowns. Mixed with the scent of an English garden on a summer evening, drifts of expensive perfumes floated across the footlights, which consisted of massed candles set in long shallow troughs, protected with a shield which threw their light directly onto the sylvan stage.

Prospero's island came alive for me that night, with rustling trees forming a natural backdrop and soft grass beneath my bare feet. As Ariel, I ran and leapt with delight, feeling the spring of earth beneath me and breezes in my hair, my voice coming back to me through space, echoing from the walls of Abbotswood. I was exhilarated, inspired, loving the beauty of this natural setting and delighting in every round of applause.

And being closer than usual to our audience, so close that individual faces could be picked out with ease, I was aware of David Hillyard sitting in the front row. I was also aware of others: of his sister, looking supremely elegant, and poor Harriet, as overdressed as a fairy on a Christmas tree, and, farther away but somehow startlingly near, the unmistakable Red Deakon sitting with arms folded, watching intently. I suppose I should have accepted such undivided attention as evidence that he found the play absorbing and the acting compelling but I preferred to think only of David and to wonder whether he found my performance tonight as good as previous ones. It was tremendously important to me that he should.

Then something happened before the final act which, as it turned out, was not unduly worrying, but which disturbed me at the time.

My father disappeared.

Clancy came to me in concern. He had waited in my father's room—"I felt he ought to lie down, Miss Aphra, not being himself tonight, and I told him I'd have some coffee waiting there. He seems overtired, and coffee, I thought, would help him along"—but he had not arrived.

The Eagle at the Gate 67

Together we searched, and it was I who found him in the sunken garden, sitting in the arbour, his head resting against the back of the stone seat and his eyes staring into space. It seemed almost a full minute before they focused on me and realised who I was.

I could think of nothing to say. There seemed no reason why he should not relax out of doors instead of in his room. Others of the cast were doing the same. I had even seen Elizabeth mingling with the audience as they strolled in the gardens and obviously enjoying their admiration. And the interval was only for a quarter of an hour, so why bother climbing those stairs in the east wing on such a warm night as this? Even now, with dusk rapidly approaching, the air was mild. I told Clancy to bring the coffee here, and when it arrived, my father and I drank it together, and then we went back to the screen of trees to await our entrances, still not talking. His listlessness told me that tonight there would be no final bow together, and somehow I knew that he would leave the rest of the cast to make their appearances at the flickering footlights edging that grassy stage and that I would be with them, taking no more than my due. And Caliban, I suspected, would scarcely even bother with that.

I was right. My father, grave and unsmiling, took no more than a single call and then withdrew. The ungainly figure of Caliban disappeared amongst the wooded backdrop, and when I ran offstage after the solo call to which Ariel was entitled, I found him leaning against a tree, well shadowed.

He said wearily, "Thank God that is over. We must rise early tomorrow, Aphra, and get away from this place. That means we must retire soon. The others can burn the candle at both ends if they wish, but not you or I, child."

I was bitterly disappointed. The exhilaration of the evening had made me wide-awake and eager for the enjoyment to come.

I said softly, "Why do you dislike Abbotswood, Papa? How *can* you dislike a place so lovely?"

Perhaps it was Caliban's hideous makeup which made me feel that I was not talking to my father. Even his voice had been skilfully disguised for the part. The halting, subnormal speech of the half-animal slave had never once faltered, despite his below-par performance. Now, at least, his voice was his own, but for me that was not enough.

When he made no answer, I said, "Please, Papa, go upstairs and remove that makeup and let everyone see you as you are. *I* want to see you as you are."

"Dear child, you know me as I am."

"Not tonight."

"That shows how well I played the part."

I answered gently, "You didn't, Papa, and I think you know it. I hope you never play Caliban again."

Barney came searching for us.

"They're calling for you, Mr. Coleman, sir. Mr. Hillyard wants you to make a speech."

"No." Never had my father been more emphatic. "No speeches. Not from me, at any rate."

"But Mr. Hillyard sent me to fetch you! And can't you hear them clapping? Miss Lorrimer and Mr. Mayfield are out there taking all the bows. . . ."

"Let them. The audience is applauding Prospero, not me. It is George's night, and I am glad to let it be. So I'll leave him to make the speech."

My father turned and walked back to the house, and the audience didn't even see him because all eyes were on the stage, and the gardens surrounding them were in shadow. I went, too, because I knew he wanted me to, but disappointment went with me. That he should retire early, feeling as he did, was obviously necessary, but that I should be debarred from the ensuing festivities seemed unfair. I resolved to slip downstairs after he was abed. I even hoped that David would send for me or come in search of me. The hall was to be prepared for dancing, he had told me, asking that I should save every one for him.

Oh, no, Papa, I thought secretly, you would not really want to deny me such enjoyment! And tomorrow you will say as much, when you are in a better mood. When we climb the stairs to our Pimlico flat, you will be glad to think that your daughter went like Cinderella to the ball; you won't begrudge her a moment of such delight or an hour of happiness in a place like Abbotswood.

We were waylaid as we went indoors. Truman met us with champagne, at the head of a line of servants. He peered intently at my father through shortsighted eyes and

The Eagle at the Gate

said, "I venture to think you will be glad of refreshment after performing, sir."

My father waved the offer aside, acknowledging the remark with no more than a shake of the head. Embarrassment made me accept a glass at once, and the pause delayed us sufficiently for others to catch up. My father was quickly surrounded by chattering members of the audience, and I refused to come to his rescue. Fatigue was no excuse for bad manners, I thought crossly, and I felt that the old family retainer was hurt. I could see his faded eyes peering in my father's direction, and in an effort to atone I asked how long he had been at Abbotswood.

"Man and boy, miss. I started as a hallboy in the late Sir William's time. My father was one of the gamekeepers here, so we lived in a gamekeeper's cottage on the estate. My grandfather before that was coachman at Abbotswood—"

"To the gentleman who kept eagles?"

"So you've heard of them, miss. Through Mrs. Stevens, I have no doubt. She will never let it rest."

"Let what rest?"

"The mistake about the eagles. Things like that should be forgotten, I always say, but Mrs. Stevens does like to gossip. A sad fault in an otherwise excellent housekeeper."

I supposed that age and a sense of male superiority made him feel he had the right to criticise a fellow servant, but because of my father's taciturnity, I lacked the heart to rebuff him by turning away.

"What mistake about the eagles?" I asked. "Do you mean breeding them in captivity?"

"Exactly, miss. My father always said it were a terrible mistake. Caged eagles were bound to turn savage, he said, and confining them to the woods was as bad as caging. I once heard of a wolfhound that reverted to natural instincts and savaged his master, so when it happened at Abbotswood, I suppose it weren't surprising. And that king eagle were a monstrous-sized bird, from all accounts. That was why it were called the King, though as it turned out the Assassin might have been more apt."

"You mean—?" My stomach gave a sickening lurch. "You mean it savaged its master?"

"Clawed him to death, miss. A terrible thing, it were. Didn't Mrs. Stevens tell you? Oh, dear, then I wish—"

The bent shoulders lifted and fell in resignation. "She likes to talk about it, so I took it for granted. But no matter. Everyone knows the story. It is one that will always be remembered at Abbotswood, I fear. Would you like some more champagne, miss?"

I looked at my glass in surprise. I had gulped almost the lot.

Going upstairs with my father a short while later, I thought how impossible it was to associate tragedy with this lovely house. The mellow beauty of panelled walls and the richness of antiques surrounded us, imparting an air of unassailable security. Yet two violent deaths had occurred here, and two stories lived to testify to them. But death could often be violent, in war or in peace, and the fact that it had struck twice in this peaceful place had done nothing to destroy Abbotswood's beauty. It still stood serenely in its sylvan setting, seemingly untouched by sorrow. These ancient walls had seen too much of life not to accept the fact that it could end abruptly, and in a place centuries old tragedies were bound to happen; a rider could be thrown; fatal illness could strike. Throughout the generations Abbotswood must have known happiness as well as sorrow. It was characteristic of life that happinesses were taken for granted, and the sorrows remembered.

Once in his room, I felt ashamed of my vexation with my father, for he was too tired to remove his heavy makeup. Clancy had to do that, and I was shocked by the pallor beneath. He complained now of nausea as well as thirst, but I was able to persuade him to drink water instead of wine. There was very little of the Châteauneuf left, I noticed, and knowing my father's partiality for wine, I guessed that if the bottle remained in his room, he would undoubtedly finish it, so I unobtrusively removed it and disposed of the dregs down the washbasin in the ornate Edwardian bathroom which served the east wing. The bath was as big as a sarcophagus and stood imposingly on a mahogany plinth. I was very impressed by it, for hip baths were still predominantly in use. After removing my stage makeup, I climbed into that bath and relished the luxury of water coming from gushing taps. Tomorrow we would be back in Pimlico, back to the hip bath routine, but I knew that I would be taking with me a yearning to

The Eagle at the Gate

live at a standard I had never been born to and that after this visit to Abbotswood life would never be the same again.

I did not slip into the white Grecian dress until after I had settled my father, so he would not suspect what I planned to do.

He said good-night wearily, and I knew he would quickly be asleep, so I would not have long to wait before going downstairs again. I could hear tantalising strains of music rising through the open windows, and my feet itched to dance to it. Tomorrow I would tell him that I had disobeyed him, and then my conscience would be cleared, and because I owned up he would forgive me. So I felt little guilt as I kissed him good-night.

I halted on the gallery above the main hall. A passage from the east wing led directly to it, so I was able to pause there unnoticed and gaze on the scene below. A string quartette was seated on a dais in one corner, and the place was awhirl with movement and colour. Such a sight caught at my breath, for scenes like this were never part of a struggling actress' life. The most that ever came her way were small backstage parties at the end of a run, or Christmas or New Year's Eve celebrations onstage after a performance, together with all theatre staff from the back and the front of the house.

I was looking into a world that I was never likely to see again, so I feasted my eyes upon it, taking in the glitter and the whirl as if trying to photograph it in memory. Never had I seen such jewels, such silks and satins, such elaborate and ornamented coiffures, such a flutter of osprey and ostrich feathers, such opulence, such elegance, such wealth. Nor had I dreamt that it could be taken so much for granted. Complacency sat on the well-tailored shoulders of every man and on the made-up face of every woman. The recollection of Harriet Hillyard's condemnation of paint and powder caused me to smile. If by such things she assessed the qualifications of a lady, then few in that crowded ballroom could rank as such. With the death of Queen Victoria and the advent of Queen Alexandra, makeup had become fashionable. It was well known that King Edward's lovely wife spent hours being enamelled and painted, perhaps to boost her confidence in her private battle against total deafness or to compete with her husband's mistresses. Who knew? Everyone loved her and forgave her—even her notorious unpunctuality would be forgiven when she finally arrived, looking as exquisite as a picture, and everyone knew that he forgave her, too, even though punctuality was a fetish with him. Women might come and go in the king's life, but Alexandra's place in his heart was unassailable.

My thoughts ran on, transferred out of my own world into that of a society which I only knew by hearsay. I seemed to be suspended in time as I stood on that gallery before finally descending the stairs leading down to it. I saw Elizabeth Lorrimer waltzing within the arm of a very military gentleman who was obviously enamoured of her, and George Mayfield surrounded by a group of admiring women. I saw Miles Tregunter waylaying a passing waiter bearing a tray laden with champagne glasses; he replaced his empty one and picked up another with mechanical precision. I hoped he would not disgrace the Thespians tonight by drinking too much.

Then suddenly I saw a red-haired man standing with arms folded, looking up at me.

That was the second time he had caught me out. I knew at once that not a detail of my expression had escaped him, that he knew how enthralled I was, how impressed and awed and excited. As before, I withdrew abruptly, stepping back into shadow. In a few minutes I would descend, taking the stairs as calmly as if I were walking down them onto a stage, and by that time I hoped the objectionable Red Deakon would have disappeared.

Instead, he came up to me. I saw him reach the stairhead and stand there looking at me. I could not escape.

"Isn't Cinderella coming to the ball?" he asked. "Pray, let me escort you. There is no need to be awed by any of it. It is all quite artificial."

"Awed? I am not the least awed. Why should I be?"

"Why, indeed? You can hold up your head amongst the lot of them."

"There is a certain inference there—"

"What inference?"

"That all this is unfamiliar to me."

"Well, isn't it?"

He looked down, as I did, on the glittering scene. He said, "I suspect that life in the theatre is more real than this—the life backstage amongst those who work for their living, I mean. Why be ashamed of it? *I* am not."

"You?" I echoed. "But you belong to this world."

"On the contrary, I am only admitted into it. That is not the same thing at all. I was not born into it any more than you were, Miss Coleman. The fact that Deakons have won a name for themselves here in Kent is nothing to go by. Our family business was founded many years ago by a blacksmith over at Lamberhurst who found he had an ability to make things other than horseshoes. He came of a family of ironworkers who had their own marl pit and extracted the iron ore from the marl by their own primitive methods; from that they developed their own bloomery—that is the forge that produces the iron—but smithing didn't enter into their scheme of things then. Only this man, the original Red Deakon, was interested in actually making things out of the iron itself. He was as uneducated as his forebears; couldn't read or write or even sign his name. But he founded Deakon's Forge over in this part of Kent when the marl pit at Lamberhurst dried up and the seam of iron ore ran out."

My interest was caught.

"You must be very proud of him."

"Of course. The Deakons have always been proud of him. It was he who handed down to us our knowledge of iron craft." He held out his hands, and I saw that they were strong and calloused. "That was six generations back, Miss Coleman, and now Deakon's foundry is the leading one in the whole of Kent and beyond. Sussex ironwork has died out, but not ours, and it will never die out so long as there is a Deakon to go on working alongside his men, fighting the iron, bending it to his will, doing more than sit at a desk handling the business side. These are the hands of a blacksmith, Miss Coleman, not the hands of a gentleman."

"But even so you were born here, born to all this. That is why you can pretend to despise it."

"Pretend?" He mocked, "*I* am not the one who is pretending. It is you, Miss Coleman. Don't be taken in by the velvet curtains."

Taunted, I turned away. His hand shot out, and I felt the strength of those calloused fingers about my wrist.

"When you leave Abbotswood," he said, "forget it. Don't think of it, or yearn for it, or hanker after it. . . ."

"I notice *you* are not averse to the place. You are an accepted guest here, which means you are a frequent one. I suppose that makes you feel you can afford to mock."

"It makes me feel cynical, no more. There has been a shifting of values since King Edward came to the throne. The old queen would never mix with her son's friends—rich industrialists and Jewish merchants who were responsible for the incredible wealth of the Victorians. But now people like the Deakons are socially acceptable because we have money—which means we know how to make it, not that we inherited it."

"Then perhaps that marks an end to hypocrisy."

"Or the beginning of a different kind—the pretence that a man is a gentleman because he, like I, has been to a university although his forebears could not even write their own names; the pretence that his friendship is valued for its own sake, not because of what he has. If Deakon's crashed tomorrow, society's open doors would be as firmly shut as in Victoria's day." He gestured to the ballroom below. "Take a look at the people down there, Miss Coleman. They are no more real than puppets, slaves to fashion not only in dress but in morals. The number of women wearing tiaras actually bought for them by their husbands can be counted on the fingers of one hand, and the number of wives dancing with their lovers instead of with their husbands are too numerous to count at all. In so-called society husbands turn a blind eye to any liaisons their wives may form, so long as such liaisons are to their own advancement."

"You are a cynic, Mr. Deakon."

"I am a realist, Miss Coleman. And now I see David Hillyard coming in search of you. A pity—I was about to ask you to dance, but I am sure you would prefer to dance with a gentleman rather than with a blacksmith."

He gave a mock bow, and was gone. Frequently, throughout the evening, I saw him dancing with Claudia Bentine, but I had no further meeting with him before I left Abbotswood and was glad of that. He had too great an ability to make me feel uncomfortable and an equal ability to suggest that he saw right through me, and I knew that if he did not actually despise what he saw, he was amused by it.

I saw David briefly before we departed next morning. He came down to the courtyard to see us off, placing a basket at our feet and a rug over our knees. Because he could see that my father was unwell, he did not prolong the parting, but I felt—I hoped—that it was as regretful on his part as on mine.

No one else was astir. I looked up at the shuttered windows of Abbotswood, and suddenly Red Deakon's cynical observations echoed in my mind, and I found myself wondering how many women were in bed with their lovers instead of with their husbands—and vice versa. Certainly the free-and-easy manners last night had been a shock to me, the blatant familiarities, the risqué stories, the language—language I would never have expected to hear on the lips of women who were regarded as ladies. They seemed to think it was clever or funny, and it never failed to be greeted with gales of laughter. If poor Harriet Hillyard believed theatrical folk were loose-living, I wondered what she thought of these. Sitting on the outskirts, a wide-eyed and dreamy wallflower, she had seemed to retreat into a world of her own, seeing only the glitter and the gold, and perhaps, I had thought, that was a good thing.

As much as some of their manners shocked me, their affectations of speech irritated me. Everything was "too, too *deevy* . . ." and even more irritating was the habit of adding Italian terminations to English words, irrespective of their being verbs, nouns, or adjectives. "Oh, bother*ino*, my stupid mamma forbade me to be darling Tony's partner*ina*, and here I am, stuck with that too too horribl*ino* Horace Prendergast. . . ." It all seemed very stupid to me, and I admired Claudia Bentine's tolerance. Her own behaviour was exemplary. She was the perfect hostess, gracious, dignified, and her brother's behaviour had also been beyond reproach. I had been proud to be dancing with him, proud to have had his almost undivided attention. In between duty dances, he returned to me constantly.

Now I heard him thanking my father for coming to

Abbotswood at such short notice—"And with not a little self-sacrifice, I suspect, sir. You are fatigued to a degree, I know. But I hope this small gift will sustain you on your journey."

To me he said not a word about meeting again, nor repeated his determination not to let me go out of his life, and I left Abbotswood convinced that such a declaration had been only a momentary piece of flattery, soon forgotten. I felt inexpressibly sad and did not look back as Abbotswood's drive hid the house from view, but as we passed beneath the stone arch framing the main gates, I looked up at that predatory eagle's head. Oddly enough, it no longer appeared menacing. Merely proud.

We travelled ahead of the rest of the company, and as the Abbotswood carriage deposited us at Folkestone station, I wondered if they were even astir. David had refused to let us travel from Hythe because it meant changing trains en route. He had come to my father's room before we left, to tell him so. His thoughtfulness never flagged. I had lain in bed last night, remembering it, also the disappointment he had been unable to conceal when I left the ballroom early in case my father should waken and need me. Lying there, listening to the distant strains of music and wishing that I, like the rest of the cast, had remained until the end, I had relived that enchanted evening.

During the journey my father again complained of nausea and could eat little from the basket of food provided for us, but he did drink some of the wine—again, a Châteauneuf-du-Pape—and after that he dozed fitfully. I was glad when we finally drew into Charing Cross Station. From there we took a cab to the converted Pimlico house in which at present we occupied a top-floor flat. Our style of living rose and fell according to our fortunes, and a flat instead of furnished rooms marked a high peak. But now, looking up at those attic windows as my father searched for his keys, it seemed no more than a cage to me—cramped, unpretentious, unworthy of an actor-manager. Perhaps my father would have fared better in his profession if he had not devoted himself to the Thespian Players.

I paid off the cabbie, and as the man carried our bags up the front steps and I followed with David's picnic hamper, I heard my father muttering, "That's odd—very odd. I know I had them ... sure I had them...."

He was still fumbling for his keys, and I recalled seeing them on his dressing table as he made up for Caliban. He had automatically emptied the pockets of his suit before changing into his costume. I reminded him of this, adding that he must surely have picked them up and would come across them later. I took from my reticule the key which my mother had always carried, thankful that my father had not bowed to convention and forbidden his daughter to have her own latchkey before the age of twenty-one.

After the spaciousness of Abbotswood the flat seemed even more cramped, although my parents had furnished it with as much taste as they could afford, mainly with secondhand pieces picked up at auction sales and stage props picked up for a song. But once our own door closed behind us, my father looked around with relief, as if he had feared he would never see the place again.

He leant on me as we went into the living room and sank gratefully into his favourite chair beside the iron Victorian grate. The small sitting room suddenly seemed too restricted to hold me, stifling, claustrophobic. I unpinned my hat and said I would make some tea, but first I put my father's feet on a footstool and fetched a pair of carpet slippers.

The kitchen, neat as it was, now seemed little more than a walk-in cupboard, and as the kettle sang and I went into my tiny room to unpack, I realised that the whole flat would have fitted into the two bedrooms my father and I had occupied at Abbotswood.

Abbotswood ... Abbotswood ... my mind revolved about it. I was thinking of it as I busied myself with the tea and searched hopefully for some biscuits, inevitably finding the tin empty, so I unpacked the remainder of David's hamper. Game pie was hardly right for afternoon tea, but there was a pot of gooseberry fool which might tempt my father. I spooned some into a small bowl and set it on the tray, and when I carried it into the living room, he met me with a smile.

"How good it is to be home, Aphra. We must find a permanent theatre near London for the Thespian Players, for I swear I shall never go on tour again."

Neither he nor I could have suspected how prophetic those words were.

After I had drunk a cup of tea and settled him with a book, I went out to buy food. I had to pick up the threads of my normal life, busy myself with household tasks, accept my lot and stop dreaming about the might-have-been and the never-would-be. I was Aphra Coleman, daughter of an actor, reared in an uncertain and often precarious profession, whose life, at best, was bounded by a top-floor Pimlico flat which had been provided for her by an industrious and devoted parent. I felt ashamed of my discontent and almost wished, like he, that I had never crossed the threshold of Abbotswood or glimpsed another world.

But the streets of Pimlico crowded in on me. I thought of the sweet air of Abbotswood and the spaciousness of its grounds, the well-proportioned rooms and tall windows, the balconies and terraces, and no matter how hard I tried, I could not but compare them with the rows of terraced houses standing cheek by jowl, the hard street pavements, the smoke-laden atmosphere of London.

As I climbed our stairs again, I felt an unaccustomed depression, suddenly convinced that there could never be any escape from the narrow confines of this world or from the struggles and uncertainties of our life.

Looking into the future was something few theatrical people ever did. To do so was like gazing into a crystal ball clouded with uncertainty, but now I found myself facing up to it and wondering if my father ever bothered to do the same and, if so, whether he saw what I now saw —old age restricting his acting, failing health, and perpetual lack of security. I thought of the many actors who, in old age, had been thankful to accept the shelter of actors' homes, charitable institutions for those in need. Appalled by such thoughts, I took the remaining stairs at the run. Whatever happened, I would never allow my father to end his days that way.

He was asleep when I entered, his book on the floor. I tiptoed to the kitchen and put away the food I had bought, then went quietly back to the living room and noticed, for the first time, that he had fetched the bottle of Châteauneuf and that a glass, half full, stood on a small table beside him. Enough was enough, I thought, and carried it away. I disposed of the contents of the glass and washed it. I also put the bottle out of reach and resolved that when he wakened, I would scold him a little for helping himself in my absence.

Feeling slightly better for busying myself, I went back to the living room. My father was still asleep, exactly as I had left him. Perhaps it was the fact that he had not even moved that first frightened me, but that unexpected leap of fear swiftly became a terrifying certainty when I realised that his sleep had a certain rigidity about it, unlike a man sleeping naturally.

SIX

Barney said kindly, "You're welcome to stay as long as you like, Miss Aphra. Mabel and I would be happy to have you. Of course, you might find the kids a bit noisylike, but maybe that'd be better for you than fretting alone in that flat."

His kindly eyes were full of concern; his voice was gentle. It seemed to me that ever since the shock of my father's death I had been surrounded by the kindness of friends. Even Elizabeth Lorrimer had hurried over from Chelsea to see me as soon as she heard the news, though I could make little sense of what she said just before she departed. "You will be all right, won't you, darling? I mean, there won't be any difficulties over your rights and so forth?"

"My—rights?"

"I mean, you'll be entitled to anything your father left? The law can be very funny sometimes, you know."

I suppose my lack of comprehension must have been evident, for Barney had interrupted firmly, "You'll excuse me, Miss Lorrimer, but this isn't the time to bother the poor child with all that. Can't you see she's too shocked?" And somehow he had edged her to the door.

Even now the time immediately following my father's death is hazy in my memory. I recalled running downstairs and hammering on the door of the flat below, and getting no answer, and then knocking on the door of Barney's place in a nearby street, and being greeted by his wife, who took one look at me and helped me over the threshold, pushing aside a bevy of wide-eyed youngsters as she did so. It is strange how it is always the small things, never the big things, which imprint themselves on the mind in moments of shock. I don't even remember running distractedly through the streets to Barney's place, although our Pimlico landlady, who lived on the ground floor, claimed that she saw me rushing out of the house "white as a sheet, the poor girl, and why she didn't come to me, so near at hand, I don't know. . . ." But I do remember stumbling into the cabbage-smelling passage of Barney's tenement, with Mabel's arm supporting me, and the dreadful pattern of the wallpaper shouting at me, and Mabel taking charge and saying, "We'll have to fetch the doctor, love. I'll come back with you right away, and you can leave everything to me. . . ."

The rest of the company had reached London an hour or two later, and by that time old Dr. Fosdike had been and gone. "Heart failure," he had pronounced. "Your father did tend to overdo things, though I shouldn't have expected a man of his age. . . . But I can see no other symptoms. None whatever."

I must have told him about the nausea and the thirst and the fatigue because he did murmur something about possible food poisoning. "Though I expect you ate the same food as your father, did you not?"

I had nodded, then remembered that we had not shared a meal during the whole of Sunday and Monday, so it was possible that my father had eaten something which had disagreed with him before he arrived at Abbotswood.

"He complained of thirst, you say. Did he drink a lot of water?"

"No. Mostly wine."

"Regrettable. Most regrettable. I recall your father had a great partiality for wine, Miss Coleman . . ." at which I told the doctor indignantly that he had never drunk to excess, which was true.

"There is nearly half a bottle left. You can see it for yourself!"

The old man, tired from years of battling with illnesses in a mixed neighbourhood which could never be relied upon to pay his bills, patted my hand and told me not to get agitated, but I had insisted on showing him the half-full bottle, just to prove that my father had not imbibed too much wine that day. I also showed him what remained of the contents of the picnic hamper, which I had shared without any ill effects. He had taken the wine to be examined. "A mere formality, my dear. It is as well to find out whether it could have deteriorated—cheap wines often do. But I don't suppose anything adverse will be found."

I didn't suppose so, either, since the wine had come from Abbotswood's cellars, so I was not surprised when such confirmation came.

So death from natural causes it was, and now the funeral was over, and Barney was coming home with me to go through my father's things. "We'll have to talk about your future, Miss Aphra, and about the Thespians, too. I can deal with all that because your pa left me to handle a lot of things, so I've a fair idea of how everything stood, but going through his personal belongings won't be easy for you, I dessay."

I found it hard to answer and walked beside him through the London streets, feeling too unhappy even to think about the future of the Thespian Players. Barney must have sensed this, for he said in his fatherly way, "It'll be good for you, Miss Aphra, to have something else to think about. Mr. Mayfield has already suggested taking over the company and keeping you on the payroll, so you won't have to worry about the future or have the responsibility of anything. And he has played second lead to your father for so many years he knows all the parts backward. Handing over the reins to him isn't a bad idea, if I may say so, though I dessay Miss Lorrimer will have a thing or two to say about it, but we can leave those two to fight it out between them. All *you* need do is let me have the ledgers and the files and the business papers, and I'll pass them on to a solicitor and let him handle the transfer. That way you'll get a fair and proper deal, all cut-'n'-dried."

With so much kindness to bolster me, I was able to sit down with Barney and sort out the papers relating to the company from the mass of unrelated matter hoarded by my father over the years: back numbers of the *Era;* press cuttings; theatrical programmes; old photographs; the typical mass of stuff which actors accumulate. And all the time I knew that I was welcoming this opportunity to postpone going through my father's more personal things, the intimate things which I could not share with Barney or with anyone else. But sooner or later I would have to open that black metal deed box which he kept on top of his wardrobe.

The knock on the door came when we were surrounded by a mass of papers, with files stacked on the floor and the contents of drawers tumbled into a heap on the table.

"I'll answer that," said Barney, "and whoever it is, I'll get rid of 'em. You won't want to bother with anyone right now."

I was thumbing unhappily through old theatre programmes when he came back, looking very startled.

"It's the gent from Abbotswood, Miss Aphra—that Mr. Hillyard."

David came striding into the room, holding out both hands and saying something about being shocked beyond belief. "A woman on the ground floor let me in. She told me the news."

Behind him Barney's expression changed from surprise to speculation. He decided to be businesslike and said briskly, "If you've come about another booking for the Thespians, sir, I can handle that, same as before."

"Another booking? I am afraid not, Mr.—er—?"

"Wills, sir. Barney Wills, the late Mr. Coleman's stage manager."

Barney looked slightly huffy over this lack of recognition but was pacified by David Hillyard's friendly handshake. "Of course, I remember you well. It is a pleasure to see you again, and I am glad Miss Coleman has someone so reliable to lean on. My visit is by chance, however." He held out a bunch of keys. "I was coming to London, so decided to deliver them personally. Keys are valuable things."

I wondered how he had found our address, but he explained that easily. "The manager of the theatre in Canterbury provided it. I guessed he would have corresponded with your father when booking the Thespian Players." He broke off. "I am deeply distressed for you, Miss Coleman."

I was still unable to accept sympathy without the threat of tears and said quickly, "How kind of you to bring the keys, Mr. Hillyard. I hope you did not come out of your way? But I am very glad to have them." For want of something further to say, I added, "Would you care for some tea?"

"Not for myself, but you look tired and could surely do with some. If you will permit me? I presume this door leads directly into the kitchen. It may surprise you to know that I make very excellent tea. You will share some, Mr. Wills? From the look of things, the pair of you have been extremely busy."

I think Barney was as astonished as I when he tossed his hat and gloves onto a chair and, without waiting for permission, disappeared into the tiny kitchen. I heard the gush of water into a kettle, the chink of teacups.

"Making himself at home, isn't he, miss?" Barney's mutter was a mixture of disapproval and admiration. "I suppose he means it kindly."

"I consider it most kind, Barney dear. And I could certainly do with some tea. You, too, I'm sure."

Barney glanced at the heavy fob watch suspended on a chain across his flowered waistcoat, which had been a Christmas present to him from my father a year or two back. He had insisted on wearing it for the funeral, combined with a black tie as a mark of respect, an incongruous combination which had not worried him at all.

"Well, you know me, Miss Aphra—come six o'clock and I'm ready for my pint at the George and Dragon, and that's right now."

"I hadn't realised it was so late! Please don't feel you have to stay—"

"Will you be all right alone, miss?"

I smiled. If he was concerned about leaving me in the flat with a man of very short acquaintance, he had nothing in the world to worry about. I had felt all along that David Hillyard was trustworthy.

After Barney had gone, he lingered while I drank the tea, and when I had finished, he carried the tray out to the kitchen. I had not imagined that a man in his position could be so domesticated. This was a new side to him, and somehow endearing. He then offered to continue helping me where Barney had left off. "It looks as if you have a great deal of sorting to do. I can at least help with that." He hesitated. "This will be painful, I know, but have you gone through your father's personal things yet?"

I shook my head. "There won't be much. What there is will be in his deed box, which I would have been unable to open without his keys."

After that there was nothing more natural than for him

to get down the heavy metal box for me, and I was glad he was there when I opened it, because although it contained little, the experience was distressing. On the top were pictures of my mother, some alone, some with my father, and some with myself in various stages of childhood. There was a faded spray of roses; the dried-up petals scattered as I picked it up. "She wore a spray of roses at St. Saviour's Church," he once had told me. That had been on their wedding day, of course. Surprisingly, there was a selection of single gloves, mostly right-handed, in various fabrics and colours, and somehow the sight of them was even more painful than the photographs and the roses, for it had been my mother's habit to wear only one glove, usually the right one, carrying the left and all too often losing it. "It is your mamma's one extravagance," he used to say. "We must seek fame and fortune, Aphra, my child, to keep her well supplied with gloves!" But not until this moment had I realised with what indulgent affection he had regarded this weakness of hers, or how tenderly he had treasured the remaining gloves which could never be worn again. Even now they held the imprint of her hand, the creases where her fingers had curved, the gentle stretching across the palm.

My eyes blurred, so that I scarcely saw other things he had treasured: a pair of baby shoes, my own, of course, and an old-fashioned teething ring tied with a bow of faded pink ribbon, on which I must have cut my first tooth; pictures I had drawn as a child; crude birthday cards I had made for him. Then came a bundle of letters tied with a white silk shoelace; from one of my mother's shoes, no doubt, because the letters were also from her. I recognised her writing and laid them aside. Someday I would read them, but not now. This was not the time to intrude into the private life of my parents.

Tears blinded me then, and I heard David say, "Leave the rest to me, Aphra. This is too distressing for you."

I obeyed because I was too overwrought to do anything else. I moved from the table to my father's chair beside the fire and sank into it, clutching his sad mementos and turning my back on the metal box which revealed the past so pathetically. So it was David who emptied it of the few papers which remained, first glancing through them in case there should be anything to distress me further.

The Eagle at the Gate

They consisted only of a few share certificates, which surprised me because I had not known that my father possessed any securities at all and when, later, I learned that they had decreased in value, I regretted this only because the small provision he had tried to make for the future had proved to be a vain effort. There were also documents concerning his ownership of the Thespian Players and a few contracts for parts he had obtained prior to forming his own company, but nothing else. And no sign of a will.

The fact that he died intestate didn't matter, David assured me. Since my father had no other living relative, his few possessions would automatically come to me. He was compassionate and understanding and very protective. I told him that George Mayfield would very likely take over the company and that I would remain a member of the cast. "So you see I have nothing in the world to worry about." But he was disturbed all the same. Like most people unconnected with the theatre, he imagined that an actor-manager must be very prosperous and was distressed that I should be left in such straitened circumstances.

It was dusk by the time we had finished. Whatever his own plans had been, he dismissed them and insisted on taking me out to dine. "I suspect you have eaten little all day, and that won't do at all." There was kindness in his voice and in his eyes, and he looked after me with genuine concern, finally commanding me, before we parted, to go straight to bed.

"Tomorrow you start a whole new life, but first you must get a good night's sleep, and then you need to get away from here. That is why I am taking you back with me to Abbotswood. I shall collect you at ten o'clock tomorrow morning."

As before, everything was cut-and-dried, forestalling any opposition.

I went back to Abbotswood in a state of incredulity. I had neither expected nor hoped for such a turn of events, but I welcomed it with open arms, for I knew that it was the best thing that could possibly happen to me. How could it be otherwise, when it was his desire as well as my own?

SEVEN

I was sitting in the arbour, and Claudia was coming toward me. She wore a dress of pale blue silk with flounces at the foot, so that it swirled about her ankles like a dancing blue cloud. It was tied about her waist with a matching sash, and her ivory leghorn hat was bound with a blue ribbon. The streamers floated behind her, and her parasol of thin ivory silk swayed gently as she walked. It reminded me of a gigantic moth with translucent wings, the kind which hovered amongst the flowers at this time of day and which David loved to watch.

Once he had caught one and placed it on the back of my hand. "Feel how soft it is, how gentle its wings flutter. . . ." I had lifted my hand and let the tiny thing fly away, and he had watched it go with regret "That is how I would feel," he said, "if ever you tried to escape from me."

I deliberately turned away from that recollected moment, back to the present one. Claudia looked much less than her forty years, I thought. Her figure was that of a young woman, slender of hip and long of thigh, with a narrow waist that needed no lacing. Her carriage was erect and graceful. She carried her years and her loneliness well.

"Why do you favour this spot?" she asked. "The sun rarely penetrates this sunken garden."

"I like its air of tranquillity," I answered, not mentioning that one of the last memories I had of my father was of him sitting here alone.

She folded her parasol and sat down beside me.

"And you, poor child, have need of both peace and tranquillity just now."

A more effusive woman might have patted my hand or put an arm about my shoulders to demonstrate her sympathy, but Claudia was never effusive. In the month I had been here, I had learned that well. Even on arrival she had offered no conventional condolences, perhaps because she knew I would find them hard to accept. Trite words of commiseration, I had learnt, meant little and were therefore intolerable. I was grateful for this woman's reserve because it made no demands; neither did it intrude.

"You will find," she continued, "that life will give you its own tranquillity. It is all a question of knowing when to accept and when to relinquish, when to hold on and when to let go."

I said nothing, because that was another good thing about Claudia:—conversationally she expected no effort from a listener. I was able to be silent and to savour the quiet of early evening, with the hum of bees hovering amongst the roses and the scent of mignonette expanding with the promise of dusk.

"You are looking better," Claudia said. "You have colour in your cheeks. Resting here at Abbotswood is doing you good. That will please my brother."

"It is kind of you to have me here."

"My dear, we are delighted. You must stay as long as you wish, though I do warn you that winter in the country can be very dull unless one hunts. And this is not good hunting country on the whole. One has to go to Leicestershire, where I was born, for that."

I was surprised to hear that she came from the Midlands. I had taken it for granted that she was local-born.

"Winter evenings can be particularly dreary in the country," she continued. "One has to make one's own amusements. Of course, there are occasional hunt balls, and visits from friends and soirées, and musical evenings, but after your interesting life I fear you would find that sort of thing very dull."

Since we were now only into June, I murmured something about not imposing on her hospitality for so long, at which she smiled and said, "David will have something to say about that, I am sure. I strongly suspect that his idea of inviting the Thespian Players to perform here was solely to meet you again. Harriet told me that when visiting Bristol, he went to see you at the Theatre Royal every night, though how she found out about that I have no idea. She herself was never allowed freedom in the evening, though I believe David was permitted to take her to the theatre on one occasion."

"Your cousin lived in Bristol?"

"Not exactly. She was at school there."

"At school! But surely she was too old? When we played Bristol, I was already seventeen——"

Claudia answered calmly, "It was one of those specialist schools which these new-thinking doctors who specialise in mental disturbances consider so admirable. Schools for the nervous, the highly strung. 'Asylum' is such a horrible word; a cruel word, I always think. So when a chance came to give her the benefit of the Bristol establishment, naturally I seized it. David and I used to take it in turns to go to Bristol to visit her, but never together because joint visits made her too excited. The week the Thespian Players were at the Theatre Royal, David extended his stay from the usual two days to seven. Now I know why."

I was suddenly too self-conscious to reply, though the remark was made most kindly, so I changed the subject by asking if the progressive establishment had helped her cousin.

"Indeed, yes. She is a calmer person, though she still gets facts hopelessly confused and always will. Poor Harriet."

As if summoned, there was Harriet coming toward us. Like Claudia, she wore a blue dress, but adorned with great slabs of patterned flowers. Again I had the feeling that she tried not only to emulate her elegant cousin, but to outdo her. If Claudia wore a blue dress, so too would Harriet, but it would be far more striking, far more noticeable.

Standing in front of us, she said, "That hat is much too plain, Claudia. So unbecoming! I could make it far more beautiful." Patiently Claudia removed the hat and held it out. Harriet snatched it and ran away, carrying it as though she had won a trophy.

"Aren't you afraid she might——" I broke off.

"Spoil it?"

"Well, it *is* a very lovely leghorn."

"She will do no more than gather flowers to bedeck the brim. Why not, if it makes her happy?"

I decided that Claudia Bentine was one of the most patient people I had ever met.

Dismissing the subject of her cousin, she said, "I was sorry I had no opportunity to meet your father when he was here. I hope it isn't too painful for you to discuss him now. I could see you were very proud of him, and not without justification, though like everyone else I was sorry not to see him play Prospero. He was a very good-looking man, I understand, though behind that alarming makeup it was impossible to see his features."

"Have you never seen pictures of him?"

"No, alas. Theatregoing passed out of my life many years ago, and here at Abbotswood no periodicals dealing with the arts come our way, and the daily press seems to deal only with things in the metropolis. Your father was mainly famous outside London, I am told. You will think my ignorance of the theatre very regrettable; but I have always been content with a domesticated life, and my brother has always been away so much. He is the member of the family interested in the arts. Beauty in all forms holds a strong appeal for him—music, painting, horticulture, wildlife. There are hothouses here at Abbotswood in which he grows rare and exotic plants, but no one is allowed inside except as an invited guest in case he should leave the doors open and admit dangerous draughts. He keeps the door locked to maintain the correct temperature. Personally, I find the hot steamy atmosphere too overbearing to enjoy going there; but he may show his rare blooms to you sometime, and I am sure he will want you to see his collection of butterflies."

"I had no idea he collected butterflies."

"Indeed, yes. Some are very rare. He doesn't catch them, of course. I don't think David could bear to put even the smallest creature to death. Tropical specimens come from dealers all over the world. My brother is very clever. I have always been proud of him. He could master certain subjects at school far quicker than other boys of his age. Natural history was one. Chemistry was another. This has proved very valuable since he came to help me at Abbotswood, for apart from managing the estate, he has set up his own laboratory for the study of crop diseases and to find antidotes. There is a disused oast-house beyond the park, with twin roundels. One he uses as an office, the other as a laboratory. People are beginning to experiment with fertilisers and disinfectants nowadays, but David won't allow a single one to be used until he has broken down the formula and then reproduced it himself, and if it fails to measure up to his exacting standards, it is discarded. He has found all sorts of antidotes for vegetable poisons and saved a lot of crop damage in consequence. Compared with my brother, you will find me very dull. I sew, I read, I run the household, I entertain, I take part in local charitable affairs—a very different world from yours."

My father's words echoed in my mind. "It isn't our world . . . *places like this, houses like this, people like this are not for you. . . .*" And then I was recalling his unwillingness to come to Abbotswood, his reluctance to meet people here, his eagerness to get away, and wishing with all my heart that he could have seen the place as I had seen it and was now getting to know it. Had he done so, he would have been forced to admit that my instincts about it were right, and his wrong. Abbotswood was fulfilling all my expectations.

"If my father seemed a little unsociable," I said, "it was because he was tired and unwell."

"I noticed he did not attend my party and wondered why. I had no opportunity to speak with him at all. I am even more sorry now and feel that coming to entertain us at Abbotswood at the end of a demanding tour must have put a great strain on him."

"I am sure he didn't regret it," I lied, and thought what a pity it was that my father had not met this woman, whom I found myself liking more and more.

Footsteps sounded on the brick path surrounding the sunken garden, and, despite myself, I looked up eagerly, for by now I knew David's quick, light tread and always experienced a leaping delight at the sound of it. I was unable to hide my reaction, even though I knew Claudia Bentine was watching me. If I had taken the first step toward loving her brother during my first visit here, I had progressed well into that state since my return and could not disguise it.

Looking at him now, handsome and well groomed as ever, I wanted to stretch out my hands to him and feel his smooth white ones, always so well manicured and well tended, take hold of them.

His hands had a beauty which was unusual in a man. Despite their masculinity, there was an aesthetic quality about them which implied a certain fastidiousness and refinement, even a delicacy and grace. I would watch their movements with a feeling of sensuous pleasure which the hands of no other man had ever stirred. But David awakened much unfamiliar feeling in me, feelings of an almost primitive quality which held promise of unknown depths and excitement.

My delight in seeing him was immediately counteracted by the sound of another tread, heavier and less welcome. Down the steps leading into the sunken garden, between the clipped yews and quaintly fashioned peacocks and figures, came Red Deakon. It was our first meeting since my return to Abbotswood, and as he approached, I realised what a powerfully built man he was. Perhaps his craft had developed his physique in this way, although there was something more than brute strength about it. He had the stride and the carriage of an athlete, but I compared him, to his detriment, with David Hillyard, as all men would be compared in my mind from now on.

In contrast with David's impeccable tailoring, Red Deakon wore a hacking jacket of rough tweed, a rider's stock and breeches, and tall leather boots.

"Here is Red to see you, Claudia. He has ridden over with the new balcony designs. While he shows them to you, I will carry Aphra away."

David had fallen into the habit of calling me by my Christian name even in the presence of others, as if formality between us were not only unnecessary but not even to be contemplated. I felt that Claudia was as aware of this as she was of my response to him, but I was indifferent to the opinons of others because only David's were of any account to me now. When he held out a graceful hand, I accepted it gladly. As I did so, Red Deakon bowed, but I spared him no more than a courteous glance.

Claudia said, "Don't you also want to see the designs, David?"

"Later, sister. Later."

As we moved away, I caught a fleeting glimpse of her expression. She had forgotten us and was looking only at

The Eagle at the Gate

Red Deakon, and her pleasure was as obvious as mine had been when David appeared. Somehow I knew that this pleasure had nothing to do with the blacksmith's mission. Perhaps, when one is infatuated with someone, one recognises similar infatuation in others, but strangely enough I felt no sympathy. For an older woman to be attracted by one many years her junior, or for a man to be attracted to a woman many years his senior, was not unknown or all that unusual, so my distaste for the idea of these two being lovers was unreasonable. I was glad to turn my back on them and departed willingly with David, but the rapport between them lingered in my mind, awaking reactions which I could neither define nor understand.

I recalled that the man had shown no surprise when seeing me. No doubt all news of Abbotswood penetrated to the village, for it was the manorial house and had ruled over local affairs ever since it had been built in Norman times. I was already learning a lot about Abbotswood's history, spending hours in the library when David was occupied on the estate. The room had become a sanctuary to me because no one else visited it. This was not surprising since it was the darkest room in the house, being the one remaining chamber from original Norman days. Harriet, searching me out one day, had shuddered and described it as creepy, but I felt no such reaction. I loved the arched ceiling spanned by its original massive beams, the sunken fireplace, the stone arches surrounding mullioned windows. Even the shadowy light was soothing, and in my imagination I could picture the original owners of the house dining here in Norman austerity, for, Truman had once told me, this room had been the dining hall when the first owner, Rupert de Friemont had built Abbotswood. It had been known then as the Domaine de Friemont, being changed to Abbotswood when becoming a monastery in 1459, founded by a descendant who renounced worldliness for a life of meditation and holiness.

Truman, I had learned, was a mine of information and loved to reveal it. Coming across me in the library one day, straining my eyes in the permanently dim light, he had lit an oil lamp and brought it across to me. Gas had not been extended to this rarely used room, and he was full of concern for my eyesight.

"I did not know the library was occupied, Miss Coleman; otherwise, I would have knocked. I am the only member of the household who comes here now. Not even Mrs. Stevens is very diligent about keeping the place dusted, let alone this rare collection of books." He seemed pleased to find me engrossed in them and busied himself lighting other oil lamps until I was enveloped in a friendly glow. "I used to attend to this room personally when Sir William was alive. He would entrust no one with these volumes, except me. It was his grief that neither of his sons spent much time here, though as far as Mr. Lawrence was concerned, that was perhaps unfair. As elder son he had many responsibilities, and Sir William had brought him up to be very much aware of all he owed to Abbotswood as the heir, *and* the time he should devote to it even though his tastes lay elsewhere. Young Jasper was free of all that because he would never inherit and never had any desire to. Alas, Mr. Jasper caused his father many an anxiety, for all his ability to charm his way out of scrapes."

Truman had broken off at that point, possibly aware that he had been indiscreet, and for the same reason I did not encourage him to go any further, much as I wanted to. I was becoming more and more interested in the story of the Bentines because it was all part and parcel of the story of Abbotswood. Safe in the library, I could delve back into its history and into the lives of former owners whose biographies had been recorded for posterity and had remained as part of the archives of the house when bought by Sir William's father. Had he purchased Abbotswood because he admired it or because of its woods and his wild notion of breeding the eagles which ended his life so appallingly?

If I stayed here long enough, perhaps I should find out. Meanwhile, there were De Friemonts and their descendants, with names like Dubois and Bezant and De la Rue, whose portraits, stiff with ruffles or military uniforms, looked down on me from the library walls. The De Friemont line had died out in 1815, when the first Bentine had purchased their ancient home and started a new epoch in its history. But the first Bentine era had ended in tragedy, and the third had known tragedy, too, although that was no more than one of life's coincidences and no indication that a curse had been placed upon De Friemont successors. *Some*one would have purchased Abbotswood when the original line was no more, and it was better that such a house should be taken over than allowed to fall into decay. There was much evidence of rebuilding throughout the years until only this one room remained of the original Norman structure, but the place had lost none of its impressiveness, none of its dignity and beauty.

"Come back, Aphra," David teased. "I don't like it when you escape me, even in your thoughts."

His beautiful mouth smiled down at me. Even that quickened my blood, and when I felt his fingers entwine my own, the sensation increased. There was sensuality even in his fingertips, and his eyes made no secret of it. His face became suddenly tense with longing. "I want you," he whispered. "You know that, of course. And don't tell me this isn't the time or the place to make love to you. I know that only too well, but it doesn't prevent me from wanting to."

Our footsteps halted. The fingers of his other hand touched my cheek gently and then ran exploringly down my throat and within the curve of my neck, stroking, caressing, massaging the little hollow at the base with an insistence that was both gentle and urgent. My body turned toward him instinctively, and I felt his arms go round me and the hardness of hip and thigh pressing against my own. My eyes closed as his lips came down to meet mine.

I had expected his kiss to be gentle. It was not. It was hungry and demanding. It excited me and made me hungry, too. I felt his strong teeth against my lips as his mouth enveloped mine. I felt yielding and fragile within his domination, incapable of resistance, but no thought of resistance even stirred because I wanted what he wanted, and I wanted it just as passionately.

It was he who broke away. "Not here, not here," he murmured, "but I must have you, Aphra. Don't make me wait too long."

I knew then that he intended to become my lover and that I wanted him to be. But beneath this awareness and the terrible urgency of our need for each other I felt a disappointment which was almost painful. So it was to be seduction after all. My bed, my body. Tears pricked my eyes as I wondered how I could have been fool enough to dream of anything else—I, who had nothing else to offer.

* * *

We were standing within the shelter of a tall beech hedge which curved toward the house. The running footsteps beyond were instantly recognisable. Harriet was coming.

By the time she rounded the corner we were standing well apart, but the shock of her appearance transfixed us. She wore Claudia's hat, the crown smothered in exotic blooms and the brim slashed so that it drooped in scallops about her face. She halted in front of us, preening.

I think I cried out in dismay but cannot be sure because David's explosive reaction drowned everything else.

"How did you get those flowers? How dare you break into my hothouse!"

He was beside himself with rage. His normally pale face was suffused with colour, and his hands trembled. He took an angry step towards his cousin, arms outstretched. I thought he was going to seize her, but instead, he pulled the hat off her head and looked down at the mutilated blooms as if he could have wept.

Harriet's beaming smile changed to sulkiness.

"I didn't break in! I know where you keep the key, so I unlocked the door *and* locked it after me when I left. Why should you be so cross? Blue flowers like that and those lovely crimson ones don't grow outdoors, and they were absolutely right for that hat. I saw them through the windows, and they were just what I wanted. Claudia will be pleased, I'm sure. I told her I would make it beautiful for her."

David flung down the hat and turned away. I could see he was fighting for self-control, and my heart went out to him. Already those exotic blooms, plunged out of a tropical atmosphere into a northerly one, were turning brown at the edges in premature death. But my heart was concerned for Claudia, too, whose elegant hat was ruined.

I picked it up. "We must hide this," I said.

"No," said Claudia. "Give it to me."

She and Red Deakon had walked across the lawn from the sunken garden, so we had not heard their approach. Since they had come from the same direction as we had, I wondered in dismay whether they had seen me in David's arms. It seemed more than likely, since we had only just drawn apart and there they were, standing nearby, with Red watching Claudia in concern.

The Eagle at the Gate

Mutely I held out the hat and saw the grief in her eyes. She turned it round and round in her hands, not speaking, and then she gave it to Harriet. "You must have enjoyed doing this," she said gently, "so I also hope you will enjoy wearing it."

Harriet smiled with childish delight and plonked the creation back on her head; then she went skipping away to the woods, singing happily.

"David." His sister moved to his side and touched his shoulder with a sympathetic hand. "Being angry doesn't help. She doesn't understand. You must forgive her, as I do."

"I wish I had your saintly virtue!" With a visible effort, he controlled himself. "You are right, of course. You always are. Normally I can cope with Harriet, but the sight of those flowers was too much."

"I know how you feel. In future, keep the key where she cannot find it."

David answered bitterly, "Is there *any* place she won't ferret in?"

"She doesn't visit the oast-house, except when you are there. She knows that is forbidden."

"She knew the hothouse was forbidden, too. But your suggestion is a good one. I will keep the key in my office in future. Forgive me for losing my temper. You, too, Aphra. I am ashamed now, of course."

There was nothing I wouldn't forgive him, and I felt he knew that. I think he also knew that I understood and sympathised with his outburst.

Red Deakon spoke for the first time.

"Come, Claudia—a glass of wine will do you good after a shock like that. You conceal things well, but not from me."

He placed a solicitous hand beneath her elbow and turned her toward the house, and I was surprised by the gentleness of that strong blacksmith's hand. For me, he had no eyes at all, and I was glad of that because I was in no mood to face his mocking discernment. I wondered if he remembered, as I did, our conversation on the gallery, his warning to forget all about Abbotswood, and his insistence that it was no place for me. Now I viewed him with suspicion, for it was obvious where he considered his own place to be—at Claudia Bentine's side. And she was mistress here.

I think I had already recognised him as an ambitious man, but I had believed his ambition to be confined to Deakon's Forge. Now I was not so sure.

David said, "What a worry Harriet is! We really must do something about her, Claudia."

His sister looked back over her shoulder. "We will keep her here, where she is happy and well looked after."

"I merely thought that perhaps a return to Bristol might be beneficial."

"No, David."

Clauda's decisive tones closed the subject, and David took my arm and led me in their wake.

Truman served the wine with his customary air of dignity and solicitude, then left the decanter and departed.

We seated ourselves in the drawing room, David and I opposite each other by the fireplace and Claudia with Red Deakon on a sofa. Conversation was aimless and polite—the weather, crops, village news, all of which left me out because I knew nothing of such matters—but then Claudia thoughtfully included me by asking my opinion of the new balcony designs.

"Do show them to her, Red. Miss Coleman is very interested in everything pertaining to Abbotswood."

So it was as obvious as that, I thought regretfully as the man brought the drawings across.

I avoided his eyes, though there was no reason for doing so. He had probably been too engrossed in Claudia to notice David and me out there in the garden. But I detected mockery in his voice as he said to Claudia, "I have noticed Miss Coleman's interest myself."

My head jerked up a trifle indignantly, and he met my glance with an amused air before returning to his seat. I was so disconcerted that it took me a moment or two to focus my attention on the drawings, and I was glad when David joined me. He was unperturbed by, and possibly unaware of, any underlying mockery in Red Deakon's words, but I was sure it had been there. So the man did remember his advice, his warning to me not to be taken in by the velvet curtains. His arrogant assumption that he could treat me with disdain inflamed me further, so that

I found it hard to praise what was very admirable work. I left David to do that and ignored the man for the rest of his visit.

But courtesy demanded that I should bid him good-day before leaving. By that time we had all moved into the hall and Claudia was walking ahead with her brother.

Red Deakon said, "I have been debating whether to call on you, Miss Coleman, ever since I heard of your return, but circumstances persuaded me that I might not be welcome. You might have found visitors trying, particularly those you do not like. But I want you to know how sorry I am about your father's death. It must have been a grief and a shock."

Although the words seemed trite, I was surprised by the feeling behind them and found myself thanking him, adding that it would always be a grief and a shock.

"I understand. Time masks things, but contrary to general belief, it does not always heal. You will find your work a great refuge. Work always is. And I have heard that theatrical folk are tremendously compassionate when any of their members are in distress."

"That is true, but so are other friends."

"Meaning Hillyard and his sister? I am sure their concern must mean a lot to you."

Did he always put a double meaning into anything he said, or was I wrong in imagining an underlying implication, a suggestion that this invitation to stay at Abbotswood meant a great deal more to me than a friendly gesture? Were he and Claudia watching me with something more than kindly interest? Did they imagine that I was scheming to remain?

I felt my cheeks flush and turned away.

"Don't misinterpret *every*thing I say, Miss Coleman. I know I have a disconcerting habit of speaking the truth, which doesn't endear me to many people, but don't imagine inferences which are not there. I mean it in all sincerity when I saw that I am sorry about your father, but remaining here too long will be no help to you. Grief leaves one too vulnerable, and you could therefore suffer more. So I also mean it when I say that a speedy return to work could be your salvation."

"*And* that you are sorry I returned to Abbotswood?"

"That, too. But surely you expected it, or have you forgotten my advice to forget about the place? I still hold by that. Fortunately you will not be here forever."

Twice within the last hour I had been reminded that I did not belong here—first by Claudia, subtly pointing out that this was not my world and discouraging any lingering visit by stressing the boredom of country life in the winter, and now by this red-haired man, who, I felt, had been primed by Claudia to urge me to go. It could be nothing to him whether I departed or remained, so I was even more convinced that he was her ally. What hurt most was the thought that this woman, whom I liked, did not like me in return. Seeing me in her brother's arms must therefore have increased her desire to see me gone.

EIGHT

"I want you," David had said, not "I love you." There was a big difference, and as I reflected on it, alone in my room, I saw the wisdom of an early departure. I had to make a final break with Abbotswood whether it hurt or not, which meant a final break with him. But I was inexperienced in loving a man the way I loved David Hillyard and was caught in the trap of my own desire.

In a way I was also challenged by the combined attitudes of Claudia Bentine and Red Deakon; to depart would be to capitulate to them. There would be a certain ignominy about it, too, as if acknowledging that I did not fit into this background and never would. In leaving, I would be admitting that I was no more than an impoverished play actress who had been charitably housed and fed for the past month, and in remaining, I would be imposing on this charitable kindness. Either thought was galling.

A tap on my door heralded a maid bearing a heavy copper jug of steaming water, some of which she poured into a flowered bowl on my marble-topped washstand. The jug was fitted with a lid to keep the contents hot, and she placed it aside for my use should I wish to replenish the bowl. Before leaving, she drew the heavy curtains across my windows, although it was scarcely dusk. They were not velvet, this time, but pink damask to match the bedspread and bed hangings. I scarcely glanced at them, though they had impressed me very much on arrival. After seeing the Pimlico rooms again, everything at Abbotswood seemed more beautiful than ever, but already I was becoming accustomed to the luxury of this bedroom which was in the west wing, the wing occupied by the family. I even thanked the maid mechanically and scarcely heeded her respectful bob on departure. As quickly as this had I begun to feel at home here, so perhaps Red Deakon's reminder that it could not last was salutory and much needed.

I went downstairs in a subdued frame of mind, and I went slowly, taking my time and glancing idly at the walls as I did so. Unlike the library walls, which were covered with portraits of bygone De Friemonts, the rest of the house displayed very few. This surprised me, for I would have expected to find some Bentine portraits in the wing occupied by the family.

"You look thoughtful, sweet Aphra."

David awaited me at the foot of the stairs, both hands out-stretched, and immediately my despondency vanished.

"I am surprised to see no Bentine portraits," I said as my footsteps quickened.

"I understand they were a family who disliked being painted."

"That seems inconsistent with people who enjoyed acting."

He shrugged, not interested in the Bentines. "We must talk," he said.

"Yes. We must talk of my departure. I have been here too long."

"Too *long!* You have been here no time at all."

"A whole month."

"That *is* no time at all. You need longer to recover from your father's death."

"Work will help me to do that."

He almost pulled me into the drawing room, firmly closing the doors behind us. Then he turned and placed both hands on my shoulders.

"What has put this idea into your head?" When I made no answer, he said, "Was it my behaviour this afternoon? Did I frighten you? Oh, my sweet Aphra, forgive me, but waiting is so hard and I am not a patient man. I have waited for you for a very long time. . . ."

"We have known each other only a few weeks."

"Much longer than that. Much, much longer. In some previous existence, I am certain, for the moment I first saw you I knew we were predestined for each other. Don't smile, my love—these things do happen, although I never believed it until you came into my life. I made you come into it, but you know that already. Chance might have taken me to that theatre in Bristol, although I am not

The Eagle at the Gate 105

wholly convinced even of that, but I dared not leave it to chance to arrange our meeting. I had to organise that myself, so I invited the Thespian Players to Abbotswood."

And his sister had permitted it because he was her younger brother, whom she loved. I had already noticed Claudia's indulgence of his whims, her maternal feeling toward both her younger relatives. But I suspected that her indulgence would stop if it meant tolerating any emotional entanglement with someone whom she considered socially beneath her brother.

How had Red Deakon described the people who flocked to Abbotswood on the night of her birthday? If he had not actually used the word "snobbish," that was what he had meant, and now I wondered if it applied to her, too, and even, in a way, to himself since he now appeared to be so close to her.

David gave me a little shake. "Aphra, did you hear what I said?"

I nodded, too emotionally choked to speak. But I had to be sensible. The future had to be faced, and I knew this was what my father would wish me to do. I had already gone against his wishes in returning to Abbotswood, although I felt that were he to know of it, he would surely be grateful to David Hillyard and his sister for befriending me at such a time, but however I felt about Red Deakon, I knew he was right when he said that work would be my salvation. I could not hide here forever, imposing on hospitality which others might regard as charity. Perhaps I had even been thoughtless, selfish, in remaining so long.

"Then if you heard me," David said with a touch of impatience, "why don't you say something?"

"I have said it already. I must go. I know what you want of me, but that isn't what *I* want—"

He interrupted furiously. "I don't believe you. You wanted it this afternoon, and if I kissed you now, you would want it again. For God's sake, Aphra, don't pretend to me that you are frigid!"

His arms slipped from my shoulders to my back, drawing me close, pressing my body against his own. He whispered excitedly, "I know you feel as I do . . . the heat, the longing. . . . That is desire, my darling; a physical need, an ache, a yearning that can be satisfied in only one way, with one person. I shall be your lover, and you will never want any man but me. And oh, the things I shall teach you, things we will do together all our lives because we will be lovers all our lives."

I broke away. I was crying. I wanted so much more than that. I wanted children and a father who would give them his name.

"No—no—"

"My darling, have I spoken too soon, urged you too soon? But waiting is so difficult, and now you are threatening to go I have even less time. When I brought you here, I thought I would be content to watch you slowly recover from sorrow, that I would cherish you throughout the months until convention allowed me to speak, but I am a passionate man, my love, and why should we wait a whole year just because convention demands it?"

I was still. I felt the tears drying on my cheeks. I stared at him in disbelief. A year, he had said. The conventional year demanded for mourning and which forbade the possibility of marriage. . . .

"My love, why do you look like that? What have I said to surprise you?"

"A year—the conventional year of waiting—"

His smile was joyous.

"You hate the idea, too. Oh, sweet Aphra, how glad I am of that! So you won't go away, will you? You will stay and we can be married very quietly, and a fig for society's ridiculous ideas!"

He seized me again, and I clung to him. We kissed; we let our urgent bodies press close, yearning, demanding, longing, promising. . . .

The double doors opened. We jerked apart, but David left one arm about my waist as we faced his sister.

Claudia was so shocked that she remained where she was, both hands on the ornate gilt doorknobs. I even thought she had gone a little white, but was too delirious in my happiness to be really aware of anything else.

"Claudia! I am glad it is you because you must be the first to hear the news and to congratulate me. Aphra is to be my wife."

She made no answer. She closed the doors quietly, came into the room, and stood a little way off, studying us. Then she said, "You don't mean it, of course. Miss Coleman would not do such a thing so soon after her father's death."

I had the extraordinary feeling that she was seizing on that as an excuse. Certainly I knew that this news was the last she wished to hear. I had been right. Claudia Bentine wanted her brother to be involved with me in no way at all, particularly in marriage.

"Oh, come," David protested. "Marrying me won't make her mourn her father any the less, though it will certainly bring happiness into her life and therefore help her bear his loss the better. And you surely don't uphold that nonsensical idea that she should wrap herself in gloom for a whole year? Grief doesn't switch itself off at the end of a prescribed period! I intend to marry Aphra as soon as possible and as quietly as possible. We want no fuss, no pomp and ceremony, no disapproving congregation witnessing our wedding as if we were committing a sin, and if that is the way *you* feel about it, you can stay away, too."

It was not the first time I had seen that ice-cold anger in David's face, nor was it to be the last, but at this moment it thrilled me because it was in my defence.

His sister clasped her hands tightly. I could see the tremendous effort it cost her to control her feelings.

"If it is what you wish, David, then I wish it too, but I beg you to wait awhile. . . ."

"No. There is absolutely no necessity. Aphra is alone in the world, and therefore no one can interfere."

Claudia turned to me then. "Are you sure you are not marrying my brother for that very reason, Miss Coleman?"

The remark outraged David. It angered me, too.

"I can only think that surprise, or shock if you so prefer to call it, has made you speak without thought, Mrs. Bentine."

I was amazed at the steadiness of my voice. So, perhaps, was she, for she said not another word. Not that David gave her any chance to. "That," he said, "was very cruel of you, Claudia, and I can't forgive it."

"I did not mean to imply that she was calculating, merely that she might be carried away by her need for someone to care for her. After all, she is young and has known a father's love and protection all her life—"

She floundered helplessly, and David laughed. "My

dear sister, I can assure you that what Aphra wants from me is not a father's love, and what I feel for her doesn't remotely resemble it!"

Three weeks later he had his way. Claudia accepted the situation, but not without one final appeal to me. On the eve of the wedding she came to my room and made one last plea.

"It isn't too late to draw back," she urged. "You are so young, too young to know your own mind...."

"You must have been about my age when you married Lawrence Bentine."

She answered evasively that the two cases were different, then pressed on. "To marry at a time of emotional stress can be a tragic mistake. I wouldn't want you to suffer. And you would miss your life in the theatre, I am sure."

I said gently, "I believe you are really thinking of your brother, not me. This saddens me, because I have liked you from the start and hoped you felt the same about me. Please, Claudia—try to." She gave a little start when I used her Christian name, and I think it was that which made me realise how steeped in convention this woman was. In polite society one did not advance to Christian name terms until one had known a person over a period of time, and no young woman would ever address an older one in such a way until invited to.

"You see how you wince at the informal manners of my theatrical background," I continued. "You must forgive me for calling you Claudia, but I am so accustomed to hearing David refer to you that way that inevitably I think of you by your Christian name, too. And now I am no longer to be Miss Coleman, surely you don't intend to address me as Mrs. Hillyard instead? We will be sisters-in-law!"

"I see your mind is made up," she said with an air of sad resignation. "Is there nothing I can do to dissuade you?"

I cried, "Why should you want to? Is it because I am comparatively penniless? The only capital I have is the little my father left and the profits from the last tour, which will come to me when the company is wound up, plus the sum George Mayfield is to pay for scenery and props. I admit I am not a social catch, if that is what you want for David."

"Don't talk like that, don't think like that!"

"What else am I to think? What other reason could you have for not wanting me to marry your brother?"

She opened her mouth, then closed it tightly. Then she gave a despairing sigh and left me. She had lost, and I had won, but I felt no triumph as the door closed behind her. The thought of my coming marriage would have been even happier had I felt that I was really welcome at Abbotswood.

If George Mayfield's letter had not arrived on the morning of my wedding, I would have paid greater attention instead of scanning it hurriedly and pushing it aside. So its full implication did not occur to me until several weeks later, when I found the letter thrust into a drawer of my dressing table. By that time it was too late to take up his offer, even had I wanted to, and I felt little compunction about my delayed reply because the world of the theatre was now behind me and I had no desire to re-enter it.

"Everything is signed, sealed, and settled," he had written. "I am engaging the cast as before, running things exactly as your father did, which means that there is still a place for you as leading juvenile, and because of your sad loss, my dear Aphra, I intend to raise your salary by ten shillings a week because I know you will need it. We go into rehearsal on October 1, which means that I will want you back to sign your contract no later than September 30. I believe it was your father's wish that you should have a tryout as Imogen, and I am willing to comply. This won't please Elizabeth, but she really is getting too old for ingenue parts, and in any case, she is too buxom to impersonate a boy convincingly. There are plenty of strong leads for her still—the Shrew, Lady Macbeth, Portia—she will be effective in all, and so her vanity will be satisfied.

"There is just one thing I must ask you—about that booking your father is believed to have made at the Hippodrome, Folkestone. Do you know anything about it? No confirmation has come to hand, nor did he confide the details to Barney, who, as you know, combined the job of road manager with that of stage manager and will still do so. He is therefore kept informed of such matters, but your father gave him no details of this particular booking—understandably, poor man, since he was more ill than any of us realised. I wrote to the manager of the theatre, but the letter was returned by the post office. I then went along to the *Era* offices, only to learn from the sub-editor who keeps records of these things that the theatre closed many weeks ago and still appears to be on the market. But I recall that Charles went specifically to Folkestone to clinch the booking when we all went ahead to Abbotswood. I can only conclude that he was unaware of the theatre's closure and failed in his mission. Such a mistake seems unlike Charles. Did he confide anything in you?"

By the time I read this through thoroughly David and I had been married for several weeks. I wrote posthaste to George, telling him why I would not be rejoining the Thespians and relishing the surprise with which my news would be received amongst the cast, and by way of atonement I promised to drive into Folkestone as soon as possible and call on the gentleman who, I knew, was taking over the theatre.

"The *Era* seems to be lagging behind with its news," I finished, and then I signed my new name with pride. *Aphra Hillyard*. And the embossed letterhead filled me with equal pride, for it was now my permanent address, my permanent home, the thing I had dreamed about and longed for and thought impossible to achieve. *Abbotswood, Kent*.

David entered as I signed the letter. He stooped and kissed the back of my neck. His lips lingered, and with his mouth against my skin he murmured, "Whatever you are doing, you can put it aside. My demand is more urgent. . . ."

He carried me over to the bed, ignoring my laughing protest that luncheon would soon be served *"There's time, there's time,"* he whispered, and with urgent hands he pushed my clothing aside and almost without waiting claimed me. And, as usual, my senses leapt to meet his. One of the first lessons David had taught me was that this delight could be enjoyed not just in the generally accepted hours of night and that it was a husband's right to claim it whenever he wished. Love was not ordered by the clock.

"You must blame yourself, not me, if I am an impatient

lover," he murmured later as we lay languorous and content after forgetting the world and everything in it.

He turned on his side and looked at me, stroking the damp and tumbled hair from my brow with a gentle hand. His palm was smooth and dry and, for such a moment as this, surprisingly cool, and all unbidden I found myself comparing it with the strong, rough one of Red Deakon. Immediately the enchantment and wonder of this moment disappeared. I saw him again at my wedding, standing with arms folded as I walked down the aisle on David's arm. His eyes had been fixed on me, his face unsmiling. I had almost imagined there was pity there, until we were beside his pew and it appeared to be mockery. At that I had looked away swiftly, and during the small reception at Abbotswood I had avoided him studiously. No cynical guest would be allowed to spoil this most wonderful day of my life.

From the moment we left the family chapel to the moment we went upstairs to the suite of rooms Claudia had allocated to us, I had eyes only for my husband. It did not matter to me that at this time of year and at such short notice, David could spare no time from the estate to take me on a wedding trip. That would come later, he promised, in the spring perhaps. Paris in the spring was at its best, and after that there would be Rome, Florence . . . wherever I wanted to go. But to be wherever he was was honeymoon enough for me.

I had not thought of Red Deakon since my wedding day, and why I should do so at such a moment as this, I failed to understand.

After a while David roused, slipped off the bed, and crossed to an embroidered bell rope beside the fire.

"We will lunch up here," he said. "After loving you, I am in no mood for Harriet's exhausting chatter and Claudia's trite conversation about house and garden and village affairs. I would prefer to sleep the afternoon away with you."

So luncheon was brought up to us, and a table set in our adjoining sitting room whilst I rebound my hair and David lay on the bed, watching me.

"Who was the letter to?" he asked idly. "The one you were writing when I came in." His smile teased. "If you have an admirer, God help him—and God help you."

"You surely would not punish me just for being admired?" I laughed. "That can hardly be classed as an infidelity!"

"No, but I would never permit any demonstration of it. You are mine, and no other man can cast covetous eyes on you."

"Tyrant!" I laughed again, not taking him seriously, and tossed George Mayfield's letter across. "I was answering that, belatedly."

He scanned it, then said, "Why bother to reply at all?"

"Because it would be ill mannered not to! George is a friend."

"Not any longer. You have put those people behind you. Remember that, sweet Aphra."

"You're not serious? Why, you welcomed them all to Abbotswood not so long ago!"

"As performers. Paid performers."

"Then I was a paid performer, too!"

"That is true, but I have lifted you out of those ranks."

I laid down my hair brush, my cheeks pink.

"You loved me, that was why you married me. Not to lift me up in any way, not to elevate me to your side. If I was good enough to marry, I was your equal, and still am."

"Yes, now that you are Mrs. David Hillyard."

"I was as much your equal then as I am now." I heard a rising note of anger in my voice, and when he laughed, I bit my lip, because there was no kindness in his laughter, only ridicule. Then it ceased abruptly, and his voice became caressing.

"You do rise to the bait, don't you? But I swear you are more desirable when you are angry than when you are calm, sweet Aphra. You must become accustomed to my teasing, though I confess I enjoy making you squirm a little."

"Like that poor butterfly you imprisoned in your palm that day?" The words came out spontaneously, surprising me as much as him.

"Yes," he answered after a moment's reflection. "That isn't a bad comparison at all." He tossed George Mayfield's letter aside. "Well, answer this if you really want to, although the man can scarcely expect a reply after these long weeks of waiting. I declare he must wonder about it and think you very forgetful."

"All the more reason for me to reply at once—and I am sure he will understand when he hears about my marriage."

"Perhaps. Though you *are* a little absentminded, aren't you, darling. Are you aware that you have forgotten to put your shoes on again?"

So I had. They lay where they had fallen, kicked off as he carried me to the bed. I laughed and slipped my feet into them, glad that all was well between us again.

As we lunched, I told him of my intention to drive into Folkestone to see what I could learn about the reopening of the Hippodrome. "I feel I owe it to the company since my father arranged the booking. Something must have gone wrong because he never made mistakes about such things."

David was silent. I looked at him, sensing a preoccupation, almost an embarrassment. He met my glance and said compassionately, "Don't waste your time, my love. Your father never went near the Hippodrome."

"I know. He told us that."

"He also told us that the owner of the Metropole was to be the new licencee."

"Yes—?" I spoke uncertainly, puzzled and not a little alarmed by my husband's guarded voice.

"It was a pack of lies," he said bluntly. "A story made up for our benefit. The owner of the Metropole may be acquainted with your father, and your father with him, and I know for a fact that he did indeed stay at the Metropole that night—rather surprisingly since it is an expensive hotel and, judging by the little he left you, he was far from monied. But very possibly he scrounged hospitality in the way theatrical people do, trading on their public name."

"*He would do no such thing!*"

My husband said gently, "My darling, you must control yourself. Emotional instability can have dire results. Look at Harriet."

I felt my face drain of color. This was not the gentle, thoughtful man I had fallen in love with, but a detached stranger with cold eyes and brittle voice. I heard my fork clatter against my plate. Instantly David's hand reached across the table and covered mine. His eyes were warm again, his voice gentle. How could any man switch from warmth to coldness and back again so quickly?

"My dear one, I am making allowances for the fact that your grief over your father is still very recent and therefore still acute. That was why I was keeping quiet about the things I had found out."

"What things? There are no things to *be* found out!"

"My poor sweet, of course not. Forget it. Forget everything, and don't think any more about Folkestone. Just why your father preferred to go there instead of coming to Abbotswood might best be left undiscovered."

"I—I don't like your implication—"

"I am not implying *any*thing!" He spoke now with elaborate patience, as if humouring someone slightly demented. "I am simply giving you the facts. For some reason best known to himself your father decided not to come here until the last possible moment *and* to get away as quickly as he could. We have only his story that he drove up to Abbotswood in a hired carriage and slipped in through a side entrance because the drive was crowded with arriving guests. In actual fact, all visitors had arrived by lunchtime, so a furtive entrance later in the day was unnecessary."

"My father was never furtive!"

"Well, my darling, he was on that occasion." David dabbed precisely at his mouth with a table napkin, laid it aside, and pushed back his chair. His actions had an air of dismissal, closing the subject, but I was not prepared to let it go.

"You have been spying on him, checking on him, and I don't like it."

"Checking, yes. Spying, no. I was concerned about his sudden death and for your sake tried to ascertain his movements before he came here. I recall your telling me that the doctor who examined him toyed with the idea of possible food poisoning, so I called on the manager of the Metropole and learned that he did indeed stay there, but the man was not pleased at the implication that food poisoning could have been contracted at his hotel, any more than I was pleased at the idea that it could have been contracted at Abbotswood—not that it was, of course, since no one else was affected. But if Claudia had heard such a suggestion, she would have reacted the same way. And now, my love, think no more about it. Your father is dead, and whatever secrets he had died with him."

"He had no secrets."

My husband smiled gently.

"Do you really believe that? Is there any person in the world who doesn't have *some* kind of secret? But I am moved by your loyalty to him, your trust in him. That is as it should be and as I wish it to remain. If you hold me in such loyalty and trust throughout our married life, I shall be more than content."

He came round the table and kissed me lightly on the brow. "And now I must get back to work. How do you propose to amuse yourself this afternoon?"

I shrugged. I could give no thought to amusement. Nor was I prepared to dismiss everything so casually.

"If my father said he had booked the company to appear at a certain theatre on a certain date, then he spoke the truth. He never made mistakes about such things."

"He did this time, my love—or else he was *not* speaking the truth. The owner of the Metropole told me himself that he made no bid for the lease of the Hippodrome. Running an hotel like that one is more than a sufficient occupation for any hotelier."

I heard my husband cross to the door, but I didn't watch him go. I was staring unseeingly at my forgotten food. I heard the door open and his footsteps stop; then his voice came back to me, very gently.

"I am afraid you must face one other fact, Aphra. Prior to your father's death he was obviously—shall we say disturbed? His strange whim to disguise himself as the hideous Caliban, what sort of masochism was that in a man so proud of his looks? And the performance he gave that night was distinctly erratic. I hope I was the only one in the audience who detected his lapses of memory, his confusion—"

My head jerked up.

"He was unwell! You know that! You commented on it before he left Abbotswood next morning."

"I did indeed. And I shall continue to agree with you on all points."

"What do you mean—'continue to agree'? Stop sounding as if you were intent on humouring me."

"But I am, my love. You make it necessary when you are in moods like this." He came back and kissed me, but I could not respond. "Very well," he said with sudden impatience. "If you want to sulk, sulk, but I thought you had more emotional control, more stability."

"If you are suggesting that I am mentally disturbed—"

"My darling, I am suggesting no such thing. How touchy you are, just because I happen to have found your father out in some peccadillo! There must have been women in his life; no doubt he had an assignation with one in Folkestone."

"And you didn't check on that," I taunted. "Didn't you ask at the Metropole if my father took a woman to his room?"

"Good God, do you think I would stoop to *that*? You are distraught, Aphra. Hysterical. I never suspected that you could be like this. Had your mother such tendencies? These things can be hereditary, I believe." When I stared at him speechlessly, he went on. "I have never questioned you about your parentage—"

"Are you doing so now?"

"No. Just wondering. I suspect you know very little about it, and perhaps that is a good thing."

The door closed behind him. I couldn't believe that the man who left the room had been my lover only an hour or so before.

NINE

That I had quarrelled with my husband after such a short spell of marriage seemed impossible, but the ugliness of the scene lingered with me. Even more disturbing was the discovery that tenderness and love could be replaced so swiftly with anger and raised voices, although in all honesty I had to admit that the only raised voice had been my own. Not once had David's cultured tones become louder; it was I who had cried out in protest, whereas his precise inflections merely sharpened his words, imparting a razor edge which was more deadly than any blaze of wrath. Certainly my own emotional outcry had left him unmoved, and only I felt the worse for it.

To stay in that room for the afternoon would be intolerable. I would be taunted by the echo of his words and by his inferences about my father's duplicity and my own emotional instability. And his hints about my parentage, the doubts he cast upon it, were unforgettable, too. He had given me no chance to ask his meaning. He left me feeling angry and bewildered and, in a strange and sickening way, frightened.

I flung open the vast Sheraton wardrobe which dominated one wall. When entering this room for the first time, I had admired its beauty, the gracious lines, the gleam of walnut and mahogany, the oval medallion designs on the doors, inlaid with the typical shell motif which marked some of Sheraton's finest work. Only when coming to live at Abbotswood had I realised how extensive had been my father's knowledge of antiques and how much he had taught me, and never did I fail to experience a feeling of wonder and admiration when I opened these magnificent doors. Sometimes my fingers would linger, feeling the beautiful patina of the wood—but not now. Now I saw only the array of clothes within. Mine, all mine. The whole room was given over to me, with a dressing room leading off it for my husband. We lived very splendidly here at Abbotswood, surrounded by beautiful furniture, walking on fine carpets, eating off the finest plate, drinking from the purest crystal, and finally withdrawing behind magnificent curtains when night came.

These were the things which I had found so enviable when I first entered this house. These were the things which had awed me, promising a life of elegance and dignity such as I had never known and which quickly became the dominant desire of my life—next to my husband, of course. Abbotswood and David Hillyard had quickly become synonymous in my mind. But now I belonged to both and found that it was still possible to be hurt, even in surroundings like these.

Trembling, I seized the nearest coat to hand, a finely tailored velour with velvet trim. The line and cut were excellent, from the narrow waist to the long and sweeping skirt which covered my trailing dress. On the shelf above stood an array of leather bandboxes, all containing magnificent hats made especially, and hurriedly, for my trousseau and all paid for by David.

This evidence of his generosity seemed to taunt me now. *You are ungrateful . . . ungrateful . . . ungrateful to treat him with angry words when you have so much to thank him for. . . .*

I slammed shut the splendid wardrobe. I would walk vigorously across the park until I was calm again. I had walked a lot since coming to Abbotswood, for I had yet to learn to ride. To be able to handle a horse was apparently a desirable feminine accomplishment in a countrywoman—one of the many desirable accomplishments, such as handling a gun or a rod or reins by day or flirting genteelly with the nearest male by night, encouraging him with suggestive glances and tittering stupidly behind a fan when his hands strayed to waist or bosom, though what sensual delight could be experienced from curves rigidly encased in whalebone, I could not imagine.

Artificial, the lot of them. Red Deakon's verdict sprang to my mind. I hated to admit that the man could be right about anything, but I had quickly learned that he was right on that score.

Before marching out of the room, I picked up my letter to George Mayfield, determined that he should have it. I would put it in the leather mailbag in the hall, to ensure despatch. Not for the world would I drop an old friend.

Claudia was in the hall, conferring with Mrs. Stevens. They both looked up as I descended the stairs, and I saw the housekeeper's eyes flicker over my purple coat. I could almost read her thoughts. *Well, I suppose purple is a mourning colour, but somehow, on her, it doesn't look it.* . . . David had said almost the same thing. "You must wear that colour all your life, darling. It looks magnificent with your dark hair, and when you wear it, it ceases to be sombre or mournful." But I could sense Mrs. Stevens' disapproval and knew she was thinking that, bride or no bride, it was too soon for someone in mourning to advance from regulation black to the graduated tones of grey and purple which were officially acceptable after the requisite twelve months.

Then her eyes lowered, avoiding my glance. Not since I had become Mrs. David Hillyard had the woman tried to engage me in conversation. Such familiarity with a member of the family was taboo, unless that member initiated it, and even then it would be confined to the most impersonal interchange. That was not the kind of conversation Mrs. Stevens enjoyed; she had demonstrated as much when showing me into the room in the east wing. I had come here then as a touring actress—a paid performer, as David now put it—and as such I had not been on a par with the family or even with the local gentry. Now I was suddenly elevated, no longer a person whom she could approach for a friendly gossip, and a great deal had probably been said about *that* in the servants' hall. "Don't know what society's coming to, that I don't. Why, only the other day Lord Ashford's heir married a Gaiety girl! The young rakes nowadays don't seem to give a fig for position or breeding. All they want is some brazen young thing from behind the footlights, and all *they* want in return is a title and the income that goes with it. Of course, Mr. Hillyard hasn't a title and never will have, and nor will the mistress, but still they *are* gentry and Abbotswood is a great house."

Claudia's glance was more kindly. She had made an effort to accept her brother's wife and even to make me feel at home, but my position here was not all I had expected or hoped for. She was mistress of Abbotswood, and if I were to take any part in household affairs, only she would decree it. The most she had permitted me to do so far was to arrange flowers. There were no other ladylike duties available for me apparently. I occupied a nebulous place, not exactly a relative because in some subtle way I had not yet been fully accepted as such, yet still not a guest or a visitor who would ultimately depart.

She dismissed Mrs. Stevens and came to meet me. "Are you going out?"

"Yes. For a walk."

Her grey eyes surveyed me. Despite her air of reserve and the subtle barrier between us, I still had the feeling that she was basically a kind woman, and I wished she would emerge from her antipathy and accept me for what I was, her brother's wife who bore her neither animosity nor envy. But always there was this veiled sort of feeling, this guardedness which forbade me to get to know her. That this guard could disappear I well knew, but only in the company of Red Deakon.

"You are hatless," she reprimanded gently.

"Yes. I like to feel the wind in my hair."

"But—"

"But it isn't 'done'? It isn't 'correct' when in mourning? Does sorrow have to be observed in these regulated ways? Do signs have to be displayed? I shall always grieve for my father, with or without a hat." That sounded facetious, but I had not meant it to be. "Oh, Claudia, can't you understand? Conformity doesn't always mean sincerity." I touched her sleeve, and she withdrew slightly. That hurt a little. It was like a rebuff, so I walked on, saying over my shoulder, "I *like* going without a hat, and I am going without one now. I will keep to the park, so the only people to see me will be the estate workers, and I daresay they disapprove of me as it is."

"Aphra, wait!" I was surprised by the note of pleading in her voice and stopped in my tracks. She came to my side and said, "Forgive me. I was not meaning to criticise."

This overture made me so happy that I smiled at her at once. Spontaneously I reached up and kissed her cheek.

"Enjoy your walk," she said, "and if you *would* keep to the park—"

"—it would avoid disapproving tongues in the village?"

"Country people are insular and easily shocked. It is as well, and perhaps kind, not to offend their codes. To you, those codes may seem narrow, but to them they are the guidelines for social behaviour."

She watched me descend the front steps, those steps which had impressed me so much when I first drove up to them at David's side. That day now seemed surprisingly long ago because so much had happened to change me from the rather naïve and wide-eyed girl stepping into a world hitherto undreamt of. I was now a woman; wife and mistress of a man I loved; an inhabitant of this magnificent house, accustomed to come and go by the entrance used only by members of the family or their personal guests. So now I lifted my skirts and descended with accustomed ease, marvelling that so soon did one grow used to things. Would this acceptance become indifference one day, even with me? I doubted it. I could not imagine myself ever taking Abbotswood for granted.

The brisk walk lightened my spirits, and perhaps the brief encounter with Claudia helped, too. At least there had been some small overture on her part, which I hoped indicated a thaw in her recent chilliness. I would welcome a return of the friendliness she had shown to me when the Thespians were here.

The immediate grounds surrounding the house gave way on three sides to woodlands, part of which formed the offstage wings for the open-air theatre in the dell, but the fourth, sweeping down from the front of the house, stretched from the drive to a wide area of lawn which terminated in a ha-ha constructed several centuries ago. Beyond it lay the park where deer roamed, so tame out of the rutting season that they would eat from one's hand, and beyond the park spread Abbotswood's farmlands, overlooked by the ancient farmhouse where the factor lived, and less obtrusively by the oast-house which David used. Hops had once been grown at Abbotswood, hops to rival any in Kent, but these had been dropped in favour of more profitable agriculture and cattle. So the disused oast-house now provided different but equally valuable use.

In my determination to drive away anger and despondency, I walked farther than I realised, and by the time I reached the oast-house I felt considerably better. There was nothing like exercise and fresh air for lifting the spirits, and with this welcome release came a desire to restore things to normal, to rectify what could only have been a misunderstanding, to win back my husband's good humour and to be happy again. I felt ashamed of my outburst, and eager to say so. So I knocked loudly on his office door.

I stood there, waiting for his summons, but none came. Yet I was convinced that the place was not empty. No sound reached me, but I was conscious of a strange awareness, a feeling that silence had descended abruptly when I knocked.

I hesitated, turned away, went back. I knocked again, then tried the door. It opened at my touch, revealing the round interior, a brick-walled chamber dominated by David's businesslike desk. It was, like himself, immaculately tidy. So were the shelves and cupboards stacked with papers and files. The whole place had an atmosphere of orderliness which I was quite sure extended to the laboratory beyond.

I was still aware of that strange, listening silence. I called, but my voice only echoed in the round room and up the wooden stairs curving to the matching chamber above, the loft beneath the pointed roof topped by its ancient cowl. I had never been inside an oast before, and curiosity urged me to explore. Beside David's desk was a door communicating with the second roundel, but when I tried it, it was locked. It would be important to keep a place like a laboratory locked when not in use, of course, but I would have liked to see inside.

Disappointed, I turned away, then halted at a sound from above. A metallic sound. Someone was up there. It could only be David, so I gathered up my skirts and ran up the wooden stairs, calling his name. I had reached the aperture in the floor before he had a chance to reply, my head and shoulders emerging into a shadowy chamber which was almost a replica of the room below, except for the lofty pointed ceiling terminating in the cowl. A shaft of light pierced down from this point, emphasizing the darkness elsewhere.

"David?" I climbed the rest of the way and stood uncer-

The Eagle at the Gate

tainly beneath the spotlight, assailed by the odour of dust and stale hops and a nauseating smell which I could not define.

I repeated sharply, "David? Are you here?"

My voice whispered round the bare walls and came back to me mockingly. I looked around, trying to penetrate the shadows as my eyes grew accustomed to the gloom. The place was empty. There was nothing here but the dust of years and chaff left from the drying of hops over the centuries. Particles crunched beneath my feet as I stepped forward. Then I stumbled to a halt, arrested by that metallic noise again and the realisation that the crunching beneath my feet was caused by something harder and more substantial than dry leaves and chaff. My toes stubbed against something which rolled away a few feet and then lay staring up at me. I saw sockets where eyes had been and a gaping jaw stubbed with decaying teeth. A skull lay amongst scattered and broken bones, grinning up at me.

I stifled a scream, and as I did so, the light blotted out and a fierce rush of air swooped over my head, forcing me to my knees. I knelt there, crouching among the bones of this charnel house, too terrified to move.

Something *was* there, but it was not a human being. It was a shadowy creature of terrifying strength, trailing this metallic sound behind it but able to rise and blot out all light. I could feel it poised, ready to strike, a gigantic bat out of hell.

Another rush of air flung me face down, my cheeks pressing against sharp fragments of bone. The stench of death was in my nostrils, and beside me the metallic noise was sharper. It fell against my ear, and I felt the weight of a chain drag against me. Dear God in heaven, what monster was kept here to devour human beings? Paralyzed, I lay there, incapable of producing either movement or sound, feeling the acrid taste of horror in my mouth and the clench of terror in my stomach. I heard the heavy beating of wings as the monster swooped again, nearer this time, closer than before, skimming my head and dragging at my hair. Pain shot through my scalp as a strand was plucked from its roots. Scream after scream forced their way through my parched throat. I could hear them from a long way off, and the sound of footsteps also from a long way off, and a voice calling something unintelligible beneath my fast-disappearing senses.

Then silence. I had not fainted after all, for I lay there listening and waiting, aware of a voice speaking soothingly, but not to me. "There, there, Conrad—no need to struggle, no need for fear. You weren't expecting an intruder, were you? But you're safe now. I am here."

It was David's voice at its most gentle, with overtones of love which I myself had heard at our most tender moments. So the nightmare was not over; I was still in this charnel house, which seemed even more unreal with the introduction of my husband's voice, for only in some bad dream would he seem so familiar with the place and with the creature that inhabited it.

The chain was dragged away. I heard scratching noises as the monster settled down. And then David was helping me to rise and exclaiming irritably, "My dear Aphra, what *are* you doing here? In God's name, don't ever frighten Conrad like that again. He will attack in self-defence, and who can blame him?"

Somehow I was down the stairs. After the gloom from above, piercing sunlight through the open door of the oast-house almost blinded me. Then David was pressing me into a chair, and I saw that one hand and forearm were encased in a leather glove with a heavy sheath gauntlet reaching to the elbow.

He said, not ungently, "Whatever made you lie on the floor like that? You should have made for the stairs."

"I—I couldn't. The thing almost knocked me down." I fought to control my shaking voice and somehow managed to ask for water. By the time David fetched it from his laboratory—I saw now that the door stood open—I had managed to achieve a certain self-control and was even brushing feebly at my dusty clothes and taking great gulps of air to steady myself. But the glass rattled against my teeth as I drank.

"Now," David commanded, "tell me why you went up there."

"I heard a sound and thought it was you. In God's name, David, what do you keep there?"

A broad smile spread across his face. He even laughed as he said, "You actually didn't see him? Most people are awed by the sight of Conrad. He is the most handsome eagle ever kept in captivity."

"An *eagle!* In that dark graveyard? I saw a skull—"

David shrugged. "Of course. When he captures a rabbit or a hare or any other creature, I let him bring it back to his eyrie if he is too satiated with other kills to eat it at once. That wasn't a human skull you saw."

I stared at him, speechless, and he laughed again.

"My dear Aphra, have you any idea how comical you look, all wide-eyed and terrified and dusty into the bargain? What would my sainted sister think if she could see you now? A good thing she isn't around, although even if she were, she would know we hadn't been coupling on the floor since I am not in a dusty state myself."

He shook with mirth. I cried out to him to stop.

"There is nothing to laugh at! That place is littered with bones. Why don't you clear it up?"

"Because Conrad likes to peck at them." My husband spoke as if I were a child who had to be patiently taught. "I can see I must introduce you to him and he to you."

"No!" My voice was too taut, too sharp, betraying alarm in a way which annoyed him. I took another drink of water. "I'm sorry. I will be all right in a moment. But you can't blame me for not wanting to meet a creature that has pulled out my hair by the roots."

I put a hand to my scalp gingerly. David examined it and remarked indifferently, "A few hairs, perhaps. No more. An eagle's defence is in his talons. Had they touched you they could have penetrated your skull. So it was only his beak which accidentally dragged at your hair. Don't make a fuss about nothing." He forgot me then, tilting his head upwards, listening. "He is quiet now. I put his hood on to tranquillize him."

"You seem more concerned about him than about me."

"Of course. You are big enough and old enough to take care of yourself. Common sense should have made you dive for the stairs. He couldn't have flown down after you. For one thing, his chain would have stopped him, and for another his wing span is too great for him to get through the trapdoor. And don't call him a creature. He is the most noble of birds, the king of birds. But he has to be protected and cared for. He could have damaged his plumage *and* his nervous system plunging about like that. My poor Conrad."

He moved to the stairs and was gone before I could protest. I rose, endeavouring to smooth my hair and brushing ineffectively at my skirts. I would have walked out into the sunlight had I not looked such a sorry sight, but I had to restore order to my appearance before returning to the house and Claudia's discerning eye.

That moment's delay was perhaps unwise. On the other hand, perhaps not. Perhaps David was right in saying that I should meet Conrad face to face and overcome my fear of him. As he descended the stairs with the eagle perched on his leather-covered arm, even my unsettled nerves were lulled into admiration, for never had I had seen such plumage, such markings, or a head poised so nobly. Beneath the mask of his leather cap his aristocratic beak jutted proudly, and in his silence there was a dignity which made me ashamed of my own display of fear. Had the creature really been more terrified than I?

"Come and look at him, Aphra. Touch him. Feel the silkiness of his feathers. Don't be alarmed. When hooded, he can sense things, but not see, so you are quite safe from attack." He was caressing the plumage with pride and affection.

I could look, but not touch. The power and size of the bird awed me, but reaction from those terrible moments was still with me. I saw the great talons and the steely muscles of his legs beneath the jesses of soft leather which bound them, and recalled that there had been no protection for me from the strength of those muscles or the sharpness of those terrible claws. Inches long, they curved over the thick leather gauntlet protecting my husband's arm, and as I took a hesitant step forward, I saw them clench suddenly in a vicelike grip and David's arm brace to bear the thrust and weight.

"He senses your nearness, my love. See how he clings to me instinctively. Sometimes he will hold on like this for so long that my hand is numb by the time he decides to fly from it. His strength and weight are so great and his talons so dagger sharp that this glove has to be made of three thicknesses of padded horsehide leather to withstand them. Come, we will take him outside and launch him. He has not eaten today, so he should be ready for the kill. When I

The Eagle at the Gate

want him to perform really well, he has to be content with pecking bones up there; that way he works up an appetite. You'll find a satchel in the cupboard over there; it contains his lure. Fetch it for me."

I stood irresolute.

"There's no need to be nervous! I hope you are not going to be like Claudia and Harriet, holding back at the sight of him. He is harmless so long as I am in control. He will do whatever I want of him. I bought him from a zoo when he was a year old, so I have had him long enough to train to my will. Now he is more than eight and strong enough to live for another eight. He is a crowned eagle, the biggest and most formidable of all species. In his native South Africa he would kill and eat monkeys and slay even fair-sized buck. Here he has to be content with hares and rabbits and partridge and pheasant and the occasional sheep when no one is looking. I shall never forget the first time I saw him kill a sheep. One crash onto the creature's back and his talons pierced the throat, killing instantly. I saw the spurt of blood and Conrad's beak thrust into the wound, drinking it. That was the biggest thrill I've ever known because I knew then that I had succeeded. I had brought out the hunter in him, even though he had been born and raised in captivity. I had released the killer instinct of his ancestors over the past million years. What is the matter, my love? Why look at me that way?"

"Because when you talk like that, I don't know you."

He smiled.

"That means you are at least getting to know me, but to know me completely, you must get to know Conrad, too. He is my other self, aren't you, Conrad, my handsome?"

I turned away, murmuring that I couldn't go outside until I had tidied myself, but in reality hoping that David would leave me alone. Instead, he answered impatiently, "Well, hurry. It is plainly time for Conrad to be fed; otherwise, he wouldn't have dived at you like that. It was lucky you met him in darkened quarters; outside in daylight you wouldn't have stood a chance. You'll find a clothes brush in my desk over there. I'll get Conrad's lure meanwhile, but don't delay. I dislike being kept waiting."

"You have never told me that you kept an eagle as a pet," I said as I brushed myself down and finally smoothed my hair.

"I would have told you eventually."

"Claudia has never mentioned it either. Nor Harriet."

But Mrs. Stevens had given some indication, had I been alert enough and curious enough to question her, when she first told me about the Bentine eagles and remarked that Mr. Hillyard would have disagreed with rearing them in those restricting woods. The comment had been lost on me then, but not now, for it clearly indicated that only an expert handler would have been so knowledgeable.

I heard David saying, "Claudia and Harriet are nervous of him and were doubtless afraid that I would promptly bring him up to the house to display to you, had they told you about him. I am glad they didn't because any stories they related might have instilled into you their own ridiculous feelings. Instead, I shall instil mine. You must learn to love him as I do and on no account fear him. If you fear him, he will sense it, and then I shall have to continue to fly him alone, which is not nearly so enjoyable as with an audience—even an audience of a timid woman." He gave me a sidelong glance, tinged with amusement. "Of course, it is vastly entertaining to see him terrify people."

He had taken the lure bag out of the cupboard with his free hand and now said impatiently, "Surely you are ready?"

Reluctantly I put down the clothes brush and followed.

"We'll take him over to the park, away from the farm. I don't want to lose a good factor, and the man gets fearful for his livestock when Conrad is around. It is useless to remind him that they are my livestock, and so the loss of an occasional sheep is my loss, not his. That was probably a sheep's skull you saw in Conrad's loft. There now, we'll settle him down on this branch and make him come to the lure."

Deftly he removed the bird's long chain from a swivel attached to the leg and then perched him on the chosen spot. I saw a bell fixed about the ankle. "That is to trace him by should he go astray," David told me as he took out the lure. "If I ever lost Conrad, I don't know what I should do, there is such rapport between us. I doubt if any other eagle could take his place."

"What if he should turn on you, like that Bentine eagle?"

David laughed contemptuously. "Plainly, that man had no idea how to handle the bird. I am Conrad's master, and he knows it."

As he spoke, he tied the lure onto the end of a line. It consisted of half a dead rabbit with fur and bones still intact. The remains of an uneaten kill? I suppressed a shudder, then found myself watching, mesmerised, as David removed the eagle's hood. I saw a pair of ferocious eyes blink in the sudden light, snapping open as if springs released the heavy, predatory lids. I saw the powerful head and neck, the strong, curving beak, and the ripple of sunshine on his glossy plumage.

"Just look at that tail," David enthused. "The crowned eagle has the longest tail of all. In the Middle Ages, when eagles were trained for falconry, hunters called it the train and covered it with a leather bag for protection when travelling. The disadvantage of so long a tail is that it can become entangled among trees and consequently damaged, but no knowledgeable handler takes such risks, which shows just how ignorant that Bentine ancestor was, allowing his birds to fly loose up there in the woods. No wonder one killed him in frustration!"

David whistled softly, and the eagle jerked to awareness, watching the lure being swung in ever-widening circles. Then, to my surprise, he rose almost perpendicularly to the sky.

"Isn't that magnificent? Only the crowned eagle can rise like that. Other eagles simply take off in the ordinary way. Now watch him. He will perch forty to fifty feet above us, waiting and watching until he is ready to launch. See how he chooses an unencumbered branch, with no entangling offshoots to hinder him? There he goes! Now see the height he will climb to before he dives."

The immense bird soared higher and ever higher until he was no more than a speck in the sky. I remarked that he was too far up to see the food, but David shook his head. "The higher he flies, the farther he can see. Eagles have fantastic eyesight. Sometimes they focus on a quarry more than a mile away and land straight on target. Look out—here he comes!"

The distant speck grew larger, zooming down with wings nearly closed, nose-diving at such incredible speed that within seconds of plunging he was crashing to earth. I saw the steely legs thrust and brace, the back rise, the body straighten, and with a tremendous thud the eagle landed upright on the swinging lure with such force and weight that it was half buried in the earth. Then the talons were digging it up and tearing the flesh into shreds as if it were tissue paper.

"What do you think of *that?*" David demanded proudly.

It was an awe-inspiring performance, and I said so.

"I knew you would be impressed, but you must appreciate more than his flight. Look at those talons. They can lacerate and kill. An eagle's bite rarely amounts to a serious injury, just vicious pecks of flesh out of a person. When I began to train him, I wore a fencing mask because eagles can grab people by the face and disfigure them for life or blind them. Don't shrink like that—he won't touch you while I am around. Besides, he is intent on food at this moment. When he has finished devouring that, he will launch again for a real kill, and that is when the excitement begins. The lure is only an appetizer." Glancing at the velvet collar of my coat, David finished, "Lucky that isn't fur. Many a tame eagle has mistaken a lady's fur collar for an animal and landed on it. The talons go right through and into the neck, killing instantly."

If my first encounter with the eagle had not been so terrifying, I might have overcome a resistance to the bird which remained with me permanently. Despite this, his performance during the next half hour was impressive; the beauty of his flight, the magnificence of his wingspread— nearly eight feet from tip to tip—and the dexterity of his flying technique were remarkable, but his ruthless killing, both in the air and on the ground, made me shudder. Time after time he soared, dived, rolled over onto his back in midair to clutch at some creature in flight, never once failing to trap it with those dreadful talons, and time after time his hurricane descent to earth killed unerringly. Wildlife, it seemed, existed only to be slaughtered by this

The Eagle at the Gate

king of the sky; great or small became his instant victims, even to the lowly field mouse, which he would grasp with his foot as if it were a coin folded within a human palm, then convey to that gluttonous beak and swallow whole.

His appetite was voracious, but even he could apparently reach satiation point. With distended crop, he finally viewed a litter of flesh and bones and turned away indifferently.

"Had enough, my handsome? Very well, we'll take the remains home to your hideout. Help me gather them up, Aphra. There's an oilcloth bag in the satchel. Flesh *and* bones, remember. There's enough here to tide him over until I fly him again."

I looked at the massacre and refused. "The place looks like a battlefield. Don't ask me to touch it." I turned away, unable to look any more at that swollen bird, now hooded and waiting somnolently on a nearby perch, his swivel and chain linked to my husband's wrist. Nor could I look at David, for I was repelled by his indifference to such slaughter.

"My dear Aphra, you're not squeamish, are you?"

"About unnecessary killing, yes. You allowed the creature to continue just for the sport of it."

I walked away, leaving David to scoop up the remains and shovel them single-handed into the oilcloth bag, apparently uncaring about bloodstained fingers so long as his precious eagle could have a well-stocked lair. The beauty of its flight was now, for me, a thing forgotten. All I could recall was the lightning swiftness of his killing and the barbarism of it; killing for killing's sake and for my husband's enjoyment. And all I could hear was the echo of the victims' screams, the violence of the eagle's crash landing, and the dreadful tearing of his talons.

The horror of my first encounter with the bird came rushing back, so that I broke into a run, stumbling through long grass blindly. I had to put as much distance as possible between myself and the eagle. Or was it his master I wished to escape from, a man whom I believed I knew and who now showed an entirely different side to his character?

I must have run in a complete circle, for within minutes I was face to face with David again. He was striding toward me, Conrad perched upon his arm once more and the oilcloth bag bulging from the leather satchel. I stood still, trying to quell my breathlessness but unable to control my thumping heart. A strange reaction was setting in. I wanted to face neither my husband nor anyone up at the house. Claudia's shrewd glance would tell at once that I was upset, and if Harriet observed it, she would be delighted. Mrs. Stevens could be observant, too, in an inquisitive and unwelcome way. Only Truman's faded eyes would show concern for me, and that was something I had no desire to face either.

David smiled at me indulgently.

"What an emotional creature you are, my love, running away like that just because you couldn't bear to look on death. In the country one learns to accept it; wildlife preys on wildlife. It is in the nature of things." He had reached my side and now stood looking down at me with teasing eyes. "You must learn how to bow to the inevitable, my darling. You cannot change the laws of nature."

"I cannot always enjoy them either."

"In time you will cease to feel that way. Why don't you go for a walk to clear your mind of these bogies?"

I nodded. That was exactly what I needed. He fell into step beside me, but when the oast-house came into view, I turned away, feeling that I never wanted to go near the place again.

David said, "Let me know any time you plan to come down to the oast-house, and I'll see that the trap into the loft is shut. Normally, it stands open to assist ventilation. By the way, you haven't told me why you called."

I admitted that I had come to see him because I hated the way we had parted after lunch, whereupon he looked at me in surprise, as if unaware of any discord, any rift.

"My love, I don't remember our parting or what immediately preceded it. Only what happened before that. Those are the moments of marriage to remember, the moments that bring us close not only physically, but spiritually. Everything else is unimportant." He leaned across and kissed the tip of my nose, and the eagle's glossy feathers brushed my hand. They felt like silk, but even so I shrank away.

David said gently, "You need never fear him when I am around. You need fear nothing when I am around. I

The Eagle at the Gate

shall always take care of you." His beautiful mouth curved with that sweetness which never failed to touch my heart, and I parted from him feeling a great deal happier.

Stepping out briskly, I thrust my hands into the pockets of my coat and my fingers closed on the letter to George Mayfield. I had forgotten to put it in the mailbag for the postman to collect. By now he must have been and gone, so the best thing to do was go to the village and mail it from there.

This reminder of George inevitably reminded me of my father, and as I walked, I found myself recalling the facts David had thrust at me concerning his visit to Folkestone. Reluctant as I was to believe that the booking at the Hippodrome had been a mythical one to cover my father's delayed arrival at Abbotswood, I also had the facts contained in George Mayfield's letter as confirmation. Like it or not, I knew I had to acknowledge that there was something wrong with my father's story, and knowing him as I had, I also knew that he had never taken women friends to hotels like the Metropole. The *affaires* in his life were conducted less publicly and amounted to no more than trifling dalliances to assuage intermittent longings for Petronella. A carefully laid plan to journey far afield for an amorous meeting was unconvincing.

Equally unconvincing was the idea that he had travelled all the way from Canterbury to Folkestone on the vague off chance of booking a future date at a theatre which had closed down and for which the *Era* had announced no prospective reopening. Whatever I had said about that journal's being behind with the news, I knew it to be well informed and up-to-date in all theatrical matters. Such was the paper's function. Every actor and every management in the country studied it regularly, and my father had been no exception. He had known which theatres were playing to capacity, which had vacant dates and when, which were closing and which reopening, because such knowledge was vital to him as actor-manager of the Thespian Players.

I could no longer pretend, even to myself, that I believed my father's story. He had obviously paid a visit to Folkestone to kill time and to avoid staying at Abbotswood longer than was necessary, and he had chosen Folkestone because it was conveniently situated. A distance of only four miles meant that he could journey to Abbotswood shortly before the performance started and so spend the minimum of time at a place he had initially been determined not to visit.

Every thought awakened another thought; every reminder brought yet another reminder. It had taken all possible persuasion to make him accept the booking at Abbotswood and when he finally arrived, he did so as unobtrusively as possible, at a time when everyone in the household would be changing and so miss his arrival, and he had slipped in by a side entrance instead of approaching the front door. On top of all that was his avoidance of people and his determination to get away from the place as quickly as he could.

But what reasons lay behind such behaviour I should never find out now.

Thoughts of my father, coupled with physical exercise, drove my encounter with the eagle, and my husband's obsession with the creature, completely from my mind. I was forgetful of other things, too, and it was not until I had walked the mile and a half from Abbotswood to the nearby village, and arrived at the small general store, which also served as a sub-post office, that I realised I could not mail my letter to George Mayfield after all. I had intended to go no farther than the park this afternoon and therefore left my reticule behind, so I lacked even a penny for the stamp.

I halted with my hand poised on the iron latch of the shop door, aware that I was a conspicuous figure in my elegant purple coat, with my hair even more windblown than before. It was a gusty day, and the elements had done their worst. I could feel the heavy coil of hair in the nape of my neck, threatening to break free of its pins. I could also feel the curious eyes of villagers, watching and speculating and eyeing my clothes, and I could hardly blame them because the gentry did not walk hatless in village streets; they rode by, well mounted on fine horses or driving in shining landaus or broughams, behatted and gloved as befitted their station. For the young bride from "up at the house" to walk abroad with a disregard for ladylike appearances was, to say the least, surprising; even faintly shocking. (But she'd been one o' them play actresses, hadn't she, so mebbe she knew no better. . . . Mrs. Bentine, now, she were different. *She* wouldn't've wed afore she were out of mourning; *she* would've waited a respectable time and she would certainly *not*'ve "come out of the black" too soon. . . .)

I dropped the latch and descended the short flight of worn steps to street level, and as I reached it, down came the rain. It was one of those sudden deluges which could wet a person to the skin if he didn't run for shelter, so I ran. (And *now* look at her, running she is! That's no ladylike behaviour!) Before I even reached the grove of trees beyond the village, my hair was drenched. It would have been wiser to have sought shelter within the village store and braved the censorious eyes of shoppers. Serves me right for being cowardly, I decided as I stood beneath the protection of overhanging branches, a high stone wall at my back and the curious eyes of villagers now mercifully left behind.

There was nothing to do, but wait here for the rain to pass, and I prayed that this would be as quickly as it had come. I could feel water trickling from my hair to my neck and down within the collar of my blouse. A fine sight I must look, and what a blessing David could not see me now, or Claudia, or anyone from Abbotswood! It was all very well to defy country conventions, but I now had to live with them and if I wanted to be happy at Abbotswood, I would have to conform more willingly. And since above all things I wanted to be accepted as one of the family, I must learn to behave like one of the family.

I was aware of faraway village sounds. Bell ringers were practising in the church tower; a distant vendor was crying his wares; a muffin man's bell was ringing; and from behind me, beyond the wall, came a dull roar, like furnace fires, accompanied by clanging and the throb of machinery. And suddenly there was the additional sound of hooves coming to a halt beside me.

"Mrs. Hillyard! You will get soaked standing there—wet trees give little protection in rain like this."

I knew that voice, and my heart sank. I might have known that this man would come along to witness my discomfiture; he always seemed to appear at embarrassing moments and to make no secret of his reactions. I looked up into Red Deakon's face with as much composure as I could muster, with my wet hair hanging in bedraggled strands from my brow and my skirts muddied at the hems.

As I expected, he was laughing. I could see it in his eyes, although he did not give way to it.

"Pray, come inside and shelter, and when the rain is over, I will drive you home."

To decline would have been peevish, and to remain where I was would have guaranteed that I would have looked a great deal worse before I finally trudged back to Abbotswood, so I had no choice but to accept as graciously as I could. I had not noticed the tall wrought-iron gates a few yards to my left, set within the high stone wall. Now I saw that they stood open to the lane, and beside them, carved into stone pillars, was the name DEAKON'S FORGE.

He dismounted, and I had no choice but to hurry beside him through those gates, and truth to tell, I was grateful for the offer of shelter.

We halted within a courtyard, and I looked around with interest, despite the rain running into my eyes. To the left were a long range of stone buildings, with walls so thick that noise from within was heavily muted. Only the outer wall facing the lane was close to the dull roar of furnace and the heavy clang of iron, so that the great disturbance was directed away from a distant house which stood at the end of a long driveway to the right. From where we stood I could see only part of it, for a screen of trees followed the curve of the drive.

After shouting for a stablelad to tend his horse, Red Deakon hurried me toward the house. I ran beside him, head down, and the sight of my soiled skirts dismayed me. Even when dry, they would be badly stained. I hated the thought of returning home in such a sorry state and prayed that I would be able to slip upstairs without meeting anyone, particularly David, who was fastidious not only about his own appearance, but about mine.

At the front door I lifted my head and looked about me again. The drive had bridged a shallow river, little more than a very wide stream, which encircled the house like a moat, with lesser streams running from it like veins from a main artery, and most of these seemed to have been diverted toward the well-concealed ironworks. But it was the house which caught my attention. It was a long, two-storied building, constructed of stone, rather erratic and uneven in design, but with predominantly a late-seventeenth-century air, and beside and above the white front door, which boasted no more than a single step, were sash windows set in creeper-covered walls. I could tell at a glance that the house was large without being a mansion and that it had been preserved with pride and care.

As Red Deakon unlocked his front door and ushered me within, I wondered how many generations of Deakons had worked to turn this place into the house it now was. Then we were inside, and he was taking my wet coat and handing it to a woman who came hurrying from the rear of the house. "Hang that up to dry, will you, Meg? And then bring some tea as quickly as you can. Mrs. Hillyard has unfortunately been caught in the rain and would welcome refreshment, I'm sure."

"Of course, of course, the poor lamb."

The woman's smile was warm and friendly, lacking both censure or criticism. She bustled away, leaving the master of the house to look after me. We were in a long, narrow hall with white panelled walls, and at the end of it a white staircase covered with red Turkey carpeting ran up to a fine landing. There was an unassuming charm about the place which I liked; it was the charm of homeliness and comfort, putting me at ease immediately. Even my prickly guard, which always went up when I met this man, had subsided a little, and I found the idea of tea decidedly appealing.

"Come into my study, Mrs. Hillyard, and you can take off those shoes and dry your feet in front of the fire."

Somehow I was not surprised to find myself in the room before he had finished speaking. Red Deakon was the kind of man who never wasted time, nor apparently did the kindly Meg, for no sooner had he installed me in a comfortable chair and unceremoniously removed my shoes than in she sailed without knocking, kicking the door open with her foot because her hands bore a laden tray. "I forgot to tell you," she said, "there's been a bit of bother down at the works. That Jenkins again."

She set the tray close to my side: seed cake and scones and homemade jam, thick with strawberries from the look of it, and a tea service which I knew to be Rockingham because my father had once bid unsuccessfully for a similar one at an auction in one of London's salerooms. During rests between tours he would spend hours in such places, frequently taking me with him, but rarely buying because for the most part prices were beyond him. I wondered if I would ever cease to be reminded of my father. Even in this man's house it seemed that there were things which could call him to mind.

I picked up the beautiful teapot and began to pour as my host answered his housekeeper's remark.

"The usual kind of trouble, I suppose. Helping himself to scrap iron?"

"What else? You're too indulgent with those men of yours. No Deakon before you ever allowed the workers to take home even so much as an ounce. All scrap had to be melted down and reused. But you are asking for trouble, letting them have a free ration for their own use. Give them an inch and they'll take a yard, and that man's doing so. He makes things to sell, that's my guess—trivets and door knockers and the like."

"What the men do with their allocation of scrap isn't really my concern. Originally it was intended to make things needed in their homes, but if they need extra money and don't exceed their free allocation, it is up to them. And Jenkins is the only one who ever abuses this privilege. I take it the foreman has been up to see me about it?"

"Not half an hour since. And don't you go turning a blind eye this time!" She gave a final glance at the tray and commanded us to eat well. " 'Waste not, want not!' " she quoted. "Well, I have things to do. . . ." And off she bustled.

Red Deakon's amused glance met mine. Then his eyes went to my hair.

"It will dry all the quicker if you loosen it, Mrs. Hillyard, and if Meg should come in and see you sitting with it about your shoulders—as no lady would, of course—she won't be in the least perturbed. As you may have gathered, she is rather unorthodox herself, and she has been part of this household long enough never to be surprised by anything. So shake your hair free, and relax."

I was glad to, but as I pulled out the pins, I winced. Red Deakon was watching, so did not miss that betrayal.

"You are hurt! What happened?"

"A mere nothing. My hair caught in some brambles—"

He was stooping over me, parting my hair gently.

"There's a nasty spot there, coated with blood, as if a strand has been pulled out by the roots."

"I told you—some brambles caught it."

"Pretty fiercely, from the looks of things."

"I walked headlong into a bush. I am more accustomed to city streets than country lanes."

He was already walking through the door as I spoke, and returned a minute or two later with a bowl of water. By then my hair was streaming over my shoulders.

He insisted on cleansing the spot. The water was soothing against my scalp, and I was grateful for it.

"It's nothing serious," he commented, "but it must have been a nasty jab. There was dried blood at the roots, tangling the nearby hair. It should feel better now." He finished lightly, "But take care how you walk about our country lanes, Mrs. Hillyard. We don't want you scalped. That hair is too beautiful."

I was thankful he had accepted my story and thankful to let my head fall against the back of my chair. He laid the bowl aside and sat down opposite me. I was aware of his glance moving from my hair to my throat and was startled when he said, "That brooch—where did you get it?"

I touched the cameo which had been my mother's. Even as a child I had been attracted to it. It was unlike most cameos, for the carving was not of a traditional head, but of a dragon with a gauntlet of chain mail in its mouth. It was one of the few pieces of jewellery my mother had possessed, and all I knew about it was that it had belonged to her own mother and to her grandmother before that. It was not a big cameo, and its value lay in its unique design; but I was surprised that a man like Red Deakon should notice it.

I could tell him nothing of its history; as far as I knew, it had none—like my mother herself—but his interest prompted me to unpin it and hand it across. He studied it for a while and then handed it back without comment, but for the first time I saw this man's face free of mockery or amusement. With unaccustomed self-consciousness I re-pinned the brooch on my blouse. In bending my head the curtain of my hair fell forward, masking my face, and I let it remain there until this strange self-consciousness passed. I could feel steam rising from my hair and to speed the drying process I ran my hands through it, lifting and shaking it to admit the heat of the fire. And so we sat in silence until I could bear it no longer, for I could feel his eyes upon me all the time.

"My hair is dry—I must go—"

"It isn't nearly dry, and the rain has not stopped. Rest assured that I will get you back to Abbotswood sooner than you would have reached there had you walked."

I was glad he made no comment about my being in the village hatless and alone, nor asked what brought me there. An afternoon walk was a harmless enough occupation anyway, and perhaps I had imagined those censorious eyes of the villagers. I could think of no reply, nor did I want to meet his eyes when he appeared to be studying me so carefully, so I let my glance wander about the room. I was surprised to see it lined with books, for I did not associate this man with intellectual pursuits. I noticed volumes devoted to Kentish history and others titled *Families of Kent* and *Noted Kentish Families,* and thought how dearly I would like to delve into them.

"This house must be very old," I said. "I thought seventeenth century at first glance, but now I am not so sure. The sash windows and the Georgian front door are surely additions, because stone doors were no longer in use then." I could see a surround of about six inches between the edge of a large Persian carpet and the walls. "How old is it?"

"This particular room, as old as the Norman remains at Abbotswood, or so my father believed. He spent most of his days, after retirement, studying the history of this area and I am happy to have inherited his library—and to have added to it. Plenty of Norman remains have been identified in and around the village. The first Deakon who came here from Lamberhurst—"

"The first Red Deakon?"

He nodded. "He walked all the way across country, looking for a place in which to start all over again, and he stopped only when he stumbled on those buildings which now house Deakon's Forge. They were derelict cow byres, and standing away over here was the ruin of a small chapel—this room. It had nothing but a stone floor and crumbling walls; the windows were gone, and the roof was open to the sky, but he troubled to look no further, for here was also the commodity he most needed—water. Those streams out there, and the narrow river which surrounds the house, all come down the hills at the back and run into a small lake beside a natural clay pit beyond the ironworks. To call the foundry a forge is a misnomer now, but that is what it was when my namesake started, and we will never change it. So here was all he was looking for! Red clay, water, the essential things he needed to start his bloomery, plus walls which could be repaired and plenty of timber to fire a furnace when he built it. The whole abandoned place was ideal or could be made so—so he took it."

"*Took* it? You mean he helped himself to it? Did no one turn him away?"

"No one, for the simple reason that no one lived within miles. There were ruins of an old manor house, in such a state of decay that the only thing to do was to utilise the broken stones and timbers elsewhere, but before he started, he sought out the parish priest at Hythe. The man had no knowledge of the place, but parish registers revealed that a family named Neuton had once lived at the now nonexistent manor house, so presumably the land and the tumbledown cow byres and the ruined chapel were theirs, but the family had disappeared. That was a period of destitution for Kent following the Union with Scotland; prior to that, there had been a flourishing weaving industry over Cranbrook way, but the Union killed it. Many families emigrated; others went across to Flanders to work the looms there. Those who remained had to fight for survival as best they could."

"And your ancestor did the same."

"He had no alternative. The seam of iron ore in Lamberhurst's marl had run out, and the area was no longer worth working. So he settled here, sleeping in the old cow byres by night and working on them by day, hauling stones and timbers down from the ruined manor building and digging the clay and extracting the marl and then the iron ore. He also built his furnace."

"*And* the Deakon family business." My interest was caught. "And when he had built his furnace and rebuilt the cow byres, what then?"

"This. A cottage out of the ruined chapel. The floor was sound, and he raised walls from it and built a roof and reed-thatched it himself. He made it dry and weatherproof, and he continued to work on it for the rest of his life. He also went on searching for members of the Neuton family, and years later he succeeded. He found an old lady living over beyond Canterbury who had married into a branch of it. He had money then, and he paid her a good price even though she could produce no deeds for the property. She accepted it gladly. She also appeared to be the last of the line, for no further branches of the Neutons were traced. After the deal he went on building and extending, and succeeding generations did the same, each according to the needs and fashions of their time, and the result is a hotchpotch of different styles, different tastes."

No, I thought. The result was a home, mellowed by time and loving hands.

"Since it became mine," he continued, "I have done nothing to it, except to make this room my study because it is the heart of the house, from which it originally drew life. I don't regard it as idleness to let an old house which pleases you lie fallow in your time. Good places, like good pictures, are meant to be appreciated. But of course, you know that, don't you? You are attracted by beautiful houses, are you not, Mrs. Hillyard? I have observed that from the start."

So he was remembering the velvet curtains, and my excitement up there on the gallery at Abbotswood, and how I had come back and married into the family. In retrospect it all seemed very ambitious and calculating. This was apparently how he saw it, and now he was reminding me, mocking me again.

I reached for my shoes.

"They are still damp," he said, and took them from me and replaced them in the hearth. "And as I told you, your hair is not altogether dry."

"Even so, I must go. They will be wondering what has happened to me."

"And very shocked they would be if they knew. Is that what you are thinking? Would it surprise you if I told you that Claudia would be pleased to know that you are safe and sound in this house and that she would not mind in the least if she knew you were alone with me?"

"It would surprise me very much."

The Eagle at the Gate

"But Claudia is a surprising person."

I made no comment. To me, Claudia was predictable, judging her brother's wife by conventional standards, deeming her not of his class and therefore unworthy of him. Though she might appear to have accepted me, I knew otherwise. I knew that she schooled herself into a pretence of it, but that was as far as it went. I would go on liking her because my instincts made me, but would her socially disciplined mind ever accept me as her equal, let alone her brother's? People hidebound by prejudice never yielded. But how could I say any of this to a man who so obviously admired her?

There came the sound of wheels on gravel, gradually slowing down and finally stopping altogether. From this room we could not see the area of the front door, and it was not until Meg entered unceremoniously that I saw who the caller was.

"Mr. Hillyard is here for his wife—"

David thrust her aside. I saw her indignant glance as he came into the room and shut the door on her.

"Your servant made a mistake, Deacon—"

Red Deacon interrupted. "Meg is not a servant. She is the widow of a cousin, and she runs the household for me. This is her home, and I dislike her being referred to as a servant, or treated as one."

David cut right across that. Tight-lipped, he said, "I had no idea my wife was visiting you, but the woman assumed this to be my reason for calling. Before I could even ask for you, she announced that I would find Mrs. Hillyard in the master's study."

His eyes were as cold as his voice. I shivered as he looked at me, but I could not turn my glance away. He frowned at the sight of my hair, streaming over my shoulders like an abandoned whore. I could sense the thought even though he did not express it. And my feet— propped on the fender, shoeless. I could imagine the picture I presented, sitting beside this man's fire in an easy chair, with my shoes off and my hair loosened. Somehow I had to retrieve the situation. I bundled my hair up again with hands that I forced to be steady, and said calmly, "Mr. Deacon gave me shelter from the rain. I am sure you will wish to thank him, as I do."

To that, David said nothing, and we were gone within

minutes. He ushered me firmly to the door and then into his carriage.

If he had spoken even one word during the drive home, things would have been easier, but he remained silent. Not even when we were well away from Red Deakon's house did he give vent to anger. It was "not done" to create scenes in public, even in isolated country lanes with not a soul in sight.

The rain had stopped. I sat erect, clutching at dignity, only realising then how much greater poise a woman had when holding a parasol in gloved hands, her head crowned with an elegant hat, her hair smoothly coiled beneath it. I was at a disadvantage with my hair disorderly and my hands bare, with not even a reticule to hold. All I could do was carry my head high. As we approached Abbotswood, I braced myself for the moment when the lodgekeeper emerged to open the gates for us. Poor Miss Hillyard might be excused for eccentricity, but I was expected to emulate Mrs. Bentine, who would never go out in public looking as if she had been playing truant and had to be brought home like an errant schoolgirl, hatless, gloveless, with hair awry. But that was how young Mrs. Hillyard would appear to the lodgekeeper. I put up a tentative hand and touched the loose coils of my hair. How badly I had redressed it without the aid of hairbrush or mirror!

The gates were ahead. I saw the big stone arch with the eagle's head looking down on us, and then David wheeled the horses to the right and drove along a lane skirting the walls. So he was ashamed of me and was taking me home through a side entrance. I looked back; the lodgekeeper had not heard the sound of approaching wheels and therefore had not emerged to find out whether they were heading for Abbotswood, but the eagle at the gate seemed to be watching us with contemptuous eyes. And suddenly I was remembering my father's warnings, such as never to take people at their face value, and that menace could lie behind a mask, and that throughout life predators could lurk like eagles at the gate. I wondered now if he had noticed this one when he came to Abbotswood that day and if he had remembered that quotation. I also wondered how the Bentine family had felt about this reminder of their grandfather's death, cast for perpetuity in stone.

But to me the carving appeared no longer inanimate. The awareness of Conrad, secretly housed in his oasthouse lair, seemed to have imbued it with life, and I knew that never again would I look upon it without feeling the taste of death in my mouth.

David chose the entrance which brought us directly to the east wing, so that we entered the house through a part which was used only for visitors and was therefore shut up. I smiled faintly and said, "So you are ashamed of me, are you, David? You wouldn't wish the staff to see your wife looking unkempt?"

He made no answer, and we walked in continued silence through those endless corridors, past the rooms which the Thespian Players had occupied and finally past my father's and my own. How awed by them I had been, even to the extent of stroking the velvet curtains and thereby exposing myself to Red Deakon's discerning gaze! I thrust aside the recollection of that moment and walked on with my husband, our feet soundless on thick carpets, with portraits of long-forgotten De Friemonts and their descendants looking down at us from the walls. Despite age and neglect, their faces were compelling and strangely alive.

I said, "I cannot believe that no single member of the Bentine family ever had their portrait painted. Are you sure they have not been hidden away—and why, I wonder?"

My voice had a note of bright defiance about it because that was how I felt. I had had enough of my husband's stony silence. I wanted to goad him into speech, no matter how angry. Bringing me home so ignominiously was bad enough, but to be threatened with an impending scene, a scene to be staged when *he* decided and not before, sparked an answering anger in myself. But against his adamant refusal to be drawn, I was helpless and finally gave up any attempt. And so at last we reached our rooms, and with elaborate courtesy he opened the door for me. I saw his well-manicured hand, his pale white hand, resting on the chased gilt door handle, and in a remote corner of my mind I wondered which was the more elegant and refined.

He closed the door.

"Now," he ordered, "take a look at yourself."

I suppose, by Abbotswood standards, I did look untidy. My hair had dried in a soft cloud and had obviously been bundled up in a hurry, and the rain had certainly made a mess of my clothes; the lapels of my purple coat were crinkled with damp, the velvet collar curled, but I did not look as bad as I had felt or had been made to feel by my husband's disapproval. So I shrugged and said, "My coat will have to be cleaned and pressed, but no harm will have come to it because the material is good. And rainwater is kind to the hair. It makes it soft and glossy."

He exploded, "Have you no sense of decorum, no shame? And to think that if I had not called on Claudia's behalf, with a query about the balconies, I might never have found out!"

"Perhaps I am lacking in decorum—it isn't ladylike, is it, to appear hatless in public?—but I have absolutely no cause for shame, nor have you."

"No cause! Visiting a man's house *alone*, sprawling beside his fire with your hair down? Do you call that nothing to be ashamed of? I wonder you didn't take off your blouse and skirt and dry them before the fire along with your shoes!"

"I didn't think of it. What a pity! That would have been a great deal more comfortable than sitting in damp clothing."

He half raised his hand as if to strike me. I flinched instinctively, and he withdrew, but with an effort. It was he who trembled now, not I, though I was conscious of a sick feeling in the pit of my stomach. This seemed to be a day for emotional scenes with my husband. I turned aside from him, taking off my coat as I did so, and before he could stop me, I had rung for Mrs. Stevens.

"Don't you dare let a servant see you as you are!"

"I don't intend to," I replied coolly, and went into the bedroom and removed my skirt. By the time he followed me I was already stepping into another and then seating myself before my dressing table mirror and picking up a hairbrush. By the time Mrs. Stevens knocked on our sitting room door I was immaculate again. I gave her the coat and skirt, asking her to have them cleaned and pressed and offering no explanation for the state they were in.

My cool behaviour momentarily took the wind out of my husband's sails, but when the housekeeper returned a minute later, the garments still over her arm, my triumph died.

"I turned the pockets out on my way down, ma'am, and found this—"

It was my letter to George Mayfield. Before I could take it, David had done so, and Mrs. Stevens once more left us alone.

"And what is this?" he demanded frigidly.

"The envelope speaks for itself surely? You knew I would write to him. I went into the village to mail it."

"Why the village? The mailbag is in the hall."

"I forgot to put it there, so decided to post it myself. Unfortunately, I went without my reticule, so could not buy a stamp."

"You forgot to put it in the mailbag, you forgot your reticule, you went to mail a letter but forgot to take a penny for a stamp. . . . What is the matter with you, my dear wife? You are becoming singularly absentminded, and this concerns me. Or were you dreaming again? I recall your telling me, during that drive from Canterbury to Abbotswood, that you were much given to daydreaming. These are Harriet's traits. Perhaps I should seek help for you, too."

He could not have punished me more effectively had he struck me. I threw him one expressive glance and walked out of the room. Behind me, I heard him tearing the letter into shreds. I could not be sure, but I thought I also heard quiet laughter, but when I whirled round, all I saw in his face was concern and pity, and that was worse.

TEN

I had to forget David's cruel remarks. By now I knew well enough that he had many facets to his character and that I had to accept them. One should never expect perfection in anyone. Certainly he would never find it in me. So I had to reject that scene, convince myself that in comparing me with Harriet, he had spoken only with a momentary desire to wound, as people do when angry, and that no sooner had the words been spoken than he had regretted them. In due course he would admit as much and another little fracas in our marriage would be forgotten.

But the scene he had created in Red Deakon's house was less easy to forget. The memory of it humiliated me, and as humiliations do, it rankled. Such experiences in private were bad enough, but in front of others, involving others, they were less easy to forgive. Particularly this one. David's attitude in finding me in Red's study had been insulting, particularly to Red, who was merely being hospitable. Such misjudgement demanded an apology, but this was something my husband would never make. In intimate moments with me he might repent, but never would David admit to another man that he had been wrong in any way. That was one facet of his character which would never change.

So it was up to me to put the matter right. The question was how to create the opportunity. After such an incident I could hardly pay a casual social call.

I also had the feeling that Red might have been amused by David's jealousy. The suggestion of being involved with me would appear entertaining to him, for all along he had seen me as someone inexperienced and naïve. It was older women like Claudia whom he admired and was attracted to. So it was best not to revive the incident by going out of my way to apologise for it.

But what about Meg? David had slighted her, and Red had been angry about that. The least I could do was make amends to her somehow.

After breakfast next morning I harnessed the governess cart, an old-fashioned affair drawn by a gentle pony which Claudia's coachman had taught me how to handle because it was easy for a beginner, and without telling anyone where I was going, I went to call on her. By the time I reached the house Red would have gone to his forge, so I ran no risk of being confronted by him.

Meg opened the door, and her warm smile put me at ease.

"I've called to say how sorry I am about yesterday. My husband made a mistake. Not realizing who you were, he was unintentionally cruel."

The smile became compassionate, and somehow that made everything worse. I wanted no one's pity, any more than I really wanted to apologise on my husband's behalf. Meg's compassion made me aware that no wife should be put in such a position.

"So long as you were not upset," I said lightly.

"I can recall nothing to be upset about, bless you."

Red's voice came from within the hall. "Who is it, Meg?"

I froze. I wanted to bolt. I felt suddenly brazen, a very forward young woman indeed, calling at this man's house so soon after being the cause of a scene in it. But I had no time to turn away; he was standing there, regarding me with the familiar quizzical look on his face.

I announced as casually as I could, "David called yesterday with a query about the balconies—"

"And forgot to mention it." Red was laughing. As I thought, the whole incident had entertained him vastly. But at least I had hit on an excuse for being here.

I blurted, "Claudia merely wanted him to enquire how the work was progressing—" (True? Untrue? I had no idea.)

"Suppose you come along and see for yourself," Red suggested after surveying me for a brief and, I felt, speculative moment. "I am on my way back to the forge now."

I should have recalled that a smith began work before breakfast, knocking off for it only after the hearths had been lit, dowsing troughs filled, and apprentices allotted

The Eagle at the Gate

to the men who needed them most that day, for it was common knowledge that smiths were amongst the earliest starters of all labourers. Only when the great bellows were drawing on the hearths could they sit down for their first meal of the day. Even the master smith put in the same hours as the hearth stokers, bellows men, strikers, and harriers, from six in the morning until six in the evening and even longer when necessary. To a dedicated craftsman, work was his life, as acting had been to my father.

I accepted the invitation willingly, for I had never seen a blacksmith at work on anything but the shoeing of horses, which was exclusively the harrier's job. Leaving the governess cart behind, I walked with Red down the long drive and over the bridge to the sheds. Not for the first time I was aware of his great height, but not until later did I really become aware of the power and strength of the man.

The clang of hammers on anvils echoed like bells, all at varying pitches, as we approached the forge, but Red would not let me enter the place until I had discarded my outer clothes in his office, put on an enveloping overall, and covered my hair with a scarf. ("Enough damage was done to that lovely hair of yours yesterday, without getting it filled with iron dust today," he said.) I felt ridiculously self-conscious as he tucked it away carefully and knotted the scarf to make sure that no strands were uncovered. I could not understand why I found his nearness disturbing, but not until he moved away from me could I lift my eyes.

"You can see everything except the new furnace room for sheet iron—the place would roast you alive," he said as we entered the heart of the forge, the main blacksmithing chamber, where raised hearths stood in pairs down the middle, back to back, with great cowls directing the heat and smoke out through the roof, and anvils placed within arm's reach. These were clamped onto solid baulks of timber, rough-hewn sections of tree trunks, which, Red explained, not only absorbed some of the shock when the hammer struck the anvil, but had the springiness to give "lift" after each blow. "This enables the smith to strike more rapidly and at the same time with less effort. The lightest hammer weighs at least two pounds, and sledges weigh anything up to seven, twelve, or even twenty, so I like my men to conserve their strength. Iron handling isn't for the weak, but there's no sense in misusing muscles."

The glow of the hearths attracted me, each pumped to varying degrees of colour, by which the experienced smith could judge temperatures at a glance. Surrounding each small and glowing area was the yet unburnt fuel, ready to be raked toward the centre when needed. I watched an apprentice wield a slice, a long-handled shovel which scooped up a handful of fuel and manoeuvred it to the point where the heat was developing; one glance from the watchful eye of his senior directed the lad unerringly. Another boy deftly flicked a spray of cold water from the dowsing trough, with a brush of twigs, directly onto the areas of hot iron indicated by his trainer. "A tin could be used for the job," Red explained, "but most of my smiths are experienced men who prefer the old-fashioned bundle of twigs, a well-tried accessory which can reduce the area of intense heat to exactly the right temperature in the least possible time. Plunging can dissipate heat too quickly and too greatly."

The whole atmosphere of this place excited me. The noise and the heat, the dramatic effect of leather-aproned men swinging mighty hammers onto iron gripped in immense tongs by other men who turned and manipulated the material to exactly the required angle, the smell of red-hot metal, the hiss of steam, and the varying glows of colour from each hearth—all were as thrilling as any stage set to me.

"Hardly a place for women," Red shouted above the din, "but you want to see it all, don't you?"

How did he guess? Was he as intuitive as that about me? When my head jerked up in enquiry, I saw that he was smiling broadly. "You have an expressive face, Mrs. Hillyard. You give yourself away every time. Now why turn aside when I say that? Do you want to hide your feelings from me always?"

I certainly did. Instead of becoming less self-conscious with this man, I was becoming increasingly so. The knowledge that I was an open book to him made me feel very small indeed.

"May I see the balconies for Abbotswood?" I asked stiltedly.

"By all means. This way—but watch out for your skirt hems. Iron dust and scaling penetrates everywhere."

I felt his hand beneath my elbow as he led me away, and somehow I was glad that his men were too absorbed in their tasks even to glance up. I lifted my skirts as we went, for what he said was true. The stone floor was ingrained with the iron dust of centuries, but I did not care. I preferred good honest dirt like this to the floor of Conrad's charnel house.

The recollection of David's pet eagle struck a jarring note, sinister and frightening. I wondered if Red knew about the creature and presumed so, since Claudia and Harriet and, therefore, everyone else did. One could hardly exercise an eagle out of doors without people seeing it.

Minutes later I was able to forget all about David and Conrad and everyone at Abbotswood, for the next shed astonished me, stacked with wrought-iron railings, gates, ecclesiastical screens, balustrades, weather vanes, brackets for inn signs, and ornamental work of all kinds. Red pointed to a stack and said, "Those are the remainder of Claudia's balconies, waiting for the finishing touches. The rest are completed and waiting to be fixed, as she knows."

As she knows. My query on her behalf now seemed ridiculous and certainly unconvincing. No wonder Red had regarded me so quizzically at the door of his house. I felt my cheeks flush and stooped swiftly, ostensibly to admire the work but actually to hide my colour.

It was easy to praise the design of oak leaves and acorns, beech and fir and chestnut, all trees which grew prolifically at Abbotswood. Here and there, a medallion of fir cones and catkins formed a centrepiece. I knew the designs were Red's own work and complimented him.

He shrugged. "It is easy to produce a design when one knows well what appeals to a customer." (Particularly well, in Claudia's case?) "I am glad she decided to get rid of the eagles' heads, despite your husband's fondness for them. Being an eagle fancier himself, of course, that is understandable." He glanced at me and finished nonchalantly, "I saw that great bird of his on the wing yesterday. Were you present at the exercise?"

I nodded.

"And that was when you were caught up in the bramble bush, I suppose?"

Now why did he mention that? Was he hinting that he guessed the truth and had seen through my trumped-up story?

"I trust your head is less painful today," he added.

"A bramble scratch soon heals."

"It didn't look like a bramble scratch. It was a clean peck which went deep."

"Thorns very often do."

I evaded further comment by asking if I could see some of the ironwork being formed. "Those leaves and branches must demand a great deal of skill."

"I will show you anything you wish to see." Again his hand was beneath my elbow, and again I was unreasonably aware of it and unable to draw away. He led me through an arch into a room where workers stood at long metal-topped benches, hammering and twisting and shaping small pieces of iron into all kinds of adornments.

A man was sweeping scraps from the floor and depositing them in a wooden truck. Like all workers, he wore a thick leather apron, but in his case deep pockets dragged it downward at each side. I saw Red's glance go to them.

"There's no need to burden yourself with those pieces, Jenkins. All scrap can go into the truck for the boys in the salvage shed to sort out. In that way everyone gets their fair share when it comes to the free allocation."

So this was the man about whom the foreman had complained yesterday and whom Red had defended when Meg reported the incident. Indulgent as he had appeared to be at the time, he was nevertheless making it plain right now that petty pilfering could be detected.

"Of course," he continued, "if you need more pieces for special jobs in your home, you have only to come to me. You won't find me unsympathetic."

Shiftily the man emptied his pockets, muttering that the stuff had only been there because he didn't want to mix up too many different sizes and weights in the truck, and with a nod Red passed on. I thought I saw a touch of amusement in his face, and when he met my glance, he nodded.

"I know full well what he does with those scraps and

that he's been helping himself to them for a long time. He has a very profitable sideline, making oddments for villagers. If I were in his place, who knows, I might do the same. But it is time he realised that others don't help themselves behind my back and that I'm not a man to be underestimated."

Only a fool would underestimate a man like Red Deakon, I thought. Certainly I never would. His will would be as strong as the iron from which he made his livelihood.

The morning passed all too quickly, and we were back in the heart of the smithy again, where the hearths glowed and the anvils clanged. I was aware of disappointment because we had come to the end of the tour. I didn't want to leave. This had been the most interesting visit I had experienced since living at Abbotswood, a direct contrast with Claudia's restrained tea parties, formal dinner parties, and elegant soirées. There was a down-to-earth vigour in this place, somehow emphasizing the lack of it in my present way of life. This forge was Red Deakon's whole existence, and he was dedicated to it; but just how much the craft itself meant to him I did not fully realise until we were passing a row of anvils and a man, swinging a sledge with sinewy arms, swayed and missed his aim. The mighty hammer fell with a crash, and the man was on his knees, gasping for breath.

In one stride Red picked him up and carried him across to a wall bench, where he unbuttoned the man's shirt and felt his heart. "It's home for you, Piper, for as long as necessary. If you won't obey the doctor's orders, you'll obey mine. You know damn well I've forbidden you to lift a sledgehammer, let alone swing one. When the doctor passes you as really fit again, you can take over a light striker's duties. Those small hammers are quite enough for a man of your years to handle. Don't look so worried— you'll be kept on full smithing pay. I can't afford to lose a man like you. What the devil made you swing that thing? And did you imagine I wouldn't find out?"

The man leant against the wall, breathing heavily, muttering between gasps, "Young Ballard there don't know how to do it—can't get the knack of the thing somehow."

"Nor will he, until you kill yourself by overstraining

that heart of yours, it seems." Red shouted above the din for a mug of strong tea. "And when you've drunk it and rested awhile, I'm taking you home—and no arguments. And stop muttering that the job is urgent. I know it is. I'll finish it myself, and young Ballard will learn from me just as ably as he'll learn from you, I'd have you know." He gave the man's shoulder a gentle shove. "You can sit there quietly and watch."

Back he went to the anvil throwing off his jacket and waistcoat, rolling up his sleeves, casting aside his necktie and loosening his shirt, picking up a leather apron and donning it. Then with a heave he lifted the mighty sledgehammer and swung it above his head, holding it poised in both fists and shouting, "Now, young Ballard, when that iron comes back from the heat, *watch!* Watch every movement and the way every strike lands."

I saw the iron, which had been returned to the fire to maintain heat and malleability, brought deftly back to the anvil between giant tongs, and *crash* went the sledgehammer right on target. A striker standing alongside delivered a lighter blow with a ball-peen hammer before the next mighty crash, and so it went . . . crash and strike, crash and strike . . . like the rhythm of some gigantic drum and tinkling cymbal, a rhythm set by Red and maintained by him as the iron between the tongs slowly turned under his direction. No words, just a glance and a nod, an indication from the master just how far to angle the iron to meet the next mighty blow; no more was needed between these men.

I watched, awed and fascinated, as Red lifted the tremendous sledge by its yard-long haft, swinging it from the anvil and up over his back until the massive weight was poised above his head for the powerful descent and final impact. The grace and apparent ease of the entire motion were deceptive, for the power demanded was betrayed in every muscle of his body, from neck to thighs.

I saw the admiration on apprentice Ballard's face, the longing to achieve such a standard. Under a man like Red, he would, and yet another expert smith would be turned out by Deakon's Forge.

I became aware that others were watching, too. Work was thrust back into the fires and bellows uttered their gurgling noise to maintain a steady temperature during this

The Eagle at the Gate

brief, stolen respite. The master was working among his smiths, as his forebears had worked, and there wasn't a man in the place who was going to miss that.

Some had learned their craft from Red, others from his father and grandfather, but somehow I knew that none of them had ever envied their employer so much as he secretly envied them. He was a blacksmith at heart and always would be. Running the business had robbed him of none of his skill and strength. Did he come here alone, when the forge was empty, to indulge his passionate love of the work? I suspected so. How else had he maintained such a standard? That rhythmic swing and crash, swing and crash was the art of a true master blacksmith.

A brief pause while the iron was returned to the fire.

"Get back to work, you men! This isn't a performance —this is what we are here for, the lot of us!"

The men grinned and obeyed; the anvils rang again. Red mopped his face and swung the sledgehammer high once more, and back came the red-hot iron and the crashing rhythm started again. I saw his chest gleaming, the strong hairs on it drenched in sweat. I saw the massive muscles of his arms and shoulders and back rippling with every movement, and I saw the exultation in his eyes as he worked. He was like all the gods of myth and legend, come down from Olympus. He was the reincarnation of Hephaestus, Vulcan, the biblical Trubal-Cain, and the Norse god Volundr. I was carried back thousands of years, long before Julius Caesar's legions set foot in Britain, to Syria and Egypt and elsewhere in the Middle and Far East, where the craft of smelting and manipulating copper, bronze, and iron was carried out exactly as now.

I heard an echo of my father's fine voice reading to me from the Bible. ". . . the smith fighteth with the heat of the furnace, the noice of the hammer and the anvil is ever in his ears, and his eyes look upon the thing he maketh; he setteth his mind to finish his work, and watcheth it. . . ."

For the first time I saw the real Red Deakon, a man who could conquer iron and revel in his victory. A man who could create a thing of beauty out of a base metal which was still the most precious, the most valuable in the world.

When the smiting process was gone, the iron was heated

again and then carried to a metal-topped bench to be clamped at one end in a vice, and then, taking a pair of mighty forceps, Red seized the heated end and bent it slowly to his will. He had forgotten me, but I did not mind. I was willing to wait for him to look at me again, and when the job was done, when the metal had been shaped by his strength and was plunged into the dowsing trough to be tempered, I still did not mind when, without so much as a glance at me, he went straight back to Piper, resting on his bench.

The old man nodded his approval. "You did a grand job, sir. You can still beat the lot of us."

Red grinned. "When you've finished that mug of tea, I'm taking you home. That's an order."

I felt superfluous. I walked toward the door without looking back. I had forgotten everyone in the place, except the master of it. I could still see his face and the enjoyment in his eyes, the swinging sledgehammer, the rippling muscles. And the kindness of him when he looked at a tired old man.

"Aphra!"

I had reached the door and stepped through. I was about to let it fall behind me when Red caught it. Outside, we stood looking at each other. He still wore his leather smithing apron, and the sweat was still on his massive chest. The power and the strength of him seemed vibrant at such close quarters.

He pulled a handkerchief out of his pocket and wiped his hands carefully; then he removed my headscarf and my hair tumbled down about my shoulders.

He said quietly, "That is the second time I have seen you look like that, the second time in two days."

There was nothing in so trite a remark to make it sound like a caress, but it was almost as if he had stretched out a big, gentle hand and touched my hair.

I went back to his office and shed the voluminous overall. He did not follow. I pinned up my hair and donned my hat and coat. When I crossed the courtyard, there was no sign of him, and when I drove away in the governess cart, I looked exactly as I had looked on arrival—young Mrs. David Hillyard from Abbotswood. But somehow I didn't feel like her anymore. Something had happened to me, and I didn't know what it was.

ELEVEN

I told no one of my visit to Deakon's Forge. At lunch Claudia mentioned the balconies, saying they were progressing well from all accounts and promised to be more worthy of Abbotswood, and still I said nothing. I felt as if I were cherishing something very precious, something I wished to share with no one, so I let her continue talking about Abbotswood without interruption.

Her pride in the place was intense. It was almost as if she regarded it as a sacred trust. I wondered whether this had been her husband's attitude, whether she believed she owed it to him to carry on in the same way, or whether this passionate devotion went deeper than that—to a feeling of guilt and a need for atonement, as if in being a good chatelaine of his home, she could somehow compensate for failing him as a wife. Or was she doing it for his brother's sake, so that if he ever returned he would find his inheritance well preserved, well cherished?

Guilty her love for Jasper Bentine may have been, but the heart cannot be controlled, and I had often looked at those carved initials in the arbour and wondered what he had been like. Lawrence, too. I had not yet seen those ancient photographs of amateur theatricals staged here at Abbotswood and thought it would be interesting to see what the brothers looked like.

That same evening, as I sat with Claudia sewing for a coming charity bazaar, I remarked that she must be looking forward to seeing the last of the workmen and all the mess their work entailed. The old balconies were already being removed to make way for the new.

She nodded, and said, "But they are completing it in record time, thanks to Red's supervision. He has been wonderful, and I shall miss his frequent visits. He always seems to bring a breath of life with him, a breath of the outside world. Here at Abbotswood we are perhaps a little too self-centred."

"You should get out more."

"I get out sufficiently. Local affairs, shopping in Canterbury or Folkestone, visits to friends. . . ."

"Well," I said briskly, "once all the mess outside has been cleared up, you must entertain more. I remember your birthday celebrations. What a success they were! I know that was a special occasion, but we could surely stage another production down there in the dell. Not a professional one, but amongst ourselves and with friends. We could rehearse through the winter and put it on in the spring."

Harriet, who was with us, clapped her hands in delight. "I could do my Ophelia again! Or better still, Juliet. I have always wanted to play Juliet and we could use one of the new balconies, with the terrace below as a stage. Oh, if only I could persuade David to be Romeo—how handsome he would look! Was *Romeo and Juliet* ever put on in the old days, Claudia?"

"Not that I recall, dear."

"I would very much like to see those photographs of bygone productions," I said.

Claudia said that she doubted if they could be found. "I have not seen them for a very long time."

"*I* know where they are." Harriet told me, "and one day I will get hold of them and show them to you. It won't be easy, but David always says that if one wants something badly enough, there are always ways of getting it."

Claudia said that if the photographs were stored away in one of the attics, she would not hear of Harriet risking a broken ankle to get them. "Some of the stairs are now perilous, and the floors also. I forbid you to go up there."

Harriet said nothing. She sat there, hugging herself. She loved to have secrets.

"Has David ever shown you his butterflies?" Harriet asked out of the blue.

We were at dinner the same night, the four of us, and there was one of those lapses in the conversation which I frequently found very welcome, because conversation at meal times was always stilted, etiquette demanding that in front of servants a family should never discuss personal matters. Consequently subjects were all too often confined to generalities—the weather, the farm, the orchards, local affairs, snippets of court life reported in the newspapers but never discussed in any critical way. One did not criticize royalty because even country society strove to emulate it.

I admitted that I had yet to see the butterflies and added that I would very much like to.

"You have been married to my cousin all this time and never seen his pride and joy!" Harriet exclaimed. "Why, I do believe he is more proud of his butterflies than he is of that horrible hothouse."

"My hothouse is not horrible, Harriet dear. I have noticed that you have a great liking for it."

"Is that why you have hidden the key again?"

"I cannot risk anyone entering without my knowledge and—"

"And stealing precious flowers to make a hat more beautiful."

"And allowing the temperature to drop and damage the plants."

"They are not much use, shut away behind glass, and they are certainly not much use outside it. Those flowers died very quickly, and my poor hat looked very sad then."

David gave his cousin a patient smile, and she turned back to me.

"Make him show you his butterflies. They are really quite beautiful, aren't they, Claudia? Some of them anyway. I don't like the dark-coloured ones, those moths which fly into your face on a summer's evening, but some of the tropical ones are wonderful. Bring them out after dinner, David, and let us all have another look at them."

He agreed willingly, and later, when we were gathered in the drawing room, he unlocked a cupboard and carried glass-covered cases, one by one, across the room.

"Let me help," Harriet cried, fluttering beside him as if imitating a butterfly herself, but Claudia patted a seat beside her and said gently, "Why not join me here, Harriet, and then we can look at them together? There is plenty of room for Aphra, too." She turned her smile on me. She had been very pleasant to me throughout dinner, perhaps because David had been somewhat withdrawn. His manner toward me had not thawed since bringing me back from Red's house yesterday, although he had been courteous enough in front of others.

Somehow I felt that Claudia had sensed the strain between us and was anxious to comfort me. Had she guessed that we had quarrelled?

Once the cases of butterflies lay before us, my husband's manner changed. Pride lit his face, and one by one he named the various species for my benefit. Monarchs and royal admirals I knew, but there were also giant sulphers and orange tips, owls and morphos, silver spotted and great spangled fritillaries, pearl crescents and mistletoe hairstreaks. "There are imperial hairstreaks, too," he said. "They come from Australia, and as yet I haven't been able to obtain a specimen, but I have a dardanus swallowtail from Africa—this is the fellow, with his long tails and creamy yellow colouring with bold black markings—and look at this peacock! Did you ever see such vivid colours? It is one of the world's most beautiful butterflies, and one of the cleverest. It has a special sound-making apparatus at the wing bases, to deter bats from attacking it when it hangs in trees during hibernation. Others even manufacture their own special brands of poison. You didn't know that butterflies were so astute, did you?"

"Isn't David clever?" Harriet demanded with pride. "He knows all their Latin names, too."

"I won't bother my wife with those," he said. "That would be a little too much to expect her to take in."

I saw Claudia look at him and knew that his disparaging, yet somehow indulgent tone had caught her attention. For myself I chose to ignore it. I leant over the glass cases to hide my swift rush of anger and pretended to be absorbed in their contents. And indeed, I found them very beautiful. Even in death the colours were vivid, and I asked if this were the reason for keeping the cases in a cupboard.

"No—for safety. If by chance the glass covers were broken, their fragile wings could be broken, too."

He put the cases away, again declining Harriet's eager assistance, and after that he seemed in better mood, though I suspected he would have enjoyed gloating over their contents by himself for the rest of the evening. How-

The Eagle at the Gate

ever, his impeccable manners were back, and he was attentive to the three of us until at length we went to bed, and even more attentive to me when we were alone. He insisted on brushing my hair, a practice he had indulged frequently during the very early days of our marriage, marvelling over the thickness of it, praising its dark colour, and insisting that *never* should I allow it to be frizzed according to current Edwardian fashion. "In fact, my love, I would have you resemble poor Harriet in no way at all."

"*I*—resemble Harriet!"

He gave a vague but somehow significant shrug. "Well, sweet Aphra, there have been moments recently when I confess to feeling uneasy about you, anxious about your behaviour. That is why I am going to insist that you rest more. I do this only out of concern and love for you. Breakfast in bed and rise late—"

"No! I hate to lie abed once I am awake."

"I know you do, but I think perhaps you are a little tired these days and that is why your behaviour is becoming rather—unpredictable. No doubt the shock of your father's death, and the excitement of moving out of your own world into this one, placed a strain on you. I recognise the symptoms, and before long I fear that Claudia will recognise them, too. I am not suggesting that you are actually becoming deranged, but I would not wish anyone to imagine that you were tending that way. And now come to bed and sleep...."

He cradled me in his arms that night as if I were a child in need of care, and terrifyingly, I found I was thankful for the feeling of protection it gave me.

The days began to slip by like beads upon a string, graduating down from the round full days of summer to the shorter days of early autumn. They passed peaceably, with no further misunderstandings, lulling me and reassuring me, but enveloping me in a cocoon of idleness, for such was the routine of life at Abbotswood. While the domestic wheels turned busily, I remained outside all that, a member of the family and therefore not expected to lift a finger except to dress myself, and if I had asked my husband for a maid to help me even with that, he would have provided one. He humoured and indulged me, but sometimes I felt he did so with unnecessary watchfulness. If I forgot the smallest item, I was now careful to hide the fact from him, even though it was no more than normal forgetfulness. But somehow I felt he regarded forgetfulness as totally *ab*normal because he himself was incapable of it. David never forgot a thing. He was too meticulous.

I was amazed to find that a life of leisure can pall. My life as an actress had been constantly busy, either with performances or with rehearsals, studying new parts, memorising lines, even working on my costumes because my mother had taught me to do so. Until the Thespian Players had been able to afford a wardrobe mistress, she had undertaken that work, and after her death I had continued to care for my own theatre wardrobe, as well as make my own clothes. I knew of no actress who was not handy with her needle because necessity made her so; even Elizabeth Lorrimer had not been above making things or altering things. But in my new social world a lady did not demean herself that way; it would cast a sad reflection on her husband were she to do so. To sew for charity, yes; that was entirely permissible. So I was glad to help Claudia by making things for her pet charities. I hated being idle.

I also spent quite a bit of time with Harriet, exhausting as her company could be. She had abounding energy, although it was frittered away without any results to show for it. But the main thing was to keep her happy, Claudia said, and this I found easy to do so long as I allowed the stream of her volubility to flow unchecked. I learned to work on Claudia's charity sewing whilst listening only fitfully to my cousin-in-law's chatter or to roam in the park with her in the same way. I even tolerated her inaccurate rendering of some of Ophelia's speeches, applauding at the precise moments she expected me to. If I so much as hesitated, she would face me with outraged indignation. "You're not clapping, you're not clapping! You couldn't have been listening *at all!*" And only a prolonged demonstration of applause would appease her.

I would never have believed that the days at Abbotswood would be lethargic and even stifling, for such a state had never been associated in my mind with so highly a desirable way of life. Laziness was unfamiliar to me; so, too, was the feeling of inertia it created. Perhaps I would have accepted it more easily had I not been reared in an atmosphere of hard work and financial anxiety, two conditions totally unfamiliar to the family I now belonged to. Despite David's claim that his sister was hard pressed for money, there was no evidence of it—or else their ideas of being "hard pressed" were by no means allied with reality as I knew it. But I very quickly realised that Claudia was an able mistress, one who kept her hands well in control domestically and whose authority was recognised and respected by the household.

I felt superfluous, and so, in time, the library became an even greater refuge, for it offered escape from boredom, from the repetitiousness of days which varied only as far as the weather was concerned. What to wear and when to wear it, what to do and when to do it, whether one could walk in the park or whether one should stay indoors—these seemed to be the major decisions of life, occasionally relieved by calls from neighbours on Claudia's at-home days or driving with her to return such visits on theirs, and always the conversation was the same, the trivialities of news, the tidbits of gossip, and if I managed to smother a yawn, I knew full well that it would be noticed. One had to do more than smother yawns. One should not yawn at all.

Late September brought a St. Martin's summer which lasted well into October, with warm, sunny days. We made the most of them, spending much time outdoors, and when Harriet asked me to go blackberrying with her one day, I was glad to. Even that represented a break in the tedium of life, a change of routine.

The sun was warm on my back as I stooped to pick the ripe black fruit, and I found the occupation enjoyable, except for coping with Harriet's petulance if my basket appeared to be filling more rapidly than her own. "You are stealing mine—I know you are stealing mine! You could not possibly have so many if you were not!" After that I surreptitiously dropped fruit into hers, so that she kept ahead of me. Humouring Harriet could become very wearing, and I thought not a little resentfully of the many times David had done the same to me, so that I was now very wary of giving him the slightest opportunity or excuse to do so. As a result, he had been unable to taunt me about my absentmindedness.

To atone for all this, however, was his physical passion for me, a passion which seemed to hint at greater depths, although he was the gentlest and most considerate of lovers. This side of him never failed to awaken a response in me, so that I believed our physical union to be perfect.

Perhaps the warmth of that late September afternoon lulled me into a false sense of security, leaving me unprepared for the shock it was to bring. The shock was only mine, for it affected Harriet in no way at all, which somehow made my reaction appear very silly indeed.

We came upon David unawares. He was sitting within a small clearing, intent upon something on his lap, so absorbed that he did not even hear our desultory voices or our movements amongst the blackberry bushes. He was absolutely still and, incongruously on such a day as this, he wore gloves, but what struck me most was the ecstatic expression on his face and the curve of his lips, which suggested the greatest relish. When Harriet called his name, he scarcely glanced up; his eyes merely flickered toward us and then back to his lap.

Harriet went skipping across to him, crying, "What have you there, David? What is it? A game of some kind?"

"Yes," he answered without shifting his gaze this time. "It is capital sport, but it is also highly interesting. You can watch, if you like. You too, Aphra."

I reached the spot just as Harriet cried excitedly, "A caterpillar, a caterpillar! You've caught a caterpillar!"

I looked down and saw a vividly striped creature impaled upon a piece of white card. A pin pierced the end of it, and the body curled from that point, arched in agony. Beneath it was a tiny pad of cotton wool.

"David! Let it go, for pity's sake! What are you doing?"

"Studying it, of course. Look closer—you will find it fascinating. I have been hunting for just such a specimen for a long time, and today I struck the whole colony." He nodded toward a jar on the ground beside him. It was more than half full of similar caterpillars, desperately trying to escape, their bodies wriggling beneath the tightly fitting lid, which had been punctured in places to admit air. So he was intent on keeping them alive—and if I could lay my hands on that jar, I would be intent on releasing them. Something warned me not to try, but to await the right moment. Meanwhile, Harriet was holding the jar aloft and laughing in glee at the helpless antics within. I turned my glance away, repelled by her childish relish, and saw once again the expression on my husband's face. The similarity between them was a shock to me, but mercifully David's contained another quality—intelligent interest.

"This is what is called its defence posture," he said practically, "and these vivid yellow and black stripes are called aposematic, which is derived from a Greek word meaning 'a signal.' This disguise has been developed to ward off predators. Birds quickly learn the appearance of such a species and know that its poison means death. Isn't nature wonderful? Without these natural protections, and others, there would be no chrysalis and consequently no butterfly."

"Let it go," I begged. "You are torturing it!"

David laughed.

"I do believe you are a sentimentalist, my dear. I have no intention of letting it go. Did you know that this tiny creature can give off a poison in self-defence?"

Harriet squealed and jumped aside, and David laughingly told her to be quiet. "I am giving my wife her first lesson in natural history and she obviously has a lot to learn—including not to be squeamish. Lean closer, Aphra, and you will see all its little spines erect, those fine hairs standing upright. That is where the poison comes from. Other species collect poisonous substances secreted by plants. Those contain cardenolid heart poisons, but specimens like this—which manufacture their own—actually produce cyanides. These cyanides even circulate in the blood of burnet moths, those common or garden moths which haunt heathlands where the burnet rose grows. Don't imagine they are defenceless little creatures. They are harmless enough to human beings—unless one managed to collect a massive amount of their secretion—but they mean death to their natural enemies. My goodness, but this little chap is killing himself in the effort to pour all that poison out of his spines, though he hasn't a notion of what threatens him!"

"*He* isn't killing himself, *you* are killing him! And I suppose you mean to do the same to these?"

I sent the jar flying out of Harriet's hands. It fell on the soft earth with a bump and the lid flew off. The creatures went wriggling away amongst the grass, but David was quicker than they. In a flash he was on his knees, picking them up with a gloved hand while clutching the card with the impaled caterpillar with the other. "You must be out of your mind!" he raged.

"She is, she is!" Harriet chanted, jumping up and down. "She is mad, mad, *mad!*"

I stormed at her, *"Be quiet!"* and her voice cut off as if I had struck her.

"Hold the jar for me, Harriet, while I put these fellows back."

She tossed her head at me then, feeling important because her cousin had turned to her for help. "You see?" she taunted. "David can do without *you*, but he can't do without *me*. I should think he will never trust you again. Will you, David?"

He snapped back at her, "Do keep quiet and hold the jar still. I can't hold onto this one *and* handle the others unless you do."

"Then let me relieve you of it!" I cried, and snatched it from him. As I did so, I pulled out the pin and the caterpillar curled itself round my finger in one last paroxysm until I shook it free. I knew it was dead as it fell to the earth. The card went flying away on the breeze.

David was outraged. He confronted me with a white, contorted face.

"My God, but you'll be sorry for this! You've made me lose a sample of its poison! I could have extracted it from that scrap of cotton wool and analysed it. Those creatures cause a lot of damage in our orchards, and *some* antidote has to be found." He held the jar against his chest, as if defending it from me. Then his fury changed to sudden laughter. "Mark my words, Aphra, you are going to be very sorry you did that. Very sorry indeed. Wait—just *wait.*"

The rash flared up quickly, spreading from my hand to my forearm. By the time I dressed for dinner the whole area was a violent red.

"Didn't I say you would be sorry, my love? I will order dinner to be sent up for you. I wouldn't like Claudia to see that rash; she might fear contagion. Wrongly, of course. It is a perfectly harmless caterpillar rash and in time will disappear. That poison is only fatal to other wild-life."

"In that case, we can reassure her."

"You would be wise to go to bed. You can have a meal on a tray."

"I don't wish to, and I see no necessity to go to bed just because of a rash."

He shrugged. "Please yourself. But remember, you have only yourself to blame, so don't expect me to sympathise. Such squeamishness! I have no time for it. If people were unprepared to experiment with live specimens of any form, no progress would be made. But if you do insist on coming downstairs, wear something concealing. We have a guest for dinner, and I have no wish for you to draw attention to that rash. It would arouse comment, and I should be embarrassed to have to admit that my wife acts irresponsibly at times."

I had already chosen a gown with a deep fall of lace from the wrists, and I stepped into it without bothering to reply. Beneath the long sleeve my arm felt on fire, the pain so intense that I found it an effort to speak, but I managed to ask who the guest was.

"My sister's most intimate friend—Red Deakon. Naturally, I haven't told her that I found you visiting his house alone. Nor, I imagine, will he."

He put a world of implication into his voice, but I said nothing. I knew that my sister-in-law and Red Deakon were friends but had no desire to learn the extent of their intimacy.

Now I recalled how he had once scorned the morals of Abbotswood guests, his contempt for wives who flaunted their lovers and husbands who displayed their mistresses; his dislike of the intrigue and hypocrisies, the blind eyes and the silent consents. And now David was hinting at a personal relationship between Claudia and the very man who had condemned such behaviour, the man who had stirred me so strangely that day at the forge. Was it possible that his moral standards were on a par with the rest?

Hard on the thought came another: that both he and my sister-in-law were free to live their lives as they wished. They hurt no one in the process, no husband, no wife. So in that respect they could not be condemned. I wondered how long they had been lovers and why they did not marry. Many a wife in many a successful marriage had been older than the husband.

I had not seen Red since I had paid that memorable visit and now felt an extraordinary self-consciousness at meeting him again beneath my sister-in-law's roof.

That was how I always thought of Abbotswood—as Claudia's house, though legally it was not hers. Sometimes I wondered what would happen if Jasper Bentine never turned up to claim it. What the legal procedure was in such cases I had no idea. Could the law decide to hand it over to her? I imagine not, but of far greater concern was the possibility of the unknown Jasper's reappearing some day, for that would certainly mean the end of our life at Abbotswood. Perhaps he would allow his sister-in-law to remain—he had loved her, David said—but one thing was certain: her Hillyard relatives would have to go, and all my fine dreams about belonging to the place would be over.

Claudia's aptitude as a hostess was very evident that night. When entertaining—whether a single guest or, as on the night of the Thespians' performance, nearer a hundred—she was at her best. She looked beautiful, and she gathered us all under her wing with charm and ease. She had gone to much trouble in planning the dinner, and this mark of her esteem for Red seemed significant. They made a handsome pair, and although I still believed that I preferred David's type of looks, I had to admit that Red's were undoubtedly striking, due mainly to his powerful physique.

I contributed little to the conversation. The intensity of the rash, which was rapidly spreading, made me feel unequal to the effort; but David was at his best, and in Red's company Claudia expanded. Harriet, inevitably, chattered sixteen to the dozen, relating how we had gone blackberrying, and how Mrs. Stevens had promised to see that Cook used the fruit for blackberry fool tomorrow, and how *she* actually picked the greater number. "But Aphra kept stealing from my basket to make it seem that *she* was picking the most!" Claudia sent me a commiserating little smile, and it was at that moment that she noticed my untouched food and the way in which I was merely making a pretence of eating—and then her eyes went from my

The Eagle at the Gate

fork to my hand, half covered by the fall of lace, and her eyes widened.

"My dear Aphra, what have you done to your hand?"

Harriet announced gleefully, "It isn't what *she* did; it's what the caterpillar did! And David warned her, didn't you, David? You said she would be sorry. I could have told you that you'd get caterpillar rash, Aphra, I really could."

Claudia exclaimed, "But a caterpillar rash can be extremely painful! Has it been treated?"

I tried to say that it was nothing to worry about, but a thousand red-hot needles seemed to be throbbing in my hand, and when I tried to speak, I failed. My lips moved helplessly, and I closed them again because I felt, ridiculously, that I wanted to cry. Harriet's taunting, coupled with David's indifference and the throb of pain, were getting the better of me. I wanted nothing so much as to rush out of the room and find someplace where I could be alone.

To my surprise, Red Deakon was at my side, gently lifting my sleeve. His muttered exclamation seemed to annoy my husband.

"It's nothing to make a fuss about," David said impatiently. "A caterpillar rash disappears as quickly as it flares up. The best thing to do is to let it take its course. And it will teach my wife not to meddle."

He sounded bored, and he went on eating as if nothing must be allowed to spoil his meal. I saw his sister sitting very still, and although I could not be sure, because we were dining by candlelight, she seemed to have gone rather pale.

"Surely you have an antidote for it, David? Something in your laboratory, perhaps?"

"Not a thing," he answered indifferently. "The best course *is* to leave it alone and to avoid picking up caterpillars without gloves in future." He looked across at me and smiled. "A little suffering is good for the soul, my love."

Red Deakon burst out, "Well, if you are not prepared to do something for it, Hillyard, I am. I have an effective application for this sort of thing at the works. The men sometimes contract skin troubles of one kind or another from the vegetation surrounding the marl pit. I'll be back soon."

David shrugged and let him go. Claudia continued to sit very still, and Harriet looked at the door, round-eyed, scarcely believing that the dinner guest had walked out of the room and out of the house. After that we scarcely spoke until he returned.

So it was Red Deakon who treated my painful hand, and he did so with surprising gentleness for so strong a man. David looked on, saying that a lot of fuss was being made over nothing, but if his wife was going to be childish about it, then perhaps it was best to humour her. "But Harriet didn't get into such a fret when she had that nettle rash last summer!" At that Harriet prinked with self-gratification.

"And now I think your wife should go to bed," Red Deakon said when he had finished.

"I suggested that before dinner, but she can be very stubborn at times."

"Or perhaps stoic," Red murmured. "That rash must be extremely painful. I suggest you send for a doctor first thing in the morning, and if you happen to have a sleeping draught, Claudia?"

For the first time, Claudia seemed to come out of her abstraction. Her silence had been very noticeable, and beneath my pain it puzzled me. That she should be concerned for me was gratifying, but that she should actually be worried seemed unnecessary. Yet that was what her stillness suggested—an inner tension and anxiety out of all proportion with the sudden appearance of a rash which, though painful, was not serious. And somehow I felt that Red Deakon was aware of it, too, and knew the cause. During the incident he had glanced at her once or twice, as if her stillness were telling him a lot.

Claudia pushed back her chair, saying she would fetch the sleeping draught and bring it to my room. She even slipped her arm about my waist as we went upstairs, but we said nothing; I, because I was unequal to it, and she, presumably, because she did not want to. But I was glad of the sleeping draught because I did not even hear David come to bed.

The Eagle at the Gate

Next morning the doctor confirmed my husband's verdict that the rash would heal itself in time and grudgingly admitted that the treatment it had received was adequate and could be continued. It seemed more than adequate to me. The intense burning had lessened, and I was grateful to Red Deakon for leaving me a supply of the medication; but this put me under yet another obligation to him, which I regretted.

About noon I was sitting in the arbour, reading, when he sought me out.

"Truman told me I would find you here. Apparently this is a favourite spot of yours."

So Truman had noticed that. . . . The old man's faded eyes missed nothing. I had come to regard him as a sort of watchdog about the place. And it was true that I found the privacy of the sunken garden very much to my liking, the arbour particularly. Harriet rarely pestered me here because it got very little sun, but perhaps lovers whose trysting place it had been had appreciated its shade. I knew that the romantic associations in my mind were attributable to the entwined initials carved in the seat beside me. Had they really stood for Jasper and Claudia, and had they really been lovers, she and the man who killed her husband? And did Red Deakon remember the affair? I did a rapid calculation and worked out that he must have been about eleven at the time, for I estimated he was about thirty now. A boy of eleven was at an impressionable age, and there must have been a deal of talk in the neighbourhood when the nine months' bride of Lawrence Bentine was widowed so tragically.

Everything that happened "up at the house" made news in these parts, so everyone associated with the event would have been the target for gossip as well as for sympathy. "Poor young Mrs. Bentine" particularly. What would she do now that she was bereaved? Would she leave Abbotswood or remain? Surely she would marry again, being so young? And was it true that her brother-in-law loved her and had seized the opportunity to kill her husband to get him out of the way? Cain and Abel, Cain and Abel! God must surely bring him to justice! It were no use him running away; fate would catch up with him. He must be guilty, of course, to panic and disappear like that. And he had always been the reckless one, in and out of scrapes all his life, but never a scrape so serious as this. . . .

An eleven-year-old boy must have heard all this, and wondered, and remembered.

In the short months I had lived at Abbotswood I had learned how virulent local gossip could be, and not merely amongst the villagers. Every tasty morsel exchanged over the Crown Derby and the Sevres in elegant country houses was tinged with malice, like poison in a perfume. Behind gracious Queen Anne or William and Mary façades, tongues wagged as energetically as behind cottage doors. Abbotswood was no exception. Its serene front and bland windows were as great a disguise as any for gossip in the servants' hall, not to mention in the drawing room when visitors called. Sometimes I suspected that this was their object in calling, though Claudia held herself aloof from it—perhaps because she had once been the target herself. She would preside over the teacups serenely, leaving her guests to indulge their malice between themselves, but never joining in, and sometimes, when the scandal became too much or the tongues wagged too hard, she would do her best to distract Harriet's avid attention, for her cousin drank in every word.

My marriage to the eligible David Hillyard had been a nine days' wonder, and I was well aware that in the eyes of many he had succumbed to a scheming little actress; but this amused me more than it worried me, and I paid it no heed. My sister-in-law's dignity was an object lesson to me; she was an example of the perfectly mannered, detached onlooker who had erected a screen between herself and the world, but I also knew that this screen stood between herself and me and that never would I be allowed to see behind it. Only this man, this confidant, her "intimate friend," knew what it concealed. Why not use the word "lover" and be honest about it? I thought with sudden impatience as he came toward me. These petty disguises for truth had not existed in the theatre. There nothing was hidden. Perhaps that was why "the profession" had earned its reputation for immorality. The thought made me smile. In the world I now belonged to, immorality was as frequent as in any backstage dressing room. I would have respected Claudia's association with Red Deakon had it not been concealed behind her pose of the gracious lady of Abbotswood, the mistress above suspicion.

I had judged Red to be more honest, a man who never concealed his feelings or his actions, if anything, a great deal too forthright. I felt sure that if he loved a woman, he would not be afraid to proclaim it to the world, so any covering up of their relationship must be Claudia's wish, not his.

"I came to check on the progress of my men," he said, asking with a gesture if he could sit beside me, and when I nodded, he flicked aside his coattails and did so. "So I thought I would take the opportunity to see how you are today."

"Much better, thanks to you. I am indebted to you, Mr. Deakon."

He shook his head a little impatiently. "Even if that were true, which it is not, I am sure you would hate to feel indebted to a man you are still trying to dislike."

There was nothing to say to that. To contradict it would be untrue; to admit it an embarrassment. I shied away by telling him that the doctor had examined my hand this morning and approved his medication, at which he said wryly that that was a big concession from old Dr. Claybury. "He has no time for quacks, and nonqualified treatment comes under that category in his mind. In actual fact, the medication is an old herbal one handed down through my family. The Deakons were too poor to afford doctors in those days, so home recipes had to be relied on." Almost without pausing for breath, he finished, "You didn't say how it happened."

"The rash, you mean? I thought my husband mentioned it, or Harriet did. Being town-bred, I had no notion that it was unwise to handle caterpillars without gloves."

"And you were blackberrying, and could not avoid them...."

I nodded. I had no intention of revealing any more, but to my surprise he said, "I hope you didn't let the creatures get away. That would have displeased your husband. I gather he likes to collect specimens. Claudia has told me how hard he works at finding antidotes for such poisons—and others."

"Yes. He is very clever."

"Clever indeed." His keen blue eyes looked at me for

a long time; then he asked abruptly, "Do you miss the theatre, Mrs. Hillyard?"

"I have little time to think of it." Not for the world would I have admitted that I had all too much time and that I thought of it all too frequently. In recent weeks my memory had veered more and more towards days which seemed carefree in retrospect. The anxieties and uncertainties were now eclipsed by memories of friendly camaraderie and heartwarming applause, not to mention the curtain calls my father and I had shared. How proud he had been at such times! How proud *I* had been! But those days had gone, and anxiety had gone with them, replaced with all this—this lovely house and grounds, this sweeping park and farmlands, this social elevation and life of leisure.

Red Deakon smiled faintly. "No time?" he echoed. "Does life keep you so busy here at Abbotswood? Do you find the social round so all-absorbing? I am surprised. I should have expected a young woman like you—" He broke off, and with a gesture which was half in dismissal and half in apology, he rose, but for a moment he stood looking down at me. "Your husband must be very gratified by your contentment."

With a bow, he was gone.

After his departure I found it impossible to concentrate on my book again.

I had not seen David all day. He had risen before I wakened, and the sleeping draught had been so effective that I had not even heard him stir; but now, as I went indoors, I felt apprehensive about meeting him again. The memory of his indifference was acute, and I found it hard to forgive. Equally sharp was the recollection of his callousness, although I supposed that many a scientist involved in such work would have regarded my reaction to the killing of any tiny creature as sentimental or squeamish, as my husband did.

But I was disturbed in other ways, chief of which was the subtle change in his attitude towards me. I could not believe that in so short a time his ardour could have cooled, and when I remembered our passionate moments, I believed it even less. Yet there seemed to have crept into his manner a certain criticism, a watchfulness, as if he were now beginning to observe in me certain characteristics which had not been there before, characteristics which caused him anxiety. This awakened an uneasiness in me, an increasing self-doubt, so that I became tense, afraid of doing and saying the wrong thing, or, alternatively, defiant. Then again, I would be overanxious to please because I so desperately wanted to restore the rapport of our early days together.

It seemed impossible that rapture could fade so quickly. I had always imagined that love grew with marriage, strengthening with the years, that bonds became stronger and more durable, binding two people together as closely as my parents had been. Through all their struggles they had remained united; hardship had drawn them together, not thrust them apart. And there was certainly no hardship to divide David and myself. We were cushioned in comfort here at Abbotswood. In such conditions no chill wind could reach us. Yet I felt touched by uncertainty, though unable to put my finger on the cause. I felt it as I went upstairs to tidy my hair—there had been a wind even in the sunken garden today, and David never liked to see my hair windblown—and I felt it as I descended for luncheon. Truman was crossing the hall to the dining room and turned at the sound of my step. His faded eyes lit up, and a gentle smile spread across his wrinkled face. I always had the feeling that Truman liked me, and his presence in the house gave me a feeling of comfort. I still recalled the time he had stood on the threshold of my father's room in the east wing, telling me in a tone of dignified reproof that it was his task to unpack for the gentleman. I remembered, too, his scrutiny of my father's old carpetbag, so unlike the quality luggage normally brought by guests. Now that I knew Truman better, I realised that his scrutiny had been prompted by interest, not disapproval.

I had brought that big bag with me when I returned. As my husband had told me derisively, I was a sentimentalist, but at that time his attitude had been different. Because that carpetbag had gone everywhere with us on Thespian tours, I could not part with it, and David had been amused but fondly indulgent. He had told Truman on no account to dispose of it, but to store it with other luggage, and the old man had carried it away as if it were made of the finest hide instead of threadbare carpet. I think he had endeared himself to me at that moment.

Any apprehension I had felt about meeting David again proved unnecessary, for he greeted me at luncheon with all the fondness he had ever shown and enquired how I felt.

"Much better, as you can see."

I held out my hand and pulled up my sleeve to show the improvement. He lifted it to his lips and lightly kissed the palm and the wrist.

"That will show how little I regard such rashes," he said. "Didn't I tell you it would heal itself?"

" 'In time,' you said. I think you must agree that Mr. Deakon's application did it good."

"Why do you call him Mr. Deakon?" Harriet demanded. "Everyone calls him Red, though I do think it a very funny name. It is on account of his hair, I suppose."

"I have known him too short a time to be on Christian name terms."

David laughed. "That would make no difference to Deakon. I am quite sure he thinks of you as Aphra." His beautiful mouth was touched with an expression I could not quite fathom. Amusement? Indulgence? Derision? Or a reminder that he had not forgotten the informality of that scene in Red's study, my loosened hair, my shoeless feet. Whatever lay behind that meaningful curve of his well-shaped lips, it was not exclusively for me, for it was still there when he turned to Claudia and said. "Don't you agree, sister? *You* know Red more intimately than anyone. Perhaps you have even heard him refer to my wife by her Christian name? The man has little regard for formality, but what can one expect from a blacksmith?"

Claudia was entirely unruffled. "I would not say that I know him 'intimately,' but I do know him well. He is a good friend. And I would hardly call him a blacksmith."

"That is what he calls himself, and I admire him for it," I put in. "It shows a lack of pretension, and there is too much of that in the world."

"Oh, I know you admire him very much," my husband said lightly.

The Eagle at the Gate

"I admire his lack of affectation, his honesty."

I was surprised by this admission, for I could never have imagined myself expressing admiration for Red Deakon in any way, but in my new social world he was certainly the most genuine person I had met. Not that this made me wish to avoid him any the less. That blunt honesty of his caused him to see through situations and people to an embarrassing degree, including myself.

Claudia changed the subject by asking David if he would let her use some of his hothouse plants to decorate the hall for the charity bazaar she was holding at Abbotswood the next day. "Some which will suffer least from a change of temperature, of course. If we choose them this afternoon and keep them in a warm room overnight, they should survive well, don't you think? And I will give instructions for the hall to be well heated. The days are drawing in, and people will be glad to be warm indoors."

David agreed that acclimatization would help the plants to survive and said that if she would send someone down to the oast-house, he would hand over the key. "I will also jot down the names of various plants you can safely move. All are labelled."

"So *that* is where you keep the key now," Harriet piped. "You have been hiding it from me, I know, just because I picked a few flowers." She pouted. Harriet could brood and fret over any slight, real or imaginary.

David pushed back his chair and patted her frizzed head in passing. "Naughty children must be punished," he said lightly.

"I am *not* naughty! I am not, I am not! Didn't I help you yesterday? Didn't I hold the jar for you, as still as could be, after it was knocked out of my hands? Aphra did that, so she is naughty, not me!"

"That episode is closed, cousin. Aphra has been punished for it."

"How?" Harriet demanded, changing from tearfulness to glee. "How did you punish her?"

"I didn't. Nature did. You saw it for yourself. And my wife is penitent now."

I gasped. "I am not in the least penitent and have no reason to be!"

David had reached the door. He stood quite still, looking back at me.

"Then you must learn to be, my dear wife. Anyone who meddles with my work will be sorry."

"They are quarrelling again, they are quarrelling again!" Harriet bobbed up and down in her chair excitedly. "They quarrelled yesterday, and *now* listen to them!" She enjoyed any hint of a scene.

Claudia cast her a warning glance, indicating Truman's presence. He was standing by the sideboard with that air of self-effacement which well-trained servants assumed, as if merging into the wall panelling, ready to pop out only when plates had to be removed. Nevertheless, one had to be discreet at the table, for even automatons had a certain life in them and might be able to listen and think and talk. This attitude toward servants was one to which I would never grow accustomed.

Harriet shrugged. "Oh, Truman is as deaf as a doorpost, everyone knows that. May I choose the plants for tomorrow, Claudia?"

"You may help, dear, and if Aphra would be so kind as to collect the key?"

My sister-in-law never made a request without some motive behind it; in this instance, to make peace with her brother. Her manipulation could not have been more obvious, but I knew her concern was for David's happiness, not mine.

I stipulated that I would collect the key only if I had my husband's assurance that the trapdoor to the eagle's loft was firmly shut.

"I gave you my word on that," he said, "though the request is silly. You know he cannot get through the trap or descend the stairs. And I cannot imagine why you are so anxious not to meet him again."

"When did you meet him?" Harriet demanded of me. "Have you been flying him again, David? You know I like to watch."

"From a safe distance, you mean. As for when I've been flying him, I exercise him almost every day, as I am sure you very well know since you miss so little that goes on."

"But how does Aphra know you keep him in that loft?" Her tone was jealous. "You never told *me*. I thought you just kept him in a cage somewhere."

"I wouldn't do anything so cruel. He needs space to

The Eagle at the Gate

move around, and the loft is big enough to give him plenty of that. It also protects him from the elements when the weather is bad. But wherever I kept him, I can't imagine you wanting to call on him." He laughed suddenly. "Not as my dear wife did, at any rate."

Claudia turned to me anxiously. "You didn't actually visit the bird up there? My dear, was that wise?"

"As it turned out, no."

Harriet asked gleefully, "Did he attack you?"

David said solemnly, "He pulled her hair, cousin," and Harriet subsided into giggles.

"Oh, I would *love* to have seen that, I really would!"

"You are a bloodthirsty woman," David told her good-naturedly as he finally left us.

When I reached the oast-house, the main door stood open again and so, this time, did the one to the laboratory. And David had fulfilled his promise—the trapdoor to Conrad's loft was firmly in place. I called David's name and heard him answer in an abstracted sort of way, "I'm in here. You can come in, but don't disturb me for the moment."

I entered the second room, then paused, considerably startled. The circular chamber was handsomely equipped, but I was reluctant to go farther. The walls were lined with jars, and pots of Italian majolica, all labelled in gilt lettering; there were also drawers with names of medicines in Latin printed on them, and dried poppy heads and herbs and strange plants hanging in bunches; and in the centre of the room, with a long chimney going straight up to the cowl in the pointed roof, stood a stove. The floor of the room above had been removed so the chamber seemed incredibly high, the circular walls narrowing to the apex so that they closed in like a huge trap. The whole place gave me a feeling of claustrophobia; to look up made me dizzy. Or was that due to the faint odour of drugs which lingered in the air?

There were also other odours: of mice and guinea pigs in cages. Their squeaks and squeals and scratchings also filled the room. There were croaking noises, too—frogs and toads kept captive in moist tanks. To me, there was something horrible about such imprisonment.

David spared me not a glance. He was stooping over a

marble-topped table. His hands were encased in rubber gloves, and he was wielding a sharply pointed instrument as delicately as if it were an artist's brush, except that instead of applying colour, its incisions made little spurts of red splash onto the marble.

He was dissecting a frog.

I turned away sharply, and he must have sensed my revulsion, for he said, without looking up, "No squeamishness again, I beg you. Come and take a look. That will help you to overcome any ridiculous reactions."

"No. I will wait in your office."

"Please yourself. I have almost finished. But why wait outside? There are books here which you should find interesting." With a slight inclination of his head he indicated a collection across the room, and because I did not want to provoke him into annoyance, but also because over there I would have my back to the marble table, I went across and studied them. There were volumes in English, German, French and Italian, all dealing with poisons, venoms, and the deadly properties of shrubs, plants, and insects, even of pond life. Every possible branch of toxicology seemed to be covered. Claudia had spoken the truth when saying that her brother was clever.

"There—I have finished." Satisfaction was in his voice. "And now I can attend to you, my love. I suppose you have come for the key."

I turned then, and saw him brushing fragments of dead frog into an enamel container, which he carried across to the stove, leaving other sections behind. I felt faintly sick and struggled to hide it, but when he had shut the stove, he looked across at me and shook his head.

"My poor Aphra, how sensitive you are! You must not come here in future if you are so easily upset." His tone was a mixture of patience and impatience and immediately made me feel foolish.

"The books are interesting," I said, "but rather beyond me."

"Of course. I expected that. Though there *are* women who have mastered these subjects, and chemistry is taught in many schools for young ladies these days."

"So I understand, but as you know, I had no conventional schooling. I was taught 'on the road,' so many hours a day, according to the law."

The Eagle at the Gate

"By your father, an actor."

"By my father, a scholar. He was an Oxford man with a First in history and the classics, so my basic education was by no means sketchy."

He sighed. "There you go again—touchy as ever. I swear you are getting worse."

"Perhaps it is your taunting, your derision, your patronage which are getting worse. Do you do it deliberately, I wonder?"

His astonishment was genuine. So was his concern. He came toward me and was about to put his hands on my shoulders when I jerked away. He still wore his rubber gloves, and they were streaked with blood.

He laughed and pulled them off. "Forgive me, my love—I would hate to stain that pretty blouse." He dropped the gloves into a sink and turned the tap. "I am sorry my work repels you, but it is very useful, very necessary, and someone has to do it."

"Where did you qualify?" I asked, to my own surprise as much as his.

"In Vienna. But I was interested in toxicology long before that. Ever since I read of the work of Louis Pasteur and other *savants* of his kind. It is my ambition to produce some revolutionary antitoxin, some serum, which will benefit mankind as greatly as Pasteur benefitted medicine. That is why Claudia equipped this laboratory for me. Improved crops, better harvests, healthier cattle—think of the benefit all that would be to the human race."

"I thought Claudia had very little money."

He stared.

"Wherever did you get that idea from?"

"From you. You told me long ago that she was forced to maintain Abbotswood only on the income left to her by her husband."

"But I did *not* say she was penniless, though I do think it the greatest folly for a woman to have control of her own income. The last amendment to the Married Woman's Property Act was a most foolish piece of legislation. But as for the things you are now saying, the lies you are accusing me of telling, really, my dear, I don't know where you get your strange ideas from! Do all theatrical people live on their imaginations?" He finished with a touch of ruffled pride. "I would have you know that the Hillyards were wealthy Midland industrialists. *I* was not the pauper when we married."

I flinched at this unnecessary reminder of my own poverty.

"No," I admitted. "I was. Sometimes I wonder why you did marry me. I am well aware that I had nothing to offer you."

"Except your very desirable self. What more could I want?"

His gentle tone and his swift change of mood made my heart soften immediately.

"I am glad I please you in that respect, at least," I said, and went to him without hesitation when he held out his arms to me.

With his lips against my hair, he murmured, "On that you can be assured, my darling—although of course you still have many things to learn, and I, many things to teach."

He stopped any questions with a kiss, so long and so impassioned that I forgot everything, even the strange implication beneath his words.

At length he put me aside.

"You must go, my love. I am sure Claudia will be waiting and perhaps wondering what detains you—although she knows there are no comfortable facilities here for lovemaking." He laughed, and I was happy again. "And now the key of the hothouse. I will show you where I keep it, so you may replace it if I am not here when you return. But on no account are you to let Harriet share the secret, and I beg you to lock the hothouse door when leaving and to keep it closed when you are there. Many of those plants are useful in my work. That is why I grow them, and they must not be jeopardized."

We went through into his office, and he took the key from a small drawer, one of a nest of three beneath the rolltop of his desk.

"Remember," he said, "the middle one."

I had been in the hothouse only once before, shortly after my marriage, when David had shown me his most prized blooms. I could well appreciate Claudia's distaste for the humid atmosphere, but to me the heady perfumes were as bad. There were bitter aromatic smells also, floating in intermittent clouds as we passed clumps of trailing vines and fantastic creepers. The green house was divided into three linking sections; the first, given over entirely to unusual shrubs, David had not paused to show me, knowing I would appreciate his rare and colorful flowers more, but as I walked with Claudia and Harriet through this preliminary section, its light made greenish by the abundance of foliage climbing the windows until they almost spanned the domed glass roof, I decided that not everything in nature was beautiful. There were gaunt branches terminating in freakish growths and crouching trees with tendrils creeping across the moist earth. If one allowed one's imagination to run riot, the idea of them clutching at one's ankles could be vivid and frightening. But I had to take a stern hold on my imagination were I to please my husband and give him no reason to accuse me of harbouring strange ideas.

The more outlandish growths seemed to fascinate Harriet as much as they repelled me. The sight of cancerous lumps adhering to barks and roots drew her eyes immediately. I fancied that Claudia found them as distasteful as I, for she turned her head away from the more repulsive ones. Her cousin, on the other hand, would contemplate them with rapt attention, and once she stooped, and lifted a spikey arm outthrust across our path.

"Do you think it is alive?" she demanded. "It *looks* alive, doesn't it? Can you imagine how it would feel about your throat, Aphra, digging these spikes into your flesh so that you bled and bled?"

Claudia protested, "Harriet, *please!* Don't be ghoulish!" To me, she added, "Let us get out of this part and into the orchid house. I have no taste for this sort of thing."

I agreed, but Harriet only laughed. She dropped the branch, and I could have sworn that it twitched once or twice before lying still again.

Certainly the second hothouse, leading from this one and into yet a third, was more to my liking. I closed the door on the nightmare growths and only regretted that we would have to pass them again on our way out, but by that time Claudia and I had our arms full and I was so intent on carrying my precious burden without damage that I spared not a glance right or left. At the entrance a gardener placed our selection in a large barrow and carefully wrapped them with sacking whilst I locked the door behind us. Turning away, I caught one last glimpse of those hideous growths and was glad to leave them behind.

Harriet was chattering beside me. "Do you know how the place is heated? I do. David once showed me. He would never show *you*, of course. He doesn't trust you the way he trusts me."

I checked a smile, remembering how David would not even trust her with the key.

"I expect you think the place is heated from inside," she prattled on. "Well, it isn't. It has its own boiler room out here—look." She pointed to a small brick building adjacent to the north side. "The boiler is fed with coke, and there are dials and all sorts of things to make the temperature go up or down, but David won't let anyone fiddle with them, not even me." She spoke regretfully, as if cheated, and I thought the lively intelligence she showed was somewhat surprising in view of her backwardness.

I went straight to the oast-house. The office door was closed, but unlocked. David was not there, and his laboratory was shut up; but he had left his desk open, and I dropped the key back into the little drawer—the middle drawer of the nest of three—and went away.

When I returned to the house, there was a visitor waiting in my sitting room upstairs. It was Elizabeth Lorrimer, and I could never have imagined myself so glad to see her.

TWELVE

She looked magnificent, clad in green velvet with sables which seemed almost good enough to be real, and on her head a huge hat covered in matching velvet and swathed with sable-coloured tulle and ostrich feathers. An enormous muff completed the outfit, apart from high-fitting laced boots of brown leather with curving Louis heels of green.

She held out her arms to me with a sweeping theatrical gesture, and I returned her embrace warmly.

"And now let me look at you," she commanded. "Turn around, turn around! I must say you do it just as gracefully as onstage—that was your mother's teaching, of course. Dear Petronella—I see you still wear her brooch. I'm glad your new magnificence hasn't made you discard it."

"I wear it almost all the time. Fancy you remembering it!"

"Naturally, I remember it. Dear Petronella even wore it at the church when they went to make their vows. How the years fly! I was a very tender juvenile in those days, of course, barely into my teens." Her eyes flickered toward me and away again, and I kept a careful control of my expression, for I knew that she had joined the Thespian Players in her early twenties. But what did her vanity matter? She was here, and antagonistic toward me as she had sometimes been in the theatre, in retrospect it meant no more than the average professional jealousy. It was good to see her, and I said so for about the fourth time.

"You look radiant, Elizabeth. I take it that life under George Mayfield's management is not so bad after all."

"Dire, darling, absolutely *dire!* He will never be the manager or the producer your dear papa was; otherwise, we wouldn't be playing a date like Folkestone."

I started.

"Folkestone? The Hippodrome?"

"Where else, darling? It is the only theatre in the town, and a shabby one at that. Mind you, I do hear it is going to be done up quite a bit and that the new lessee has great plans for it; only there wasn't time to put the work in hand before opening the place again. I suppose he had to get business in as quickly as possible, and being a businessman, he would get down to that right away. And there's money behind him. There must be. He wouldn't own an hotel like the Metropole otherwise."

"So it *was* true! Papa *did* go there to negotiate a booking! I heard from George Mayfield that no one knew anything about it, and when he wrote to the theatre, the letter was returned—"

"Very likely, since the place was closed at the time, and I gather there were one or two unexpected hitches before completion. As soon as the *Era* heard that negotiations were finally under way, they announced it, and I have to hand it to George—he didn't let the grass grow under his feet. And that is why our winter tour has opened there— *As You Like It*, dear, not *Cymbeline*, which I think your father planned. George, the fool, says he doesn't see me as Imogen! Can you imagine anything so stupid? I fear he isn't going to be so good on casting as dear Charles was, but still—" The velvet shoulders shrugged. "Rosalind is a nice part, and I am good in it. Would you like to see the reviews, darling? I have them here." She was opening a vast reticule (green leather with big brown tortoiseshell handles), still chattering as she did so. "Rave notices, my dear, absolute *raves*—for me, of course. If they are like this at Folkestone, you can imagine what they will be like when we reach the number ones—Birmingham and Manchester and Glasgow and Edinburgh. Oh, we've a very good tour lined up, but all on the strength of your dear father's name. *He* made the Thespians famous the length and breadth of the provinces." She dabbed at her eyes with a lace handkerchief, and I was touched by the fact that they were genuine tears. Tiresome as Elizabeth had often been, on the whole her heart was in the right place.

I was delighted by the press notices and said so.

"I do believe you sound a little envious, Aphra. Don't tell me you miss life on the boards already?" She looked around. "Not with all *this* in your life! I must admit I had an ulterior motive in coming to see you. Not that I wasn't anxious to see your dear self, of course, but naturally we're all agog to know how you're getting along. Miles Tregunter declared you'd be too uppish to receive me—the beast. I shall be delighted to tell that man that you welcomed me with open arms. You look surprised, darling. You needn't be. I've had more than enough of him. He borrowed ten pounds from me during the last tour and never paid it back. Besides"—she gave a self-conscious giggle and fluttered her eyelashes as coyly as any leading juvenile—"George Mayfield had to engage a second male lead to take his former place in the company, and the man is—well—you know what I mean, darling."

I did know. She meant that the new second lead had succeeded Miles Tregunter in her life. I smiled and said that now I understood why she was looking more blooming than ever, which pleased her so much that she generously dismissed herself as a topic of conversation and turned to me.

"And how *are* things with you, Aphra? Are you happy? Oh, you must be, with that gorgeous man! Though I must confess I found him a bit stiff and not a bit forthcoming, and you could have knocked me down with a feather when I heard you had actually married him. You were a cunning one, arranging to travel alone with him from Canterbury that day! I would never have thought you had it in you, really I wouldn't. But there you are, still waters run deep and so forth. *And* you pulled it off! What a triumph! No title, of course, but many a Gaiety girl has done no better." She put her head on one side and studied me reflectively. "I must say I expected you to be looking —well, a little less peaky, if you know what I mean." She winked knowingly. "Not enough sleep, perhaps?" She followed this with a loud laugh, the kind of laugh indulged in backstage, raucous and full of meaning, recalling all the things I disliked about the theatre and the many aspects of theatrical outspokenness with which I had never felt at ease; the aspects my parents had tried to shield me from, particularly my father when he became my sole guardian from the age of fourteen.

She leaned forward confidentially and said, "Tell me, dear, is it any different in higher circles from the lower?

I don't suppose so, since all men are made the same way and all want the same thing. . . ."

This was the sort of woman-to-woman gossip I most decidedly did not want, and my expression must have said so, for she gathered up her almost-genuine sables a trifle huffily and said, "Oh, very well, dear, if you think yourself too good to let your hair down with old friends, I'll take myself off. I won't intrude again, of course."

"Elizabeth, please—don't take me wrongly!"

"How else can I take you? But I'm sorry for you, I really am. How long have you been married? No more than a few months and looking decidedly off colour. I hope he's kind to you, this husband of yours. I hope he doesn't abuse you in certain ways, and you know what I mean by that. And I do hope he isn't a snob and that he doesn't despise you because of what you are, although surely he knew about that when he married you. . . ."

A footstep outside the door made her break off, and by the time the handle turned she had changed the subject swiftly. She was on her feet and kissing me good-bye, cooing that it had been lovely, just *lovely* to see me, and looking so well, too! "Positively radiant, darling, positively radiant!"

David walked into the room, showing no surprise at all.

"Truman told me you had a visitor, my love, and who it was. Welcome once again to Abbotswood, Miss Lorrimer. A carriage is waiting to drive you back to wherever you came from—"

"Folkestone," I announced. "The Hippodrome, Folkestone. You remember, David—the theatre my father tried to get a booking for and apparently succeeded."

If I had expected him to be surprised or embarrassed, my anticipation was wrong. He looked merely puzzled, as if he had no idea what I was talking about.

"Well, to be fair, darling," Elizabeth gushed, "it was George Mayfield who actually fixed it all up, but of course your dear papa did make the preliminary approach."

David looked politely bored, waiting by the door to usher her out.

I went with her, saying I would go down to see her off. "And thank you again for coming to see me. Anytime you are this way, anytime at all, please come again."

"I promise to. I would have come earlier in the week, but you know what the opening date of a tour is like— one is never out of the theatre. Today was my first free afternoon; there have been run-throughs every day, polishing up the production, and tomorrow being Saturday means a matinee as well, and of course, we're off on Sunday. Nottingham and then Leicester, leading up to the really big number ones."

By then we were walking down the main stairs, and soon I was waving good-bye from the front steps, concealing my impatience to get back upstairs and face my husband with this proof that my father had neither lied nor pretended and that he, David, had been sadly mistaken when he made those awful accusations.

Face to face with him again, I scarcely shut the door before demanding an apology.

He stared. "For what, in heaven's name?"

"You know perfectly well for what."

"My darling, such grammar! Five minutes in the company of one of your theatrical friends, and you lapse again."

I took a deep, steadying breath.

"Sometime ago you declared that my father lied to me. You said you had checked with the owner of the Metropole Hotel, who told you that my father had stayed there—"

"That is correct. He did."

"But you also said that the man was not connected in any way with reopening the Hippodrome."

My husband's well-defined eyebrows raised in surprise.

"My dear one, you are imagining things. You must be, for I haven't the faintest notion of what you are talking about. How would *I* know the affairs of an innkeeper? And surely you do not imagine I would question a stranger about his investments, his business plans?"

"But you said you did, you *told* me you did!"

"Upon my life, I said no such thing. For your sake, because of the implication that possible food poisoning might have hastened your father's death—not caused it, mind you, not caused it!—I tried to find out if other cases of food poisoning had occurred at the Metropole. None had. And so I told you, to set your mind at rest. But all this rambling, these wild ideas, these stories you invent—

my dear Aphra, you fill me with the greatest anxiety. And now there's the matter of the key—"

"What key?" I asked, startled.

"The key of the hothouse, of course. What other? Why did you not put it back, as I told you to?"

"But I did! I went to the oast-house specifically for that. You weren't there, so I put it in the little drawer you took it from—the middle drawer—"

"Don't lie to me, Aphra. I have been in my office all afternoon. After we left the laboratory, I gave you the key, and then after you had gone, I cleaned up my lab, locked the door, and spent the rest of the afternoon at my desk. You did not come near. So give me the key now, and I will say no more about it. But understand this, never again will I entrust you with it."

My brain was reeling. We had gone over and over, round and round, repeating and repeating, accusing and defending and arguing until I could stand no more.

"I haven't *got* the key, I tell you! I put it back! The middle drawer in the nest of three at the top. *I put it back, I put it back!*"

"You are hysterical. Pull yourself together. Do you want the whole house to hear?"

"I want the whole world to hear! I want it to hear the truth!"

"The truth is that you are out of your mind. You are unbalanced. How can you ever hope to become mistress of Abbotswood in your state of mind?"

I burst out laughing.

"Mistress of Abbotswood! You forget your sister is that."

"She won't be forever. She is a widow, remember. She may marry, even after all this time. She is still attractive. Many men find her so and one in particular. I would not be surprised if she married Red Deakon. Ah, that disturbs you, doesn't it? You are very much aware of the man yourself—"

I cut in sharply. "Even if she does marry him, or anyone else for that matter, and leave Abbotswood, *I* won't take her place. You and I will have to go. We have no claim, no right to be here."

"There are always ways if one wants something badly

The Eagle at the Gate

enough. Look at all I have done for Abbotswood, all I can yet do. I deserve to rule here."

"You are talking nonsense. There is no way you can ever become master here. And why are you trying to convince me that I am unbalanced, out of my mind? Is it some sort of private torture you enjoy practising, like impaling caterpillars, or imprisoning butterflies until they die of fright, or watching that eagle of yours kill the helpless? What sort of sadist are you? And what wild notions fill your head that you can imagine yourself ever becoming master of Abbotswood, or I its mistress?" I turned aside wearily. "It is you who is insane, not I."

He seized me by the hair, jerking my head round until my face was upturned; then he struck it with the back of his hand, across and across, hard. I staggered, and he let me go. I sagged to the floor at his feet.

Someone was knocking at the door. David had gone, and I was alone. I had dragged myself to a chair and remained there in the dusk, thankful that the gas had not yet been lit, grateful for the shadowy room.

The door opened, and Claudia entered.

"I heard sounds, and then I saw David racing across the park—" She broke off. "Why are you sitting in the dusk? Ring for the gas to be lit."

"No."

I saw her peering at me, puzzled, questioning.

"Something *is* wrong," she said.

I let my head fall against the back of the chair. "Ask David," I answered wearily. "On second thought, don't bother. He will only tell you that I stumbled and fell."

I heard the sharp intake of her breath. She came across and pulled my chair half round to the window. It was a solid, heavy chair. I was surprised by her strength.

She studied me for a long moment, then said in a carefully controlled voice, "Tell me."

"He is trying to convince me that I am mad."

"I don't believe it."

"On the other hand, he may only be trying to convince himself."

"I tell you, I don't believe it."

I shrugged. "As you wish."

She was silent then. I hoped she would remain so or

leave. More than anything, I wanted to be alone. My face was throbbing. It would probably swell. A quick swelling or a slow one? I posed the question in a detached sort of way, not really caring. A swollen face would be nothing compared with going out of my mind—

Who said I was going out of my mind? Who put the idea into my head? Not I, not I. . . . I must reject it, fight it. Everyone forgot little things, sometimes even big things, but that did not mean one was going mad.

Claudia's voice came to me out of the dusk.

"Have you been provoking him? It is foolish to provoke a man, any man. You have only yourself to blame if he lost his temper."

"Does a man, any man, strike a woman if he merely loses his temper?"

"David would never do that. I don't believe it. I won't believe it."

"Then I suggest you light the gas and see for yourself."

She withdrew sharply.

"You are a foolish girl, Aphra. Young and foolish and wilful. You wanted him so much; you set your heart on him, didn't you? Oh, I could see that! You were enamoured of him, as you were of Abbotswood. You set him on a pedestal, and now you are whining because he has fallen from it; but I know David as he really is. He is my brother; I have known him all my life. I know the *real* David as nobody else can, and I won't have you maligning him or accusing him of brutality. Not my David."

" 'Your' David is my husband, which means that I know him as only a wife can."

"I don't want to hear more! I will listen to no word against him. If he hit you, which I don't believe, you must have driven him to it. Did you fly into some petty tantrum and then flare at him the way highly strung people do? Because if you did, and he warded you off, it must have been accidental and entirely your fault. His hand caught you perhaps; no more than that."

And never would she believe more than that. She would never be my ally in this house. She never had been.

"I tried to warn you," she went on. "I tried to discourage the whole idea of marriage between you. Remember?"

"You never wanted me here, I know."

"Because it isn't your world! I feared you would be bored here, stifled, and then David would suffer, and *that* I would never forgive. My brother is brilliant. He needs understanding and affection and sympathy. A petulant wife, a bored wife, would be the worst possible thing for him. I would have opposed any young woman whom I believed might become that kind of wife to him. I like you, Aphra. I could even be fond of you, but not if you hurt David. If only you had returned to your own background, to the theatre, the kind of life you were born to, I am sure you would have been a great deal happier and my brother would have been spared disappointment—because it must be a big disappointment to him if you are hankering after the theatre again. This scene between you —it occurred after your actress friend called, didn't it? I saw her leaving and recognised her at once."

"Elizabeth's Lorrimer's visit had nothing to do with it."

"Well, whatever the cause, I won't have David worried or upset. He cannot work in such conditions. He is a sensitive person; he needs peace and harmony in his life." Her white hands gestured helplessly. I saw them flutter in the shadowy room, with the helpless, bewildered movements of the night moths her brother liked to catch.

"Recriminations are useless," she said finally, forcing a brisk note into her voice as if to emphasise that the matter was closed. "You are married to him for better, for worse, remember that. And you owe him everything. Everything." A pleading note crept in now. "Brilliant people are often temperamental, and I admit that dear David is—well—just a little, now and then. Bear with him. Try to understand him more. Remember, a wife cannot run away at the first little upset in her marriage."

"But they do, don't they—not in actuality, but in the other ways? Like taking lovers and meeting them secretly and carving their initials for all eternity in trysting places." I was appalled by what I said, but my voice ran on. I could not believe it was mine, nor could I stop it. "J and C. Jasper and Claudia? Was he *your* escape?"

I heard her gasp, and I wanted to call the words back. I had hit out because I was frightened and hurt and rebuffed by her lack of sympathy—and because what she said was true. There could be no running away; in this day and age right was always on the husband's side. A wife was her husband's possession, and if he abused her—in whatever way he abused her—the world did not wish to know.

Claudia moved to the door. Her feet seemed to drag. I wanted to cry out that I was sorry but could not.

"I think it would be as well if you dined up here tonight," she said dully. "Harriet—the servants—they notice things."

So even in the dusk she had seen my bruised face.

A thought struck me. There *was* one way in which I could demand her help.

"Claudia, wait! Did you see me lock the door of the hot-house?"

"Of course."

"What did I do with the key?"

"You went down to the oast-house to give it back to David. I saw you go."

"That doesn't prove that I arrived there, but it might help if you told him. You see, he doesn't believe I did. His office was empty, and I put the key in the place he took it from, but he says it isn't there now, that he never left the office and I never entered it. But I did."

"You don't think—Harriet again, perhaps? That somehow she discovered the new hiding place? She does tend to wander everywhere, and I cannot keep an eye on her all the time—and she *can* be a little naughty every now and then. Not that she means to be. She doesn't understand that some of the things she does *are* naughty, like helping herself to things that she wants. I wouldn't want you to be blamed for something not your fault. All the same, it doesn't seem likely that it was Harriet, does it, because if David had been there, he would have seen her. You must have made a mistake. Perhaps you left the key in the lock. Perhaps you merely shut the door and I took it for granted that you turned the key. It is so easy to make mistakes, to think you have seen something or done something." She finished thoughtfully. "Come to think of it, I can't be absolutely *sure* that I saw you actually turn the key, though I did see you close the door. Perhaps you dropped the key somewhere, or put it on a ledge while we were choosing the plants—yes, you might well have done that, so your hands would be free. Don't you think it would be best to go back and find out? I'm sure David would be pleased if you did, and then all would be well between you again. The light hasn't entirely gone. It is only shadowy indoors at this hour."

It was not to appease David that I thought the idea a good one; it was to satisfy myself. If the door was locked, I should know that I had done the right thing as far as that was concerned. If open, well, I would have to face the realisation that I had been very absentminded indeed. Had I really left the key inside? Could I possibly have dropped it? Had I actually imagined that visit to the oast-house to return it? Fear sent doubt chasing through my mind in the tortuous way that only self-doubt can.

"Very well," I said, "I'll do as you suggest. And I will also take your advice about dining up here. I would prefer to anyway."

She nodded and said she would have something sent up to await my return, and I dragged myself out of the chair and into the bedroom, where I flung a cloak about my shoulders. To avoid meeting anyone in the household, I went out by the east wing, past the disused bedrooms where only visitors slept, past the room I had occupied and the one my father had occupied, aware of the deserted air of the place and the long-empty corridors—thickly carpeted, luxurious, waiting for people to inhabit them again. Somehow it all seemed alien now. The whole house seemed alien. A place in which I had never belonged, nor ever could.

Shock hit me as the door of the hothouse swung open in my hand. I stared down at the empty keyhole, my fingers still on the heavy iron knob and my mind trying frantically to recall my every movement during the earlier visit. It was I who had unlocked the door when the three of us had arrived, I who had turned the knob, I who had taken out the key—or had I? Had I left it in the lock, ready to be turned again when we left, and when we did so, had I taken it out but forgotten to turn it?

Or had I carried it in my hand after closing the door when we entered and kept it there as we walked through the jungle ahead? If so, what had I done with it then? Dropped it or put it down somewhere, as Claudia suggested? If the latter, then I must have put it down in one of the glass houses farther on, amongst the tropical flowers and plants from which we had made our selection, for we had scarcely lingered in this first one, except during that moment when Harriet had lifted that strange, lifelike branch and let her imagination run riot.

I stepped inside, closing the door behind me, and leant against it. My head as well as my face had begun to ache, making thought difficult and reasoning almost impossible. I was so certain that I had taken the key down to David's office and replaced it in that small drawer—but had I? Had I suffered some mental aberration and imagined the whole thing? Was David's anxiety about my mental state justified after all?

Things he had said now echoed in my mind. ". . . *there have been moments lately when I confess to feeling anxious about you. . . ."* "*I recognise the symptoms, and I fear that before long Claudia will recognise them, too. . . .*" "*These are Harriet's traits; perhaps I should seek help for you. . . .*" ". . . *Had your mother such tendencies? These things can be hereditary, I believe. . . .*"

I was shaking. I folded my arms about my body, hugging myself in an effort to be still and trying to think calmly and quietly and sanely. The shock of my scene with David had unnerved me, but all I had to do was to reason carefully, and logic would come to my aid. I must retrace my steps, from the time the three of us entered the hothouse to the time we left. We had walked through this first section, and Claudia and I had gone ahead into the next one, leaving Harriet to follow. There we had stopped—yes, I remembered it distinctly; we had stopped to admire the orchids, and yes, I had had the key in my hand. I remembered transferring it to my left one and reaching up with my right to touch a miraculous bloom and marvelling over its beauty. We had lingered here— how long? Just long enough to admire that miracle of nature. But we had lifted no orchid plants from their shelves, for they were too fragile, too precious, too delicate to risk moving, so I would not have put the key down in there.

It was in the third section, that riot of colour and nameless blossoms, labelled with Latin derivations I could not even remember, that we had made our choice, and this had taken a long time. Pot after pot we had picked up,

The Eagle at the Gate

checking the names with David's list, weighing colour against colour to achieve perfect harmony, then replacing and reselecting until we had the number we needed as well as perfect blending. Then we had carried them through, one by one, to the entrance, ready to hand to the gardener, who waited just inside the door with his commodious wheelbarrow and protective sacks. So almost surely I had put the key down in that final greenhouse, on one of the shelves or on the low stone edging which divided the centre path from the earth beds on either side, but where, I could not tell.

I must have picked it up mechanically, I decided, for I had definitely taken it back to David's office and replaced it. I clung to that recollection, convinced it was not imaginary. But I had to prove it, and to make absolutely sure I had not left the key here was the first step.

It was growing darker. In this humid place the light had a strange luminosity, the dusk of twilight reflecting on the domed glass roof and on the walls which were built up in plate glass sections set in iron frames. Had Deakon's Forge manufactured those frames, I wondered, also the intermediary doors with their iron panels to the lower halves and the heavy iron knobs—duplicates of the main door except that they did not lock? That was irrelevant thinking, and I dismissed it. I knew what I had to do, and the quicker I started, the better. I would return to the house and ask Truman to give me a lantern; better still, I would ask him to come and search with me. A witness would be useful perhaps, even a shortsighted one. He could at least testify that a search had been made.

Decision calmed me, and I walked briskly back through the orchid house and then through the one which I secretly called the jungle, and reached for the door.

It was locked.

I shook it again and again. I rattled the knob, turning it this way and that in increasing frustration. The door was not self-locking, so it *had* to be open, but however frenziedly I tried to force it, it refused to yield.

I shouted, despite the fact that I knew no one could hear me. This stifling place was situated well away from the house, though I could see the walls of Abbotswood with their rows of windows, like blank and guileless faces staring out into the gathering dusk. Lights had been lit, which somehow emphasised the approach of night, and one by one curtains were drawn, shutting out the world and myself. The house suddenly took on the appearance of an enemy, watching from a distance but not revealing itself, withdrawing behind a barrier, unapproachable, hostile. All its graciousness was lost; it became formidable, terribly unfamiliar, an enemy world harbouring someone who had deliberately trapped me in this stifling place.

There seemed no other explanation, but strangely enough, instead of frightening me, it only angered me. I had no patience with stupid practical jokers.

I took a hairpin from my hair and thrust it between the lock and the door, and felt the bolt firmly in place. This was no accidental jamming. It had been deliberately turned, and very quietly, so that no grating noise should penetrate between those solid glass walls or echo beneath that solid glass dome. While I had been in that last greenhouse of all, someone had silently approached and locked me in.

I banged on the metal framework of the door, but the only effect that had was to give vent to my fury and make the side of my fist sore. I took off my shoe and hammered on the glass, but the only result was a hollow echo all around. It needed a great deal more than the dainty heel of a lady's shoe even to scratch that thick panel of plate glass.

Perspiration began to bead my forehead; my scalp felt damp. It was useless to panic, for that only sapped energy and made thought incoherent. I forced myself to reason calmly.

For the door to be locked from the outside meant that someone either had a key or had passed this way and seen it in the lock, and knowing it should not be there, turned it without looking inside, and then no doubt removed it to take back to the master. I knew that most of the workmen on the estate called David the master because he exercised so much authority. So it might have been a gardener who had inadvertently locked me in. No less than six were employed at Abbotswood, with four undergardeners, and all knew that the hothouses were Mr. Hillyard's exclusive territory and not to be entered. But surely they also knew that he never left the key in the

The Eagle at the Gate

lock, at any rate on the outside, whether he were there or not? The smallest detail never escaped his attention.

"Hasn't forgotten a thing, has he, Miss Aphra? Planned it all down to the last detail. Just like a campaign. . . ."

Barney's words came to me like an echo from the past —a distant past, or so it now seemed. And how right he had been, how sound his observation of my fastidious husband who never put a foot wrong, who never made a mistake and had no patience with those who did.

Anyway, I thought, returning to my predicament and forcing myself into calm thinking, there had been no key on the outside when I arrived, so none could have been seen there by anyone passing. Not that anyone was likely to pass at this hour of the day. Estate cottages, where outside workers lived, were situated away over in the park. One reason why David had chosen this site for his hothouse, he had once told me, was its isolation. No one was likely to disturb him when working there.

Perspiration began to trickle from my scalp to my neck, running in rivulets beneath my blouse. I shed my cloak; if I were cooler, I might think more clearly. And so I began to reason again. First, I commanded myself, remember that there is only one key to this place, so no one is likely to have a duplicate, unless one was made secretly, and who would be likely to do that? Not Claudia, who disliked the humid atmosphere, or Harriet, because if she had tried to get one made, to whom would she have gone? Not to anyone in the village, because that would have awakened comment and would surely have reached Claudia's ears and possibly David's. I had no doubt that Harriet would like to have keys for all of Abbotswood's secret places, but to obtain them would be another matter. As for the gardeners, it would be more than their livelihoods were worth to take an impression of the lock just so that they could feast their eyes in secret on Mr. Hillyard's rare collection. So that left only David himself, who, after all, must have found the key where I placed it and come up here to make sure that the door was locked. And of course, he had no idea I was inside, nor would he have seen me in either of the distant sections, especially in the gloom.

There—it was all quite reasonable when one came to think about it, and nothing to be frightened about at all.

He would be angry about the unlocked door, of course—that had been a stupid oversight on my part—but no harm was done. Except to me, trapped inside and unable to escape until someone came by in the morning or missed me. When I was absent from our room tonight, and the dinner Claudia had arranged to be sent up was found untouched, Claudia would remember where I had gone and I would be released instantly.

Claudia. It was Claudia who suggested I should come here. Claudia was on David's side, not mine. There shouldn't *be* sides, but there were. Two enemy camps, with forces lined up against me.

There goes your imagination again, Aphra Coleman. No—Aphra Hillyard, of course. The heat was confusing me. I was Mrs. David Hillyard of Abbotswood, Kent. I lived at last in that grand house which had overwhelmed me at first sight and awakened in me such ambitious yearnings, such dreams of security and happiness and comfort. Somehow only the comfort seemed to remain now; material things like good clothes and fine furnishings, and rich carpets and beautiful crystal and silver, sparkling chandeliers, shimmering upholsteries, velvet curtains . . . velvet curtains . . . and a man with red hair and mocking eyes. . . . *"Don't be taken in by the velvet curtains, Miss Coleman . . . don't be taken in by the velvet curtains. . . ."* Dear God, but it was hot! Surely, it was getting hotter? My thoughts were spinning. My clothes were clinging to my body, my hair to my scalp; my bruised cheek was wet, my forehead streaming. I unpinned my mother's brooch, that dear, precious brooch which was my strongest link with her, and unfastened the high neck of my blouse and then, very slowly, very carefully, I repinned the brooch at my breast, for I must never lose it, never lose it . . . it was important, important. . . . *"Where did you get that brooch, Mrs. Hillyard,"* A dragon with a gauntlet of chain mail in its mouth; unusual for a cameo.

I was swaying. The green jungle was coming toward me and then retreating. Take deep breaths, and again, and again. Lean against the glass door. It should be cool . . . cool. . . .

It was not. My wet blouse clung to the glass, and the glass itself was now so hot that it poured more heat into my body.

The Eagle at the Gate 203

Dizziness again. Dizziness and darkness. *"Where did you get that brooch, Mrs. Hillyard?"* Red hair and keen eyes; a strong voice and strong hands. *"These are the hands of a blacksmith, not the hands of a gentleman."*

Through consciousness which seemed to ebb and flow, sounds penetrated: the creaking of pipes; the rustling of plants as they breathed. Did plants breathe? Of course they did; they needed to, in heat like this. If they failed to breathe, they would stifle as I was stifling. I was stifling because I couldn't breathe . . . couldn't . . . breathe. Dear God, help me to breathe, *help me to breathe!*

A leap back into coherent thought told me that the creaking sounds in the pipes were expansion caused by a rise in temperature. Did one have moments of lucidity in the midst of delirium? It seemed so.

But I wasn't delirious. I was perfectly sane, perfectly calm. All I had to do was wait for someone to come, for Claudia to remember where I had gone. She would remember, wouldn't she? She wouldn't let me smother to death just because she didn't want me at Abbotswood or because she didn't want me as her brother's wife? Of course, I should never have revealed my knowledge about Jasper Bentine being her lover; I should not have flung it in her face like that, although it was no more than a wild guess. To let her know that I suspected her secret had been unwise and perhaps cruel. But cruelty begets cruelty, and I had hit back because her brother had been cruel to me and she did not care. It was only David she cared about, no one else. And certainly not about a little actress from nowhere who had dared to step out of her own world into this one.

Were these monster growths actually breathing? Were they stretching their limbs and testing their strength and getting ready to attack? Was that long spiky arm, which Harriet had believed to be alive, actually crawling along the ground toward me? I watched it, mesmerised, a dark shape in the gloom, and suddenly I heard screams echoing through the nightmare place, rasping against the glass walls, resounding beneath that distant dome where a vast network of vile limbs intertwined, writhing in the heat . . . stretching, reaching, growing longer and longer until they were vast tentacles moving relentlessly downward . . . and then came a helpless, terrified sobbing which was as loud in my ears as the screams had been, and tore at my throat in the same way. And the heat added its merciless torture until my brain seemed to go berserk and my body lost all strength.

No screams now. Just helpless whimpering and nameless dread. *So this is what suffocation is like.* The thought seemed to run like a cool, remote current in distant channels of my brain, which were already removed from this area of reality.

This is what madness is like, too.

But even madness could have isolated moments through which reason forced itself, and such a moment came to me now. If the temperature was rising, someone had caused it to. Someone had restoked the boiler; someone had fed the glutton with its meal of coke, and fed it well, and then had turned up the dials until the heat was a throbbing, living thing, burning up the air in my lungs, choking the life out of me. Was he still there, waiting until the temperature rose to a point which would mean death to a human being? Or had he gone away, not caring if these rare plants died too, so long as I went with them?

My paralysed mind marvelled that at such a moment as this I could be stirred to anger—white-hot, blazing anger which dragged me to my feet and hounded me to fight. I had slumped to the ground—hot, clammy, steaming ground; not even the stone path running down the centre of this fiendish place was cool. It burned with a life of its own, just as that thing stretching toward me had a life of its own. *Can you imagine how it would feel about your throat, digging its spikes into your flesh so that you bled and bled?*

Leaping terror hurled my body against the door again and tore screams from my throat in one last frenzied cry for help. My fists pounded as ineffectively as before, and I rocked backward and forward, slumping more heavily each time, beating my body against the doorframe until it vibrated in a way which gave me immeasurable delight. I would conquer it. I would conquer it! See, you devil, you cannot trap me forever! The vibrations echoed with dull booming sounds; I could feel them shivering up the glass until those fiendish limbs overhead trembled.

Then something slid down about my neck like a writhing snake, shaken free from the tangled mass above. I clutched at it and felt it squash beneath my fingers, a soft, pulpy mass of vegetation falling to pieces in my hands. I went wild with laughter then, screaming my derision, shouting to those monsters above to come down and do their worst, and I turned and stamped on the spiky arm sprawling along the ground, and the stench it gave off seemed to multiply in the heat . . . the ever-rising heat . . . the ever-increasing aroma of overripe vegetation seeping into my brain like an anaesthetic. I had to do one last thing before it sent me down into oblivion. *I had to smash that glass wall and smash it well.*

I almost fell upon the pot containing the freak plant with the spiky arm (*You see, you see! I am not afraid of the likes of you!*), and I dragged it to the door and then up onto the stone paving which marked the boundary of moist earth beside the stone centre path. The glass wall ran right down to the base beside the door. If I could lift this thing, hurl it, crash it through that wall even if I crashed through with it, the air would be sweet outside, sweet to die in.

I prayed for strength, and it came, one last superhuman effort which racked my whole body and gave it power. I heard a crash like thunder, and I fell to the ground and covered my head with my arms, and when at last all was quiet, I lifted it slowly and faced the cold air which flowed straight toward me through a gaping hole. And I stayed where I was, breathing deeper and deeper, and I did not mind when my burning body began to shiver, because it was alive, *alive*.

Sounds. Voices. Running footsteps. And faces—Claudia's, and David's, and Harriet's too. And then Truman, kindly old Truman holding a lantern high so that it shone straight onto me through the glass panel of the door. The sight of me shocked him so much that he could do nothing but stand there staring, struck dumb. Claudia looked shocked, too, and for all the world as if she were distressed. What an actress she was! And there was Harriet, eyes agog, and David . . . but he was not even looking at me. He was staring at the gaping hole in the glass wall and the broken pot with its contents spilled half in and half out of the hothouse. His lips were white, and suddenly his handsome face crumpled and did not look handsome anymore.

I cried feebly to be let out. I heard my voice gasping that someone had locked me in, someone had tried to kill me, and Truman came to life like an elderly puppet jerked to action. I had dragged myself to my knees by then, swaying amongst the broken glass and unable to find the strength to rise. I was kneeling like that when the old man put his hand on the knob and turned it, and the door opened at his touch.

THIRTEEN

No one believed me, of course. Least of all, David. He stood outside, too stunned to move, regarding me in total disbelief. I could see it in his eyes and in his white, contorted face.

Claudia and the old man helped me rise, and Claudia picked up my discarded cloak and wrapped it around me, and all the time I went on insisting that the door had been locked. "I was trapped, I couldn't get out . . . it got hotter and hotter . . . someone turned up the temperature, someone tried to kill me!" My teeth were chattering. My limbs were shaking.

"She is overwrought," Claudia said. "We must get her to bed. Step carefully, Aphra—there is glass everywhere. My goodness, what heat!"

My knees threatened to sag again. Truman held me on one side and Claudia on the other. The old man kicked a path through the broken glass to the open door, and still David stood outside, rigidly staring. Even in my state of weakness and confusion I knew that beneath his disbelief was a blazing anger.

Suddenly he shouted to Truman, *"Fetch someone!* This damage must be repaired at once!"

"Sir, it will need a glazier. We have handymen and gardeners on the estate, but no glaziers."

"I know that, you fool. It will have to be boarded up for now, but first thing tomorrow a glazier will have to be fetched—better still tonight, if one can be dragged from his fireside." He was in control now. He stepped through the open door and pushed the old man aside. "Don't waste time helping my wife. She can stand, as you see." He seized my arm impatiently. "Let us get her out of here and the door closed. I don't want *every*thing destroyed, although God knows there's little chance of anything surviving a chill blast like this!"

Claudia said, "I will take care of Aphra. Leave her to me."

"Gladly."

He dropped my arm as if he could not bear to touch me. So it was Claudia who peeled the sodden clothes from my body, who put me to bed, brought brandy, and finally said, "I will have another room prepared for David tonight. It will be better if you—if you are left alone." I knew she had been about to say, "if you do not meet," and then thought better of it. "I will let everyone know that you are not to be disturbed, and tomorrow you will feel better and be able to tell us what happened."

"I have told you. The door was locked. Someone must have locked it outside and gone away—except that they also turned up the temperature till the place was hotter and hotter and I was suffocating. So whoever it was went into the boiler room after locking me in."

She stroked the hair back from my brow.

"You don't know what you are saying. You are confused. The lock must have jammed somehow, so it couldn't be opened from inside, or else you were turning the knob the wrong way. You saw for yourself that it opened as soon as Truman touched it. As for the abnormal heat, something must have gone wrong with the boiler. You are overwrought. Tomorrow you won't say these things. You will have forgotten all about it."

To answer was a waste of effort. To protest that never in my life would I forget one moment of that nightmare was useless. I felt too weak to embark on any argument but rallied sufficiently to murmur that everything I said was true and would still be true tomorrow.

"Tomorrow," she said firmly, "you will rest. To come downstairs and meet a lot of people would be exhausting for you."

I had forgotten that tomorrow was the day of her charity bazaar. The entire hall was to be given over to it, and people would be milling everywhere. To come "up to the house" was a day in the life of every villager, and a sorry sight I would look if I put in an appearance. I closed my eyes, too exhausted to say more, conscious only of relief because I would not see David again tonight. I was not ready to face any more of his anger.

The Eagle at the Gate

* * *

I was driving along a country lane in one of the broughams from Abbotswood, and I looked at the hands controlling the reins and was surprised to see that they were Elizabeth Lorrimer's. "I had no idea you knew how to handle them," I said, and she replied, "Don't be silly— I drove your parents to St. Saviour's when they went to make their vows. You were not there."

"Don't *you* be silly," I retorted. "How could I be? I was not born then."

"Naturally. Do you find the air chilly? I will put up the hood." And without even pausing, she lifted her arm, and up went the hood behind us, and I wondered how I could have imagined we were driving in a brougham. It was a phaeton, and the vehicle became heavier and heavier and hotter and hotter, because suddenly it changed from a phaeton to a travelling coach, with Elizabeth up on the box, still driving, and I shut up inside with the doors locked. I tried to open the windows, but they, too, were locked; the air was getting hotter; I was stifling. I banged on the coach roof, crying to be let out, but that only started her laughing, and she drove the horses faster and faster. Then suddenly the coach stopped, and David opened the door. "Why don't you come out?" he said. "There is nothing to stop you. You had only to open the door and step down."

So I stepped down, and Elizabeth had vanished. There was only David and myself, and the big stone eagle overhead. We were outside the gates of Abbotswood, and David took hold of my shoulders and forced me to look up at the eagle. I saw then that it was Conrad, fearsomely alive, with his diabolical gaze fixed on me and his wings spreading for flight. He began to move. Very slowly, he began to swoop. Not with the hurricane dive I had witnessed before, but with a terrible relentlessness that mesmerised me. I saw his murderous beak and his killer's talons and could not move for terror.

And then I saw Elizabeth again, standing aside watching. "The creature is a snob," she said. "It despises you because of what you are. Did you know what she was when you married her, Mr. Hillyard?"

David shook his head, released my hand, turned his back on me, and walked away, and the eagle's flight increased until it was directly overhead, and beneath the immense span of its wings all was darkness around me. I screamed, and suddenly I saw that it was not an eagle at all, but a dragon with a glove of chain mail in its mouth, and there was Red Deakon holding out a big gentle hand to me, but the more I tried to grasp it, the farther away he went until I began to sob in terror. He was disappearing and I needed him. Then he had gone, and I was shut up in the coach again, suffocating, choking. . . .

I wakened violently. I was alone in the vast bed, and my nightgown was drenched, as my clothes had been up there in the hothouse; but relief surged over me. It had all been a nightmare: the smothering coach, the predatory eagle, the peculiar menace of Elizabeth's words—"It despises you because of what you are. . . ."

What did she mean—*what* I was? A naïve young actress enamoured of a dream? A silly girl who regarded a fine country mansion as an enchanted castle? Or someone out of her mind, irrational, given to strange fancies and morbid fears, who imagined her life was threatened just because she found a door locked on her, who forgot her own actions and believed she had done things which she had never done—such as returning a key to its hiding place?

I lay very still in the dark and silent room; then my hand groped across the bed to the side my husband occupied. It was cool and empty; so Claudia had been as good as her word and persuaded him to sleep elsewhere tonight. But perhaps there had been no need for persuasion. That white, twisted face which had looked at me through the smashed wall of the hothouse had told me plainly that he had no desire to come near me.

I rolled over from the hot and rumpled area in which I lay, to the cool, unoccupied side of the bed, and there I remained with my nightmare still haunting me and the claustrophobic feeling of that locked coach threatening me just as vividly as that hour of purgatory amidst a jungle growth. I knew there would be no further sleep for me tonight.

I was wrong. I slept suddenly and deeply, waking late in the morning to find Claudia beside me with a tray. It was past ten o'clock, she told me.

"I brought this myself because I felt you would not wish anyone else to see you at the moment."

She meant the maids, of course. Because of my appearance. The reminder prompted me to lift an exploratory hand to my face. I was thankful to feel the swelling much less, but a mirror across the room reflected a dishevelled young woman with an ugly discolouration across one cheek.

"No one expects you to come down." Claudia told me comfortingly.

Of course not. Everyone would expect me to keep discreetly out of the way.

"I feel well enough," I said honestly. "If you are afraid that people will comment on my marked face, I promise to tell them that I bumped into the iron frame of the hot house door. That seems a feasible explanation, don't you think?"

She answered, without looking at me, "I am thinking only of you."

Oh, no, I thought. You are thinking of David, who must be protected at all costs. Never let the smallest hint of misconduct fall upon him.

"I have persuaded David not to come near you today. I confess this is as much for his sake, as for yours. He is distraught because of the devastation you caused. Why did you panic, my dear, just because you turned the doorknob the wrong way? And what a thing to do, smashing that glass! You were lucky to suffer no cuts. I suppose that was because you had the presence of mind to throw yourself to the ground. But it really was nonsensical behaviour. You must have realised that the instant you were missed you would have been rescued. *I* knew where you had gone—"

"Oh, yes," I interrupted. "You knew because you sent me there."

She corrected gently, "I merely suggested you should go there to check on the missing key."

"Which was not missing, after all, since it was used to lock me in. And to let me out. *Some*one must have unlocked the door again when I was overcome by the heat, someone who sent the temperature soaring."

"Now, Aphra," my sister-in-law said patiently, "don't start making those wild accusations again. No one will believe you, and you will only succeed in making yourself ridiculous—and, of course, angering David even further. We forgave those terrible things you said last night because they were obviously the ramblings of an hysterical girl, but in the sane light of day and after a good night's sleep, there is no excuse for persisting with them."

"Except that they are true. Someone did lock me in, and someone did turn up the temperature, which means that someone deliberately tampered with the boiler for one reason only: to kill me."

She gave a patient sigh.

"My dear Aphra, no one *could* have done. After I left you, I went straight down to the drawing room, where Meg Deakon was waiting to see me. She is Red's cousin-in-law and keeps house for him."

"I know."

Claudia looked surprised, and I recalled that she knew nothing about my visit to Red's house. David had declared that she would not hear of it from him and certainly not from Red because Red would not want her to know that another woman had visited his house alone.

"She had brought a lot of things for today's bazaar," Claudia was saying. "She is a splendid cook, and always so generous. Red had driven her here, and we all had a glass of sherry wine together. Harriet joined us, and then David. So we were all together and can testify to this. Ask Red and his cousin, if you like! After they left, Mrs. Stevens came in to ask whether you had decided to dine downstairs after all, because the tray I had sent up had not been touched. Then I remembered you had gone to the hothouse, but that had been more than an hour before, so David insisted on going to find you. Naturally we all went."

"And Truman? Why Truman?"

"Frankly, my dear, I don't know, but he is a fatherly old man and was very concerned. He went to fetch a lantern, I recall, because it was almost dark by then. And I remember David saying that if you were in the hothouse, it proved you had the key after all."

"The door was unlocked when I got there. That was why I was able to go inside."

"And why it was unlocked when we rescued you."

I said no more. What was the use? I drank the coffee gratefully and never had it tasted so good, and I promised to eat all my breakfast, so Claudia departed well satisfied.

After she had gone, I rose, bathed, and dressed with care. It was important that I should put in an appearance downstairs and that I should look well and confident and fully in control of myself. I chose a cashmere morning dress of chartreuse green which was a good foil for my hair. I also took from a drawer in my bureau, where I had stowed away souvenirs of the past, my old box of theatrical makeup, and very carefully, very discreetly, I disguised the telltale marks on my face with a stick of Leichner No. 2, blended on the cheekbones with a touch of No. 5. The swelling had almost gone, but if anyone noticed it I would simply use the mythical collision with the hothouse door as an excuse.

Studying myself critically, I decided that, considering all I had gone through since Elizabeth's visit yesterday, I looked passably good. It was wonderful what a good night's sleep could do—except to blot out memory, of course. David's behaviour, the unbelievable things he had said—*and* denied—coupled with his violence, could not be obliterated by a good night's sleep or by pleas from his sister, any more than the marks of his action could be fully obliterated by a delicate application of greasepaint. The marks and the memory remained.

I was crossing to the door when sounds from my husband's dressing room caught my attention, first the soft opening and closing of the outer door, then light footsteps moving across the room. One of the maids, I concluded. But they would have finished cleaning the room by now; I had risen very late indeed. And those footsteps had been hurried. Why would a member of the domestic staff run across a room? Servants never ran; they were trained not to. They had to be as unobtrusive as possible, doing nothing to attract attention. Every menial household chore had to be accomplished before the family was astir in case the sight offended. It had astonished me, when I first lived at Abbotswood, to learn that the cleaning out of grates had to be done shortly after dawn, not merely to enable fires to be alight by the time the family descended, but because such tasks should be carried out unobserved, and if by chance one descended early and came across a maid on her knees brushing the stairs, one had to pretend she was not there, and she would cast down her eyes for the same reason and shrink to the side of the staircase in a vain attempt to be invisible. The elevated member of the family would then sweep by because to acknowledge the servant when engaged in such a task would have been embarrassing on both sides.

So I hesitated. If a maid had arrived tardily to dust and tidy the dressing room, it would be unforgivable to humiliate her by opening the door and discovering her guilt.

What compelled me to wait and to listen, I had no idea, but I did so. There was scarcely a sound, merely a faint rustle of skirts now and then, but very little of that. Whoever was here was not cleaning the room. The minutes ticked by, telling me nothing.

And then came the lightest of coughs, and I knew immediately who it was. I opened the door, and I was right. Harriet was on her knees before a low drawer which ran across the base of a wardrobe and to my surprise she was wiping the surface with a soft duster.

My entrance so startled her that she fell back on her heels, the cloth still in one hand and the other plunging immediately into a pocket of her skirt. We stared at each other in mutual astonishment.

"I—thought you were asleep!" she gasped. "Claudia said you were staying in bed."

"And so you decided to be especially quiet?"

"Of course." She rose then, no longer disconcerted. Harriet could rally from any embarrassing moment more quickly than I. "I came to fetch a handkerchief for David. He is busy downstairs helping Claudia with things and getting his hands so dusty that I offered to fetch one for him."

She moved across the room, her free hand still hidden.

"And I suppose that is what you thrust into your pocket when I came in?"

"Of course," she said airily, and went on her way, saying as she did so, "You did a terrible lot of damage to David's plants. Killed most of them, I shouldn't wonder. What a wicked thing to do! He is terribly angry, I can tell. I always know what David feels and what he is thinking. We were very close until you came." She stopped in front of me. "You look surprised, but why? Cousins have been known to marry, and the difference in our ages would not have mattered—and I look very young. David had often told me how young I am. Men don't worry about age differences the way some women do. Look at the Brownings.

And Red Deakon and dear Claudia. Not that she will stay young forever, the way David says *I* will."

She went skipping away down the corridor, singing to herself, not caring whether I believed her story about the handkerchief or not. And I certainly did not. The excuse had been thought up very hurriedly; Harriet had a certain measure of cunning in her childish mentality, but not enough. I knew full well that David's clean handkerchiefs were kept in the top right-hand drawer of a Georgian dressing chest, and when I opened it, there they were in a neatly stacked pile. What was kept in that long low drawer, I had no idea, but when I stooped to find out, it was locked.

Now what are you up to, Harriet?

No one but she would ever know.

If she had not thrust that hand into her pocket so hurriedly, I might have thought she was merely trying to open the drawer, ferreting in her insatiably curious way, but that quick concealment puzzled me.

I paused on the gallery and gazed down into the hall, just as I had gazed on that night so long ago. Now, as then, it was a whirl of activity, but of a different kind. The bazaar was to open officially at noon, but already the place was packed with villagers, looking with awe at the magnificence which had so impressed me in those early days. There were also members of the local gentry, friends of Claudia's who shared her charitable activities. Tables had been set up on all sides, displaying handmade crafts, needlework, crochet and knitting, and homegrown fruit and flowers—but no vegetables, unless Abbotswood wished to lose its very competent housekeeper. I could imagine Mrs. Stevens turning up her nose at such an odour in *her* spotless household!

How Mrs. Stevens must be hating it all, I thought; how she would bemoan all this trampling on the carefully polished floor, the fingermarks on panelled walls, not to mention the mess which would be left behind! I had overheard her protesting to Claudia that it was all very well to admit the hoi polloi ("Half of them only come because they are curious to see inside Abbotswood, if Madam will forgive my saying so"), but how much better it would be to hold an event like this outdoors in summer, to which

Claudia had soothingly replied that she well understood the housekeeper's feelings, but opening up the hall at this time of the year had been considered a tactful answer to the head gardener's plea to keep the public off his lawns and flower beds. "And after all, Mrs. Stevens, it only happens once a year, when Christmas is in the offing. We must inconvenience ourselves sometimes for the sake of charity."

One had to admire Claudia; when she undertook something, she carried it out wholeheartedly. There she was now, walking from table to table, checking that everything was in order and admiring every display, however modest. No one would have suspected that any disturbance could ever take place in her impeccable house. She was the country lady of the manor to perfection. And there was David, being affable to everyone, smiling his charming smile, having a word here, a word there, congratulating here, congratulating there, and receiving bobs and curtsies in return as if he were lord and master of this place—which, in the eyes of most people, he probably was. And certainly, in his own eyes, he deserved to be.

A footfall beside me—and there was Red Deakon, a yard or two away, looking at me as intently as on the night of the ball. The situation was identical, except for the clothes he wore and the company down there.

"I saw you from below," he said, "and came up to enquire how you were."

"How I am?" I jerked.

"Your sister-in-law told us you were indisposed."

His amber-brown eyes were studying my face. Had my concealment been poor after all? My hand flew to my cheek.

"It—it was nothing! I bumped into the door of the hothouse, that was all."

His frown was quick and puzzled. "But Claudia said you merely had a headache and had retired early."

We were talking at cross-purposes. He was referring to last night, when he and his cousin's widow had taken wine with the others and I had officially gone to bed early. The slip was mine, but before I could cover it up, he asked, "Did the collision with the hothouse door follow our visit? Surely you did not rise and go out after retiring to bed?"

"No, no—it happened before that."

"I heard this morning that there had been some damage

to your husband's precious greenhouse, but I paid little heed. The village glazier does a lot of work for Deakon's, fitting glass into wrought-iron frames for summerhouses and the like. He arrived much earlier than expected today, asking if he could be spared to attend to urgent repair work on the hothouse up at Abbotswood, which naturally suggested glass had been broken. I must have misunderstood him. Or I hope I did?"

"No, not exactly—that is, I was clumsy. I bumped into the half-open door, it closed with a crash, and the vibration caused some glass to shatter."

"But you were unhurt?"

"Oh, yes."

"To bump into an iron door frame would be extremely painful. That accounts for your slightly swollen cheek, I take it, and it certainly accounts for your headache last night. I could tell Claudia was concerned about you, and now I am not surprised." He glanced down into the crowded hall. "Are you sure you feel up to facing this throng?"

"Perfectly sure."

"Then let me escort you."

He held out his arm, and I placed my hand upon it, and so we descended into the great hall, side by side.

"A rather different gathering from the night of the ball, Mrs. Hillyard."

"Very different, Mr. Deakon."

"And rather more to your liking perhaps?"

"To a certain extent."

"But not entirely, because, being very feminine, you like to dress up and look beautiful, and that is as it should be—provided it is for the right people and amongst the right people. But may I say that, to me, you look as lovely in that simple dress you are wearing today as you did on the night of the ball?"

I was tempted to say that I could never imagine myself looking lovely in his eyes, then deemed the words to be coquettish and accepted his remark as a polite compliment instead.

"You are not wearing your brooch today. It is unusual to see you without it."

"And surely it is unusual for a man to notice such a small item of jewellery?"

"In the ordinary way, perhaps, but that is no ordinary brooch. The design caught my eye because I have seen it before."

"Where?" I asked in some surprise.

"I will show you one day if your husband will permit me to take you."

We had reached the foot of the stairs, and before I could reply, David was beside us, saying, "And where must I permit you to take my wife, Deakon?"

He lifted my hand and kissed it, looking at me with tender concern.

"For a country drive to bring some colour into her cheeks. No wonder she has been suffering from a headache—colliding with the door of a hothouse would lay anyone low. With your permission, I would be happy to speed her recovery with a breath of fresh air. I have a call to make over at Chilham this afternoon, and Meg wishes to do some shopping in Canterbury, which, as you know, is only a few miles distant. She would appreciate feminine company, I know. You would be doing both Meg and your wife a good turn by giving your consent."

"You make it plain that it would be churlish not to, but alas, I fear my dear Aphra may not be quite up to it—"

I interrupted forcibly. "Indeed, I am. In fact, an outing would do me a power of good. Do you not agree, Claudia?"

Wherever David was, there was his sister sure to be— or so it seemed today. She was so close at this moment that she must have heard our conversation.

"Indeed, I agree." To her brother she said, "If Aphra is well enough to come downstairs, she is certainly well enough to go for a drive. This affair will come to an end by three o'clock. I see Meg very busy at her homemade cake stall over there—I will urge her to leave whenever she pleases, for I would not wish to delay her shopping. And her stall will be cleared ahead of all others, that I know. There is a buffet luncheon from twelve to two, for those who wish to take it—that solves *that* particular problem!" She turned to me then. "My dear, I am delighted to see you up, though I did advise you to rest today. Do you really feel equal to all this? Would you not prefer to stay quietly somewhere until dear Meg and her cousin are ready to leave?"

She sounded and looked completely sincere, but so did

my husband. Anyone seeing him kiss my hand, and the anxious way in which he hovered about me, would have believed him to be the most devoted husband in the world. But I could detect the ice beneath his manner and knew I was not forgiven. I had done untold damage to his rare and precious plants, and my punishment had yet to come. Punishment, too, for making wild and terrible accusations. Only he attended to the boiler house, so only he could have been responsible for sending the temperature soaring. I knew, even as he kissed my hand, even as he remained close to me throughout the remainder of that morning, even as he chose the daintiest morsels for me from the buffet luncheon and urged me to eat, that underneath this guise of tender solicitude, he was waiting like a predator, like an eagle at the gate. . . .

But I could be unforgiving, too, and my bruised face, which began to throb again unexpectedly, reminded me of the cause.

We left Abbotswood before the bazaar was over, but not before my husband had cornered me and commanded me to stay at home.

"You will do as *I* say. You will await me in our sitting room at three-thirty. By that time I will have made my farewells to all the important guests, and Claudia can be left to entertain them to tea."

He said it with the most charming smile. Anyone watching would have thought he was murmuring endearments.

I smiled back.

"I regret I shall not be here. Meg knows I am to join them and therefore expects me. I do not intend to keep her waiting. I know what you wish to talk about, and I will gladly do so when I return."

It was folly to defy him, of course, but it would be equal folly to yield. Nor was it in my nature to. I could neither bend the knee nor retract any accusation I had made, for however great had been the pressure of fear, my mind had been perfectly clear on that point. My imprisonment had been as deliberate as the slow and suffocating death planned for me. The only thing that was not clear, and never would be, was the reason for it.

It was a long drive to Chilham, and to save Meg's time, Red drove straight to Canterbury and deposited her there, promising to return at an appointed time and to pick her up at the cathedral gates in the Butter Market. So we visited the Elizabethan village alone.

Its fame as a beauty spot was justified, but Red gave me no time to linger. He drove straight to the village church, tied up the horses, and led me inside.

"This," he said, "is what I promised to show you."

It was a memorial brass set in the stone floor, close to the altar. It showed a monk with tonsured head, and above was a shield, and in one quarter was a dragon with a gauntlet of chain mail in its mouth.

There was no inscription. Merely a name, with a date below. MEDRITH NEUTON, 1631.

"This must have been one of the last memorial brasses to be made in Kent," Red told me, "for the art fell into disuse later. 'Medrith' was the original version of Meredity, and 'Neuton' eventually became Newton. Does it mean anything to you—the shield, or the name? I think it must, since your mother's brooch bears the same device. Was Newton her maiden name?"

The extraordinary thing was that I had no idea. My mother had never referred to her life before she married my father, nor had he. And I, totally incurious because as a family we lived entirely in the moment, had never associated her with any other name than Coleman. I hastened to explain that this was not so ridiculous as it sounded. "Theatrical people live only for the day, never for the past or the future."

"Which is why you hankered after security so much," Red Deakon said gently. "I recognised that, even from a distance."

"You mean—the way I stroked the velvet curtains—" Somehow the memory of that moment was so vivid that I could not look at him.

"Yes. It touched me. I could not help smiling."

"In mockery, I thought."

"Then you were mistaken. But I felt sorry for you somehow. You must not resent that or the warnings I tried to issue later. You seemed so vulnerable. And you were. You still are. That is one reason why I brought you here." He touched my shoulder, and I had an almost overwhelming instinct to draw close to him. "I am not probing, but somehow I feel you need to be given an identity other than being the daughter of a well-known touring actor. To establish what might establish—other things. When I saw that brooch, I recognised the symbol immediately, for the family from whom the original Red Deakon bought our lands, the widow whom he traced over here near Canterbury, bore the name of Newton, and they were descended from this same Medrith Neuton who lies here. He sought refuge in a monastery on the death of his wife when she was smitten by the plague in 1611, but their children lived, and his two sons entered the church. One became a Roman Catholic priest, and the other a Protestant. The Protestant priest married and had a family. Always there were Newtons in the church, as priests or pastors, in high office or lowly. This is as much as the Widow Newton knew of their history. I believe I once told you that after my father's retirement he spent his life recording the history of these parts and the stories of local families. The Newtons were one, but their story is incomplete. It would be interesting now to trace them further. There may have been other descendents, though from the widow's records it would appear that the family eventually died out. But when Kent fell on hard times, many people from these parts emigrated." He finished, "Your mother's marriage lines may help. They would give her maiden name."

Of course. But where were they? In my father's deed box, surely, locked away with other papers he had left. I had kept the box exactly as found, but I had no recollection of any marriage lines.

"They must have been lost," I said. "I know my parents were married at the Church of St. Saviour in Chelsea, because my father told me so, and Elizabeth Lorrimer, too. She was there."

I was staring down at the memorial brass, remembering another, plus the inscription beneath. "Here lyeth bvryed ye body of Aphra Nevton wife of Medrith Nevton Gent. . . ." The pathetic wife who had died of the plague, who had achieved "many virtues" during her short span on earth, had been outlived by her husband by twenty-three years. Why he was buried here and not by her side would remain a mystery. Perhaps he had been unable to stay in a part of the country which held so many memories of her; perhaps he had fled with his children from a plague-ridden area, or perhaps the monastery in which he eventually sought refuge had been in these parts, and his final burial took place in this little church because other Newtons were buried here, too. I saw other memorials bearing the name, carved in stone upon walls and tombs.

I wondered now whether my parents had deliberately gone in search of that other country church; whether their visit had not been accidental and, if so, why my father had told me that it was. Too late, now, to find out.

"The fact that my mother possessed a brooch bearing this symbol, handed down from her mother, does not prove that she was a descendent of this family. The brooch might have come into my grandmother's hands some other way. Purchased in a secondhand jeweller's, perhaps, or received as a gift from someone."

"True. But St. Saviour's will have a record of the marriage, of course."

And how was I to get to Chelsea to see it? Not with David's vigilant eye upon me.

We left the church then, and as I went I had a curious feeling, a feeling which I had never fully experienced before, not even when I married. For the first time in my life I felt that I was beginning to have some identity, that I was discovering roots, that somewhere in the world I actually *belonged*.

But it was not at Abbotswood.

I knew the scene with David would have to be faced, and soon. I told myself I was ready for it, but when I returned home, the appointed time had still to come. He had already changed for dinner and gone downstairs to the drawing room, so I knew he intended to keep me dallying. Only when *he* decreed would any scene take place or any matter be settled. He was master of Abbotswood, legally or not. And certainly he was master of me.

He began to demonstrate this at once, but not in the way I expected. It seemed that his action in striking me had changed only my feelings, not his, for when I went down to dinner, he greeted me with the greatest affection, enquiring how I had enjoyed my outing and remarking on the colour it had brought to my cheeks. He even kissed me. I felt the sensual touch of his lips against my own and knew that despite our violent antagonism, he was desiring me again. Tonight he would claim my body, and be-

The Eagle at the Gate

cause I was his wife, I would be expected to submit. I knew all too well how expertly he could arouse physical passion in me, in ways which now seemed to have nothing whatever to do with love, ways which were useful to a man when he did not want to satisfy his lusts with an unresponsive woman.

Was that what I was now to become, merely a body to serve and please his own?

In sudden rebellion I moved away and saw Claudia watching from across the room. As always, her face was unreadable, but when I joined her, she too commented on my improved appearance. "It is good to see you looking yourself again, Aphra. And you *are* yourself again, are you not?"

Meaning that I would make no more wild accusations or do any more upsetting things.

"I feel splendid," I agreed, sitting down beside her and spreading my skirts. I had chosen carefully tonight and taken pleasure in doing so, for to look my best was to feel my best, and when feeling my best, I could hold my own. So I wore a gown of emerald velvet with a deep plunging neckline; both the colour and style looked dramatic with my dark hair and white skin, and the design of the gown showed my figure to advantage. David had always admired my figure; I had the smallest waist in all Kent, he had often declared, and the loveliest breasts.

Had I been wise to choose a gown tonight which seemed to emphasize these parts of my body, parts he so loved to touch? In the early days, when he stripped me and then fondled me, his caresses had delighted me as much as himself, but how would I feel when next he did so? Would I remember those smooth white hands becoming brutal and striking me, or would his expert lovemaking cloud my senses yet again?

He brought me a glass of wine and stood before me, smiling, with that meaningful curve of his lips which I knew so well and which suggested so much. His eyes held more than desire; they were full of secret amusement, teasing, taunting. He was laughing at me. He was telling me that *he* would take control, *he* would call the rules, and *he* would make the moves in a game which was to be played beween us privately, and that only he would know what kind of game it was, and it would start and finish when he decreed and in whatever way he decreed, and it would last for as long or as short a time as he wished.

He held my glance with an almost mesmeric control. It took almost as much mental strength to turn away from him as it had taken physical strength to hurl that plant pot through the glass, but for the time being at least, it broke the spell.

When I turned my glance away from his, it settled on Harriet, whom I had not even noticed. There she was, beside the fire, staring moodily in our direction, watching everything, missing nothing, but not understanding anything. My husband's attentiveness to me, the kiss he had given me, even the smile he savoured me with appeared to her, and perhaps to his sister, as being prompted by nothing but love and a sure sign that I was restored to favour again. And poor Harriet did not like that. She was jealous.

David said, for all to hear, "You must go to bed early tonight, Aphra. I shall take you myself directly after dinner. You won't object to our leaving you so soon, will you, dear sister? I dare say you will be glad to retire early yourself after so strenuous a day. But it was a great success, was it not? I understand the affair raised a goodly sum. What a pity I could not donate some rare and costly plants to increase your funds, but alas, fate robbed me of the best—"

"Not fate, your wife," Harriet put in.

"Hush, cousin. That is unkind. You know that poor Aphra is distraught—or was, last night. Could she have behaved in such a way otherwise? She was not herself. We must remember that. We must take very great care of her so that she never has such lapses again."

I saw Claudia look at him then. It was a strange look which I could not fathom, but there was so much about Claudia that I could not fathom. Sometimes I felt that she looked upon the world from behind a mask, but that the world would never be allowed to see behind it in return. It was a kind of one-way viewing which enabled her to see everything that went on, yet remain anonymous.

Harriet demanded, "Aren't you going to punish Aphra for what she did? I felt sure you would punish her."

She sounded disappointed, and she probably was. I

was getting to know Harriet by now, or as well as anyone could get to know her. Once I had hoped to make a friend of her, to help her, even to understand her, but I had abandoned any such hope by now, as I had abandoned hope of ever getting to know my sister-in-law or winning her liking. Claudia still held me at arm's length. No matter how concerned about me she had been last night or how solicitous this morning, I was left with the feeling that it had been due to no more than a sense of duty.

My husband admonished gently, "Now, Harriet, that also is unkind. People who are not responsible for their actions must not be punished, because punishment will not help them."

"*David*—" Claudia spoke urgently, but I cut right across her.

"I was entirely responsible for my actions," I said. "I smashed that window deliberately, and I gave you my reason. Apologies won't help, and in any case I don't consider that I should make any, and since apologies from whoever was guilty won't help either, the best thing to do is to forget all about the business. If," I finished, "one can."

"My love, I do so agree." David spoke in a humouring tone of voice which said all too plainly that he did not agree at all but was willing to let the world believe he did. "But one thing I must make clear, sweet Aphra, and that is that not one except yourself was guilty in any way at all. No one shut you in; no one tried to suffocate you or frighten you to death. Can you name one good reason why anyone in this house should behave in such a way, any reason at all why someone would want to kill you, or any person who would profit by your death to the remotest degree? Of course, you can't."

The awful thing was that he was right. There was no more reason why anyone should try to kill me than there was for my husband to claim that I was mad.

But someone had. And he did.

"And now," he said, "here is Truman to announce dinner, and after that we can all go to bed and never refer to this unhappy matter again."

He was as good as his word. When dinner was over, he took me by the arm and led me upstairs. Claudia kissed me goodnight and went into the drawing room, but Harriet remained in the hall, watching our departure. I could feel her morose glance following us until we were out of sight. She had been sulky all evening.

I don't know what I expected when we reached our room: recriminations or forgiveness, hatred or passion. I was not yet ready to forgive David for striking me; the shock of discovering a violent side to his nature was still too vivid for that. But, as Claudia had reminded me, I was still his wife, which meant that he still had the right to sleep with me.

The gas jets had been left burning, the bed turned back, our nightclothes laid out. Reluctant to undress, I unpinned my hair, shook it free, and began to brush it. The hiss of gaslight filled the room, whispering, threatening. If he is going to punish me, I thought, let it be now. Let it be over and done with. Whatever he does, I shall only hate him the more.

My hands paused. Hate him? Did I hate him? I hated the man who had struck me, yes. I hated the man who enjoyed watching an eagle at the kill. I hated the man who had looked at me last night with that distorted face, caring less for his wife than for his precious hothouse blooms, and the memory of those things made me hate the man who came to me now and began to unbutton my gown, although his every movement was gentle. I hated every gesture of his smooth white hands, but I endured them, and when at last I stood naked before him, I waited for whatever he planned to do next because he had the physical power to overcome any resistance.

I felt his touch run over me. How dry and cold his hands were! I shrank instinctively, and they closed about my waist in a grip which was anything but loverlike. His fingers dug into my flesh, forcing me to be still. "You liked it once," he whispered. "You liked a great deal more than this. My God, how you liked it, how you cried out for more!"

"There was no threat behind it then."

His hands fell away. He looked hurt. He was the injured lover, slighted, rejected. He turned the tables so quickly and so adroitly that it was I who felt guilty.

He picked up my nightgown from the bed and held it above my head for me to slip my arms into. The action surprised me as much as his sudden change of mood.

The Eagle at the Gate

When I lifted my arms, he drew the garment down as if he were covering something that had no life or appeal in it. You see, the action said, you are not so desirable after all. . . . *I* can reject *you*.

I slipped between the sheets. Now he would go into his dressing room and prepare for bed, and then he would come back and join me—and after that?

Instead, he leaned over me and kissed my brow. To my astonishment, he was laughing very quietly. "In my own good time, sweet Aphra. In *my* time, not yours."

And so began a cat-and-mouse game which was to last through the slowly darkening days of autumn, until the very eve of an event which was to bring everything catapulting to a head.

But before that happened, terror was to thrust itself into my life again with horrifying impact.

FOURTEEN

David and I were sitting silently over breakfast the next morning when Red, armed with a gun, rode up to Abbotswood to announce that a rogue fox was plaguing the village and that he and a group of men were determined to catch it. Though near, the hunting season had not yet arrived, and in any case this creature was cunning enough to outrun any field. Nightly slaughter was now a regular event in chicken runs and sheep pens, no matter how well fortified. A rogue fox's teeth could bite through the strongest wire and splinter the hardest wood, so an all-out effort was to be launched today to rid the neighbourhood of this menace.

"We're warning all farmers to keep their livestock safely locked up and to mount guard until we have caught him. We are also seeking permission to trek across their lands. Hence my call. We'll try not to do more damage than necessary, but if the creature lies low amidst crops, we'll have to beat a track to him to get within firing range. We're pretty sure that his lair is on the south side of the village, and we'll try smoking him out to get him on the run. That means he may head in any direction, including Abbotswood lands, so it would be wise for everyone here to keep away from the park and the farm in case we have to fire across either. I've spoken to your factor, and he is herding the livestock already."

"It was I you should have consulted," David said tersely.

"That's why I'm here, though my mission was primarily to Claudia since she is mistress of Abbotswood."

"Which I run for her. That makes me master here. Right now, she is in the flower room with Harriet." David pushed back his chair and finished in a tone of dismissal. "I'll give her your message and delay you no further.

You'd better be on your way, or that fox will outwit you and your village mob."

His manner brought a flush of embarrassment to my face, but Red merely looked amused. His eyes met mine briefly. "If your wife plans to go walking," he said, "I'd like to be sure she keeps away from the danger area."

"My wife's safety is my concern, but I am sure she appreciates your thought. Not that there's any likelihood of the fox heading this way if, as you believe, his lair is on the far side of the village. With a pack of yokels yelling after him, he isn't likely to slow himself down by running uphill, which he would have to do were he to head in this direction. In any case, Aphra will be with me. I'm off to exercise Conrad, and I shall do that in the park regardless of possible trespassers." He gave me a sudden smile, that unexpectedly sweet smile which he could turn on at will. "You will join me, won't you, my love? But wrap up well, there's a nip in the air today."

I wasn't sure that I wanted to watch the eagle in flight again, impressive as he was. To view from a distance would be different; it was being in at the kill that turned my stomach. But, as David often pointed out, I was unnecessarily squeamish. Perhaps Red would also consider me so, brought up in the country as he had been. But somehow I felt that the sight of an eagle killing a sheep was not a spectacle he would personally relish.

If I declined to accompany my husband, what then? A morning arranging flowers with Harriet and Claudia, their watchful eyes on me all the time? Since the episode in the greenhouse their observation of me had subtly increased. I felt that they, like David, were only waiting for me to break down again.

The idea of a good brisk walk appealed to me more than sharing their company, and to my surprise, David made no objection. "Keep to the woods," he advised, "and don't forget my warning to wrap up well. It can be cold among those trees, out of the sun. Wear that warm tweed coat with the fur collar and little matching hat. Promise?"

His voice was full of the most tender concern, worthy of the most devoted husband. Perhaps that was why Red, about to speak, thought better of it and remained silent.

Dutifully I promised, and although I felt such coddling

to be unnecessary, I knew I would keep my promise, for I was in no mood to risk incurring my husband's censure. The situation between us was already strained enough.

I watched Red ride away and was sorry to see him go, for in an increasingly insecure world he seemed to represent stability. It was ironical that here at Abbotswood, surrounded with all the necessities of life as well as the luxuries, I should have a feeling of insecurity, but it was like a gathering cloud casting an ever-widening shadow. In retrospect, the footloose theatrical days of my life seemed safer than the present, which was equally ironical since the first attraction of Abbotswood, to my inexperienced mind, had been the wonderful security of it. Within these walls, I had believed, apprehension and uncertainty could never exist; a person would be cherished and protected, and fear of the future would be unknown. Yet now the future seemed wrapped around by doubt and a nameless dread, and there was I in the midst of it.

David was speaking, saying something about my looking peaky this morning and that I would be wise to get out in the fresh air as soon as possible. "Sure you won't come down to the park with me, my love? A pity. The sky is wonderfully clear and the weather dry, an ideal day for Conrad. Eagles hate to fly in the rain; their wings become too heavy when wet. They will seek cover and refuse to come to the lure for hours until dry again. Not even hunger will drive them out."

"Perhaps that's not surprising since they know they will gorge themselves eventually."

David laughed and agreed. He was all amiability to me now, and somehow I felt that this had not passed unnoticed by Red. Pride made me glad that we had presented a picture of marital harmony because I would have hated him to suspect that things were not right between us, thus recalling his earlier warning that Abbotswood and the people in it were not for me. Strange that both Red and my father should have warned me in the same way.

David went to his study to deal with the morning mail, and I upstairs to don outdoor clothes. The woods it would have to be, dislike them as I might. I could never overcome the sense of oppression they gave me—a claustrophobic, shut-in feeling which was nonsensical. Sometimes my imagination was too vivid. Anyone more sensible wouldn't allow a certain picture to enter her mind whenever she set foot in those woods, the picture of that earlier Bentine being clawed to death by his noble king eagle, but I could never shut it out. The place seemed haunted by the event, and since I had become acquainted with Conrad, the scene was even more vivid to me, for I had seen those great talons at work.

When I went downstairs, David was in the hall. He came over and kissed me. "I waited to make sure you had obeyed me," he said. "Knowing how forgetful you are, I wouldn't have been surprised to see you wearing the lightest of coats." He buttoned my fur collar high about my neck. "I must take great care of you, my darling. You are very precious to me."

Did all men vacillate between anger and tenderness, the way my husband did, leaving a woman bewildered and uncertain? My father had never done so. Temperamental outbursts in the theatre, frequent among actors, had been no more than passing episodes, accepted by everyone without concern. They could be prompted by jealousy, forgotten lines, delayed cues, misplaced props, wrong entrances and exits—the thousand-and-one backstage irritants which could upset a performance or a rehearsal and explode into scenes which ended as abruptly as they began, leaving neither rancour nor bewilderment. But David's moods were different because they were not only unpredictable but unfathomable, swinging from cruelty to sentiment, from coldness to passion within the space of minutes.

How long would his present mood last? I wondered as I walked up to the woods. I could anticipate his returning to the house, after a morning with Conrad, in a very good mood indeed, for I knew how stimulated he always was after flying the eagle, but if the bird did not perform well, if the killing didn't prove entertaining enough, his mood would be quite the reverse.

Before entering the woods, I looked back. At this point I was high above the park. There was no sign of my husband or of the eagle; the skies were empty of that giant wingspan. Perhaps David had not reached the oast-house yet, or the lure needed breaking into smaller hunks until Conrad himself captured something more substantial, or perhaps David had decided to carry him to a far distant point across the miles of parkland just in case those armed villagers did invade the area. I stood for a moment, looking down on Abbotswood's spreading acres, and thought how serene and lovely they were under the morning sun. But now I found myself regarding them dispassionately, not with any awe or envy or longing, as in the early days, but with almost critical detachment, as if viewing a splendid painting, admiring the work but not wanting to own it.

I turned away. Before me, the woods spread darkly, closely packed tree trunks reaching toward the sky, interlacing branches shutting out the sun. I had no wish to enter there. Perhaps it would be better to go back and join Harriet and Claudia, no matter how tedious Harriet's chatter might be or how chilling Claudia's reserve. Only impatience with myself urged me forward. It was about time I overcame this cowardice. If I admitted to David, later, that I had retreated, he would despise me and let me know as much. Then Harriet and Claudia would despise me, too. Claudia might hide it, but not Harriet.

In not wishing to face any of this, perhaps I was guilty of greater cowardice; I only knew that having resolved to take a good brisk walk, I should set about it. I would at least return to the house looking better for it and sufficiently refreshed to bear the atmosphere at lunch with greater equanimity—which meant that I would be able to bear David's unpredictability, too. I didn't trust this morning's mood. His tenderness had been assumed for Red Deakon's benefit, not mine. After his rejection last night that was obvious.

I refused to think about last night or the uneasy feeling it had left me with, the feeling that my husband was about to embark on some cat-and-mouse game in which I would surely be defeated. I could reject such imaginative nonsense on such a morning as this because alarms and fancies had no place in the sun.

But within the woods there was no sun at all. Shadow struck a chill into me, so that I stepped out briskly, stumbling a little over tree roots as I went, momentarily blinded by the darkness. After a while my eyes began to get adjusted, and I could see a rough track ahead, the very track along which David and I had walked on the day I arrived for the Thespians' performance. I had shivered then, and I shivered now. I also recalled how he had chivalrously led me back to the gardens and how, when there, he had imprisoned a butterfly in his closed palm, delighted by its desperate attempts to escape. I should have recognised that hint of cruelty as a betrayal of an unsuspected side to his character, but I had been too enamoured of him to see behind the mask.

I don't know how far I had walked, or for how long, when I first experienced the feeling that I was not alone, but I had reached the deep heart of the woods, where the shadows were at their darkest and the tall trees at their blackest. I halted, feeling that the sheer weight of silence was a cover for something deeply evil, and in that moment I also realised that something else was wrong about these woods and why I had never liked them. They contained no birdsong. Had those Bentine eagles made all wildlife extinct here, in their desperate quest for survival, or was it simply that there was no place here for anything so pure as the singing of birds?

But life of some kind breathed nearby. I could sense it, feel it, but not see or hear it. I felt a sickening iciness crawl up my spine and over my scalp, as if frozen fingers touched my skin and then ran through my hair, lifting it at the roots.

I had to get away from this place, away from this pit of darkness into sunlight, away from death into life, for this was a forest of the dead, and if I remained here, I would become one of them.

I tried to move and failed. My limbs were petrified, immobilised. Had the blood died in my veins, or had this unseen, threatening presence reached out and clutched every muscle, paralysing them?

A giant twig dropped from a branch. Then another. I saw them fall in front of my eyes, dark shapes against greater darkness. I was too conscious of the deepening blackness even to wonder what caused them to fall. Leaves, twigs, branches could drop easily enough before the wind. But there was no wind, and the trees stood motionless as a pall of deeper shadow spread relentlessly from above.

And then came the sound. Such a gentle sound. No more than a tinkle. The tinkle of a bell, tiny but crystal clear, bringing horror in its wake and a terrifying awareness that the darkening shadow from above was caused by the slow, relentless movement of wings endeavouring to find their way through a maze of branches.

Conrad was following me.

I was stumbling then, pushing frantically against undergrowth in an endeavour to find a hiding place, my frozen limbs moving as in a nightmare when one treads upon the same spot, getting nowhere. How could a numbed body move at all, how could breath force itself through lungs cramped by fear? I felt stark terror seize me, as it had seized me once before. But that had been in a different place, a different atmosphere; a stifling atmosphere, with smothering heat squeezing the life out of me just as this ice-cold fear was squeezing it now.

With a crash, the ground rose up and hit me. I tasted earth in my mouth and my cheek was seared by something hard, something sharp, but I was covered by overhanging bushes. I lay winded, my face against the ground, my hands pressing against the thing that had cut my cheek. A jagged tree root. I had tripped and fallen into a well-concealed hollow.

Although the overhanging bushes afforded protection, screening me from that predatory hunter, instinct urged me to lie still, to make neither sound nor movement even though the bird would only become entangled in this jungle growth should he attempt to reach me. Those talons could kill only when unhampered. But his nearness held menace, and I had no desire to tempt Providence.

It seemed a long time before the tinkling of Conrad's bell ceased. He had come to a halt somewhere. Then I heard something else—a sound of violent tearing accompanied by screeching rage. My head lifted, and my eyes looked through a tiny gap in the undergrowth to a clearing where the eagle had managed to land. He was within a yard of me, rending a furry creature apart with maniacal fury, the fury of frustration because the animal had neither flesh nor bones.

I knew then why my head felt cold. In my frantic dash for cover my fur hat had fallen off and acted as a lure.

Don't move. Don't breathe. Don't do anything to attract his attention. When beset by fury, anything could happen.

The bell was tinkling violently now, shaken by the eagle's rage. Surely David was out looking for him, surely he must hear? The bell was attached to the bird's leg for that very purpose, to help trace him should he get lost. How far had the creature flown thus to escape his master's vigilant eye? I could imagine David scanning the sky for him, away on the other side of the park. He must be over there, he *had* to be over there for the noble killer to be free like this, in an area which David took care to keep him away from.

But somehow Conrad had flown in here, and somehow he had to escape, as I had. I saw him rise, then heard him screech as he struck an overhanging branch and fell to earth again. I saw his great talons seize my fragmented fur cap and rend it in a further frenzy of rage as I lay praying for survival in this dark and bitter place.

Then a miracle happened. He rose perpendicularly, as I had once seen him rise before, straight up from that open space, colliding with nothing this time. That meant there was a gap up there, sufficiently wide for him to escape. I had only to wait until his shadow finally departed, and then I could drag myself out of this merciful spot and seek a way out of these sinister woods.

The shadow vanished, the tinkling bell was no more, but I had lain rigid for so long that I could not pull myself up. I seized the tree root with shaking hands and pressed hard against it, pushing my body into a sitting position. Every cracking twig beneath me sounded like a pistol shot, signalling my presence to any listening ear. And the silence still seemed to be listening; the unseen presence still seemed to be near, waiting for me to emerge so that it could pounce and kill.

Coldness had robbed my hands and feet of a great deal of sensation, and my uncovered head was numb. I felt that if I did not move soon, the numbness would spread to my face and down through the whole of my body, and then I would reach the coldness of death, and there would be no fear left in me, no sensation whatsoever. It would not matter then if my husband's carnivorous bird returned and found me.

But it mattered right at this moment. Alone and terrified as I was, the human instinct to cling to life still surged in me. Before all sensation froze in my legs, I had to force myself to rise, and somehow I managed to,

The Eagle at the Gate

clutching at undergrowth which was too weak to support me. I heard branches snap at my touch, though I could scarcely feel them, but my face was not wholly numb because I could still feel the pain inflicted by the jabbing tree root. And mire besides. Knife-sharp brambles scratched my cheeks and forehead as I pushed my way out; I felt blood on my lips, but I did not care, because the scratches and the blood had not been caused by an eagle's dreadful talons. I was safe from those now, thank God.

Unsteadily, I took a few paces, then halted. Which way, *which way?* The woods spread on all sides with deceptive little paths leading nowhere. I forced my legs to move more quickly, but they lacked direction, and soon I found myself staring down at fragments of fur. I had gone full circle and was back on the very spot where Conrad had tried to devour my cap, the spot from which he had risen perpendicularly and not returned.

I lifted my head then and saw a patch of sky. Which way was the sun moving? If I knew, I could find my way home, for the house lay south of the woods, but it was impossible to tell in this dark labyrinth. "The sun rises in the east and sets in the west. . . ." The childish lesson forced itself into my brain. At noon it would be directly overhead. So it couldn't be noon, for the space above was not lit directly from on high. Nor could I tell from which direction the light did actually come, whether the sun was approaching its zenith or had passed it.

Walk, then. Straight ahead. You are bound to come out *some*where.

The retreat of Conrad left me calmer. He must be already soaring out there above the network of branches which reminded me all too forcibly of other entwining plant life. If I could survive that burning hell, I could certainly survive this dark and chilling one. I folded my arms about my body, took a deep breath—and froze.

A branch had snapped beneath a footfall, and it was not mine, for I had not even moved. But someone else had.

Or *some thing*.

Silence. All I could hear was my thudding heart, threatening to burst my eardrums. I took a tentative step forward, then another, and another. The earth crushed softly beneath my tread; I was stepping slowly, carefully, withholding my weight.

Crack. The sound reverberated through the silent woods. Then another branch snapped, louder this time, heavier, nearer. Panic hit me. I yelled, *"Who is there? Whoever you are, come out!"*

Come out, come out, come out . . . the words bounced from tree trunk to tree trunk, laughing back at me. Then silence again.

Now I was shaking all over, and the dreadful coldness was clutching again. I forced myself to take a staggering step forward, then another and another, just as before. To my surprise my feet gathered momentum until I was actually running, reeling through the trees in an ever-bewildering path, getting nowhere, hearing the echo of my footfalls behind me—except that they were heavier and, instead of being panic-stricken like my own, they were relentless.

I stopped dead, whirled round, and shouted my challenge again. "Show yourself, whoever you are! *Show yourself!*"

I should have known that no one would because, of course, no one was there. I was alone in these woods; they were as empty as when I had entered. I sagged onto a fallen tree trunk and took deep, steadying breaths. Don't let panic take over. There's nothing in the world to be frightened of. The eagle has gone, and you are safe, safe, *safe*. Remember that. Now get to your feet and press on.

My legs moved, lifting my body. I walked forward (don't hurry, don't try to run this time!), and I made no attempt to muffle my tread because, of course, there was no one around to hear, no one following me, no tinkling bell to herald a killer. And no heavier footfall either, so I had to stop imagining things.

I knew I was lost, but to admit it meant defeat, so I walked on, my legs growing stronger as circulation increased, but dear God, it was cold in these woods. I said aloud, to give myself Dutch courage, "I promise that if I ever do find my way out, I will never come back here again. That I *do* promise! I will stay at home even if I have to arrange flowers with Harriet and listen to her prattle forever!" As for David. . . .

But I wouldn't think about David. He was up to something. He was playing a waiting game. He had told me so last night. *"In my time, not yours. . . ."* Threat or promise? Both, of course. Oh, dear God, get me out of here!

And then I saw it—a break in the trees. Sunlight. Open sky. I was running toward it, sobbing. I had reached the edge of the woods and beyond lay open country. As I emerged, I could see the village far below. I had come out in the gardens of Abbotswood, but in the opposite direction. No matter—I was out of that terrifying labyrinth, out of darkness, out of danger.

The sun was warm on my face—and then suddenly cold as renewed shadow spread over me. I was standing on an outcrop of rock covered in scrub. I could see the whole world below, and the whole world could see me. I lifted my face and saw that vast wingspan again, hovering against the sky in the way it always hovered before the wings half closed for that silent, lightning plunge. The eagle was directly over me, as if it had been waiting for me to emerge. My hand darted to my throat, choking back fear—and touched the fur collar of my coat.

"The talons go right through—killing instantly."

No time to fling the garment aside, no time to grapple with endless buttons. I leapt from the rocky outcrop and rolled beneath its projecting overhang, aware that the dread moment had come. That strong and supple body could dive into my hiding place with ease, crash landing on target.

The crash came. I heard it blast in my ears. The world reeled, then slowly steadied. I looked up and saw Red Deakon silhouetted against the sky, a smoking gun in his hands, and from somewhere a voice was screaming, *"You killed him! Damn you to hell, you killed him!"*

FIFTEEN

Much later, after Red had picked me up and seated me on his horse and taken me back to Abbotswood, I recalled his voice rapping back in anger, "Which life do you value most—that eagle's or your wife's?" and David didn't even hear. He was kneeling beside the dead bird, weeping, with neither a thought nor a glance for me.

I remember Red mounting behind me and my body leaning against his as he turned the horse's head and rode away. Neither of us spoke. We rode in silence the whole way home, and when he lifted me down and set me on my feet, he softly touched my cheek. Incredible that a hand which could bend iron to its will could be so gentle. . . .

"You're hurt. Your face is bleeding."

I tried to speak, and failed, because this was not the moment to ask how he came to be at that particular spot at that particular time. In that far-off glimpse I had had of the village, I had seen his team of men gathered in the distance, as if their task had been accomplished and now they were grouped together, talking about it. But as I turned away, one question demanded utterance.

"Did you see him earlier? Conrad, I mean."

Red nodded. "I had scarcely got back to the village after leaving Abbotswood before I saw the creature on the wing, but not anywhere near the park. Up there, near the woods, where I knew you had gone."

No need to say more. No need to ask if he remembered my husband insisting that I should wrap up well, wearing the fur-trimmed coat. Such thoughts were better silenced.

I dare not believe that David had deliberately sent Conrad after me, that he had suggested a walk in the woods for that purpose, that he had made me wear that fur-trimmed coat and cap, that he had taken the eagle there and released him, that before I emerged from the undergrowth, he had recaptured him and then, with the bird perched on his leather gauntlet, hooded and silent, had stalked me through the woods until I came out into the open and stood exposed to the sky, that he had then set Conrad free again, knowing I would be an inescapable target with my throat wrapped in fur.

None of this dare I believe, for I had no proof. Nor did there seem to be any motive for wanting me dead. A man did not need to murder his wife just because she thwarted him or because he was tired of her, or because he took a sadistic pleasure in taunting her. Remove her, and he would be cheated of that pleasure, though a sadist could always find another source for it. But whom else at Abbotswood could he mentally torture but his wife? Claudia would protect Harriet always, and as for Claudia herself, despite his claim to be master here, it was she who actually held the reins, so he would be careful never to antagonise her.

As I bathed, dressed, and repaired the signs of my frantic moments in the woods, I knew I had to steel myself for my next meeting with David, but when it actually happened, I found that wasn't necessary after all. He walked into our bedroom like a defeated man and dropped into a wing chair beside the fire. His face was white and drawn, and he stared unseeingly before him, saying nothing.

I watched him in the mirror as I finished coiling my hair, and when he still remained silent, still stared into space, I went into our sitting room and rang for Truman. The man came promptly, and I ordered a brandy without delay. When it came, I took it into the bedroom and found my husband sitting exactly as I had left him.

A solicitous wife would have tried to comfort him, but I did not. I merely held out the glass, saying, "You'd better drink this," and he took it mechanically. I went back to my dressing table and finished my toilet. I had the extraordinary feeling that I was mistress of the situation, that I could call the tune, that I could even accuse—if I had enough evidence to back my suspicions. But I had none. An unseen presence in the woods? Heavy footsteps echoing my own? I had been near hysteria, and hysteria plays tricks with imagination.

The brandy restored colour into the ashen face, and

when he had drained the glass, he looked directly at me for the first time.

"What the devil made you stand on that prominent point? I told you to keep to the woods."

"I couldn't stay in them all day."

"You could have returned home. Why walk into open country like that?"

"I lost my way."

"Or did you want to see the fox caught? Did you want to see Red Deakon wield that gun? Did you know he would be on that slope and go there deliberately?"

I threw him a contemptuous glance. "You are beside yourself."

"Of course, I am beside myself! Conrad was killed because of you."

"Because of *you*," I corrected. "Because you set him free up there—"

"I had lost him. I was searching for him. On a day like this an eagle will fly far—that is the fear of all handlers, that in ideal weather conditions they may lose their most precious birds."

"Then you should have waited to fly him on a less favourable day."

I walked to the door, but in a flash he was ahead of me.

"You seem very sure of yourself—but don't be."

I pushed past him, and he grabbed my wrist, his fingers closing hard over it. His face came close to mine.

"You will be punished for this," he whispered.

"You seem obsessed with the idea of punishment. You enjoy torture, don't you, so long as you can be the one to inflict it, whether on small and helpless creatures or on your wife? But mark this, David. You cannot break me. I don't know why you want to or what it would avail you, but I shall never be cowed. Never."

"You will be tamed as an eagle can be tamed. You will obey my will, as he obeyed."

"As he did today, marking me for the kill?"

He flung my wrist aside. "You are out of your mind. The fact that he was flying free up there was none of my doing, but it was *your* doing that he met his death, and for that I shall never forgive you. If you had not come into the open—"

"—wearing that fur-trimmed coat you ordered me to wear?"

He stared, aghast. "What are you implying? What strange fancy has seized you now? I know you are not responsible for that ridiculous imagination of yours, but be careful what you say, or I will have to take steps to repress you. You knew perfectly well that to expose yourself to an eagle's gaze, wearing fur around the throat, was asking for trouble, and I can only think you did so because you knew Red would kill him instantly, being the crack shot he is. You did know the man was to be there and that was why you came out of the woods at that point. You hated Conrad. You were jealous of him—"

"Jealous!" I laughed aloud. "If you say 'terrified,' you will be nearer the truth."

"Jealousy or fear, for either reason you made sure of his death. But you will be sorry. Oh, yes, you will be very sorry indeed. But I can bide my time...."

It was then that the cat-and-mouse game really began and, as far as my husband was concerned, it was a game played by an expert, with infinite variations. A game of advance and retreat, of teasing and torment. One day he would be smiling and tender, the next cold and withdrawn. I never knew from one moment to another what kind of mood he would be in or how he would react to anything I said or did. I never knew when he would come upon me unawares, when seek me out, when avoid me. I felt his watchful eyes even when he was not present. I also suspected Harriet of watching me on his behalf, ready to report back to him everything I said or did.

Claudia also watched. Her calm, inscrutable face revealed nothing, but missed nothing either. As she sat quietly sewing, her glance would slide above her needlework, her eyelids scarcely lifting, but everything within her span would be observed. And it was usually I who came within her range of vision, for Harriet was adept at sitting behind her cousin, out of view, so that to speak to her or to look at her, Claudia had to turn deliberately because not even she had eyes in the back of her head.

Three people watching me, three pairs of eyes never leaving me. Only at night did I really feel I was not being spied on, and even then I could sometimes feel a watchfulness in the very walls.

David continued to sleep in another room, but he also continued to use his dressing room and to come into my bedroom whenever he felt so inclined. He would sprawl in an armchair beside the fire, elegant in a long brocade robe with his nightwear beneath, drinking brandy, talking desultorily, waiting for me to undress and then watching me with his sensual mouth going slack and his eyes becoming heavy, and then, when I was in bed, he would still sit there, slowly revolving the balloon glass in his hand and staring at me above it, and I would lie there waiting for him either to come to me and do whatever he willed, or to go away.

The strange thing was that he always went away. Even when he came and lay on the bed beside me—always on top of the covers, never beneath them—and rolled his body over onto mine and opened his mouth and covered my own with it and stayed there for a long time, never removing that devouring mouth, until sometimes I wondered if this were another attempt at suffocation, some way of crushing the life out of me which gave him sensual enjoyment. But I learned that I had only to endure it and wait for him to leave me. Sometimes he would do so abruptly, but often he did so lingeringly, rolling his body away from me and lying very still on top of the covers again, and then, when I wondered if he slept at last and the tension in me slowly unwound and sleep became something I knew I could no longer hold at bay, I would feel the weight of him upon me again and the searching mouth and the hard teeth bruising my lips, and I dared not moan, dared not cry out because I knew that this was some kind of endurance test and that if I held out long enough, I could win this move in the game.

Other nights he would not come near me. I would hear him in his dressing room, and I would wait, tense and on edge, ready to force myself into some semblance of ease and indifference should the door open to admit him, and then breathing a sigh of relief when I heard him leave. He would do this for one night, two nights, for as many nights as he wished. *(In my own good time, sweet Aphra. In my time, not yours.)* And on other occasions I would awaken in the night and see his dark shape, standing above me as he looked down on me. "You cried out," he would say. "You were having a nightmare, just as Harriet used to have. . . ." But I knew full well that I had experienced no nightmare at all and that the fear had come to me after waking, not before.

The days and weeks ticked by in unremitting tension until I felt that my control would snap and that when it did, I would go crawling to him, begging to be released from this strange kind of torture. Only the knowledge that nothing would give him greater satisfaction forced me to maintain a tight grip on myself. I knew the sort of reception I would get if I broke down. *"Torture,* sweet Aphra? What kind of torture? Who is torturing you and in what way? What are you imagining now in that unbalanced mind of yours? Locked doors, suffocation, people wanting your death, although no one could remotely gain by it . . . and now *torture* when not a single hand has been raised against you? Come, my dear, you are sick . . . mentally sick . . . perhaps I should seek help for you . . . there are all kinds of new treatments being tried nowadays. . . ."

No! Never would I let him do that to me! Two could play this diabolical game, and my part in it was to wait and endure, because surely it could not go on forever, and if it did, surely there must be some means of escape, even for someone so penniless as I? I began to think wildly of running away. Not dramatically, not fleeing in the night only to be found wandering and brought back to a long-suffering husband who had immediately sent out search parties for me, because nothing could testify more than that to an unbalanced state of mind, but quietly, with everything well thought out, well planned.

I even wrote to George Mayfield, telling him that I missed the old life and the smell of greasepaint and longed to be behind the footlights again, but taking care not to suggest that this was anything more than a sort of homesickness, because pride prevented me from admitting that my marriage was a mistake, my wonderful romantic marriage about which I had been so ecstatic in the early days, days not so long ago when I counted the months back. And to make sure that the letter was not intercepted —suspicion, I found, grew in the mind as rapidly as some poisonous weed—I watched for the postman cycling up from the village to collect the Abbotswood letters which Truman always handed to him with great formality, opening the ancient leather mailbag in the hall and presenting the contents to the man after checking that all bore the one penny stamp. Then I hid halfway down the long drive, and after the postman cycled past on the return journey, I ran out, calling after him. "I was late with this! I am sorry to hinder you, Mr. Barlow. . . ." I knew he liked to be called "Mr." Barlow. Few people were so courteous to a village postman.

After that there was the anxiety of waiting for a reply and the even greater anxiety of trying to collect it without anyone's seeing it first because the formality of receiving letters at Abbotswood equalled their despatch. Barlow would deliver them personally to Truman, who would then place them on a silver salver and put them on my husband's desk in his study; so well had David established himself as master of Abbotswood that all correspondence, even that of the mistress of the house, was automatically delivered to him. But that procedure applied only to the morning mail. Midday, afternoon, and evening deliveries were more difficult to intercept, because all too often David was present. Truman would then carry the silver salver to him and present the letters personally.

Should any reply from George Mayfield come by any of those three deliveries, my only hope of interception lay in David's being in his office or laboratory or out on the estate at the time. Sometimes this happened, but not always.

But most of all, I prayed a reply would not come by the morning delivery on Sunday, the only delivery of the day, because that always arrived when we were at breakfast and any hope of interception then was out of the question.

Never had I realized how difficult life could be made by the well-organized routine of a well-organized household, and sadly for me, George's reply came by the six o'clock evening delivery one Saturday. Truman came into the room bearing the familiar salver, and we were all there, as usual, before dinner, presenting the usual picture of family harmony.

David picked up the letters, riffling through them in his pernickety way, but halting at the sight of bright blue notepaper, so totally unlike the quality notepaper used by people of his acquaintance, and I guessed at once who the writer was. The touch of flamboyancy coupled with cheapness of paper spoke for itself. It was typically theatrical. Elizabeth Lorrimer even used scented stuff, bright pink in colour.

I saw Claudia eyeing the letters too, and I think it was then that I recalled seeing her do this before. Once I had entered the study and found her with the morning mail in her hand; she had dropped the letters back onto David's desk at once, as if caught in some guilty act. I remembered thinking how strange it was that the mistress of the house should appear to be furtively examining the mail, when surely by rights, and in the absence of a husband, it should be hers to examine. But the incident had been banished by my own anxiety.

Now David put aside all letters but that bright blue one. He slit the envelope with a paper knife—never would those white fingers tear an envelope apart; every action had to be exact and precise. He took out a single sheet of paper, frowned when he saw that it was folded the wrong way, and read the brief message it bore. I could tell it was brief because it occupied only a single side, but apparently the contents required a second reading, or perhaps even a third because it was a long time before he replaced it in the envelope and put it in an inner pocket.

He picked up his wineglass then, and smiled very very sweetly.

"You look lovely tonight, Aphra. Very elegant. Do you not agree, Claudia? Harriet?"

Claudia smiled. "She always looks elegant. You have a very lovely wife."

"Indeed, yes. I am a fortunate man."

The right words uttered in the wrong tone, but if Claudia noticed, she gave no indication. Harriet had not even bothered to answer him. She had made an elaborate toilet tonight, with lots of trailing chiffon and artificial flowers entwined in her bird's-nest frizz, bracelets and necklaces jangling as she moved, and in order to attract attention, she was drifting about the room in a way which suggested more than a desire to show off her fluttering draperies. I sensed an undercurrent of restlessness in her movements, a kind of keyed-up condition which I had detected a lot recently, a sort of suppressed waiting which she was finding hard to bear. But one accepted Harriet's moods as one accepted a child's, knowing them to be unpredictable and ready to swing one way and then another without warning.

Like David's, I thought suddenly. Exactly like David's.

"My dear Harriet," he said now, impatiently, "do sit still. Must you pace the floor like that? You are forever on the go. I saw you only this afternoon, striding toward the park as if you were going on a route march. Where were you heading with so determined a step?"

"A walk. Why shouldn't I go for a walk? Aphra goes for lots of them. She takes long long walks all by herself. Did you know that?"

"And why shouldn't she?" Claudia asked unexpectedly. "Walking is very good exercise. I see no reason why Aphra should not walk as often as she wishes and go as far as she desires."

I was grateful for that. Long walks had become essential to me. They provided me with solitude, freed me from the constant feeling of supervision, and helped me physically because I found them both relaxing and stimulating—so long as I kept away from the woods. With fresh air and brisk movement, tension evaporated and I would return to Abbotswood ready for the next phase of the charade.

As a result of these long walks, I had begun to know the countryside well, for I wandered much farther than the park and grounds. I knew every country road, every twisting lane; I could plan a different route every day. The people in the village had become accustomed to the sight of me, walking hatless and without gloves, and now did not regard it askance. They even greeted me, the men pulling their forelocks and the women curtseying. There would be nods and shy smiles. I was becoming less and less of a stranger. I was being accepted, not because I belonged "up at the house," but because I was now a familiar face and one that did not ride by in state.

Once I had met Meg Deakon coming out of the village store, and her warm smile cheered me. I liked the woman and paused for a chat. Since the eagle's death I had not seen Red, though David's insistence that the man should never be admitted to Abbotswood again had been firmly overruled by Claudia, who, rather to my surprise, had pointed out that he owed Red a debt of gratitude for saving my life. To that David had made no reply, but Red had continued to supervise the balcony replacements without interference. Even so, we never met. I knew that soon the job would be done and the stonemasons working with his men would also be finished. After that perhaps Red would keep away from his own choice, or if he visited here, it would be only on Claudia's invitation.

The thought left a bleak spot in my mind. In the ever-increasing confusion of my life he represented logic and sanity and safety, and something more deeply emotional which I could not analyse.

During my chance meeting with Meg that day, I had learnt that her cousin had gone away, but that she was expecting him back the day after tomorrow. That was today. I found myself wondering if he had returned yet.

David's voice cut into my thoughts. He was still talking to Harriet. "And while we are on the subject of your aimless wanderings, I must insist that you take care not to associate with people from the village other than those approved of by myself and Claudia."

"What do you mean?"

Harriet paused in the midst of her pacing and looked at David apprehensively. That she imagined herself to be in love with him, I knew, but that she feared his disapproval so much surprised me. I had not known her to be the target for it since the day she stole those rare flowers to decorate Claudia's hat.

"I mean that later on I saw you talking to a man—one of Deakon's workers, I believe. I was cutting across from the factor's house and saw you close to the park wall, away from the lodge, talking to him. Behaviour of that kind is most undesirable, although I realise you acted in all innocence. I suppose the man accosted you, though what he was doing on Abbotswood lands I cannot imagine. Anyone on official business has to present himself at the lodge first, even tradesmen delivering goods. Who was he, and why was he there?"

"I—I have no idea! He was lost, he said. He had wandered in by mistake."

"By mistake? Through a side entrance by *mistake*? Notices forbidding trespassers are clearly displayed."

"He—he could not read! I pointed the notice out to

The Eagle at the Gate

him, but he had no idea what it said. So I told him to be off, and he went, and that was the last I saw of him." She ruffled defensively. "I do know how to treat the lower orders."

Lower orders. A person of lesser rank who had dared to penetrate our sacred boundaries. I must have betrayed my reaction because my husband said, "Dear Aphra considers us to be snobbish, do you not, my love? But I doubt if even Red Deakon would approve of his workers trespassing, and somehow, Harriet, I felt the man was not there by accident."

The bizarre head tossed. "I daresay not, I daresay he was bent on poaching, but I could hardly accuse him of that without proof, could I?"

She was more ingenious with her excuses than I could ever be, but I did wonder why it was necessary to make them.

"I am not scolding you, Harriet. I just want you to be careful. All sorts of horrible things can happen to a woman when walking alone."

"They never happen to Aphra. At least, not that she ever tells us."

"Ah, yes, Aphra—I will come to her later. All I want to know from you, Harriet dear, is that man's name."

"How could I possibly know?"

"All villagers are known to us."

"In that case, you have no need to ask, have you? You must have recognised him."

David laughed. "My dear cousin, you have a quicker wit than I suspected. Sharp as the proverbial needle, aren't you?" When she preened, well pleased, he added, "But do not be too sharp, cousin, or you might regret it. I believe that man's name to be Jenkins. Am I right? Did he introduce himself, or was it not necessary?"

"David, stop needling Harriet."

Claudia's voice was quiet, but firm. To my surprise, David made no answer. He turned to me instead.

"And now to you, my dear wife. So you are still taking long walks, are you? Alone? Always alone?"

"Always."

"I am surprised—and concerned, of course. Quite apart from the fact that I consider it unwise, you should set a better example. How can we expect dear Harriet not to wander off by herself if you persist in doing so?"

"She is no more likely to come to harm than I am."

"You would, of course, tell me if you ever had a companion on your walks? You would not hide anything from me, would you? Nothing of any kind, I mean."

"I cannot remember to tell you everything, any more than you, I am sure, tell me."

That was a mistake. I saw his frown, which said so plainly that he had a right to keep to himself anything he wished, but I had not.

"Above all, my dear wife, you would not hide letters from me or indulge in secret correspondence?"

Claudia said blandly, "Aphra has little or no correspondence, David, as I am sure you are very well aware. And now, let us change the subject, shall we?"

It was unusual for Claudia to come to my rescue, but this was the second time she had done so this evening. She had also put a stop to his tormenting of Harriet. Since David could do no wrong in her eyes, I was astonished.

He answered equably, "By all means," and immediately began to talk about the farm, and how much the harvest had yielded, and what crops were planned for the coming year. I let the conversation flow over my head, but I was aware of Harriet wandering aimlessly about the room, spinning on her toes every now and then to make her skirts whirl about her ankles, very delighted with the effect. Suddenly she took a few runs and skips, as if breaking into a dance.

"Look at me, look at me! Did you ever move as gracefully as this on the stage, Aphra? I am quite sure you did not, though I thought you were really quite good as Ariel that night you performed here. Do you remember that night, Claudia—you too, David?"

"Indeed, I do. My wife spoke her lines so feelingly, especially those about the 'fever of the mad' and—and—how does it go on, my love? Can you remember?"

"Of course. *'Not a soul/but felt a fever of the mad and play'd/Some tricks of desperation.'*"

"Precisely," he murmured. "And that was what you did, was it not, when you caused such havoc in my hothouse, and again when you were responsible for the death of a noble eagle? You must indeed have been mad to play such desperate tricks."

Claudia said abruptly, "Those things are over and forgotten, David. I beg you not to refer to them again."

"I will certainly promise not to refer to them, sister, but you cannot expect me to forget."

"Then at least give Aphra the opportunity to." She rose and crossed to the fireplace, tugging impatiently at the bell rope and saying, "Surely dinner is late? Surely it should have been announced by now?"

"You seem on edge, Claudia. Has something upset you, is something worrying you? Dinner is not due for another quarter of an hour. If you wanted it earlier, you should have ordered it earlier."

Eventually, I thought, this evening would come to an end. It could not drag on forever like this; I even suspected that Claudia felt the tension as much as I, but not for the same reason, for only I was likely to be the target for greater punishment than my husband's needling or barbed innuendo, because only I had received a letter, the contents of which I had yet to learn but which were obviously damning. Claudia had not written secretly to anyone, and the worst Harriet had done was to talk to a would-be poacher in the park. But I had appealed, behind my husband's back, for rescue. I had written to George Mayfield openly hinting that I wanted to return to the company, and I had done so because that was the only hope I had of getting away from a situation which had become intolerable. What had he said in reply? Would I ever know? Would David ever show me that letter?

Whatever he chose to do, I was certain of one thing: I would suffer for it.

Throughout that interminable evening I waited, through dinner, through two long hours in the drawing room afterwards, with Harriet singing and accompanying herself on the piano, heartily applauded by David and listened to with patient indulgence by Claudia, and through yet another hour when we lingered over tea, which Claudia always ordered before going to bed. The fact that David chose to partake of it tonight confirmed my worst fears that he intended to prolong the agony of waiting and that he knew I was waiting, fully aware of that letter in his inner pocket and his displeasure over it and dreading what was to come. He was enjoying the situation hugely.

I found myself trying to guess the form my punishment would take. Another session in the bedroom, being regarded in silence with an undercurrent of threat in his eyes, or another half hour of taunting comment as he watched me undress? "Would you enjoy it if I made love to you tonight, sweet Aphra, or would you shrink from me? You shrink from me a lot lately—I wonder why. After all, I make no demands on you now, no physical demands at all. Does it worry you, does it make you wonder if I have ceased to want you, and why? Well, my love, you must just go on guessing and wondering and waiting. I told you—in *my* time, not yours; when *I* will it, not you. When precisely I choose to put an end to our present relationship, or lack of it, will come as a surprise to you. And my God, you will be ready for me then, because you need loving, don't you, sweet Aphra? You enjoy it. You are warmblooded and passionate, but it will do you no harm to go on waiting—there, there, let me touch you, just so that you will remember what it is like. *That* makes you want me, doesn't it? But no, you must wait to be loved again. . . ."

Sadist. Torturer. A man who could charm and entice and seduce—and turn away, smiling.

I put aside my teacup. "I am going to bed," I announced, and without another word I went upstairs. I was willing to endure no more of that unbearable evening. I walked out of the drawing room without bothering to say good-night.

My bedroom door had no key. Many times lately I had thought of asking Truman to have one made, but pride prevented me, and since it would also have necessitated asking for one for the door of my husband's dressing room, and only he could order that, a key to the bedroom door would have been useless anyway.

I prepared for bed, put on a robe, poked up the fire, and sat beside it waiting. Somehow I knew that whatever was going to happen would happen tonight. When I heard his footsteps approaching, I picked up a book, pretending to read, and I did not glance up when he entered.

He closed the door quietly, came across, and took the book away from me.

"Now," he said briskly, "I suppose you want to know what George Mayfield's letter said."

"Naturally. And since it must have been addressed to me, I am entitled to receive it. Never at any time have I opened any letter addressed to you."

"I should hope not indeed. A wife has no right to open her husband's letters."

"But a husband may open a wife's?"

"Of course. However, in this instance I am prepared to let you hear the contents."

I held out my hand. "I will read it. The letter is mine."

He ignored that, and the paper rustled sharply as he unfolded it. "It is couched in the most affectionate terms. He addresses you as 'darling.'"

"That is a theatrical endearment and means nothing. 'Dears' and 'darlings' are bandied about quite freely."

"How vulgar. However, I will let that pass. For a letter which opens so fondly it is surprisingly brief."

He read it aloud.

"'Aphra, darling, surely you cannot be serious? Hankering to return to the stage when you have all *that*—a fine house and servants and everything else? Don't be silly, dear. Just remember all the pinching and scraping and those shabby theatrical digs and count your blessings. Anyway, darling, I haven't a vacancy. I hired another leading juvenile when you stepped into high society and she came for ten bob a week *less*. Of course, she isn't so talented as you, but given time and my brilliant tutorage, she will be. Your fellow Thespians salute you and love you as always, grand lady though you now be. . . .'"

I laughed spontaneously.

"You find it amusing?"

"I find it very characteristic."

Slowly he tore the letter into shreds. He was unsmiling. His features seemed to have tightened; his mouth, also. It was no longer the beautifully sculptured feature which had appealed to me so much. It was thin and white and vicious.

"So you planned to run away," he said, and his voice was no more than a whisper in the quiet room.

"Yes. If the Thespians would have me back."

I expected the storm to break then. Instead, the room remained absolutely quiet as, very leisurely, he began to undress, but all the time his eyes were upon me. I wanted to walk to the door and open it and leave that room forever, but knew it would be useless. He would seize me before I even reached it.

He seized me when he was ready. He lifted me up and carried me across the room. He said with ice-cold softness, "Do you remember once saying that you were glad you pleased me in bed? And do you remember my reply—that you still had many things to learn, and I many things to teach? Well, my love, I am going to teach you now. I will teach you all the ways in which I expect you to please me for the rest of our married life, and when I have finished, you will never dare defy me in any way again."

I have no idea how long the time lasted. I have no idea which was the darkness of night and which the darkness of my senses. I can only remember the things he did, the practices he forced on me. I was dragged into a world of sensuality at its most brutish, an onslaught from which there was no escape. Consciousness receded and became a whirlpool in which my mind was stunned and my body trapped. I was a thing racked and abused, and through the timeless moments, never-ending, never-ceasing, his voice gasped hoarsely, over and over again, *"I have waited for this, waited for this . . . it is better . . . better . . . better for the waiting. . . ."*

Sensuality built up into cruelty the like of which I had never dreamt. Nor did I know that cruelty could be so insatiable, but I learned it now. Violence bore down on me, dragging me into a seemingly bottomless pit from which only death could rescue me. And it was coming. At the peak of what must surely be the final degradation I felt his hands close about my throat, and his body, lying hard on top of me, half raised as he bore down. Behind that grasp was all his strength. In a frenzy of terror I clawed at his fingers and felt my voice straining in my throat as I gasped, *"If you kill me now, everyone will know you did it!"*

It could have been no more than a desperate whisper, though it sounded loud in my ears, but for a fraction of a second those clutching fingers loosened, and I pushed hard against his half-raised body and rolled slackly off the bed.

I heard him slump. I heard his breathing, heavy with

exhaustion, and I staggered to my feet, lurching across the room and through the door. The corridor outside was cold, but I was glad of it after the dreadful heat of that bed. It struck against my senses, rallying me into flight, and I ran, stumbling over the carpeted floor, through doors and along corridors, my bare feet silent in the night. I ran blindly, driven by only one thought—to escape from a man possessed, a man crazed with lust, a man bent on murder.

The walls of Abbotswood watched indifferently, and suddenly I hated them. They were prison walls housing monsters. I would escape somehow, anyhow, but for the present all I wanted was a hiding place, somewhere in which to recover, to rest my aching body and ease my terror. And suddenly I saw a pale glimmer of light through an uncurtained landing window and realised I was no longer in the family part of the house, but in that isolated east wing which was opened up only for visitors. That was why the curtains had not been drawn and why a feeling of total emptiness surrounded me.

I leaned against a door, trying to focus my vision which was blurred by pain and shock. There was a familiarity about the door; my fingers covered the chased gilt knob as if they had done so before—which indeed they had, for it opened into the room I had first occupied here at Abbotswood.

I stood swaying on the threshold. Pale fingers of dawn groped across the shadowy room, outlining hunched shapes which I recognised as furniture shrouded in Holland covers. There was the bed I had slept in, and there the door communicating with my father's room. I opened that, too, and went inside. More shrouded furniture, more Holland covers, and the bed in which he had spent a reluctant night. He had been fatigued, unwell, and for my sake and others he had come here, not for his own. He had had a feeling about Abbotswood, a conviction that it was unwise to come and wiser still to get away. And he had been right, my poor dear father, strained and anxious for reasons I had been unable to comprehend, and still could not.

I pulled back the Holland covers from his bed. It was unmade, so I collected others from chairs and from the dressing table on which he had dropped his bunch of keys and at which he had drunk the wine so thoughtfully provided by David Hillyard. The keys had been there; my stunned mind thrust the memory at me. Oh, yes, they had definitely been there when David had come along to see that my father had all he wanted.

It was strange that at such a time as this so small a thing should come to mind, printed indelibly and without a shadow of doubt. But of course, it was later, wasn't it, that David had picked them up from the floor, where, he claimed, they had fallen? Or had they? Was that a lie? Another lie? Another inexplicable lie which was somehow tied up with his motive for bringing us here and his motive for wanting to kill me.

Barney's words echoed in my memory. *"Planned it all down to the last detail. Just like a campaign. . . ."*

But what sort of campaign and what lay behind it? What kind of campaign could be so totally meaningless?

Stop thinking. Rest here. Check that there are keys to both doors, though you must be safe enough now. That exhausted man back in the west wing would be sleeping, and if he were not, he would surely have no strength left for further attack, and perhaps my terrified warning had registered, in which case he would wait for another opportunity to kill me, for a fourth attempt more carefully planned and which could be associated in no way with himself. Not in a hothouse or even out in the open spaces where, should he acquire another bird of prey, he could launch it to kill. It would have to be somewhere well away from Abbotswood and executed by some totally different means, so that no finger of suspicion could point to him.

But I would give him no time even to plan it. Tomorrow I would walk out of this accursed place and out of his life.

How I was to do it, where I would go, suddenly seemed immaterial. The small amount of money my father had left to me was in the bank, and to get to the bank, I would need ready cash, of which I was always kept short. I had no need of pounds, shillings, and pence at Abbotswood, where everything was paid for and my every need supplied. I found myself thinking of ways and means as I dragged myself across to the ornate bathroom which I had so admired all those months ago. From far away in this deserted wing no one would hear the rush of water except perhaps tired servants in their attic bedrooms close to the water tanks, and they would be so accustomed to the hiss of pipes that they would take no notice.

There were no towels; my torn nightgown, ripped beyond repair, would have to suffice. The important thing was to be clean, clean, *clean* again. I found a half-used tablet of soap and was grateful to the careless maid who had overlooked it. I lay for a long time in the tepid water, lathering myself continuously in some vain hope of obliterating both the marks and the memory of violence, and then I went back to the room my father had occupied, locked both doors, crept beneath the pile of Holland covers and curled myself into a ball in the middle of the deep, deep bed.

In the morning I was faced with the problem of getting back to my room unseen and of avoiding a meeting with my husband. I could hardly walk through those endless corridors clad in a nightgown ripped to shreds. And in any case I had left it on the bathroom floor after drying myself, a wet, bedraggled object which would reveal more than it concealed. Better a capacious Holland dust cover, although what the servants would think if they met me I could well imagine. "Young Mrs. Hillyard must be took out of her mind, wandering around the corridors upstairs wrapped in a sheet and looking like a ghost!" And I did look like a ghost. I saw my reflection across the room— wan, hollow-eyed, white to the lips. I had slept the sleep of exhaustion which had relaxed my bruised body, but not my mind.

I wondered what the time was. Judging by sounds from outside, plus the light, I deemed it to be somewhere around midmorning. If so, David would have gone down to the oast-house, to his office or that laboratory which I found so distasteful, and I prayed that whatever he did there would keep him well occupied. Claudia—where would she be? In the morning room, dealing with the day's menus, or going over the household accounts, or conferring with Mrs. Stevens or Truman. Would she help me, if I appealed to her, if I displayed evidence of her brother's abuse, or would she turn away, not wanting to hear or see or face up to anything against him? Divorce, I knew, was out of the question. Only adultery was grounds for divorce in this day and age.

But I needed help. I needed someone to turn to. I found myself thinking of a big man with gentle hands, but how could I go running to him?

I heard the distant striking of the coach house clock; eleven solemn strokes. Midmorning, as I thought. The maids would have attended to the bedrooms, so the chance of meeting them in the corridors was now minimal. It was a chance I had to take, for I could not ring down to the servants' hall from this empty room, summoning Mrs. Stevens to ask for clothes. The woman would be aghast, finding me hiding in this disused wing, and in such a state. Besides, I did not trust her; she gossiped too much. Very likely she would go straight to my husband, concerned about his wife's strange behaviour. I preferred to risk any embarrassing encounter on the way back to my room than have her discover I had slept the night here.

Claudia and Harriet would be having their midmorning tea now and possibly wondering why I had not joined them. My absence at breakfast would be no surprise at all, for I frequently took only coffee in my room, so I could let them wonder if I had gone off on one of my long walks. The day was right for it, which was all to the good.

So I swathed myself in a Holland cover and braved the endless corridors. Sleep had made me steadier; I was able to run, silent and barefooted. I met no one and reached the corridor leading to my room with relief, until I came abreast of my husband's dressing room and saw the door open stealthily. A face peered out through a gap of about six inches, but I recognised it.

"Harriet! What are you doing in there?"

She was forced then to open the door fully. She did so with reluctance and an air of great bravado until she caught sight of my appearance and forgot her embarrassment instantly.

"My goodness, you *do* look a sight! Why are you dressed up like that?"

I said the first thing that came into my head, that I had been taking a bath and had forgotten a robe, but her avid gaze was fixed on me with unabashed curiosity.

"You look dreadful. Quite dreadful. Are you ill or something?"

"I didn't sleep well." I had to get away from her; no time now to question her, no time to find out what she had been doing in my husband's dressing room or why she had been creeping out so furtively. Besides, I scarcely cared. Uppermost in my mind was a determination to get away from Abbotswood as quickly as possible, so I went into my room and closed the door.

When I was dressed, I rang for Truman, and when he came, I asked him to fetch the carpetbag I had brought with me to Abbotswood. "You know the one, I think. It seemed to interest you when you unpacked for my father."

"Indeed, yes, ma'am. It has a very unusual fastener, a kind seen rarely nowadays. In fact, I recall seeing only one in many a year. Old-fashioned, but better than many now used, in my opinion. Yes indeed, only once have I seen one like it. . . ."

He shuffled away, and by the time he returned I had laid out on the bed the few possessions I had brought with me to this house. Everything else, the expensive clothes supplied by my husband, the jewellery he had given me as a wedding present, I was leaving behind. Even the gabardine travelling suit I wore, with its matching velvet toque, was that which I had worn when David brought me from Pimlico.

"Do you require the carriage, ma'am? May I ask if you are going on a visit?"

Truman's eyes, like his voice, were puzzled. I had made no mention of an impending journey, given no orders for a carriage to be made ready.

"An unexpected trip, Truman, that is all."

"Then would you not prefer to take a smarter piece of luggage, ma'am? A lady in your position, if I may say so, would no doubt be happier with something rather more elegant, more feminine. . . ."

"This will do admirably," I said. "Besides, I have an affection for it—"

I broke off.

Claudia stood in the open doorway.

"What are you doing? Where are you going, dressed like that? Why are you packing that bag?"

"I am leaving Abbotswood. I intended to tell you before I went."

She said sharply. "Leaving? No, I beg you—not yet!"

Truman had gone. We were alone, standing on each side of the bed in which I would never sleep again. Her hands were twisting feverishly, with an anxiety I could not understand, for surely it would mean nothing to her if I went away. She should be glad. She had never wanted me to marry her brother.

"I suppose David will be able to divorce me eventually. I don't know how the law stands in regard to a deserting wife, only to an unfaithful one, but if there were any justice in the world for women, it would give me my freedom. Perhaps someday the law will be more understanding."

"What has he done to you?" she whispered.

I could not tell her. Faced with the opportunity to thrust the truth about her brother before her disbelieving face, I could not tell her.

I picked up the bag, my gloves, and my reticule and turned to go.

She caught hold of my arm.

"Aphra, listen to me. Don't go, I beg you. Wait awhile —a few hours, that is all I ask." Her hands fell away and began their feverish movements again. "Listen, I have something to tell you. Someone is coming. I heard this morning. I have been waiting and waiting, and at last I have heard. He arrives at Folkestone, on the cross-Channel steamer from Boulogne, about noon. I have sent a carriage to bring him here as quickly as possible. Things will be better once he arrives, I promise you. I promise you."

Caught by her agitation, I asked, "Is this why you came here?"

"No. I have been looking for you because Red Deakon has called to see you. He is waiting in the morning room, and he has brought a friend of yours with him. Miss Elizabeth Lorrimer."

SIXTEEN

I did not trouble to analyse my reaction. I was only aware that beneath my surprise was a surging gladness. Whatever his reason, the most important thing was that Red had come to Abbotswood on my account, the one person in the world to whom I felt I could turn, the one person I had in mind as I packed my father's ancient bag. Red would help me. He would drive me to the bank in Hythe so that I could draw my savings. That was a better plan than using one of the Abbotswood carriages.

But Elizabeth—what was she doing here?

I dropped the carpetbag.

"You say he brought Miss Lorrimer with him?"

"Yes. I was surprised, too. I thought the company had moved on."

So they had. To Birmingham, Manchester, Glasgow, Edinburgh? I could not remember.

"You'd best see them before David returns for luncheon. He was in a black mood at breakfast."

"So you do admit he has moods," I said unkindly. Then I touched her hand. "I am sorry—I have no wish to hurt you—I shall be gone before luncheon because I have no desire to meet him again."

We were halfway along the corridor by then, and my footsteps quickened as we reached the stairs. I went ahead of her eagerly, and then I saw Red's big figure silhouetted against the window of the morning room, I felt that in a reeling world there could be stability after all. I stood there looking at him, and he stood there looking at me, and I wondered why I had ever considered him mocking and antagonistic.

I think we both were unaware of Elizabeth seated by the fire until she rose with a rustle of stiff petticoats and sailed across the room to embrace me.

Then she stepped back and surveyed me.

"Good gracious, the child looks worse than she did last time! Just look at her, Mr. Deakon! My poor little Aphra, you look quite dreadful, you really do, and why in heaven's name are you dressed in those old clothes? I remember them well."

I scarcely heeded her. I was looking at Red again. With his back to the light I could not see his expression, but somehow I felt that his whole body had tautened and that my appearance shocked and angered him.

He came to me then and took me by the hand, and his voice was very kind as he said, "There is something you have to hear. I went to London, to Chelsea, and then to Nottingham to call on Miss Lorrimer because St. Saviour's could not help me—"

"St. Saviour's! The church where my parents were married?"

Elizabeth said gently, "No, dear."

"But you told me. You said they went there to take their vows."

"I said 'make' them, dear. Not take them. Vows have to be taken before a priest, but there is nothing to stop a sweet sentimental pair like your dear mamma and papa from making their vows together and asking for God's blessing on their union, even though no priest would give it. And I'm sure that in the dear Lord's eyes they were as good as wed because they really meant what they said. And because no convention had forced them to kneel in that church, with dear old Barney and me as witnesses because they wanted their promises to be heard, I do believe those vows meant a good deal more than in many a proper marriage service. And they remained faithful to each other for so long as they were together, marriage lines or no marriage lines."

I had no recollection of sitting down, but I found myself on a sofa with Red beside me.

"So—you went to find Elizabeth because—because there was no record in the marriage registers of the church."

He nodded.

"I checked on the Thespians' next booking, through the Folkestone theatre, before catching the train to London."

"So you expected this—you guessed."

"I wondered."

Elizabeth said in a matter-of-fact way, "You're surely not upset, are you, dear? Funny, I always took it for granted that you knew."

"So that was what you meant when you said 'what' I am. . . ."

"Oh, come now, darling, you mustn't think of yourself that way."

"I don't. I don't feel any different at all. I loved them, and they loved me, and oh, how much they loved each other! I appreciate that even more now."

I thought of them kneeling together, hand in hand, making their voluntary testimony before God, and I thought how right Elizabeth was. No man and woman in conventional marriage could have been happier than they.

"The only thing I am surprised about is that even when he died, there was nothing amongst my father's papers to hint at the truth."

"Well, by that time, dear, I've no doubt he felt as well and truly married as everyone believed him to be. I can't really see why Mr. Deakon had to go digging all this up because, after all, it can't affect you now."

"I was trying to help her establish an essential part of her identity, Miss Lorrimer. That was why I wondered if you could recall her mother's name."

"And I had to think hard, didn't I? That shows how completely she was accepted as Charles' wife. I doubt if I could have remembered her real name if Barney hadn't. She had been known as Petronella Coleman for so long, and since Aphra is now Mrs. Hillyard, all signed and sealed and settled—although, from the look of her, legal marriage doesn't seem to have made her so happy as her dear mamma's illegal one—I can't see that it matters. She is Aphra Hillyard now. That is her identity."

"Yes." Red's voice was hard. "That is her identity."

Elizabeth flung an ostrich feather boa about her neck and said, "Well, that's that, isn't it? I must say I think it was hardly worth Mr. Deakon's time to delve into all this, but I'm glad we're doing *Julius Caesar* this week, or I wouldn't have been free to travel back with him. I've left my understudy to play Calphurnia—such a small part, and all that virtue and 'Caesar's wife is above suspicion' stuff makes it a dull one too. . . ."

She kissed me warmly. It was time to go. How could I

delay them, how persuade Red to take me away from this house? He had been concerned for me, but he would also be concerned for Claudia, whom he would wish to be upset in no way at all. He was her "intimate friend"; I had to remember that.

We were moving toward the door when a carriage was heard outside. None of us glanced toward the window, though the thought registered in my mind that it must be Claudia's visitor and that the cross-Channel ferry must have docked on time.

The door burst open, and Harriet came tripping in on tiny little steps. She was a startling figure in a Japanese kimono, with chrysanthemums in her hair. Who did she imagine she was now? Yum-Yum? I saw Elizabeth's eyebrows fly up in astonishment. Characteristically, Harriet interpreted this reaction as admiration and fluttered a fan with what she believed to be Oriental skill. Something had happened to please poor Harriet exceedingly, but what it was I was not interested enough to speculate upon.

I saw Truman crossing the hall to admit the visitor, and a manservant behind him to deal with the luggage, and Claudia hurrying down the stairs, apparently too impatient to await her guest in the drawing room.

I was caught. I would have to wait while introductions were made and then make my escape as soon as possible, but there could be no appealing to Red in front of everyone. I drew back into the morning room, hoping to avoid the meeting, and saw Harriet, her hands now thrust within the wide sleeves of her kimono, looking at me with gleeful eyes.

"I have a secret," she whispered. "What it is, you will never guess!"

Nor did I wish to try, but if I could keep her here in conversation, perhaps I need not emerge from this room until everyone had gone from the hall. I very much wanted to be alone, for the story of my parents had moved me more than I had shown. Bless their dear, dear hearts . . . they had protected me with their love.

So I had never been Aphra Coleman after all. As an illegitimate child my surname would have been that of my mother. Newton. *Aphra Neuton*. There was no doubt in my mind that that ancient Kentish family had been my mother's and that when she and my father visited poor

The Eagle at the Gate

little Aphra's tomb in that country church, my mother had known her identity. Why had she gone there, why call me after so remote an ancestress? Because she had unconsciously been seeking some link with her people so that she would feel less of an outsider, living a life of which they, mostly members of the church, must have disapproved most strongly? And to keep her secret, my father had made up that story about wandering into that little church by accident and choosing the name spontaneously. Well, maybe they had. I was simply glad they had chosen it.

Voices in the hall. Red and Elizabeth had already reached it. Harriet tripped forward as if she were making an entrance in *The Mikado*, and I saw her go shuffling across the wide floor, withdrawing her fan from one capacious sleeve and flicking it open, but keeping the other hand still concealed. I saw the newcomer halt as she went fluttering across to him, and when she made her humble obeisance, he solemnly bowed in return, as if knowing that this was a game which had to be taken very seriously indeed. I was so surprised that I momentarily forgot myself. Who was this little, baldheaded man now greeting Claudia with a distinctively foreign accent?

"My dear madame, I came, as you see, as speedily as possible, but alas, when your letter arrived, I was absent from Vienna—"

He was kissing her hand, and Harriet immediately snapped shut her fan and held out her own hand languidly, demanding the same courtesy. Very solemnly, the man complied, but as he straightened up, I saw his expression change from kindly indulgence to something more alert, though what it indicated I could not tell. I only knew he was looking toward the great staircase, and so was Claudia; so, too, was Red. He and Elizabeth had been onlookers like myself while the formality of this man's arrival took place, but I knew that Claudia had been about to introduce them. Now she halted and waited, and I recognised the step descending the stairs. It was my husband's.

Claudia exclaimed, "David! I did not hear you return."

"Very likely not, since I have not been to my office this morning. I have been closeted in the library instead. I have been trying to find out why my wife likes that room so much. She has spent a lot of time there since coming to Abbotswood. She seems to enjoy shutting herself away. A very complicated person, my poor wife. Very badly in need of professional help. . . ."

No, I thought violently. I will *not* come face to face with him again. I will not meet him or talk with him. Not ever again.

The morning room was situated toward the rear of the long hall, close to a side stair which ran up out of sight. If I slipped out of the room while they all had their backs to me, I could reach it.

I succeeded. I sped silently up the unseen staircase, the staircase the servants used, and then toward the west wing and my room. I had only to pick up my bag and then leave through the east wing; no need to face any of them again. I would walk the four miles or so to Hythe. I was much practised in walking now, and anything was better than remaining in this house for even one moment longer.

On the threshold of my room I halted. The contents of the ancient carpetbag were scattered everywhere, as if flung by enraged hands. I knew at once whose hands they had been.

I was picking up my mother's precious brooch when he spoke behind me.

"Still intent on running away, sweet Aphra? Such a waste of time and effort! You will be brought back, you know. I saw you slip out of the morning room and guessed where you were heading, and naturally, being a solicitous husband, I came back to take you downstairs again." He pulled the velvet toque from my head and flung it aside. "I cannot have my dear wife committing such a faux pas as to wear a hat for luncheon in her own home."

He held out his arm with a mock bow. I ignored it. "Allow me to escort you downstairs," he said. "Everyone is waiting, and I am sure my sister's guest must be ready for luncheon after travelling so far. All the way from Vienna, by night train to Paris and then to Boulogne, followed by a tedious Channel crossing—I recall the journey well. Do you know who he is, by the way? His name is Carl Steiner. Dr. Carl Steiner. A brilliant man. A professor of neurology, now working with Sigmund Freud as a psychoanalyst at Vienna University. He also has a world-renowned clinic for the private treatment of patients. You cannot refuse to take luncheon with so eminent a guest, especially after my sister went to all the trouble of bring him here especially to place you in his care."

I saw his sister then, waiting by the door.

"Come, Aphra," she said.

I knew then that they were in this together, and that there was no escaping their machinations.

SEVENTEEN

Dr. Steiner sat on one side of me and Red on the other. I had a feeling that Red had deliberately seated himself there, and certainly David was not pleased about it. I guessed why. With the doctor on one side of me and himself on the other, I would have been well and truly guarded.

I was glad, yet sorry, that Red and Elizabeth had been persuaded to stay for luncheon. I suspected that she was considering this a very peculiar household, what with Yum-Yum over there, and the hostess looking like a Greek tragedy queen, and my husband and me not speaking to each other—and I still wearing that gabardine travelling suit which had belonged to those long-ago touring days, when surely I had a wardrobe full of elegant and fashionable clothes. Poor Elizabeth, this unexpected respite from the gruelling work of the theatre was not proving so very enjoyable after all—unlike that first visit to Abbotswood, with all the glamour and gaiety of a ball thrown in and lots of admiring men around her. The only men now present were a prosperous blacksmith who seemed to be intent on discovering the truth about other people's business, a portly little foreigner with observant eyes, and a host who looked down on her socially. No, she would not thank Red Deakon for bringing her here, and on the whole she would not be sorry to get back to the Thespians. I could read her thoughts quite plainly.

Dr. Steiner talked to me throughout luncheon, for all the world as if I were a normal human being instead of a potential patient, but later I recalled the conversation as being one of subtle question and answer, the questions being his and the answers mine. Only one incident stands out in my memory. It occurred when a bottle of Abbotswood's special Châteauneuf-du-Pape was produced for the guest of honour, and without thinking, I cried, "Not that! Not the Châteauneuf!"

Everyone looked at me in surprise, except the doctor, who said mildly, "You do not care for it, madame?"

"I have no idea. I have never tasted it, nor ever will since I suspect it killed my father."

The astonishment which ran round the table left me quite unmoved. So did David's expression, which was one of mixed fury and amusement.

"You must forgive my wife, Doctor. You can see how wildly her imagination runs, what abnormal fancies she has. That is a very excellent vintage, I assure you."

"As you assured my father?" I put in. "But it made him ill all the same."

"He was ill already, strained and overworked, as I recall. That was the diagnosis when he died. Of course, if alcoholic poisoning speeded his end, he had only himself to blame. He was greatly addicted to wine, I remember. He drank a whole bottle of the Châteauneuf the night he was here."

"No. He only appeared to. The bottle was empty because I disposed of the remainder to prevent him from drinking any more. Yes, I admit he was fond of wine."

David protested, "You emptied away a whole bottle of one of our best vintages?"

"Not a whole bottle, only the amount that remained, which was just below half."

"Then how can you say it killed him? What wild accusation is this? I selected that wine myself and sent it up to him."

"I know. But perhaps there was something wrong with it, something which caused nausea and giddiness. Perhaps it had deteriorated."

"Or perhaps it was poisoned? Is that what you are suggesting? And the bottle he accepted so willingly the next day, for the journey home? Was that poisoned, too?"

"No."

"Ah! You made sure of that?"

"It was examined after his death as a matter of routine. But perhaps there could have been an accumulation of something toxic in his blood. . . ."

"Something a doctor would overlook?" he sneered. "Such as—what?" When I had no answer, he turned to

Carl Steiner and said with feeling, "Thank God you have come, sir. You can see for yourself how badly my wife needs your help."

I thought, but couldn't be sure because I was staring fixedly at my plate, that Red began to protest, but Elizabeth burst in with inconsequential chatter which drowned everything, and the doctor supported her by turning the conversation to the theatre and then to me personally, asking about life on tour and what it had been like to be the daughter of a Shakespearean actor, and if I ever hankered to return to the stage. I avoided that question, fearing that David, who was listening intently without appearing to, might reveal that I had written to George Mayfield, behind his back, with some neurotic idea of doing precisely that. He was seizing every opportunity to present me as irresponsible and unbalanced, and Claudia was sitting there silently, not trying to prevent him. She was my enemy, too. She had engineered this man's arrival, and she had helped her brother to prevent me from leaving the house when I was ready to walk out of it. But, as David said, I would have been brought back. I was his possession, his chattel, but whatever fiendish plan they had for me, I would never cease trying to escape, whether from Abbotswood or from some well-guarded Viennese hospital.

And that reminded me—David had worked in a Viennese hospital. Toxicology. I looked directly at him as I said, very clearly for everyone to hear, "Was it in your laboratory that my husband studied, Dr. Steiner? He qualified in Vienna as a toxicologist, or so he tells me. You must see his laboratory here at Abbotswood before you leave. It should interest you."

"I would like to see it very much, madame, and it would interest me extremely."

I was glad when the meal was over and we all moved into the drawing room. Claudia had her own coffee ritual, making it herself, continental style. While it percolated, the conversation became more or less general, though I managed to manipulate Elizabeth into a seat beside the doctor this time. I thought I would escape his too-seeing eye that way, but I found myself sitting with the full light of the windows shining onto me, and I knew that not only Red Deakon observed the telltale marks on my throat. Despite my high-necked blouse, rapidly developing bruising could be detected up to my chin. I had no doubt that the doctor's perceptive glance observed it, but would he believe me, were I to tell him how such bruising came to be there? Would anyone believe me?

I had never known Red to be so quiet. I felt that he was watchful, speculative, and this seemed to be focused on Claudia, too.

It was his interest in Claudia, and his long friendship with her, that made me resist appealing to him when at last I had the chance. He brought his coffee cup across and sat down beside me. David was also beside me, unrelenting in his vigilance, but I had only to turn my head away from him and say in a low voice, "Help me escape, Red. Take me away from this house. Drive me into Hythe, that is all I ask. . . ." But the words remained unspoken.

Harriet was still playing the geisha girl, to Elizabeth's pained amusement and, I suspected, to David's irritation. She was still fluttering her fan and her eyelashes, still tripping about the room with her tiny Three-Little-Maids-from-School steps. Claudia, ever-patient where her unfortunate cousin was concerned, smiled her ever-indulgent smile, but David suddenly burst out, "Where in heaven's name did you get that costume from, Harriet? And why dress up in it for luncheon? This isn't a fancy dress ball."

"I know, but don't I wear it well? I feel like Madame Butterfly, and I look like her, don't I? Claudia dear, I am sure that if I took singing lessons I could do opera. What production was this costume for?"

"I cannot remember, dear. Where did you find it?"

"In a trunk with other theatrical costumes, up in the attics."

"I told you not to go there. The stairs are no longer safe. I must have them put right. . . ."

"Oh, they are not too bad. Very dusty, though. But the costumes have kept well. Some of them have been affected by moth, but not all. They must have lain there for ages and ages. and the photographs—they must have been taken ages and ages ago, too."

David said sharply, "Photographs? What photographs?"

"The ones Aphra was wanting to see. Or some of them.

I promised to find them for her, so I hunted in the attics. That was how I came across this lovely costume. It might have been made for me. Don't you think it might have been made for me, Aphra? Don't you, Miss Lorrimer? Red, you too—don't you think it might have been made for me?"

David said angrily, "You have no right to go ferreting about the place. Claudia, you should stop her."

"So long as she doesn't fall down the attic stairs and injure herself, I cannot see what harm she can do," his sister answered mildly.

"I am not talking about *harm*. I am talking about her rights. She has no right to rummage in places without permission."

"Then you shouldn't keep so many places locked up!" Harriet retorted, verging on a childish tantrum.

He looked at her swiftly, with a cold, sharp gaze. "You mentioned photographs. Did you find some in the attic?"

He seemed to be probing unnecessarily, but I knew only too well how my husband could worry away at something like a dog at a bone.

"Only a few. *You* must know where I found the rest...."

I saw his white fingers clench very slowly about his coffee cup.

"Where are they?" He tried to make it sound like a casual question, but in reality it was a demand.

"Hidden, and you will never guess where!"

"You are becoming as secretive as Aphra." He turned to the doctor again. "You will find my wife very difficult to draw out, I am afraid."

"Why should I wish to draw her out, Mr. Hillyard?"

Harriet piped, "Because we all know how secretive she is! Only this morning she wouldn't tell me why she was coming along her bedroom corridor wrapped up in a sheet. She said she had taken a bath, but forgotten a robe, but she wasn't coming from the direction of the bathroom, so I knew she was lying. Were you pretending to be dressed up in a Roman toga, Aphra?"

I felt a deep colour rise to my cheeks. Sooner or later that incident *had* to come out, I thought wretchedly, but it could not have happened at a worse moment than this. I stirred my coffee round and round, round and round, wishing I could stop because this persistent, aimless action revealed an inner disturbance of mind.

"Ah," said David in a satisfied way. "Harriet seems to know how oddly my wife behaves, what kind of person she is."

She agreed happily. "Indeed, I know what she is, and so do you, David. She is a bastard, that's what Aphra is."

My head jerked up. How had she found out? And was she right in declaring that David knew, too? And what of Claudia? Had she known all along, and had this been one of her reasons for considering me unworthy of her brother? Such thinking was characteristic of the age. She appeared to be shocked, but somehow I felt it was mainly because of the word Harriet used, for which she reproved her at once. "That is a dreadful term, Harriet. You must never use it."

I said evenly, "But it is true. My parents were not married, so that makes me illegitimate, and I don't mind in the least because it made not the slightest difference in my life. However, I am surprised to hear that my husband knew. He never referred to it."

"Naturally, I had no desire to embarrass or distress you." He changed the subject. "Let me see those photographs, Harriet. How many have you? Where are they?"

She became coquettish then, giggling and standing in the middle of the hearthrug, her hands concealed again in the big sleeves of her kimono. She bowed low and then produced them from her capacious sleeve with a flourish.

Red took them before David could. I leant toward him, thankful to have something to look at other than my husband's predatory eyes and the watchful ones of the others.

I saw faded sepia groups, then one of a man in period dress. Harriet, leaning over Red's shoulder, piped, "I know who that is. I remember Claudia telling us once, before David stole these pictures and locked them away. That man is Jasper Bentine."

I leaned closer, studying the man who had been Claudia's lover, the man who killed his brother here at Abbotswood, and my gaze remained transfixed.

I was looking at my father, twenty years younger but instantly recognisable.

The Eagle at the Gate

* * *

I didn't believe it. I wouldn't believe it. But I remembered how my father had refused to come to Abbotswood and, when finally forced to, arrived only at the last possible moment, leaving just enough time to apply the heavy disguise of Caliban, choosing an hour when he was least likely to meet anyone slipping in through a side door and up back stairs, all too familiar with the layout of the house. Choosing to play Caliban so that no one would recognise him? And as Caliban he had to disguise his voice as well . . . and throughout the performance he had been ill at ease, tense as I had never known him to be. And as early as possible the next morning he left before anyone was astir except David.

More than anyone, I recalled, my father had avoided meeting Claudia.

The room was spinning about me. My father, a murderer, a man who stabbed his brother and ran away, a man in love with his brother's wife, who then seduced my mother and made her his mistress? Could one live all one's life with such a man and never see through him?

Red was saying, "Drink your coffee, Aphra." He was actually holding the cup for me, his arm about my shoulders. He saw too much, this man. He had always seen too much. I avoided looking at him and saw Claudia's pale face instead, and the doctor's, too, watching me.

The coffee steadied me a little, but Red's arm gave me strength. I began to think more clearly. Now I knew why David Hillyard had engineered the visit of the Thespian Players to Abbotswood. He had visited the theatre in Bristol and recognised Jasper Bentine from those old photographs. He had come every night for a week until he was certain he had guessed correctly, and then he planned his campaign, right down to the last detail. Even to marrying the daughter of his sister's lover, her husband's murderer, because Jasper Bentine had inherited Abbotswood on his brother's death.

That was David's motive, not only for marrying me, but for wanting my death also. *"There are always ways if one wants something badly enough. . . ."* The truth stared me in the face at last. In the absence of a will, all my father left presumably came to me. But there had been no evidence in that deed box, no actual proof that Charles Coleman was really Jasper Bentine, so how could David

Hillyard be sure that Abbotswood, of which he longed to be master, would ever be mine? Even Elizabeth had wondered whether I would be entitled to what little she believed my father could have left.

The room had stopped spinning, and Red's supporting arm was no longer there; but his shoulder was still close, and somehow I know his attention was fixed on me.

Harriet was looking at David with defiant but rather tearful eyes. "You keep so many places locked," she reproached. "You make it so difficult for me to open them, and you know I don't like locked rooms or locked cupboards or even locked drawers...."

He said slowly, "My God—you got hold of a key somehow—"

She nodded proudly.

"I had it made. It was easy. All I had to do, Jenkins said, was get a wax impression of any lock I needed a key for, so that was what I did. Mrs. Stevens uses paraffin wax on her rheumaticky joints; it was easy to slip down to the kitchens when the servants were elsewhere and help myself to some. I used to go all over the house, finding every door that was locked, every cupboard and drawer. Jenkins is very good at making keys. I can thoroughly recommend him. Aphra doesn't keep anything locked, nor does Claudia, but you, David, well, you keep just about everything locked, don't you? The hothouse, your laboratory, cupboards and drawers in your dressing room. I guessed you might keep your most private secrets in your dressing room because nobody but you uses it, except Truman to see to your clothes and the maids to clean it and they daren't trespass in private places. Neither Claudia nor I, nor Aphra I daresay because all her clothes are in the bedroom, ever goes near your dressing room. It's your personal, private place. All my big secrets I keep close to me, so I knew you would do the same. Of course, I think it mean of you. I would share any of my secrets with *you* if you would share yours with me, but you never will, so it serves you right that I found them out. I don't mean those old photographs, though why you had to lock *them* away, I don't understand. I mean a bigger secret. About Aphra. Who she really is. *That* you locked away very carefully, but not carefully enough. See—I have that here as well!"

From behind the wide sash of her kimono came the final trophy, a paper which David swiftly dived for. But she was quicker, snatching it away and dancing with glee like an over-excited child. "You shan't have it, you shan't have it!" she chanted. "And I don't see how it was ever yours, anyway. It belongs to Aphra, and because you've been so mean to me I'm going to let her have it, so there!"

She thrust the paper into my lap, and Red leapt to his feet, pulling David away, but I was scarcely aware of anyone because words were leaping up at me. LAST WILL AND TESTAMENT . . . An ordinary, cheap will form obtainable at any stationer's . . . and beneath the title, my father's handwriting.

I, Lawrence Sylvester Bentine, professionally known as Charles Coleman, being the elder son and heir of the late Sir William Bentine of Abbotswood, Kent, do hereby bequeath to my beloved natural daughter, Aphra Newton, known as Aphra Coleman and born of my very dear love, the late Petronella Newton, known as Petronella Coleman, whom I always regarded and always will regard as my one true wife, all goods, properties, and lands of which I die possessed. . . .

Slowly I lifted my head. I said to Harriet, "You told me it was Lawrence Bentine who was killed."

"Did I? I can't remember. I knew *one* of the brothers was, but of course, I wasn't there at the time, so how could I know?"

I looked at my husband then, struggling to break free from Red's grasp, dangerous, threatening. I looked at his distorted face, and in that face I saw the whole tragic story of my marriage, its relentless planning and its terrible inevitability. Then my eyes went back to the will again, the will which he must have taken from my father's deed box as I sat with my back to him in that little Pimlico flat, absorbed in the personal mementos the box had yielded and never suspecting for a moment that there was anything more. But for his convenient arrival with the keys, I would have been unable to open the deed box at all; force would have been necessary, but only after a very opportune delay, by which time he would have ensured his own arrival.

To Claudia Bentine, my wife in the eyes of the law, I bequeath for life the income already settled upon her at the time of our marriage, and the revenues from those parts of the Abbotswood estates which I apportioned to her when we parted by mutual consent on July 25, 1880, any further apportionment to be left to the discretion of my daughter, Aphra, who on coming into her inheritance has the right to dispose of any further part or parts of said estates howsoever she may wish, and I pray that in the event of that unhappy house overshadowing her life as it overshadowed mine she may have the wisdom to dispose of it in its entirety and to seek happiness elsewhere, as I did.

There was no more, other than the appointment of executors and the signatures of two witnesses—Barney Wills, stage manager, and Elizabeth Lorrimer, actress.

I turned to Claudia then.

"Harriet may have been confused, but not you. Yet you did not deny being a widow that day we lunched on the terrace. But you knew all the time that my father was alive."

"Your father?"

"Lawrence Sylvester Bentine. David also told me he was dead, killed by Jasper."

Claudia's shock was stamped not only in her face, but in her frozen figure. "Lawrence—your *father?* It cannot be true!"

"This will confirms it and is probably why my husband concealed it. You honestly had no knowledge of this? David did not confide even in you?"

"A man should keep his own counsel," my husband blustered. "Women are useless. They want to find out everything and can keep quiet about nothing. Let go your grip on me, Deakon—you're hurting me!" He began to whimper. "Doctor, make him release me!"

Steiner said in a calm, friendly voice, "Come, Mr.

The Eagle at the Gate

Hillyard, you need to rest. It was wise of your sister to send for me. She was anxious about you. You have been overworking, she tells me. I am sure she is right, and I agree with her that a prolonged visit to Vienna would be beneficial to you again. You were happy there on previous visits, and you could stay in my new clinic, opened since your time. I am sure a man with your capabilities would find it interesting. You could even continue your studies—with help, of course."

I knew that meant supervision, but my husband believed otherwise. He was quiet immediately. A miraculous means of escape spread out before him, escape with dignity and importance attached to it. His face smoothed out into something almost guileless. "With assistance, you mean? Good assistants who will help me in my work? In a well-equipped laboratory?"

"You will find that my colleagues and I have a great understanding of your needs."

David read that answer in only one way. Well pleased, he said, "I would like to accept your invitation, I would indeed, but alas, I doubt if I can be spared from Abbotswood."

"I beg you not to put Abbotswood before your own desires," Claudia urged. "You know we have a most competent factor, and you have kept the accounts so meticulously that even I could continue with them. I am accustomed to keeping the week-by-week household accounts, remember, which are by no means uncomplicated." Her hands were twisting and turning in a fever of anxiety, which only I seemed to notice. "Think of yourself, David; what a chance it will be to study under Dr. Steiner. . . . Everyone knows how clever you are. Think of the opportunity!"

Well pleased, David said, "You are right, as always, dear Claudia. Very well, Doctor, I accept your invitation. I will have Truman pack a bag right away. How soon can we leave?"

"As soon as you wish."

I saw the doctor's eyes flicker toward Red, who slowly released his grip. My husband straightened his jacket, smoothed his hair with a white, graceful hand, smiled at us all with a mixture of disdain and triumph, and said, "I will put a few things together immediately."

Claudia rose. "Let me help you."

"No, sister. I need one or two things from my laboratory. It will take no more than a few minutes."

He walked out of the room quite calmly, but he was a long time coming back. In fact, he never came back at all.

They found his body in the laboratory, a broken phial on the floor beside him.

EIGHTEEN

"He was the most endearing little boy," Claudia said. "He was born when I was ten. I was an only child and a lonely one, and the arrival of this baby filled my world. I called him the angel child, and that was what he looked like. One of those golden-haired Raphael cherubs with dimpled cheeks and big innocent eyes. I adored him. Mamma died shortly after his birth, and I felt then that he had been sent for me to take care of, and when Mama's death caused my father's final breakdown and he went away forever, David became truly the centre of my life. Nothing was too good for him. Whatever he wanted he should have. He could do no wrong in my eyes. I lavished all my love upon him. I had always been maternal; my solitary childhood had been filled with a whole family of dolls, all of which were real children to me. But when David came, I had no more time for them. I had the real thing—a baby of my own."

We were in the gardens, Claudia and I. I had remained at Abbotswood, though my enchantment with it would never be revived. The place was imbued with tragedy, not the least of which was my father's unhappiness. I guessed there had been a great deal behind that, things which had driven him away other than shock over the accidental killing of his brother. That must have been the final culmination, and that was why I had remained after my husband's funeral, hoping that Claudia would finally tell me the truth about everything, but her grief over David's death had made her unapproachable until now.

But now she had come in search of me. More than a month had passed since that memorable day when my marriage had ended.

It was strange that I could now think of my husband with pity, sadist though he had been. That was part of his illness, and that was how I had to regard it because otherwise I would forever be asking unanswerable questions: Had he really been responsible for my father's death? Had he really put something in that first bottle of wine, some obscure and tasteless poison which could not be identified, which accumulated in the bloodstream, taking action only much later, due to further intake of alcohol which, when examined, proved perfectly sound? I would never know. I could only remember certain things, certain incidents, such as David visiting my father's room and sending Truman up later with another bottle of wine, the cork already drawn. But Truman could have drawn that. And after I had poured the remainder of the wine away, what had happened to the bottle? I had replaced it on the tray, which had later been removed, and a conscientious servant would have disposed of an empty bottle.

But what about the keys which David claimed had been found on the floor of my father's room? That could have been true. But he could also have seen them on the dressing table and concealed them, making their return a good excuse to call—after my father was dead. Had he known the approximate time it would take for a slow poison to work? With his specialised knowledge he could know many things at which I could not even guess.

And with what authority and charm he had relieved me of the distressing task of examining my father's deed box!

Conjecture about the wine and the keys was useless. Without proof, both meant nothing, and there would never be any proof now. Even concealing my father's will did not prove that he had been guilty of anything before that. He could have arrived at our rooms in Pimlico still believing that my father was Jasper Bentine and not discovering the truth until he saw that document. But whether my father was Jasper or Lawrence Bentine really made no difference; as daughter of either I stood to inherit the place of which David Hillyard longed to be master. Never could he have tolerated being merely the husband of the owner; such a secondary position would not have satisfied his desire to dominate, to rule, to possess. To have ranked below a wife, lesser in authority, would have been unendurable to a man who liked to pin down helpless creatures, to trap them and torture them in order to demonstrate his total power over them, even to put them to death when he so willed.

The actions of my husband after I became his wife were more obviously suspect, and it was on these that I wanted evidence. Prove that he had released that killer eagle in the hope of slaying me, prove that he had locked me in the hothouse and tried to murder me in that unbearable heat, and I would be getting nearer the truth. But I could prove neither. I could only speculate on how long he would have left me in that smothering greenhouse had I not smashed the glass and brought the others running. Now I suspected that his horror on seeing me there had been due to the failure of his schemes; his outrage, because I had outwitted him, not because of the destruction I had caused.

But Claudia had testified that he had been within sight all the time.

"Did you always defend him in all things?" I asked.

"I had to," she answered simply. "He had no one else. We were looked after by a capable housekeeper, and our affairs were administered by the family solicitor. I had a governess who taught David his first childish lessons. She adored him, as I did; he could do what he liked with both of us. But apart from our welfare being attended to, we lived a solitary life in that house in the Midlands; we were all the family each of us had, apart from an aunt who lived in Yorkshire and paid us duty visits occasionally. We were a responsibility she did not welcome, in addition to her own. You see—she was Harriet's mother." Claudia nodded. "Oh, yes, there is a history of emotional instability in the Hillyards. My father's 'moods,' as they were called, were part of the pattern of my childhood, but I soon learned that his periodic absences from home were not the business journeys my mother pretended them to be. 'Thank God,' she used to say, '*you* take after my side of the family!' But that did not comfort me, because my father's blood was in me, too, and I was afraid. Then one day he came home, apparently cured, and my parents resumed their married life, and David was born, so I began to think less and less about any possible taint in myself. He was a healthy, normal child, and such an endearing one . . . until. . . ."

I waited, then prompted gently, "Until?"

"Until he was about seven, when he started doing things that frightened me, cruel things, to animals and even to people. One day he was missing, and the household was searching for him, but he blandly turned up, spick-and-span and spotless as ever. He had been for a walk, he said—but one of the kitchen maids was missing. He had locked her in the dankest part of the cellars where she had been searching for him. She was found two days later, but only because he made the mistake of leaving the door open; the place led off the farther-most coal cellar and was totally disused, so no one thought of looking inside. The girl must have shouted for help until she could shout no longer; the thick stone walls beneath the house shut off all sound. She was unconscious when found, and she might not have been found at all if one of the servants, going down to get coal, had not seen the intervening door ajar and heard David's laughter—he was tormenting the girl with a stick, prodding her and teasing her, unconscious as she was. But he could lie his way out of anything. I recognised then all the pathological symptoms of the hereditary Hillyard disease and knew I could not handle them. So I appealed to the family doctor and forever after David was taken care of—until about ten years ago, when he was considered fit enough to take his place in society. So I brought him to Abbotswood. You know the rest."

She looked at me half-compassionately and half-guiltily. She had asked no questions about the bruising on my neck, even when Red had insisted on Dr. Steiner examining it before the man went in search of David that day. I could still hear Red saying, "I'm sorry, Claudia, but not even for you can I sit here and see those marks on Aphra's throat and not find out the cause, though I think both you and I can guess it."

"You have a lot to forgive me for," she said now, "but so, I am afraid, had your father, and I didn't deserve his forgiveness any more than I deserve yours. Trying to dissuade you from marrying my brother was not enough. I had knowledge of just cause and impediment and could have prevented it, but I didn't because, as always, I put his happiness first. I behaved selfishly, and I behaved equally selfishly toward your father. I married

The Eagle at the Gate

him, quite determined that I should never have children. It would have been better if I had been born plain, and then no man would have desired me. Where I came from, there was less chance of my marrying because the story of the Hillyards was too well known, but in the South I was merely the daughter of a wealthy Midland industrialist family, and David, of course, was not with us."

"When did you meet my father?"

"Quite soon after coming South. My aunt, a widow by then, took a furnished house in Hythe and launched me into local society with one aim in mind—to get me married and off her hands, so she would be free to go back to Yorkshire and Harriet. And marrying me off proved surprisingly easy. Within six months I had married Lawrence Bentine. He was handsome and very charming, but I was not in love with him. I played him the worst trick a woman can play on a man. Letting him have my body meant the risk of bearing children, and because of my background, I was determined never to have any. In every other respect I was the model young wife, approved of by his father, liked by the servants, socially acceptable anywhere. And Lawrence was too much of the gentleman to force physical demands on a woman who did not want them. I tried to love him, but I couldn't. I could never understand why he was not content to be master of Abbotswood with me as it,s mistress; I fulfilled the rôle so well, and from the moment I saw the place, I loved it and have done so ever since. But now of course, you will want me to leave—"

"Not yet," I said evasively. "Tell me more about your marriage to my father."

"There is little more to tell. The relationship became strained almost at once, not only because I refused to be a proper wife to him, but also because when we got to know each other, we found we had little in common. We did not value the same things. Lawrence was always reading. *I* thought reading a waste of time and the library the dullest room in the house. Lawrence hated parties, what he called artificial social affairs, but I loved playing hostess. He was interested in literature, painting, drama. It was he who cleared that space in the dell for an open-air theatre. All that dressing up and learning lines off by heart seemed silly to me. The land, livestock, farming—none appealed to him, but to me they represented security and social standing. And he hated what he called 'this mausoleum of a house.' That was something I could never understand. He would have been happier in a cottage, he said, and I really think he would. But he carried on, for his father's sake, until Jasper came home from Cambridge."

"And you fell in love with Jasper—when?"

"Very quickly. He was everything Lawrence was not—a keen rider, a keen shot, a man who enjoyed anything and everything so long as it was not intellectual. He hated being dragged into Lawrence's theatrical productions, but he enjoyed being the centre of attention, so he took part in them. I knew women fell in love with him; he was the wild type of man with a distinctly earthy approach to love, a worry to his father, I knew. Even so, I fell in love with him, and all I had denied Lawrence I could never deny Jasper—"

We had reached the arbour by then, and I looked down at the carved initials and the entwined heart, and the date —June 16, 1880.

"Yes," she admitted, "we carved that the very day that Lawrence and I agreed to separate, although we did not finally do so until after Jasper's death. After the performance of *Julius Caesar* Lawrence planned to go, handing everything over to his brother. All he wanted to do was to get away. He was glad Jasper had come back to take over. Characteristically, he provided for me well. Perhaps he thought of it as payment for freedom—"

"Not my father. He was not like that. He had a very real sense of duty."

"I know. I am sorry. But I have never been entirely comfortable about accepting his financial support when I had never given him anything."

"Did he know about Jasper?"

"He guessed. That may have been the spur to his decision. He would leave the two of us alone, he said, and seize the chance to lead the life he wanted. He had some idea of going to Paris or Florence to study painting. I don't know why I never once, throughout all these years, thought of his becoming an actor, yet he had done it so well here at Abbotswood. But I always thought of him, *when* I thought of him (because I admit I have thought of Jasper a great deal more), as living an artistic, bohemian life on the Continent. I had no doubt that there would be some woman, one who would occupy the place I should have occupied."

"And you never offered to release him, so that he could marry again?"

"My family faith would not permit it. Or that was the excuse I gave. I stopped going to mass long ago, and my brother grew up with no allegiance to any particular church. He did not believe in religion, he said. He went through the marriage service solely because you wanted it. He told me so. 'So long as I have her,' he said, 'I don't care who blesses the union!' But as for myself—before Lawrence went away, I told him bitterly that because of my faith, I would never free him, and I was adamant about it. I think I even believed the excuse myself. But the truth was that since Jasper's death put an end to any hope of happiness for me, I felt that he who struck him down should not be allowed to find happiness either. You see what kind of woman I am! I was bitter for a long time after Jasper's death, even though it was a genuine accident and no one was more affected by it than Lawrence."

"But he did not run away, as your brother declared."

"Did David say that?" She smiled sadly. "You know by now that no reliance could be placed on anything David said, or on Harriet's statements either. I once told you that she frequently got her facts hopelessly confused."

"Such as Lawrence and Jasper—"

"Yes. The brothers were extraordinarily alike in looks, by the way, though not in other respects. No two could have been more different in temperament and character. But Lawrence's decision to leave was taken before that terrible thing happened. He would go, he said, directly after the performance of *Julius Caesar*, but I was to stay because it would make his father happy to have a good mistress running the place. But he would take nothing for himself. 'There's a curse on Abbotswood,' he used to say. 'My grandfather's savage death, my wretched marriage—' And then, of course, the third thing, most tragic of all: Jasper, my Jasper, struck down in the prime of his youth. I hated Lawrence for that, though it was wrong of me. He took unjust blame and went away, out of our lives, for good. He never even drew his income from Abbotswood because he could have been traced that way and he wanted a whole new life. So there I was—neither wife nor widow—but when people began to regard me as a widow in time, I let them. Except one man—"

Red Deakon, I thought. Red has known all along.

"Red was a child of ten when Jasper was killed. He remembered all the talk, and does still. Throughout the years he has proved a good friend, particularly since I brought my brother to Abbotswood and insisted on looking after him. Later, when my aunt died in Yorkshire and I learned that Harriet was in a home in Bristol, and I brought her here, too, Red told me I was taking too much onto myself. In his very individual way he has been a good friend, but being the individual he is, he has never minced his words. He didn't spare me when I allowed your marriage to David to go through. I thought then that Red would never speak to me again. He was angry, but on your behalf. I, of course, insisted that you were doing very well for yourself—"

"I know."

"I also hoped—prayed—that marriage might be David's salvation. He wanted you, and as always, whatever he wanted he must have. Later I began to realise how much I was to blame, how much more terrible I had allowed things to become. Especially for you."

"When? On the night he locked me in the hothouse?"

"We don't *know* that he did!"

She looked at me with a kind of desperate pleading in her eyes, but I said relentlessly, "If you know something or suspect something, please tell me, Claudia."

"Even now, when he is dead?"

"Yes."

She took a deep breath.

"I saw him through the drawing-room windows, the end windows overlooking the terrace—"

"—and up the slope leading to the hothouse?"

She nodded.

"He was coming from there. It was dusk, and he was hurrying. Earlier he had gone riding across the park, and when he returned, I told him you had gone to see whether

The Eagle at the Gate

you had locked the hothouse and that I was sure you had done so when we left. I really thought I was acting for the best, pouring oil on troubled waters, but as I say, it was getting dusk. . . . I couldn't be sure that the figure I saw was his. . . ."

But she was. I remembered seeing distant lights from the house and curtains being drawn against the dusk. If they had not been drawn, would I perhaps have detected a hurrying figure silhouetted against those lights?

"It was after that dreadful evening that you became uneasy?" I asked. "Was that why you wrote to Dr. Steiner?"

She nodded again, looking down at her hands, unable to meet my eyes.

"That was one reason. The other was that David had begun to play that terrible game—pretending you were unbalanced, unreliable, in need of attention. I could see no reason for it, other than the pleasure it had given him, as a boy, to torture defenceless things. Only now do I see what lay behind it. A mentally unbalanced woman could not be allowed to manage her own affairs, her own money. So long as you were alive, he had to get control somehow. That was why the will had to be hidden until the time was ripe for him to produce it, and that would have been after one of two things happened—you finally cracked and were certified, or you died. But when I eventually wrote to Carl Steiner, I had no suspicion of David's real motives. Even the incident in the hothouse might have been all he claimed it to be—hysteria on your part. But that mental torture, the needling—these were symptoms I had seen before, and as before, there was only one way to deal with them."

"You were determined not to let me leave Abbotswood all the same."

"Because I was afraid of what would happen if you tried to. He would have stopped at nothing, once defied. You may find it hard to believe, but by that time I *was* thinking of you."

And now it would have to rest, all of it. The past had died, taking its secrets with it.

Claudia looked up. "I have remembered something," she said. "Shortly before David brought the Thespian Players to Abbotswood, there were some Bentine portraits in the hall—of the first owner, then of Sir William and his wife, then Lawrence and Jasper. The day before your arrival they disappeared. David told me he had moved them because they were inferior paintings and he could not tolerate inferior art. I made no protest, because any reminders of the Bentines were painful to me, though I had never had the courage to remove those portraits. Now it seems obvious that David did so because you would have recognised your father as a young man, and so would your fellow actors. I never asked where he stored them, but they must be somewhere here at Abbotswood. And now here is Red. He has called every day since . . . since—"

"You have a good friend in him," I said.

"Yes. He is compassionate and sympathetic, but no more than that, and never has been. Are you not going to meet him? It is you he really comes to see. The balconies were merely an excuse."

I could scarcely control my eagerness, but I halted when she called my name.

"Aphra—"

"Yes?"

"I am ready to leave Abbotswood whenever you wish. After all, the place is yours. I have no right here."

"I give you that right," I said, and went to meet Red Deakon without a backward glance.

He held out his hands to me.

"I have the last piece in the jigsaw," he said. "I have come to give it to you. There is a parish priest over near Canterbury who has turned up the archives there. When the weaving industry collapsed in Kent, a branch of the Newton family emigrated to Canada. Years later a descendant of this branch returned to his father's village. He had already been ordained into the Protestant clergy. He married and achieved the living of the parish and became its parson. He had one child, a daughter named Petronella—"

"—who eloped with a married man, an actor, and put herself beyond the pale, never acknowledged again by her religious family?"

He nodded. "Bigotry hurts many people. Her parents must have suffered for their intolerance."

The Eagle at the Gate

"Particularly her mother, who was of a romantic turn of mind, but too intimidated by her husband to dare defy him, I suppose."

"Apparently he felt the shame of his daughter's behaviour so keenly that he promptly applied for a living elsewhere and moved far afield within a few months, but in the little church he had presided over there is a memorial brass—"

"To Aphra, the lady of many virtues."

"So you know."

"My mother chose to call me after her."

"She could not have chosen better. But the chapter is unfinished. It should end where it began, in my house, on the spot where the founders of the Newton family once lived. It would be good if their last living descendant returned to it."

He cupped my face in his hands, and the touch of them made me feel as close to him as an embrace.

"When you are ready to come to me, my dear, dear love, I will show you what marriage should really be like."

I could scarcely speak, so great was my happiness, but after a while I managed to say, "I will send word when that moments comes."

It had come now.

It was some weeks after I had talked with Claudia, and during those weeks much had been accomplished. I had consulted lawyers, given instructions, made arrangements. I had agreed to sell Abbotswood to Claudia, but I was taking certain things which Truman told me had once belonged to my father, and I had given him the ancient carpetbag for himself.

"You remember packing it for him when he left, don't you, Truman? That was why you peered at it so closely that day."

"I was looking for Mr. Lawrence's initials, ma'am. They had been worked into the lining, but the lining of this bag had been removed. Then I thought, 'No, it couldn't be possible . . . it just couldn't be. . . .'" His voice broke, and his eyes misted. Quickly I kissed his withered cheek. The ancient bag was not much of a gift; but it meant a lot to Truman, and although he had not yet been told, he would be provided for, as would others. Barney and his wife, Mabel. The Thespian Players, who needed a theatre of their own. And Elizabeth, too, because she had been present when my mother and father had made their marriage vows, privately, in God's house.

"You don't have to give me anything, darling, but how too, too deevy of you! And I must say it's nice to have a nest egg for when one grows old. Not that I ever intend to, of course. Fancy your dear papa leaving all *that!* I declare, when Barney and I witnessed that will, we hadn't the slightest idea what was in it. 'Just sign here,' Charles said, folding the paper so we couldn't read above that particular spot. 'All you need to know is that you are witnessing my will, but you aren't going to know what's in it.' *So* like dear Charles to be cagey! You know, darling, I often wondered why they didn't get properly married—whether Petronella already had a husband or he already had a wife, but of course, I never asked questions. You know what theatricals are like—we mind our own business, never probe into people's private lives. But I must say, having met that Greek tragedy queen at Abbotswood, your dear papa did a lot better for himself when he met Petronella."

"One has to understand Claudia," I said. "She is greatly to be pitied." I thought of her, living alone in that great house, with only Harriet left to mother and care for.

"Well, dear, I wouldn't mind anyone pitying *me* if I had all that money! Not that I blame you for leaving that house. Remember how your dear papa didn't want to go there? Poor Charles, will I ever forget it! The company would have lynched him had he held out, but the strain it put on him must have been terrible. Sorry, dear, I mustn't keep reminding you of your father, and you a widow already, too. . . ."

Elizabeth had seemed about to say something else, then thought better of it, but I knew she was remembering that after-luncheon scene at Abbotswood and how she had gone back as fast as she could to the crazy, unpredictable, precarious, beautifully *safe* world of the theatre.

"Before you go, Aphra dear, just one thing. What do you plan to do now?"

"Precisely what my father did—seek a life of happiness elsewhere."

The Eagle at the Gate

And that was why I had sent word to Red Deakon that I was ready, and that was what he was taking me to as he drove me away from Abbotswood to the house his forebears had built over the generations.

Dear Reader:
If you enjoyed this book, and would like to receive the Avon Romance Newsletter, we would be delighted to put you on our mailing list. Simply *print* your name and address and send to Avon Books, Room 417, 959 8th Ave., N. Y., N. Y. 10019.

Book orders and checks should *only* be sent to Avon Mail Order Dept., 250 W. 55 St., N. Y., N. Y. 10019. Include 25¢ per copy for postage and handling; allow 4-6 weeks for delivery.

AVON PRESENTS THE BEST IN SPECTACULAR WOMEN'S ROMANCE

Kathleen E. Woodiwiss

The Flame and the Flower	35485/$2.25
The Wolf and the Dove	35477/$2.25
Shanna	38588/$2.25

Laurie McBain

Devil's Desire	30650/$1.95
Moonstruck Madness	31385/$1.95

Rosemary Rogers

Sweet Savage Love	38869/$2.25
Dark Fires	38794/$2.25
The Wildest Heart	39461/$2.25
Wicked Loving Lies	30221/$2.25

Available wherever paperbacks are sold, or direct from Avon Books, Mail Order Dept., 224 W. 57th St., New York, N.Y. 10019. Includes 50¢ per copy for postage and handling; allow 4-6 weeks for delivery.

ROMANCE 1-79

Nothing bound her spirit—
but one man knew the
whispered words to
make her his.

A Pirate's Love

From sun-blazed beaches to star-lit coves, languid Caribbean breezes caressed the breathtakingly beautiful Bettina Verlaine and swept her ship westward to fulfill a promise her heart never made—marriage to a Count she had never seen.

Then in a moment of swashbuckling courage, the pirate Tristan captured her and cast the spell of his passion over her heart forever. But many days—and fiery nights—must pass before their love could flower into that fragile blossom a woman gives to only one man.

Johanna Lindsey
author of
CAPTIVE BRIDE

AVON △ 40048 / $2.25   PIR 10-78